...alive with historical detail
...ion, drama and danger,' *... Post*

...is now a...
of fans around the...
She lives in Wiltshire and is marri...

Follow Joanna on Facebook or Twitter @joanna...

Praise for Joanna Hickson

'A great tale . . . the golden thread that led to the crown of England' Conn Iggulden

'An intriguing tale, told with confidence' *The Times*

'Rich and warm' *Sunday Express*

'Colourful and vivid' Elizabeth Chadwick

'A big-hearted and engrossing novel' Elizabeth Fremantle

'Thorough...

'A gripping and e...

'A bewitching first novel ...
Housekeeping

'An enthralling blend of fact and fict...
passion and politics' *Lancashire Evening ...*

BY THE SAME AUTHOR

The Agincourt Bride
The Tudor Bride
Red Rose, White Rose
First of the Tudors

JOANNA HICKSON

The Tudor Crown

This book is produced from independently certified FSC™ paper
to ensure responsible forest management.

For more information visit www.harpercollins.co.uk/green

HarperCollins*Publishers*

HarperCollins*Publishers*
The News Building
1 London Bridge Street
London SE1 9GF

www.harpercollins.co.uk

First published by HarperCollins*Publishers* 2018

1

Set in Adobe Caslon by Palimpsest Book Production Limited,
Falkirk, Stirlingshire

Printed and bound in Great Britain by
CPI Group (UK) Ltd, Croydon CRO 4YY

MIX
Paper from
responsible sources
FSC
FSC™ C007454

My books have an uncanny habit of following the timeline of the birth of my grandchildren and this one is dedicated to the beautiful Fern Ashton, another precious joy in my life to coincide with the publication of *The Tudor Crown*!

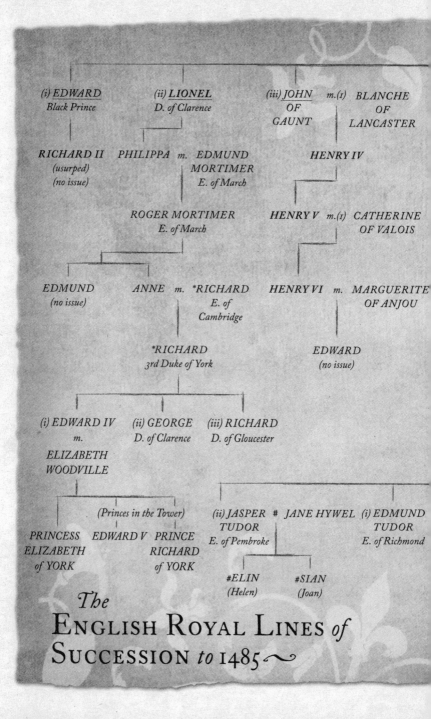

(i) EDWARD
Black Prince

(ii) LIONEL
D. of Clarence

(iii) JOHN m.(1) **BLANCHE**
OF   OF
GAUNT   LANCASTER

RICHARD II
(usurped)
(no issue)

PHILIPPA m. EDMUND
MORTIMER
E. of March

HENRY IV

ROGER MORTIMER
E. of March

HENRY V m.(1) CATHERINE
OF VALOIS

EDMUND
(no issue)

ANNE m. *RICHARD
E. of
Cambridge

HENRY VI m. MARGUERITE
OF ANJOU

*RICHARD
3rd Duke of York

EDWARD
(no issue)

(i) EDWARD IV
m.
ELIZABETH
WOODVILLE

(ii) GEORGE
D. of Clarence

(iii) RICHARD
D. of Gloucester

(Princes in the Tower)

(ii) JASPER # JANE HYWEL **(i) EDMUND**
TUDOR   TUDOR
E. of Pembroke   E. of Richmond

PRINCESS   EDWARD V PRINCE
ELIZABETH   RICHARD
of YORK   of YORK

#ELIN   #SIAN
(Helen)   (Joan)

The
ENGLISH ROYAL LINES *of*
SUCCESSION *to* 1485

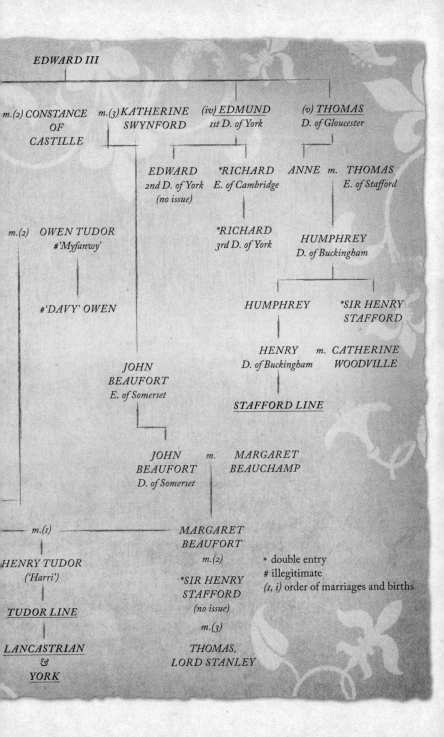

EDWARD III

m.(2) CONSTANCE
OF
CASTILLE

m.(3) KATHERINE
SWYNFORD

(iv) EDMUND
1st D. of York

(v) THOMAS
D. of Gloucester

EDWARD
2nd D. of York
(no issue)

*RICHARD
E. of Cambridge

ANNE m. THOMAS
E. of Stafford

m.(2) OWEN TUDOR
#'Myfanwy'

*RICHARD
3rd D. of York

HUMPHREY
D. of Buckingham

#'DAVY' OWEN

HUMPHREY

*SIR HENRY
STAFFORD

HENRY m. CATHERINE
D. of Buckingham WOODVILLE

JOHN
BEAUFORT
E. of Somerset

STAFFORD LINE

JOHN m. MARGARET
BEAUFORT BEAUCHAMP
D. of Somerset

m.(1) MARGARET
BEAUFORT
m.(2)

HENRY TUDOR
('Harri')

*SIR HENRY
STAFFORD
(no issue)

* double entry
# illegitimate
(1, i) order of marriages and births

TUDOR LINE

m.(3)

LANCASTRIAN
&
YORK

THOMAS,
LORD STANLEY

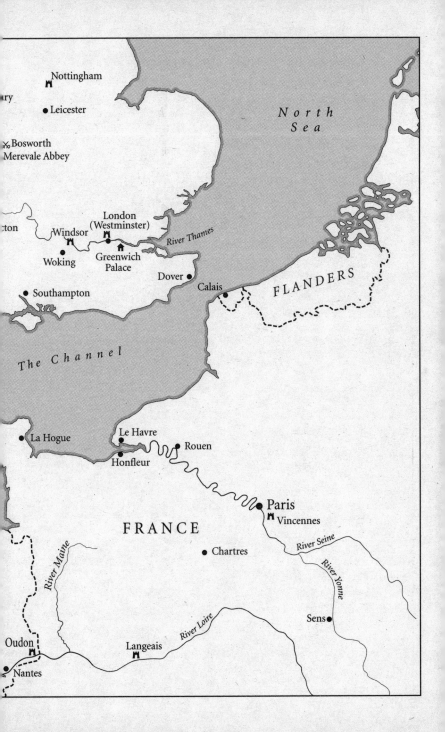

Nottingham

● Leicester

⚔ Bosworth
Merevale Abbey

N o r t h
S e a

London
(Westminster)

Windsor

Woking

Greenwich
Palace

Dover ●

Calais ●

River Thames

F L A N D E R S

● Southampton

T h e   C h a n n e l

● La Hogue

Le Havre ●

Honfleur ●

● Rouen

● Paris
Vincennes

F R A N C E

River Maine

● Chartres

River Seine

River Yonne

River Loire

Sens ●

Oudon

Langeais

● Nantes

PART ONE

I

Harri

TOSSING SPRAY FROM HER bow, the little cog swooped into another deep trough then ploughed her way up to the next luminous white crest. The wind folded the night around us with sighs and groans, turning the black ocean into a fearsome monster. We were sailing into a nameless void over waves as high as castle walls; leaving behind everything I had ever known, with faint hope of return.

The helmsman hauled on the whipstaff, swiping salt water from his beard with the other hand. 'The *Marie Gwyn* may be a small ship, my lord, but she is sturdy. She swims like a porpoise.'

'Only while on the surface,' grunted my uncle, lending his arm to steady the jerking rudder. Visibility was restricted to the narrow beam of one horn lantern and the scant reflected light of a sickle moon, which frequently disappeared behind racing clouds. Stars too appeared and disappeared like guttering candles, making navigation well nigh impossible.

3

Clearly our safety could not be guaranteed in these conditions. After countless crossings of the English Channel Jasper Tudor, Earl of Pembroke, could read the weather signs as well as any sailor and I detected his uneasiness about what lay ahead. But it had been essential to leave harbour under cover of darkness in order to escape our Yorkist enemies.

I was clinging to a cleat on the windward bulwark of the aftcastle, feeling the swell and spill beneath me as the small ship danced from crest to crest. It was the first time I had been to sea and I was filled with a mixture of fear and exhilaration.

Despite everything we managed to sail clear of the islands off South Wales and into the deep ocean, heading for the Cornish coast.

'On this wind we should reach Land's End by sunrise,' said the mariner cheerfully, 'giving us enough light to tack safely up the English Channel and across to France.'

'And enough for Edward's spies to spot us.' Lord Jasper was not reassured. My uncle's mood had been consistently gloomy ever since the dire news had reached us of King Henry's death in the Tower of London. When he cursed the Yorkists and derided their official announcement that his half-brother had 'succumbed from melancholy and displeasure' on being told of the battlefield death of his seventeen-year-old son and heir, I had echoed his contempt. I knew the old king had been somewhat weak in the head, but I too had no doubt whatsoever that Henry the Sixth of England had been murdered. It mattered not which of the three York brothers had ordered or executed the dreadful deed – Edward who now called himself King, or George, Duke of Clarence, or Richard, Duke of Gloucester – a quagmire of unlawful deaths fouled their footprints. In the fourteen years since my birth they or their adherents had scythed through the Lancastrian leadership like the grim reaper: first the Dukes of Suffolk and Somerset, then my father, Lord Jasper's brother Edmund Tudor, then my grandfather, their father Sir Owen Tudor, then Prince Edward of Lancaster, and now his father, the true anointed monarch of England; to say nothing of an unfortunate cohort of less-exalted followers.

'Only we are left to recover the throne of our forefathers, Harri,' Lord Jasper had lamented as a Yorkist army laid siege to us in his castle at Pembroke. 'But to do it we must stay alive and for that, regrettably, we must flee the kingdom.' And so on that blustery September night, the plucky *Marie Gwyn* was surfing the waves towards France, her helmsman riding the high poop-deck of the aftcastle and guiding the rudder through the connecting whipstaff one-handed, like a knight steering his charger. My uncle tried to distract himself by giving me a verbal guide to some of the nautical terms for our surroundings, pointing out the companionway or steep ladder-stair that led up from the main deck, the bulwark that stopped us tipping over the side and gave us some protection from the waves and the scuppers, or drains, which took away the seawater the ocean was hurling at us.

There were two trusty sailors on board, Bran and Dylan, fishermen from the port of Tenby who had agreed, no doubt for a good purse of silver, to ferry the outlawed Earl of Pembroke and his family across the English Channel. There we hoped to find refuge at the court of our cousin Louis the Eleventh, King of France. None of us gave voice to our fears out on the open ocean, but I think even the fishermen were anxious. They spent their lives plying the unpredictable waters around the British coast but never before had to consider the dire consequences of assisting the flight of outlaws. My own murmured prayers to the Virgin of the Sea were as much for delivery from King Edward's agents as from the power of the waves.

The rest of our company huddled beneath us in the shelter of the aftcastle cabin, most of them puking and praying for the journey to end. The unpredictable motion of the ship had felled them: my young cousin Sian and her mother Jane, Jane's brother Evan, the earl's loyal squire, who was seen to hang frequently and perilously over the ship's side, and Lord Jasper's half-brother Davy, whose habitual cheer was quite extinguished. Lord Jasper and I were fortunate not to suffer seasickness, but I had begged to be allowed to stay up on the open deck to escape the stench of vomit in the cabin. I had not needed Lord Jasper's barked warning to keep well below the bulwark, 'Because no one will be able to save you, Harri, if you go over the side.' Despite the cold wind I was warm in my fleece-lined oiled leather jacket and gradually my instinctive fear subsided, to be replaced by an illogical optimism that whatever the sea threw at us we would survive. After an hour or so observing the two men at work steering the ship, my eyes grew heavy and I curled up on the deck, wrapped my arms around a bollard and fell asleep.

I was woken by a monstrous roaring sound and, just audible through it, my name, yelled at high pitch, along with our Lord's: 'Jesu, Harri – wake up!'

The wind screamed in the rigging and the ship was bucking like a frightened horse. My uncle was alone at the helm, wrestling the whipstaff with all his might. I staggered to my feet, grabbing at a stay to stop myself crashing into the bulwark, then flung my full weight to his aid, wedged beside him, pushing as hard as I could.

The bucking eased. 'Thank God and all His Saints, Harri!' Lord Jasper gasped. 'I feared we might capsize. Bran went to help Dylan reef the sail. He sensed there was a squall coming – and he was right!'

I peered through the spray into the dim distance. Dawn was breaking and in the silvery light on the swaying horizon I could see a ragged black outline closing ominously in. 'Is that Cornwall, uncle?' I yelled.

'Land's End!' he bawled back. 'Push harder, Harri, I must haul the rudder over or we will be on the rocks.'

I set my back to the heavy wooden staff and shoved. It shifted suddenly and I nearly fell but managed to get my feet back under me, push again and the ship's bow veered noticeably away from the direction of the cliffs. The sail above flapped as it spilled wind and the boom tried to throw Bran and Dylan off their perilous perch where they were still trying to lace up the reef. They yelled with alarm.

'Keep pushing!' Fear spiked my uncle's voice. 'Saint Elmo save us! Where is Evan when he is needed?'

As if he had heard his name, the squire's dark head appeared at the top of the companionway. 'The wind is up,' he said unnecessarily, stepping over the top and clinging to the aftcastle rail. 'I thought you might need help, my lord.'

'Harri has done well,' Jasper told him. 'But there is an emergency, Evan. Can you haul in the starboard sheet there, to stop the sail flapping?'

'Aye, aye sir!' Evan quickly hauled on the rope controlling

the slant of the boom, to which the two fishermen still clung. Then with three of us on the rudder the *Marie Gwyn* became more biddable and we succeeded in trimming the ship sufficiently to allow the sailors to complete their dangerous task. The crisis over, Evan and I were able to relish keeping the sail filled and the bowsprit pointing in the right direction, laughing with relief as spray washed our faces, and the little ship once more plunged from wave to wave like a dolphin. Lord Jasper gave our laughter a puzzled shake of his head, before climbing down the ladder to seek comfort and much-needed sustenance below.

The very thought of food made me hungry. 'Did Mistress Jane say she had packed a pigeon pie?' I asked Evan. 'I could wolf down a large slice.' I was forgetting the squire's delicate stomach. His face blanched and he spewed bile. 'Holy Marie, do not mention food, Harri!' he spluttered grimly. 'You will send me to the rail again.'

I chuckled, hoping the sound would be lost in the rattling of the rigging. It was not.

'For that smirk you can polish Lord Jasper's armour when we get to France,' the squire muttered. '*If* we ever get to France.' Nausea had sobered his mood. 'More likely it'll be the Tower of London.' He jerked a thumb at the looming cliffs, now towering over our port side. 'There could be a Yorkist lookout posted anywhere up there. Or there could be a sharp rock right beneath our keel. The bottom of the sea, that's where we'll probably end up.'

Silence fell between us as we contemplated both of these outcomes. Pretty soon Lord Jasper re-appeared, a wooden bowl filled with tempting-looking pastries in his hand.

Reaching over the top of the companionway ladder to set it down, he said, 'Mistress Jane sent up some food.'

Suddenly the ship heeled violently. I reached out to grab the bowl but it was sent spinning wildly across the deck to disappear through the scupper drain-hole. I groaned in dismay, as the sail sheets snapped and strained under the onslaught of another roaring gust of wind and the canvas creaked, complaining at the drag on its seams. Evan and I had to hug the whipstaff to maintain our hold and Lord Jasper clutched at the poop-rail to avoid hurtling over it.

Bran and Dylan pushed past him, their bare feet appearing to suck the wet and slippery deck. 'Humble apologies my lords,' said Bran, grabbing the steering stick with a brawny arm and shoving it hard over so that the sail stopped creaking. His relief was obvious. 'Treacherous waters these are and there is a gale brewing in the Channel. I advise you all to go below.'

Lord Jasper had to shout to make his voice heard above the wind's howl: 'Get below, Harri. You too, Evan. I will remain up here.'

I thought it had been blowing fiercely before but another gust threatened to fling us off the ladder and when we reached the main deck, Evan and I had to clamber along, clinging to every handhold to reach the door of the cabin, which together we were able to open. Inside we found mother and child, Jane and Sian, sitting together in a cupboard bed, their chalk-white faces stark against the stained planking.

As I stumbled into the room I inadvertently kicked a pail of vomit, sending its contents slopping over the side. The stench was so appalling it made me retch and I threw myself across to the one open porthole with its shutters fastened

9

back for light and ventilation, gulping the fresh air. Spray flew in, wetting my face and making the swinging lantern fizzle and flicker.

Jane's voice rasped from a throat raw with retching. 'Where is Lord Jasper?'

Turning, I had to grab at anything that might lend support.

'He stayed up with the mariners,' I said. 'They expect the gale to increase.'

She crossed herself and muttered an Ave. It was no secret that Jane was Lord Jasper's long-term mistress and Sian was their daughter. Jane had also been nurse and governess to me since my birth and even in extreme distress her motherly instincts did not desert her. 'Have you eaten anything, Harri?' she asked.

I shook my head ruefully. 'Thank you for sending up the food but a gust blew the bowl overboard.'

With a sigh she waved at a basket wedged under the bed-slats. 'If you can eat, there is more pie. And some ale in the bottle.'

I located a mug and the leather bottle, pulled out the stopper and offered it first to Mistress Jane. 'It might soothe your stomach,' I coaxed, looking into her wan features.

'I doubt if anything will do that, Harri, but you are right, we should try to drink.' She gripped the beaker and I aimed the bottle with both hands. When she had taken a few sips she offered the mug to her daughter but Sian just shook her head and turned her face to the wall.

'Shall I try?' I whispered. Mistress Jane handed me the ale.

'Your father would want you to drink, Sian,' I said. 'Lord

Jasper always says a knight can do without meat but he cannot do without drink.'

'I am not a knight,' she snapped, but took the beaker and put it to her lips.

As she did so the ship seemed to rear up on her stern and twist dramatically and I was tossed like a leaf in the air, flung into the cupboard bed, the ale spraying everywhere. I was sprawled on top of Jane and Sian, the three of us all tangled up together, shocked and damp. When we and the ship had somehow righted ourselves we found Evan was lying in a crumpled heap in the corner and Davy was trying to extricate himself from a pile of lobster traps that had once been neatly stacked. The cabin floor was running with seawater which had rushed in through the open porthole. Miraculously the lantern was still alight, swinging wildly on its hook.

Mistress Jane tried to heave herself off the cabin bed. 'Jasper!' she cried.

I pulled at her arm to help her, meanwhile pointing out, 'You cannot go out there, Mistress Jane! Truly, it is too rough. You will not even make it to the ladder.'

'Evan – Evan can go.' She peered around in the dim light and saw Evan's huddled form. 'Oh no. Is he hurt?'

At that moment the squire raised his head, looking dazedly around. 'What happened?' he asked.

'The ship almost capsized but we still seem to be afloat,' I told him. 'Are you all right?'

Evan rubbed at his head and his hand came away covered in blood. 'Well, I am still alive,' he said.

'Do not move,' said Jane, reaching for the basket. 'I have napkins here.'

But there was a hammering on the door and a shout, 'Open up!' It was Lord Jasper. Jane threw a napkin at Evan while Davy and I fought our way across the jerking floor to haul off a heavy chest, which had slid across the entrance. With a grunt Lord Jasper managed to push the door open enough to slide in.

Jane struggled to his side, as the floor bucked and dived, 'My lord – dear God, you are soaking wet! But are you hurt?'

'Only bruised,' he said, still clinging to the door. 'Bran had tied us all to the rail or we would have gone overboard. A freak wave broke as we broached it – nearly washed us away. I came to check you were all right down here.'

He stared at Evan, at the bloody napkin. 'Battered but not broken,' the squire said hurriedly, in a shaky voice.

Jane asked, 'Can we take shelter?'

Lord Jasper shook his head. 'The gale is taking us further and further out into the ocean and the sailors can do nothing but keep the ship afloat by running with the wind.'

'Are we not going to France then, my lord?' asked his dazed squire.

'France is now behind us and we cannot turn into a wind like this.' Lord Jasper stumbled across the flooded floor to join Sian on the bed. 'We can only keep our back to it and pray that it eases soon. Come, let us keep our feet above the water meanwhile. What shall we pray, Sian?'

In her small treble voice Sian began to chant softly, hands clasped and head bowed, repeating over and over the prayer that every child knew by heart.

'Ave Maria, gratia plena,
Dominus tecum,
Benedictus tu in mulieribus,
Et benedictus fructus ventris tui, Jesus.
Sancta Maria, Mater Dei,
Ora pronobis peccatoribus, nunc et in hora mortis nostrae.'

We all crossed ourselves in mortal fear and clutched at anything we could reach to stop ourselves sliding across the flooded floor.

'Holy Mary will save us,' Sian said simply. 'She knows we cannot swim.'

2

Margaret

Coldharbour Inn, London, England, September 1471

As Sir Henry's wife, it was my duty to pray for his
soul and I knelt beside his bed in the gloom of a
shuttered chamber. Crimson drapes on the bedstead
shrouded him in deep shadow, his upper body supported
on heaped pillows beneath embroidered sheets and covers.
The monotonous rasp of his laboured breathing cut through
air that was thickly laden with the heady aroma of burning
incense. He was unconscious. For several months he had
been slowly dying from wounds received on a battlefield
and now the end was near. Even incense could not disguise
the stench of putrid flesh.

Six months it was since Edward of York had returned
from exile in Flanders bent on reclaiming the English throne
captured from him by his erstwhile ally, the Earl of Warwick.
My husband rallied his tenants and retainers and led them
off to war, to my surprise. I had thought his chronic skin
condition would exclude him from military duties. I had

also believed he was marching to join the Lancastrian army, to defend King Henry the Sixth.

After the battle, which took the life of the turncoat Warwick, news of Sir Henry's serious wounds had been bad enough but the fact that he had been among the Yorkist casualties had stunned me. My servants brought home a man I no longer recognised and not due to his disfiguring wounds; it was his treacherous change of allegiance that prompted my aversion.

Nevertheless I spent my days at his bedside, trying to halt the steady creep of rot through his flesh and praying for news of my son Henry and his uncle, Jasper Tudor, both declared traitors with a price on their heads.

Meanwhile Edward of York had reinstated himself on the throne of England and confined the true king, my cousin Henry the Sixth, in the Tower of London, then marched off to confront a second Lancastrian army on a bloody battlefield beside the River Severn at Tewkesbury.

All my prayers proved in vain and the Lancastrians were again defeated, the Prince of Wales was killed and a devastated Queen Marguerite was captured, humiliated, and taken to the Tower where her husband was already confined. Incredibly, the old king was found dead that same night, said to have succumbed to 'grief and displeasure' after hearing that his only son and heir had been cut down. Many, like me, believed both father and son had been murdered.

My husband lived on for four more pointless, agonising months.

Still I knelt by his bed and prayed, as duty demanded, but the words stuck in my throat. Instead I sought divine protection for my only son, Henry Tudor, who was fourteen years old. He had spent weeks under siege in his uncle's castle at Pembroke and then a scrawled note came saying that he and Jasper had escaped and were fleeing for France, outlawed and stripped of lands and titles, driven from their native country. There had been no news of him since.

'Holy Mary, Mother of God, and blessed St Christopher, patron of travellers, shield my son Henry from storm and tempest and guide his uncle Jasper, and the sailors who steer their ship, to bring them safely to land and protect them from their enemies of York . . .'

A sudden commotion broke into my prayers. The door of the chamber was thrown open to admit a woman arrayed in royal blue satin and accessorised with jewels so plentiful and brilliant they caught the candlelight and illuminated the gloom. 'Her Grace Elizabeth the Queen!' announced the duty chamberlain, his voice squeaking with nerves.

The consort's crown was Elizabeth Woodville's once more. She had found sanctuary at Westminster Abbey during King Edward's five months of exile, a confinement that had proved both strategic and fruitful. After suffering three daughters, she had borne the male heir for which she and Edward had both prayed so hard and upon her husband's return to London, she and her baby son had emerged from their refuge as triumphant as he. The new Prince of Wales was now thriving in his own household at Westminster Palace.

I rose from my knees in alarm. I had not attended the royal court since the change of kings. 'Madam – your grace – an unexpected honour.' My deep curtsy was unbalanced and clumsy.

Queen Elizabeth gestured for me to rise, saying, 'Stand up, Margaret, before you fall over! I hear that Sir Henry is like to die and have come to pray for a hero of York.' She moved nearer to the bed, a perfumed kerchief held to her nose against the reek of decaying flesh. 'How does he fare?'

'Not well, Madam. Doctor Caerleon says it cannot be long now.' Despite my desire to remain composed, I could feel tears slipping down my cheeks. 'But he is not at peace.' My final words emerged on a croak.

Elizabeth placed a gentle hand on my arm. 'He will be, when we tell him you are to be reconciled with the king.'

I stared at her in disbelief. 'How is that possible? Only a year ago I and my son pledged allegiance to his royal uncle in the Throne Room at Westminster.'

King Henry and my first husband, Edmund Tudor, Earl of Richmond, were half-brothers, sharing the same mother, Queen Catherine of Valois. My beloved Lord Edmund died as a prisoner of the Yorkists, leaving me a widow and six months pregnant, aged only thirteen. By God's grace, though it nearly killed us both, we had survived the birth, my son and I, and now Henry Tudor, or Harri as his Uncle Jasper insisted on calling him, was the focus of my unswerving loyalty to Lancaster.

The queen made a dismissive sound. 'Pah! We would have no court at all if every noble who once bent the knee to Lancaster was banned. Of course you will be required to take a new oath of allegiance to the crown.' Even in the dim light she caught the flicker of doubt in my eyes and her own expression hardened. 'Should that be so difficult, Margaret? Others have not thought it so.'

I could not stop my trembling chin jutting defiantly. '"Others" do not find their only son condemned to exile, your grace; perhaps even at this very moment at risk of drowning at sea.'

Elizabeth shook her head impatiently. 'Your Henry is fourteen is he not? A very suitable age to join the king's household and learn the manners and procedures of royal service. It is not my lord who is to blame for his exile; it is Jasper Tudor. He should have left him here in England. Perhaps the king will get him back for you.' She paused. 'If you were to ask him nicely.'

At that moment there was a groan from the bed. Against protocol I turned my back on the queen. 'Henry? Husband, have you pain?' I ran to a table and selected a bottle from an array of remedies. An hourglass stood nearby, its sands only three-quarters run. 'It is too soon for more poppy syrup; but no matter – Doctor Caerleon said we must keep the pain at bay.'

'Who is this Doctor Caerleon?' Elizabeth watched me pour a generous measure of the potion into a silver cup. 'I seek a new physician. Is he skilled at the trade?'

'Indeed he is, your grace, and as well as being a physician, he is also an astronomer. He studied in Cambridge and Paris.' I lifted my husband's head from the pillows and offered the cup. He sucked greedily at the viscous liquid while the queen turned from the sight and went to kneel at a Prie Dieu set before a crucifix that hung on the chamber wall. I had placed a painted triptych of Christ's Passion on the portable altar below it.

I let Sir Henry's head fall back and he took several long breaths, waiting for the drug to bring relief. Then his lips moved and I bent close to listen but his words emerged loudly in the quiet room. 'I heard what she said, Margaret.

You must take the oath. You should be at court – for Henry's sake.'

I whispered in his ear, 'Is that why you fought for Edward and gained his pardon?'

He was gasping for breath, temporarily speechless, but his eyes said 'Yes'. The fiery St Anthony's rash burned red through his beard and on his neck and cheeks, edging into the white skin of his brow, a metaphor for the black evil that was creeping inexorably up his thigh towards his vital organs.

Sir Henry regained control of his voice. 'Edward is a strong king but a fair one. He will restore your son's lands and title. I had his word.'

I set down the cup and took his hand. I shot a worried glance at the kneeling queen and bent close to his ear, murmuring my treason. 'You may trust him, husband, but I cannot. King Henry died in the Tower of London. Of what cause or by whose hand we do not know but Edward is responsible. Besides, his allies murdered my son's father.'

The dying knight shook his head and drew another rasping breath. 'You are still young, Margaret. You must look ahead, not back. Work with the queen. To secure Henry's future you will need people of power on your side. I beg you – pray for my soul and take the oath.' Sir Henry's eyes closed and he turned his head away, his chest heaving.

I dropped my forehead to his hand. Up to that moment he had not spoken for days. Now he was telling me to feign allegiance to York for my son's sake. I felt the weight of hypocrisy settling on my heart.

'He is right, you know.' The queen was at my shoulder. 'Take the oath, Margaret. Sir Henry can die in peace and you can come back to court. You should consult your doctor-astrologer. He will tell you that the sun of York now warms the realm once more and a time of reconciliation lies ahead.'

I drew a kerchief from my sleeve, wiped my tears and rose to my feet, silent. I refrained from mentioning that Dr Caerleon was an astronomer, not a caster of horoscopes.

Elizabeth said, 'I heard Sir Henry's words and they were wise.' She gazed at me intently. 'You look exhausted, Margaret, let us seek refreshment and talk some more. Sir Henry is sleeping again now. Surely wine and sweetmeats are to be had in your well-run household.'

I beckoned a serving woman from the shadows to take my watch beside the bed. Before following the queen from the room I genuflected to the crucifix and made the sign of the cross, silently thanking the Almighty that Elizabeth had only heard my husband's words to me, not mine to him.

3

Harri

At sea, September 1471

MY NAIVE OPTIMISM THAT we would survive to make landfall vanished when Dylan, trying to catch the sail sheet which had broken loose once more, disappeared with a horrific scream over the side of the ship at the height of the gale. We were all stunned by a feeling of helplessness, which turned rapidly to grief as we clung together, bucking and rolling with the ship and joining in prayers for the lost mariner as the gale swept us on into the night, into the mountainous swell of the open ocean. We were at the mercy of the waves until Bran, taking the precaution of tying himself to the rail, managed to regain possession of the sheet-rope and return the ship to the control of the rudder.

As morning approached the wind dropped at last then veered southwest, allowing us to turn our bow towards a fiery sunrise. Davy Owen found his sea legs and became a useful member of the crew, running nimbly about the decks, barefoot, obeying Bran's instructions. The sailor would not allow any of us up the rigging, however; he made the hazardous climb himself to loosen the reef on the sail. When, in late afternoon, a dark irregular line appeared on the distant horizon we greeted the sight with a collective cheer. Land Ho!

Bran guessed it must be the French coast but had no idea what part of France. In any case he did not want to get there in the dark and so decided to set a parallel course until dawn. None of us got much sleep, relieving each other on watch every two hours; I snatched a few hours' rest, making myself a nest of ropes in the lee of the foredeck, lulled by the creak of the sail above and the wash of the waves past the bow. When Evan woke me to take my turn at steering, the sun was rising over soaring cliffs, now all too clearly visible as we began a cautious approach.

Up on the poop-deck once more I heard Bran announce: 'I am going to beach her, my lord!' His voice, sharp and grim, cut through the blast of the wind and the weird singing in the stays. 'It is either that or being driven onto the rocks.'

I could see nothing but high, fearsome cliffs stretching ahead but the seaman's words gave hope of avoiding what seemed like inevitable shipwreck.

'Do what you must,' responded Lord Jasper. 'We do not want to lose another life.'

'If we can find a good shelving bay, the swell and tide are high enough to carry us up the strand and leave us there. The cog is almost flat bottomed and should come to no harm,' he added. 'I will drop you off with your baggage and launch her again at the next high water.'

'Can you sail her back to Wales alone, Bran?'

The grizzled sailor crossed himself and spat vigorously

onto the decking. 'The *Marie Gwyn* and I are twin souls. If she goes to the bottom, so do I.'

It was not a straight answer but we all knew what he meant. The ship was his life and his livelihood. He might have lost his mate but he could not live without his ship. Nevertheless I wondered if it was truly feasible to strand the heavy cog without the kind of harm to her timbers that would make re-launching impossible. It all depended on choosing the right beach.

However, we had not escaped the vicissitudes of the weather yet. As the sky lightened the wind strengthened, the waves grew higher and the coast came closer and closer. Then I saw a gap in the cliffs ahead. Sharp rocks framed a small inlet, which narrowed to a patch of sand at its apex. Wherever it was and whatever its name, it was the only place we were going.

I just had time to scramble down the aftcastle ladder to warn Jane and Sian to stay in the cupboard bed, hold tight and douse the lantern flame in the cabin before we heard Bran's cry of 'Land Ho' once more and there was a long grating sound, which I took to be the keel making contact with the sand. Waves surged and retreated, the ship moved forward and then came the grating sound again, for what seemed an agonisingly long time. I held my breath, anticipating the crack of splintering timber. But none came and eventually the *Marie Gwyn* ceased to advance and settled at a shallow angle from the vertical. Side-stepping along the newly sloping cabin floor, I opened the door and peered out to discover that the ship's bow had come to rest only a few yards from the cliff wall, and the hull had narrowly avoided a large boulder, half sunk in a crescent of golden

23

sand. Jane and Sian found their way outside and a jubilant cheer floated down from the aftcastle deck. We all joined in.

Davy appeared beside us, crying, 'We are here Mother! We have landed!', wrapping his arms around Jane's neck and then transferring his joy to Sian with a similar hug. Davy was always free with his feelings and affection. Mistress Jane was not his true dam but because she had reared him from a baby, along with Sian and me, he had quite naturally come to call her Mother. I did not do so, because I had been kept very aware, through regular correspondence from the lady herself, that my true mother was Margaret Beaufort, Countess of Richmond. And, as was Lord Jasper, my father had been half-brother to King Henry of England. My mother never let me forget my royal heritage, nor my father, Edmund Tudor, Earl of Richmond, who was dead before I was born.

Lord Jasper sidestepped down the companionway to join us and shook the spray from his hat and his hair. 'We have no idea where we are but at least we are not at the bottom of the sea,' he said. As he hugged Jane and Sian and clapped Davy and me on the back, I saw that relief had smoothed some of the deep lines of anxiety from his face.

Evan slouched in the cabin doorway, glancing up at the sky. 'The air is fresh out here but it looks as if it might rain,' he remarked.

Bran, dropping down from the aftcastle, was businesslike, as always, despite the tragedy of yesterday and the perils he would face, alone, today. He said, 'From further out, my lord, I caught sight of a spire, away up on the cliff – so it seems we have not landed in a heathen wilderness.'

Within an hour we had managed to remove our belongings and supplies from the ship and stow them in a cave, handily situated above the high-water mark. The view from its elevation showed exactly how lucky Bran had been to avoid crashing the *Marie Gwyn* into the rock-face; had he tried to beach her before the turn of the tide, a wreck would have been inevitable. But there she was, whole: she reclined gently like a stranded whale, displaying a few rows of barnacle-encrusted timbers, her mast angled towards the top of the cliffs. Ladders leaned against her lowered side and the sea had retreated a good distance from her stern, breaking waves foaming away out on the shelving sand.

The rain Evan had predicted now began to fall. Heedless of it, Bran prowled the beach assessing the best way to float his ship off when the tide returned. The rest of us took shelter in the cave, but it was cold, wet and our stomachs rumbled. Then a group of brown-habited monks suddenly appeared at the entrance, smiling in a benign way. Their leader spoke to us in a language I thought vaguely familiar and which Jane and Evan both appeared to get the gist of.

'We must be in Brittany, my lord,' said Evan. 'The Breton tongue is quite like Welsh. They are offering help if we need it.'

Lord Jasper bowed courteously to the lead monk and asked Evan to thank him and find out exactly where we were. After a further exchange we learned that we were in Finis Terre in the far west of Brittany. Quite literally, the storm had taken us to 'the end of the earth'.

'His name is Brother Hervé,' Evan added. 'The monastery up on the cliffs – the Abbey of Saint Mathieu – apparently guards the apostle's skull, a relic which attracts pilgrims from far and wide.'

'Brittany is a proud independent dukedom,' observed the earl, speaking his thoughts aloud. 'It refuses to bow the knee to France and declares itself a sovereign state. I think we can expect a welcome from its duke. We are cousins of some sort and I have been to his court on business for the King of France. Ask the brother if we may take shelter at the abbey until a message can be got to Duke Francis that the Earl of Pembroke and his family are here.'

There followed a lengthy exchange between Evan and Brother Hervé, during which it became obvious that the squire was not happy. Hearing of Lord Jasper's rank, the monk had bowed obsequiously and his eyes had begun to glitter as he started speaking so quickly that the squire was clearly finding it hard to follow. In the midst of this he sent his companions further down the cliff to the beach. Evan eventually broke away from the monk to speak confidentially to the earl.

'I think he is saying that the monastery has salvage rights on this coast. Would that mean they intend to impound Bran's ship?'

Lord Jasper's face darkened. 'I hope not but I suppose it is possible. We had better go and investigate.'

By the time Lord Jasper, Evan and I reached the beach, closely followed by the lead monk, an argument had developed between Bran and the rest of the hooded brethren, who had him surrounded. The fisherman looked mutinous but, outnumbered, he was relieved to see the earl arrive.

'They are calling the *Marie Gwyn* jetsam, my lord!' His voice crackled with indignation. 'I told them I only beached her in order for you and your family to disembark and I am leaving on the next tide. They pretend not to understand what I say but if I understand them they must understand me – is that not so?'

Meanwhile Brother Hervé jabbered away to his companions who gradually fell back from their position of confrontation. He then spoke slowly and deliberately to Evan, who translated. 'He says the abbey has a right to ten per cent value of everything that the sea washes up in this part of Brittany. There is a harbour a few miles up the coast where we should have docked and the harbour charges there are the same. Basically he is saying pay up or they will take their ten per cent in sail and rigging and then the *Marie Gwyn* will not be able to go anywhere.'

Lord Jasper fingered the hilt of the shortsword he wore at his hip. 'It is blatant extortion,' he said, frowning. 'I suppose we could threaten them in return but they are monks and that would be sacrilege. So tell them I will pay the ten per cent if they will help Bran re-float his ship. Under this threat he will probably want to leave as soon as possible.'

Evan grinned. 'I will be glad to relay your offer, my lord. I hope they are wise enough to accept.'

The deal was agreed and we all climbed back up the cliff to the cave where Lord Jasper told the monks to wait outside while he fetched what he considered sufficient coin from the heavy treasure chest we had struggled to unload and drag up the cliff. 'Tell them this is half their demand,' he said to his squire. 'I will hand over the other half when I see our friend sailing out of the bay. Meanwhile we would be grateful if they brought us some food and drink when they return to fulfil their part of the bargain. Then they may take us and our baggage to their abbot.'

I smiled as Evan borrowed Lord Jasper's air of authority to relay his instructions and handed over the money. A somewhat chastened Brother Hervé bowed acquiescence to the earl and led his troop of monks back the way they had come. Bran offered Lord Jasper his effusive thanks and disappeared to prepare his beloved vessel for the re-launch, which occurred several hours later when we had filled our bellies and monks and men assembled on the sand to put shoulders to the *Marie Gwyn*'s hull as the tide advanced past her stern. The wind had dropped to a steady breeze. We stood and watched her escape, and cheers went up as she at last cleared the encircling cliffs. Bran then set her prow to the north, waving from his lonely stance at the tiller. We could only pray that he might successfully reach his home port in Wales.

Our own thoughts now turned towards seeking asylum in Brittany.

4

Margaret

Coldharbour Inn, London, October *1471*

NEVER HAD THE TORCHES burning on the gates of Coldharbour looked so welcoming as they did on that freezing October evening when I returned from my husband's funeral, which took place a week after his death. Sir Henry had specified in his will that he was to be interred with his Stafford ancestors, in their chapel crypt in Essex. Pleshey Castle had been a sumptuous palace in the days of Humphrey de Bohun, Earl of Hereford and Essex, Sir Henry's illustrious forefather. No longer. After a hundred years of neglect, its walls were starting to crumble, hangings and furnishings, once glorious, were damp and mouldy and the hall and chambers lacked the smallest hint of comfort.

I had been determined not to spend more than one night under its leaking roof and fortunately my own trusty steward, Master Bray, had ensured that the funeral obsequies were completed as early as possible so that we might make the return journey to London in daylight. After greeting the scant congregation and consuming some of the very ordinary funeral meats, we had set off for London but even my fur-lined cloak and gloves had been insufficient protection against the chill of the dense October fog, which seemed quickly to penetrate through to my bones. It had been a long, cold, arduous ride back to the city.

'I believe there is a saying that one funeral begets the next and the doom-mongers know what they are talking about,' I complained as I allowed the steward to assist me to dismount and shook the clinging moisture from my cloak's folds. 'I am frozen to the core. I only hope the kitchen has a restorative repast for us, Master Bray.'

'I am sure Mistress Hubbard will have a cup or two of gruel left to warm our bellies,' Bray replied with a wry smile.

I frowned at his weak attempt at humour from utter weariness and irritated by his presumption that I would enjoy a pleasantry so soon after my husband's funeral. 'Gruel, like pottage, is for peasants, Master Bray. I prefer to fast rather than partake of either.'

He looked suitably chastened. 'Perhaps a blazing fire would be of more consolation to my lady,' he murmured and bowed me through the open door of the mansion. Candles and torches burned within, their light flickering off polished lime-wood panelling. Despite its name, Coldharbour Inn offered warmth and welcome.

To my delight my friend Katherine Vaux was waiting in the great hall with two servants, ready to remove my wet outer garments and wrap my shivering frame in a warm fur-lined gown. Seeing my wretchedness, she remained calm and quiet until I was seated close to the glowing fire with a cup of hot, spiced wine at my side. I rewarded her with a wan smile. 'Now that we are both widows, Kate, we can comfort each other.' There we were, both of us dressed head to foot in black, full mourning for the departed. Kate had lost her own husband five months before, slain on the battlefield at Tewkesbury. But at least Sir William had remained faithful to the Lancastrian cause, was not a turn-coat as my husband had been. My thoughts dwelt on this, but I did not need to say it. Kate and I had known each other for many years. She was the only one who truly understood my deep-seated despair about this betrayal.

She drew up a stool and settled beside me, taking my hands in hers. 'I have news to bring you good cheer, Margaret. Your son is safe.'

Her words set my heart racing. 'Henry is safe?' I echoed, clutching tightly at her fingers until I noticed her wince. 'Oh forgive me; I am so delighted and relieved. Tell me everything you know!'

She nodded. 'I will – and there is no bad news – but first you must have some warm food. I sent servants to the kitchen as soon as I heard your cavalcade arriving. I will have a trestle brought; you can remain by the fire while you eat and I will tell you every detail.'

I sighed, sat back, released my now gentle grip on her hand and watched as she was as good as her word, trestle table, linen and dishes appeared, warm water was poured into a bowl for hand-washing and beside the bowl a towel to dry my hands. Then I crossed myself and gave thanks for the food I was about to eat, and for the news I was about to receive – news I suddenly, urgently needed to hear.

'Henry and Lord Pembroke are not in France but in Brittany,' Kate began. 'There was a storm and their ship was blown far off course but, God be thanked, they were not shipwrecked.'

I crossed myself again, fervently. I too thanked God for that!

Kate went on, 'They landed on the west coast of Brittany; it has taken many days for the news to reach our shores.'

I sighed. 'Such anxious days these have been. But they are all safe you say? No one is lost?'

Kate bowed her black-veiled head. 'One of the crew was washed overboard, God rest his soul. But there were no other casualties. They are lodged at present in the monastery of Saint Mathieu, near a harbour town called Le Conquet. An application has been made to the duke for asylum.'

'Lord Jasper is related to Duke Francis of Brittany,' I remarked. 'I remember him saying he was very well received at his court a few years ago so they should be welcome there. But to be so far away among strangers . . .'

I paused to consume a few mouthfuls of deliciously soft and fragrant *blanc mange*, which my temperamental cook knew was one of my favourite dishes. He had catered for my bereaved state, which pleased me.

Kate refreshed my cup. 'Was the burial very distressing? I thought you might find it so, which is why I made sure to be here when you returned.'

I lifted the cup, reflecting, but spoke before I drank. 'I have had time to grow accustomed to the idea of losing my husband and so the burial itself was not distressing, but the lack of attendance was. None of the Staffords made the effort to come. I think he made a mistake in choosing to be buried at Pleshey, so far from family and friends.' I sipped again at the sweet strong wine. 'Tell me, did you visit the children before I arrived? How are they?'

'They are all well and happy and should be in their beds by now. They asked when you were coming back but I did not tell them it would be today in case you were delayed.' A wide smile suddenly lit Kate's dark features. 'Little Mary FitzLewis is a sweetheart, is she not? She follows Meg Woodville around like a shadow and asks questions all the time. "What are you doing?" "Where are you going?" "May I come too?"' Her voice imitated that of a small child. 'I cannot decide if Meg likes it or finds it annoying.'

'She does not chide Mary does she?' I asked. At fourteen, Meg could be unpredictable, by turns all smiles and then all frowns for no apparent reason. I did not want her upsetting four-year-old Mary, the newest arrival among the group of children I had taken as my wards. I called them my 'nestlings' – orphaned or motherless offspring of noble or gentle birth.

'No, no,' Kate assured me, 'Mary would not be such a limpet if Meg ever pushed her away. I think she secretly likes having a young admirer.'

At present I had five nestlings, and they included Kate's son and daughter, who needed a home because their mother was permanently engaged on a mission of mercy, a mission that had become the story of her life.

Kate had come to England as a girl in the train of Marguerite of Anjou, who became queen consort on her marriage to Henry the Sixth, and she had remained at the queen's court, marrying the courtier Sir William Vaux before the first change of kings. Recently, she had agreed to remain as companion to the now bereaved and dethroned Marguerite, who was still confined in the Tower of London, where her royal husband had been so recently murdered – not that anyone dared to voice this as fact.

'And you had no problem leaving the queen, or getting away from the Tower?' I almost whispered this. I was aware that Yorkist spies lurked among my servants and any reference to poor Marguerite as queen might be construed as treason.

Kate was equally careful, lowering her voice and leaning closer. 'Not from the guards, their palms are well greased; but the look on her grace's face as I left nearly made me turn back. She is so desolate and despairing it breaks my heart.'

I took a deep breath and straightened my back, forcing myself to smile brightly. 'And now you come to bring comfort to another downhearted lady, when you must often wish you could simply attend to your own grief. Will you not join me in some of this spiced wine, Kate? I think we need its consolation.'

She poured herself a cup and we raised them to each other. 'It is never a hardship to visit you, Margaret. It is a pleasure,' she said, her simple candour shining from her large, dark eyes as she added, 'and on top of that, you are caring for my children!'

'And am pleased to do so,' I responded. 'The door of my house is always open to you and your children.'

'My Joan declared today that she loves it here and never wishes to leave,' Kate revealed. 'It is such a relief to me to know that she is happy and fulfilled while I serve Queen Marguerite.'

Kate came from Anjou, but her father had been a refugee

from the Italian wars and she had the dark colouring of those from south of the Alps. Both her children were bright and intelligent and had their mother's ebony hair and olive complexion. At eleven her son Nicholas showed all the potential of a future knight and his sister Joan already showed great academic prowess, although only eight, devouring books faster than I could provide them. She was a special favourite of mine. 'Your daughter impresses me more every time I visit the schoolroom,' I enthused. 'The tutors tell me regularly how quick she is to learn. We shall have to find a truly bright husband for her if she is to be a happy wife.'

Kate made a face. 'It is a little early to be thinking of her marriage yet, is it not? But I will rely on your impeccable connections to find both my children perfect matches when the time comes.'

I set down my cup, sighed, my thoughts stirred. 'I wish I could even begin to consider such matters for my own son,' I confessed. 'But first I have to persuade King Edward to have the attainder reversed on the Richmond estates, and then to permit Henry to return and claim them. Surely he cannot be held responsible for his father's opposition to York nor his Uncle Jasper's perceived treason? He is only fourteen.'

Kate leaned closer and again lowered her voice. 'But before that you need to establish your own position with King Edward, do you not? How will you do that?'

I shrugged. 'His queen tells me that if I swear another oath of allegiance I will receive his pardon and shortly before he died Sir Henry urged me to do just that. But – oh Kate – it is totally against my inclination!'

'And mine,' she agreed. 'But now that the Yorks have an heir, Edward's seat on the throne is more secure than ever. To oppose them may be unwise. We all have to think of our children's future. Yet I cannot forget that they deprived Marguerite of her son's . . .'

She broke off because I had suddenly laid my finger on my lips. Behind her back I had seen the privy door open at the back of the hall. Through it stepped Master Bray with the eldest of my wards, Meg Woodville, the illegitimate daughter of Anthony Woodville, Queen Elizabeth's brother, born as the result of a youthful indiscretion. I had no idea who her mother was but she must have been a pretty girl because her daughter was a beauty. She must also have been persuasive because her father had acknowledged their daughter from birth, given her his name and supported her both socially and financially, at least until his marriage. Then six years ago Queen Elizabeth had asked me to take her niece as my ward because her brother's childless wife did not wish to play mother to his 'by-blow', as she called her.

Elizabeth had explained: 'His wife has brought him rich estates and he does not want to offend her but Anthony is very fond of his little girl and it seems her mother has died.' She added, apparently heedless of causing me offence, 'Meg is the same age as your son, Lady Margaret. Her presence in your household might fill a gap in your life.'

A gap caused by King Edward giving custody of my Henry to his favourite, Lord Herbert, and not to me. My anger at this heartless deed persisted but it was not advisable to refuse the queen and ironically she had been proved right. Meg Woodville had come like a bright spark into a house-hold too centred on the woes of its lord and lady, mine the result of my son's absence and the lack of further children and Sir Henry's a consequence of his fluctuating health. I had filled my barren days with worship, pleading with God and his saints to right perceived wrongs, while Sir Henry consulted doctor after doctor, fearful that a recurring rash was due to the dreaded disease of leprosy. Responsibility for a bright young soul had very soon taught me, at least, the aridness of this existence.

When she arrived aged nine, Meg had been a mass of contradictions, intensely aware of her illegitimacy but defying anyone to hold her inferior because of it. When his sister married King Edward, Anthony, like his father, had abruptly changed his allegiance from Lancaster to York, but for little Meg split affinities did not matter; she was a girl who loved on instinct alone. It must have been a disappointment to Anthony Woodville, especially after the death of his father, when he inherited the title Earl Rivers, that his wealthy wife had not produced the son every nobleman craved but he was careful not to speak of this to Meg, and she preferred to pretend that her father was not married at all.

Entering the hall, she ran to my chair and made a graceful curtsy. She was definitely a Woodville, already tall, an elegant creature in a bright-blue kirtle and lace-trimmed coif, with her burnished bronze hair tumbling down her back. I held out my arms for her eager embrace.

'Master Bray told me you were back, my lady,' she said. 'I begged him to let me come and greet you.'

I raised one eyebrow at the steward. 'And Master Bray could not deny you it would seem,' I remarked, noting colour creep into his cheeks before returning my attention to my ward. 'Have you had a good day at your studies, Meg?'

Her lips pursed into a pout. 'How could I, when I was thinking of you and hoping you were not feeling too sad?' She pulled up a stool and settled on it. 'Was the funeral very terrible, my lady? Are you glad to be home?'

Her genuine concern was gratifying. 'Yes Meg,' I said. 'It was an ordeal and I am very glad to be home. But I think you should be in your bed.'

She shook her head. 'Please do not send me away. I cannot go to bed until all the little ones are asleep. They chatter away to each other and interrupt my prayers.' She clasped her hands beseechingly. 'Please my lady, may I not have a chamber of my own?'

Kate and I exchanged negative glances. In busy noble houses where numerous servants fetched and carried at all hours of day and night, it was a general rule that children never slept alone, for their own protection. Girls shared beds and chambers with their sisters or schoolmates and also with a nurse or female servant until they were married; even young widows kept a female companion in their chamber until such time as they remarried. 'No Meg, you may not, but before you go to bed you may come with me to my oratory and say your prayers.' I stood up and looked enquiringly at the steward, who still hovered behind my chair. 'Unless Master Bray has urgent business he wishes to discuss with me first.'

He shook his head, albeit with apparent reluctance. 'Nothing that will not keep, my lady.'

'Good, then come to my solar after Compline. The chaplain will be waiting for us now. Kate, I hope you will also join us?'

After the evening Office I kissed Meg goodnight in the girls' dorter, where the young ones now slept peacefully under the watchful eye of a nurse, whose waiting pallet lay beside the door. A page lit Kate to her guest chamber and another accompanied me to the door of my solar. Inside, candles were already lit and Master Bray was waiting, his expression troubled as he took the seat I offered him.

'I think you may need to watch young Meg Woodville, my lady, if you do not want her to end like her mother,' he began, shifting his feet a little awkwardly.

Reginald Bray was not one to hold back what was bothering him, even though he knew there was a good chance I would say something to put him in his place.

'I most certainly do not!' I could imagine being sent to languish in the Tower if I failed to protect the virtue of the beloved only daughter of Earl Rivers, baseborn or not. 'What evidence do you have that she needs watching?'

'When I was in the stables on our return from Pleshey I saw a groom slip her a letter. She did not know I was there and she pushed the note into her sleeve. You might find it if you look.'

'I will ask the governess to do so but it could simply be a letter from her father,' I suggested.

The steward looked doubtful. 'His letters come quite openly with his couriers, my lady. Why should he need to send one surreptitiously?'

I gave this some thought before replying. 'Perhaps because he has something to tell her that he does not wish me to know. We must accept that the senior Woodvilles do not entirely trust me, Reginald. But I thank you for informing me of this. I will make sure we find the note. I would hate to think that they might be using such a young girl as a spy in my house.'

His head shook vehemently. 'I think it much more likely that she has an admirer at court,' he insisted. 'Did you know, while you were attending Sir Henry's sickbed, the Earl her father took her to Westminster Palace several times? Numerous young Squires of the King's Body cast eyes upon the prettiest damsels while waiting on his grace's call . . .'

'And Meg has become a very attractive young lady, something that has not escaped your notice.' I gave him a meaningful look and the blush reappeared. Master Bray was thirty years old and unmarried, as susceptible to a flirtatious glance as any young man. 'But it is true that my attention has of late been elsewhere. I will consult with Mistress Hubbard. She may have noticed something and has not wanted to worry me with it while I have had so much else on my mind.'

'You certainly have, my lady, and if I may say so, you have faced it with admirable fortitude.'

I smiled at him. I was lucky to have a man like Reginald Bray to rely on. He was not only Steward of my household but also Receiver-General of my Somerset estates. While Sir Henry had been my friend and equal, the husband I had believed shared my Lancastrian loyalties, Master Bray truly was the rock on which my life was founded, particularly now that I was a widow. 'Thank you Master Bray,' I said. 'But the past is the past, and now that we know my son is safe I can begin to concentrate on the future.'

He frowned. 'Begging your pardon, my lady, but is it not a little early yet to be considering another marriage?'

'Of course it is too early for that!' I snapped. 'I was

thinking of my son's future rather than my own, Master Bray.'

He lowered his head apologetically. 'Forgive me madam, but I submit that the two are very closely linked, however distant you find yourselves at present.'

5

Harri

The Abbey of St Mathieu, Finis Terre, Brittany, October 1471

BEING THUS STRANDED AT Finis Terre after the terrors of the sea I fell to brooding on our situation. Often a thick mist swarmed in to surround the abbey, reminding me of Wales. At night I dreamed of white mist hanging in the trees all around me, thunder rolling overhead; I crouched in thick undergrowth, fear shortening my breathing and clutching at my heart. It had been raining non-stop for days and the mighty floodwaters swept away bridges and fords over the River Severn, preventing us from crossing to join the army of Queen Marguerite and her son, the Prince of Wales. We waited at Chepstow Castle for the waters to recede; instead news came that we were too late. Our Lancastrian cause had floundered and died in the mud and blood of battle at Tewkesbury and Edward of York was back on the throne. The month was May but God had sent a spring deluge to favour the

Yorkists, just as He had sent a snowstorm at the battle of Towton ten years before.

There had been no point in staying at Chepstow and we set out on the quickest route to Pembroke Castle, while it still remained Lord Jasper's seat of power. Evan and I were among a dozen knights and men at arms who headed there at high speed, barely slowing from a canter. As we rode across a wild common near Caerwent in the continuing rain, I was astonished when a man I knew, the Welsh bard Lewys Glyn Cothi, leaped out from behind a gorse bush, dripping and dishevelled, and cried, 'Halt! Halt my lord!', making my uncle's courser shy and swerve. We halted behind him.

Lord Jasper had drawn his sword but luckily he also recognised the bard, whom I had heard many times sing his poems to gathered company. Indeed I learned that Lewys was a staunch ally of my uncle's cause, one of the secret couriers who had carried letters for him to his supporters all over South Wales.

'Hear my warning, or you ride into a trap!' The bard clutched at my uncle's stirrup.

Lord Jasper dismounted and drew him aside. I did not hear what trap it was the bard warned of but, judging by the weight of coin that fell into his open purse, it was well worth avoiding. Perched behind my uncle's saddle, Lewys directed us on a less-trodden path towards the Black Mountains, though our new destination was not revealed to those of us in the retinue.

Darkness was descending as we approached a moated castle set in a fertile valley. Lewys called it Tretower. We took advantage of the thick mist to conceal ourselves in a brake of alders clinging to the bank of the swollen river, and waited.

My uncle told me not to move from my hiding place. I was to stay by the river. But for once I disobeyed him and it was the horror I witnessed then that now returned repeatedly in my dreams, shrouded in mist and drenched in blood.

One morning, I woke with a start: someone was shaking me. I found Lord Jasper gazing anxiously into my face. He held a lighted candle and the flame was reflected in his eyes. 'Harri. You were yelling in your sleep, my boy – crying out and thrashing about. Tell me what disturbs you so much?'

I struggled to a sitting position, still trembling: 'I keep seeing that beheading in the woods, uncle – that poor old man. I do not understand why he had to die.'

In my dream, a bald head rolled in the dirt towards me, beard mired with fresh blood, the lips still moving in desperate prayer.

My uncle put the candle on the nightstand and his free arm around my shoulders. We were sharing a bed in a small chamber in the guest dorter at the Abbey of St Mathieu, on the heights above the bay where our ship had beached. I rubbed my eyes to banish the scene still branded on my mind.

A torch flaring in the mist, an old man on his knees, a sword slashing down, crimson spurts of blood coating the swordsman's boots. I threw myself back into the bushes.

I avoided my uncle's gaze for fear I would see again the hatred I had perceived in his eyes that day. We had waited, hidden, and when six mounted men rode out of the castle called Tretower Lord Jasper and his knights had pounced from ambush, stormed out of the fog and dragged them all off their horses. Five of them had been lashed to trees and the sixth, their grey-bearded leader, had been trussed and thrown to his knees. With a furious roar and one blow of his sword my uncle had struck his head from his shoulders. I do not recall every word he yelled but the final cry had been '. . . a head for a head!'

'Do you dream of this often?' Lord Jasper tilted my chin so that our eyes met at last and I nodded mutely. 'I did not realise that you saw it, Harri, so I did not explain it to you.'

'I know he was a Yorkist and our enemy but surely it is *they* who murder *our* kind, not the other way around? He was your prisoner. Why did you not send him for trial if he had committed a crime? I do not understand.'

My uncle took a deep breath and sighed. 'In war, Harri, justice is the first thing to go. Sir Roger Vaughan was a Yorkist, you are right there. But he was not just any ally of York. He was Edward's hit man and he was on the way to ambush and kill me. Those were his very orders from Edward's own pen. I found the letter in his purse. But he was more than just a paid assassin. Roger Vaughan was the villain who led my father – your grandfather Sir Owen Tudor – to the block after capturing him fleeing from the battlefield at Mortimer's Cross. By the rules of chivalry Sir Owen should have been ransomed but instead he was executed without trial, his head displayed like a traitor's on the market cross at Hereford. When I learned this I made a sacred vow to find the man responsible and mete the same rough justice to him.'

I hung my head. 'I did not know,' I whispered hoarsely.

'I did not want you to,' Lord Jasper said. 'You saw things that you were not meant to see. You disobeyed orders, Harri . . .'

Suddenly I blurted out, 'I was at the battle of Banbury under the Herbert banner. When Lord Herbert was taken prisoner by Lancastrians, Walter Herbert drew his dagger on me in fury yelling that I must have betrayed the Herberts. I thought he would kill me!' This was something I had never told anyone. I had been sold in ward to William Herbert at age four, when King Edward took the throne and uncle Jasper fled into exile. Walter was Herbert's second son and had always resented my Lancastrian presence in his Yorkist family. We were both twelve-year-old greenhorns when, as part of our military training, we were to witness Lord Herbert's superior army quash a minor Lancastrian rebellion. 'Walter had crowed that the rebels would be annihilated,' I told my uncle. 'But it was not the rout he had anticipated, his father was taken and Walter believed my death would avenge him. Yet, when it came to the moment of strike, the dagger did not plunge into me; he just stood there staring, frozen, and then he dropped the blade.'

'Thank Almighty God for that!' Lord Jasper made the sign of the cross and placed his hand on my head in blessing. 'You were both too young to be at a battle anyway.'

'Yes, we were,' I agreed. 'But strangely, after the Earl of Warwick sent Lord Herbert to the scaffold, Walter learned what it was to be a hunted man and we became unlikely allies.'

'No doubt his anger turned from you to Warwick instead,' said Lord Jasper. 'Revenge is a mighty force but I have to warn you that it is not always sweet, as many would have us believe. But perhaps you will rest easier now that we have talked about it.'

This proved to be the case. We stayed for another ten days in the abbey guest dorter, while a letter was carried to the Duke of Brittany asking for asylum, and I did not wake my uncle again in the night.

Mistress Jane and Sian were lodged in the servants' quarters outside the gates because women were not allowed in the abbey precinct. Each day, rain or shine, my uncle and Mistress Jane went walking on the cliffs beside the monastery. It was the only chance they had to speak together.

Davy and I easily lured Sian out into the open also, and the three of us chased each other along the coastal path, playing tag and stalking games around the stunted bushes. On one occasion Sian brought apples in her apron pocket and she and I sat on a rock, eating them and gazing out to sea. Davy, who rarely remained still, built fortifications in the damp sand, which we had to admire, although what we both liked best was to watch the waves demolish them.

'How can I cheer up my mother, Harri?' Sian asked suddenly, while Davy still toiled. 'She is so miserable, ever since she lost the baby.'

I stared at her, astonished.

'Oh. Had they not told you? She and my father were expecting another child, a blessing, they said, in a time of celebration for the restoration of King Henry to the throne.

'But then just before Christmas, if you remember, when my father was away attending the Parliament in Westminster, she was taken ill. She was in pain but she would not tell me what was the matter . . . until it became obvious she needed help.' Her little round face screwed up in anguish. 'There was blood all over, Harri. It was awful.'

'Oh yes, it must have been,' I said awkwardly. Sian was only a child of eleven years; I was three years her senior but I knew little enough about bodily functions myself. She remained silent so I ploughed on, 'My uncle has been sad too lately. I thought the murder of his brother the king and losing his earldom so soon after he had won it back were reason enough but if they lost a child as well then it is no wonder they are both wretched.'

'Well, what can we do to make them happy again?'

I crunched another bite out of my apple and chewed it, considering. 'I do not think they will be happy until they have somewhere to live together once more. Perhaps it would help to pray that the Duke of Brittany takes us all into his favour.'

'Do you think he will?'

I shrugged. 'Lord Jasper seems to think so, unless he just says that to reassure the rest of us.'

Sian pursed her lips. 'You can never tell with adults.'

'Perhaps Mistress Jane also worries about your sister Elin?' I suggested. 'Had you thought of that?' Elin had been staying at the home of her betrothed Will Gardiner, the son of a rich London merchant, when the Yorkists invaded, making it impossible for Lord Jasper to return to London to fetch her.

'I think Mother misses her rather than worries,' Sian said. 'In her letters Elin sounds merry as a lark. She and Will are the best of friends.'

I detected a wistful tone in her voice when she said this, as if she might be jealous. 'You miss her too, I daresay.'

'Yes but Mother more so. Elin always knew how to make her smile – or at least get some sort of reaction, even if it was only annoyance. I feel inadequate – not clever enough or even irritating enough to stir my mother's spirits.'

I shook my head. 'You should not think like that, Sian. I believe your mother takes great comfort from your presence. Imagine how lonely she would be without you. It was very brave of you both to come into exile with us. You could have stayed in your house in Tenby and lived quietly like you did before my uncle came back.'

She looked shocked. 'Oh no, I wanted to come and mother would not have let father sail without us.' She shot me a wry smile. 'It was a horrible trip though, was it not? I was so sick. I never want to go to sea again.'

I squeezed her hand. 'But then you would never see England again. The voyage cannot always be that bad.'

She said with a little laugh that made me glad, 'Still, I hope the Breton duke does not send us straight back where we came from!'

We had not noticed Lord Jasper and Mistress Jane returning from their walk: they stood with Davy beside his latest castle. Jane looked over at us and smiled, hearing her daughter's laugh, then all three of them came to join Sian and me on the rocks. The tide was coming in fast; wavelets were already undermining Davy's outer walls of sand.

'There is a silver penny for you, Davy, if the donjon is the last structure to fall into the sea,' said Uncle Jasper.

We watched in suspense as the rising water lapped menacingly into the moat around the sand tower, which slumped on one side, but stood for some minutes after the walls were entirely washed away. Lord Jasper pulled a silver penny from the purse on his belt and handed it with a courtly bow to a delighted Davy.

'Ah, yes, and for you, Harri,' he said, retrieving a slightly crushed sprig of bright-yellow flowers from between the fastenings of his jacket. 'Sometimes gorse produces flowers out of season and I found this.'

With another courtly bow, he held it out to me. 'It is yours, Harri, to wear in your hat – a flower of the *Planta Genista* flourishing in an unexpected time and place. I call it a good omen and, as the only one among us with Plantagenet blood, I think the portent is meant for you.'

6

Margaret

I QUASHED MY LANCASTRIAN pride and thought of my son's future; I would kneel at the enemy's feet. I felt a lump in my throat when I saw the lofty frame of King Edward confidently filling the throne into which my shrunken cousin Henry had almost disappeared the last time I had been at court. There was no denying Edward displayed the better image of a king, with his broad shoulders and substantial length of leg. Perhaps more significantly, his crown sat straight and secure on his head, not perched precariously, as Henry's always was.

Arriving, I was conscious that all eyes were on me but I stepped proudly into the audience chamber, reminding myself that I was there because my husband had died from wounds received fighting for this very king. I hoped my black widow's weeds were my passport to a pardon. The chamber was crammed with people and brilliant with jewels and chandeliers. It smelled of perspiration, candlewax and costly unguents.

'My lady of Richmond.' The king acknowledged my presence, using the title, which ten years ago, on his first assumption of the throne, he had permitted me to retain. From my restricted viewpoint, head bowed, I noticed him pull his feet back, so that he must have sat up straight to speak with me. Edward of York invariably addressed a lady with an air of gallantry, no matter how much he might question the worth of her loyalty. 'Allow me to offer my condolences on the death of your husband,' he said.

'Thank you, sire,' I murmured, keeping my gaze lowered. 'He was your grace's loyal servant.'

'And died for my cause, a hero and a friend.' There was a prolonged pause, which eventually prompted me to look up. Edward's blue eyes instantly fixed on mine, as if seeking the true sentiment behind them. 'And now you have come to renew your family's constancy?'

'I have, with your royal clemency.' I caught the reliquary hanging around my neck between my finger and thumb. Edward was not to know that it was the gift of my first husband, half-brother to the king he had caused to be murdered in the Tower; or that it contained a phial of water from the river Jordan, where St John had baptised Christ. John the Baptist, patron saint of my great-grandfather the first Duke of Lancaster, might shield me from my ancestors' wrath at the oath I was about to take.

Edward extended his hand. His coronation ring gleamed on his well-fleshed middle finger, a great York rose of white diamonds set in gold. It flashed the light of a thousand candles into my eyes as I knelt to kiss it. Only a year ago I had kissed my cousin's ring, which had hung on his bony knuckle like a shackle on a skeleton.

I heard myself repeat the oath of fealty: 'I humbly pledge my allegiance to your grace and to your son Edward, Prince of Wales . . .' The very same words I had used before but in such different circumstances.

When the oath was completed King Edward smiled and urged me to rise. 'Welcome back to my court, Lady Richmond, the queen will be delighted to see you here again I am sure.' He glanced in the direction of his wife's throne a few yards away. It was a dismissal and I backed carefully off the dais steps, Meg Woodville handling my copious black train with commendable skill. The queen beckoned us to her dais, allowing the next petitioner to approach the king. At this stage of his return to power these pardoning courts were busy places.

'I am glad you have brought my niece as your train-bearer, Lady Richmond,' Queen Elizabeth said. 'I do not see her often enough.'

Meg and I both made our curtsies and the girl moved forward to kiss her aunt's cheek. 'I was here with my father recently, your grace, but sadly you were unwell and we did not meet. I hope you are recovered.'

Her aunt sighed. 'I am with child again and was suffering sickness but I am pleased to say that has stopped now.'

'Allow me to congratulate you, my lady,' I said, thinking that she looked radiant for an expectant mother who had been experiencing pregnancy sickness. 'You and King Edward enjoy God's favour in your fruitfulness. May I ask when this babe might be born?'

The queen nodded. 'You may ask, Margaret, because I hope you will be there at my confinement. The child is expected next spring and I invite you to once again join my circle of attendant ladies.'

I knew there would be an ulterior motive in what seemed a gracious invitation but of course I accepted without hesitation. To have Queen Elizabeth's ear was virtually to have that of her husband and I coveted that privilege in order to pursue my son's pardon and repatriation. Still, I would have to proceed slowly and carefully; Elizabeth might also be keeping an eye on me, doubting my commitment to York.

The queen rose slowly, saying, 'Let us retire to my solar,' and her ladies scampered to organise the heavy train of her lavishly embroidered court mantle. 'I have business to discuss with you.'

There was a flurry of activity as protocols were observed, the queen curtsied to the king and we all backed carefully away from his throne before turning for the privy door behind the dais. Fashion and ceremonial were both elaborate at the court of King Edward. A speculative murmur arose among the other occupants of the chamber, probably centred around why the queen should be showing favour to one such as me, so recently on the excluded list. I noticed behind the king's throne a group of his young Squires of the Body hovering there, ready to give service if needed. The intense gaze of one darkly handsome young man seemed to be fixed on something, or someone, very close behind me – Meg Woodville.

After my discussion with Master Bray I had consulted Mistress Hubbard, the governess appointed to supervise my wards. She was a strict but kindly gentlewoman who took a sympathetic interest in all the young people but was particularly fond of Meg, who was the first to call her 'Mother' Hubbard. She had been indignant at the suggestion that the girl might be acting as a spy for her royal relatives and made a discreet but thorough search for the note which Master Bray had witnessed being handed over in the stable, finding nothing. In the absence of any evidence, I had not wished to ask Meg outright about an unknown admirer at court, but the ardent gaze of this good-looking courtier might be a clue as to a possible culprit. As soon as he became aware of my attention he quickly averted his eyes.

I snatched a glance over my shoulder when we reached the stairway leading to the royal apartments, as Meg bent to bundle my train up the steps. She was definitely red-faced but whether that was due to the ardent glances of a young admirer or her efforts as my attendant it was hard to judge. When she let out a squeal at the top of the stairs I knew it was one of delight to find her father waiting in the ante-chamber of the queen's solar. He had been reading a pocket-sized volume, which he immediately tucked into the front of his elegant doublet when his sister appeared, so that he might throw open his arms to his daughter. Unheeding of the formalities surrounding the queen's arrival, Meg dropped my train and ran into the open embrace of Earl Rivers, who swung her merrily off the ground and tried to bow to the queen at the same time.

Elizabeth frowned at his levity. 'Put her down brother,' she demanded. 'Meg is no longer a child. It is not seemly to throw her about, is it Lady Richmond?'

'Distinctly not,' I agreed, as Meg's father returned her cheerfully to the floor.

'My humble apologies, ladies,' said the contrite earl, making a second, perfect bow and slipping a sly wink at Meg. 'I keep forgetting that my daughter is now a young lady.'

'But not that your sister is the queen I hope,' said Elizabeth, nodding at the duty chamberlain to open the door to her solar.

A broad grin: 'Never that, your grace, never that!' and Anthony followed us into the inner sanctum where a fire burned brightly and the scent of hippocras hung sweetly in the air. Pages arranged seats around the queen's canopied chair and we settled down as if for a family gathering. Elizabeth's trainbearer, whom I recognised as her cousin Lady Alice Fogge, a courtier of my own age and a long-standing lady-in-waiting, gathered up her embroidery and took a discreet position in a distant window seat.

'We are here to discuss a confidential matter regarding Meg,' began Elizabeth, accepting a small crystal goblet offered to her on a silver tray. 'Please take refreshment and we will wait for the servants to leave us.'

Refreshment consisted of the strong wine, the aroma of which I had noticed. I shook my head at Meg when she made to accept a glass of the hippocras and refused it myself. 'We are fasting today, I thank your grace,' I said.

On two days a week the young girl shared my habit of eating one small fish with plain bread and drinking only water. The practice had always served me well, and now I considered it a good way to encourage self-discipline in Meg and to keep her appetite in check. It was too easy for girls who were mature in body yet still immature in mind to become plump and lazy when they lived in wealthy households. However, I did not insist that she also wore a hair belt next to her skin as I did on these fast days, to keep my mind focused on my duty to God. Ignoring the itch it caused was a knack I had acquired over the years.

Earl Rivers had no scruples about accepting the drink and raised the fragile Venetian glass in salute to his sister. 'Your health, Elizabeth. I confess I am intrigued on Meg's behalf.'

Elizabeth waited for the room to clear of servants before responding. 'It has come to the king's notice that one of his Squires of the Body is enamoured of your daughter, my lord.' She turned her gaze on Meg, who had flushed guiltily and dropped her eyes. 'And I see that she is only too aware of it.'

Anthony's brow furrowed and he glared at me. 'Do you know about this, Lady Richmond?' he demanded. 'Who is this man?'

Any reply of mine was pre-empted by the queen. 'His name is Robert Poyntz,' she said. 'And do not look so angry, brother, you of all people cannot deny that young people have feelings for each other. What we should establish is whether anything needs to be done about it.'

'We have hardly even spoken!' Meg blurted out. 'Only a few times at court occasions.'

'But you have exchanged letters I understand?' retorted Elizabeth, raising her eyebrows at Meg. 'Our Master of Horse overheard one of the royal grooms blabbing to his fellows about carrying them. Such idle gossip among servants can ruin a damsel's reputation.' Then her gaze fell on me. 'How much of this is known to you, Margaret?'

I shrugged uncomfortably. 'Very little, although I was apprised of the possibility.' I was wishing I had taken more notice of Master Bray's warning and taxed Meg with the matter of the letter. 'I was not aware of the name of the young man, however, until you told us, your grace.'

'I know his family,' Anthony remarked. 'Poyntz is a well-known name in the west. His father is dead and Robert I believe is still a ward of one of the Herberts. He will inherit several manors when he comes of age. Studying law as well as serving the king – a bright lad.'

I felt a certain amount of relief when I heard this. 'Not a *mésalliance* then?' I murmured.

'How could it be a misalliance with a Woodville?' demanded Earl Rivers, ignoring the fact that he had not actually married his daughter's mother, though he had given Meg his name.

'I am sure Lady Richmond was thinking of young Robert's suitability,' interjected Elizabeth, no doubt still acutely conscious of the furore caused by her own marriage to King Edward.

'I do not want to marry him!' cut in Meg indignantly. 'I only wrote him a few notes and talked with him in a corridor. Do I have to marry every boy I speak to at court?'

Her father's voice rose in anger. 'Hush Meg! Speak when you are spoken to and converse only with those I or Lady Richmond permit you to. There are people at court who are not necessarily acceptable. And in future do not correspond with any man save me. Do you understand?'

Meg looked mutinous. She was not used to her father denying her anything. I turned to where she sat on a stool slightly behind my chair and took her hand. 'Lord Rivers only has your interests at heart, Meg,' I said.

'Yes, and I will have words with young Master Poyntz,' he said more calmly. 'But when the time comes for you to marry I will arrange it and make sure it is to someone worthy of you and your royal connections.'

'Well said, brother.' Elizabeth drained her glass of hippo-cras. 'Meanwhile I will consult the king about the worthiness of Robert Poyntz Esquire. But Lady Margaret and I have other matters to discuss so perhaps you and Meg could enjoy some time together in my garden. I believe the sun is out.'

At this clear dismissal, father and daughter rose and left the room together and Elizabeth called to her lady in waiting, 'Cousin Alice, could you fetch a cape for Meg? Although the sun is shining, she may get cold in the garden.'

Alice knew better than to linger over a royal order and hurried to do her cousin's bidding, which left Elizabeth and me conveniently alone together. She did not waste time. 'Now we can discuss what you are going to do about your son Henry, Margaret,' she said. 'He cannot be left in the hands of Jasper Tudor. I do not understand why you allowed him to return to that rogue's custody.'

Taken by surprise, I groped for a response. 'Well, it was Henry's choice, your grace, to further his knightly training – as Earl of Pembroke, Lord Jasper was the obvious mentor.'

Elizabeth flushed with irritation. 'Do not call him Lord in my hearing, Margaret! He is an attainted traitor, without lands or title.'

Rattled, I retaliated before I could stop myself. 'And by association apparently, so is my son! Though how a fourteen-year-old boy can be condemned as a traitor I do not comprehend.'

Elizabeth's displeasure increased. 'Tread carefully, Madam! Remember at whose feet you knelt only minutes ago. Edward is very sensitive about oath-breakers.'

I took several deep breaths to calm myself before

responding. 'Forgive me, your grace. It is hard to be once more separated from the son with whom I was so recently reunited. Tell me how I may get him back again?'

There was a sudden change of mood. 'I do not know why I should help you, Margaret, but I have always found your company stimulating.' Elizabeth's candid appraisal lent sparkle to her deep-brown eyes. 'Render faithful service among my ladies during the coming months and the king will see that you support his reign. Then, your mourning period over, we shall in due course find you a suitable husband to bind you to us completely. That will give Henry a loyal family to return to and Edward will restore him to his noble status. Meanwhile, now that the Countess of Richmond has sworn allegiance to York, those who still harbour Lancastrian leanings will realise that there is little future in stubborn loyalty.'

I liked none of what she said but I swear even the ablest reader of minds would not have perceived it.

7

Harri

Château de Nantes, Brittany, November 1471

THE DUKE OF BRITTANY sent one of his officials with horses and baggage carts to bring us to his court at Nantes. We passed through great forests, crossed several mighty rivers and had frequent glimpses of the sea where it made deep marshy inroads into the land. Sometimes, as we traversed the entire length of Brittany, I rode beside Lord Jasper and learned something of what he knew of Duke Francis and his history.

'I spent a few weeks at his court several years ago, Harri, on a diplomatic mission from King Louis,' he explained. 'It was during my last period of exile and I must confess that I found Francis a good deal easier to deal with than the French king, who is a cunning ruler but an unpredictable character. Of course the three of us are related in various degrees through my mother Queen Catherine; she was King Louis's aunt and her elder sister, Jeanne of France, married Francis's uncle, Duke Jean the Sixth.'

I grimaced. 'I do not know how you remember who is related to who, uncle!'

He laughed at that. 'One day, if we are permitted to settle here for a while, I will draw you a family tree, Harri. It can be important because in Europe all the royal families are inter-married. These marriages resolve many political issues, but frequently not the problem of the succession.' He reached across from his saddle to grip my shoulder. 'Your mother will have impressed on you how proud she is to have given your father a son and heir, even if he did not live to see you born. Your line of succession to her lineage and estates is indisputable and we both live to fight for their restitution.'

I nodded, frowning. 'Yes uncle,' I said, 'but how likely is that?'

'Things can change, Harri, things can change,' he said, but I heard no great conviction in his voice.

My first sight of the duke's principal palace at Nantes reminded me somewhat of Pembroke Castle: a mighty curtain wall, with substantial towers at every angle. The surprise came when we passed under the imposing gatehouse and discovered a palace from romantic fable. We were confronted by a vast paved courtyard lined with a series of long facades of brilliant whitewashed stone, linked by elegant round towers with steep pointed roofs, glinting with serried ranks of diamond-glazed windows and embellished with sculpted lintels and balustrades. It was built to display the magnificence of the duke's court and I was open-mouthed at the sight. I had seen nothing like it. English castles tended to be spectacular fortifications from a bygone age, built to repel enemies, but here was a magnificent edifice of refined splendour, which promised luxury.

Under Lord Jasper's instructions I had dressed for the occasion in the fine court apparel I had worn the previous year to visit my uncle King Henry at Westminster Palace, during the brief months of his return to the throne. However, I had grown since then. The sleeves of the red velvet doublet, fur-trimmed, had climbed above my wrists, the front lacing was at maximum stretch and the red leather shoes with their jewelled vamps were a painfully tight fit. Climbing the curved stone staircase to the grand entrance of the palace, it was hard not to wince at every step.

I continued to suffer the silent scream from my tortured feet as Lord Jasper and I strode the length of the vast, high-beamed hall, brilliant with autumn sunlight streaming through numerous clerestory windows and scintillating from ranks of blazing chandeliers, its walls bright with colourful tapestries and frescoes. Duke Francis was holding court from the gilded dais. Our arrival induced a lull in the general hubbub and people fell back to stand and stare. The duke rose from his canopied throne to greet us, bluff and cheerful, a magnificent figure in purple satin lavishly trimmed with ermine tails.

'My lord of Pembroke – Cousin Jasper – how good it is to see you here at last and this must be the young man who calls himself the Comte de Richemont – a title I had thought I held myself!' A hearty laugh accompanied this unnerving pronouncement.

I knew that a century ago an English king had conferred the earldom of Richmond on a Breton duke but I was not aware that successive Dukes of Brittany had continued to lay claim to it. I swallowed hard and made the duke a deep bow, racking my brains for a suitable response but I was saved the trouble as my uncle spoke first.

'Our heartfelt thanks, your grace, for welcoming us to Brittany. It seems you and my nephew now have common cause against the man who calls himself King of England, who has grabbed the lands of Richmond for his undeserving brother and made traitors of us all.'

A slight twitch of the lips was Duke Francis's only reaction to this as he turned and gestured towards the petite lady in coronet and court mantle seated in the throne beside his. 'May I present my wife, the Duchess Marguerite? I believe you and she may be quite close in age, my lord of Richemont.'

The duke had taken a pretty child for his second wife, who stared ahead expressionlessly as I made my second bow. I thought she looked considerably younger than me and I gave her a polite smile, which was not reciprocated. Another lady then emerged from the crowd of favoured courtiers gathered behind the ducal thrones, a beautiful woman of mature years, clad in bright-coloured robes and glittering jewellery. She approached the duke with an exaggerated laid-back stride, which I took to be necessary to balance the extraordinary height and width of her elaborate headdress. A young damsel followed her to handle the weight of her train, a custom my lady mother held to on court occasions.

'And may I also present Madame Antoinette de Maignelais who is, I think you will agree, my lords, a jewel of my court.' The duke took the lady's hand and drew her towards my uncle, who made her a bow with a level of flourish I had not seen him display before.

'No man could disagree with that, your grace,' he said.

My eyes widened at my uncle's unusual gallantry and

then I blinked as an unmistakable snort came from the little duchess. Turning, I saw that she was smothering what I took to be a giggle behind her hand. Having made my bow to the bejewelled lady, I tentatively approached the duchess's throne but discovered, at close quarters, that her lips were not smiling but curled with distaste, disfiguring her pretty face. Nonplussed, I groped for a bland subject to open a conversation with her.

'Allow me to congratulate you on your marriage, Madame,' was the best I could do.

To my surprise she shook her head. 'Oh it is not really a marriage. Not yet at least. I am only twelve and my father made the duke promise to leave me alone until I am of age.'

Her candour astonished me and I stuttered, 'Oh – I see.'

'I am glad of it. The duke is so old.'

Again her frankness startled me. 'I think he is the same age as my uncle – not so terribly old. But I know what you mean.' I lowered my voice and bent nearer to make myself heard. 'Were you unhappy to leave your home?'

She shook her head again but changed the subject.

'They tell me you were shipwrecked, Seigneur Richemont. Is that true?'

'Not exactly. We were being blown onshore but our captain managed to sail the ship up onto a beach. It was done on purpose but the monks claimed salvage nevertheless. In the end my uncle paid a jetsam tax so we could re-launch the ship.'

'Monks?' Her brow creased. 'Were you near a monastery then?'

I told her the whole story; the terrifying storm, the loss of our crewmember and the surprise to find we were stranded in Brittany and not France. Once more her reaction was unexpected. 'The duke thinks you were lucky to land on our shore. He believes the French king would have sent you back to England; but then he and King Louis do not see eye to eye.' She frowned and gazed at me intently. 'What would happen if you were sent back?'

I grimaced. 'I do not know what would happen to me but I believe my uncle might end up on the scaffold. Yorkists executed his father and almost certainly murdered mine and he is convinced that Edward ordered the death of his half-brother King Henry in the Tower of London. Lord Jasper will never bend the knee to York.'

The duchess smiled at that. 'Just as Brittany will never bend the knee to France, however often King Louis threatens to invade us. The duke and your uncle have much in common; all the more reason to be sure you will be safe here.'

'You seem very well informed,' I observed, wondering just how much such a young lady really knew of the duke's affairs.

'Do you think I am too young to know my husband's mind?' She jerked her head in the direction of the three adults, still engaged in their conversation beside the duke's throne. 'Perhaps you think the Maignelais woman knows more of it than I do? You should warn your uncle to beware of Madame de Maignelais. She thinks she can have all men in her thrall. As a girl she became the old French king's mistress but his son, the present King Louis, detested her and threw her out of the French court, so she came here and seduced Duke Francis. Of course that was before my time – practically before I was born! She may not look it but she is nearly as old as him!' Her lip curled again. 'She

66

probably drove the last duchess into an early grave but she will not do that to me.'

'I certainly hope not!' I said.

'I am glad.' Her face lit up when she smiled. 'But your future is not so certain. I wonder what arrangements the duke will make for you? You must be anxious to know.'

'That is just what we have been discussing.' Lord Jasper had made his way over to us and caught her final remark. 'I am sorry to interrupt but his grace has invited us to his chamber, Harri.'

A table had been laid in the duke's Great Chamber and we were invited to sit and partake of a substantial meal, served by half a dozen liveried young men. There was no sign of the little duchess. The duke was there with his mistress. As the wine was being poured I was glad to hear Lord Jasper ask quietly whether Mistress Jane, Sian, Evan and Davy were being similarly provided for.

'Of course, of course,' Duke Francis assured him. 'I was surprised that you brought only four retainers with you, my lords. The Duke of Exeter foisted forty on your Queen Marguerite's impoverished court-in-exile before she threw him out.'

'Our people are family as well as retainers, your grace, and I beg you not to speak of Exeter in the same breath. We may be distantly related but he is not a relative I care to own. He does not know the meaning of loyalty and at present resides captive in the Tower of London. The only point in his favour is that while he lives he remains a permanent thorn in York's flesh. I can only say that if he found forty people willing to go into exile with him then he bribed them to do so and I warrant the bribe was never paid.'

The duke gave a hearty laugh, took a good gulp of wine and beckoned to his cupbearer for a refill before turning back to Lord Jasper. 'Now, to business. I want to keep you safe from King Louis's clutches but Nantes is too close to the French border for that, so I propose to send you to our Château de l'Hérmine in Vannes – a jewel of a palace, named for our ducal crest. It is where Madame de Maignelais' boys are being raised and so there are suitable tutors and instructors to continue your nephew's education.'

He turned to me then. 'François and Antoine are a little younger than you, Henri – I hope I may call you that informally – but there is a tennis court and it is where I keep my best horses, so you can play, ride, and polish your jousting skills. A young nobleman should not neglect that side of his education. I am sure you agree, Lord Jasper.'

'This is extremely kind and I hope we may see something of you too, Francis?' remarked my uncle. I noticed that he carefully avoided any mention of who might be the father of Madame de Maignelais' 'boys', although the lady herself sat close by, across the board. 'Of course I shall contribute towards our expenses as far as my available funds allow, although obviously my income is woefully restricted at present.'

'But we hope that will not be for long, do we not? Meanwhile the education and development of such a promising young man as Henri should not be neglected.' The duke raised his newly filled cup to us both, as we raised our cups to him.

'And yes, we shall see plenty of each other,' the duke continued. 'The hunting is very good around Vannes.' With this, he set about wrapping some kind of pancake around a portion of meat in an aromatic spicy sauce and offered it to me.

'You should eat some of this, Henri,' he said solicitously. 'You must be hungry. These galettes are a speciality of Brittany, made with sarrasin and stuffed with anything you like. You must try this pigeon. Mmmm!'

He placed it on my trencher. 'It smells good,' I said politely, 'but what is sarrasin?'

'It grows very well here in Brittany. It is a staple of our diet.'

'Of the diet of the poor and needy!' Madame de Maignelais spoke up in a withering tone of voice. 'They make these horrible "galettes", as they call them, with the dried and ground flowers of what is little more than a weed. Mountain villagers may rely on it for their staple food but we do not have to. My lord likes to humour the peasants by favouring their ways. You do not need to eat it if you do not care to, my lord Henri. I never touch it myself.'

The galette was the colour of chestnuts and oozing with the fragrant sauce; ignoring the lady's warning I took a careful mouthful and was rewarded with a pleasant nutty flavour. 'It is delicious, your grace,' I said, to a hiss of disapproval from across the board.

The duke laughed, bending over his trencher and lifting a dripping galette to his lips with relish. 'In Brittany you will grow into a fine and noble Englishman, will he not, Lord Jasper?'

My uncle wiped sauce from his fingers with his napkin and nodded solemnly. 'A noble *Lancastrian* Englishman,' he insisted.

8

Margaret

Windsor Castle, spring 1472

BEING AT WINDSOR AS lady companion to an expectant
mother who was about to go into confinement was not
like attending a hunting party. Queen Elizabeth was nervous,
fretful and hard to please. Like me she longed to ride out
into the forested park around the castle and enjoy the exhilaration of the chase but she was prevented by her advanced
pregnancy and I was restricted by my sense of duty. However,
in the end she would have a new baby to compensate her
and I never would. I thought I had managed to disguise
my frustration and renewed sense of loss but one fine spring
morning I discovered I had not.

We were sitting together in the beautiful oriel window
that Edward had commissioned in the queen's solar, gazing
out at the sweeping view it offered over the river Thames,
which flowed through the great hunting park.

'I can guess what you are thinking, Margaret. You are
wishing you were out there at the chase and not stuck in

here with your swollen-bellied queen.' Elizabeth was reclining on a day bed, her feet propped on cushions and her embroidery frame lying on the floor, having slipped through her fingers when she dozed off. 'Because if you were not daydreaming you would have picked up my sewing without my having to ask.'

Guiltily, I rose. 'I crave pardon, your grace,' I said, reaching for the frame. But she snapped, 'Leave it! I cannot be bothered to sew any more. Why should the babe need new chemises? We have plenty of old ones and it will only be another girl. I so want to give Edward a second son.'

I knew what she would say next because she asked me the question every day. 'Do you really think it will be a boy, Margaret?'

I answered, 'I think there is half a chance that it will be a boy, yes your grace.' My testy words were uttered carelessly and as soon as I said them I wished I could bite them back. It was foolish to be clever with Elizabeth. She only appreciated sympathy and sycophancy.

'Yesterday you agreed it was a male child, today you have changed your mind. That does not show consistency, Margaret. If you are not loyal to your own opinions, why should you be loyal to the king's? Which is a pity because he has found you a very suitable candidate for marriage and it is his intention to introduce you to him tomorrow.'

Tomorrow was the day the queen was due to enter her confinement and there would be a special service in St George's Chapel to seek God's blessing for the mother and child, which the whole court would be attending.

What could I say? 'My humble apologies, Madam, I wished to be amusing and lighten your mood but it was tactless. Of course I hope and I pray that you will have a son but I mostly pray to St Margaret to grant you both a safe delivery, whatever the sex of the child.'

Elizabeth glanced at me. 'I have no doubt that any prayers you make to your patron saint will have great influence, Margaret.' Surprisingly this remark sounded completely sincere; her mood had clearly softened. 'The king may want to tell you himself but I think you should have due warning. The nobleman he will recommend to you is Lord Thomas Stanley. Short of his brother of York, Edward can hardly have selected a more worthy and wealthy candidate for your hand. Stanley's first wife died at the New Year, after a long illness and Edward believes a marriage between you later this year would be both suitable and appropriate. Are you acquainted with Lord Stanley?'

I summoned an image of a mature figure in a long and expensively furred gown with a forked beard, streaked with grey. Lord Stanley was no Lancelot, but that was no bad thing. I answered, 'Only slightly, your grace. He favours life on his estates in the northwest I believe.'

'Well, he will be at court from now on because the king has made him Steward of the Household.'

'As his father was before him,' I remarked.

'Indeed. Well? Shall I tell the king you favour such a match?'

I made a brief curtsy. 'If his grace proposes it then I will, of course, give it careful consideration, my lady.'

She gazed at me steadily for a few moments then nodded. 'I will convey your response.'

I received a summons from King Edward the following day, soon after the court had escorted Queen Elizabeth to her lying-in chamber. This had been meticulously prepared, with deep-pile carpets on the floor and thick tapestries covering the walls and windows, except for one small casement, left open to let in light and air. At the entrance Elizabeth hugged her three little girls, who all looked crestfallen at the prospect of being denied their mother's kisses until she promised them that they might visit her from time to time. Little Edward, the baby Prince of Wales remained in his Westminster quarters with his household of nurses and footmen.

Only the eldest princess, six-year-old Elizabeth of York, was mature enough to sense the aura of impending jeopardy that invariably accompanied a lying-in. At the Mass for the mother and child preceding the confinement, I noticed an anxious tear escape down her soft round cheek, and I realised that even at her tender age she understood that her mother was entering a room where she faced an ordeal from which she may not escape alive.

However, having survived six births Queen Elizabeth appeared unperturbed by the joust with death that lay ahead and once ensconced in the quiet shade of the confinement chamber she seemed to settle like a nesting bird. Under my supervision, a dozen carefully chosen ladies and chamber-women would provide company and service day and night and guard their charge from any nuisance. Not even the king would be welcome to disturb the serenity in which his wife lay.

Nevertheless she was still fully aware of his affairs and reminded me of his summons. 'Should you not be attending the king, Margaret?' she inquired solicitously. 'He will be expecting you. Do not keep him waiting.' I could defer the unwelcome matter of my marriage no longer.

When I was admitted to his Privy Chamber, the king was in conference with his brother Richard, Duke of Gloucester, two red-gold heads in murrey velvet caps bending close together over a table. At thirty years old Edward of York was in his prime and when he rose to greet me, as always I was struck by his extreme height. The polite gesture was either good manners or intended to intimidate me. As I made my curtsy, I chose to consider it the former and noticed that his brother, ten years younger and considerably shorter, did not follow his example. Perhaps he did not relish the interruption – or the height comparison.

'You remember the Countess of Richmond, do you not, Richard?' the king said with a frown. 'Her late husband was a casualty of the battle at Barnet.'

His brother scowled. 'Yes, I remember her and I also remember that her Tudor son and his uncle are thorns in our flesh across the Channel.' He made no effort to rise.

'All the more reason why we should welcome the fact that Lady Richmond chooses to support our throne,' the king persisted. 'If you will not get to your feet for a lady, Richard, use them to make your exit. We can resume our consultations later.'

The young duke reluctantly pushed back his chair and made a sketchy bow, which might have been meant for me or for his brother. 'Let it be sooner rather than later, sire, or I shall be forced to take action without your consent, which I know we will both regret.'

To my surprise, instead of taking offence at Gloucester's surly tone Edward laughed and clapped him on the shoulder. 'Curb your impatience brother, all will be arranged in good time. Lady Richmond cannot wait for she is attending the queen in her confinement. I will send word very soon.'

Gloucester gave a curt nod and turned for the door. I noticed Richard of Gloucester did not appear to have grown much at all since I had seen him at court aged sixteen, when he had been granted his precocious majority and given his first military command.

'I apologise for dragging you from your duties, Lady Richmond,' the king said, offering me the seat abandoned by his brother. As was his habit he wore a short doublet, which emphasised his fine physique and drew attention to his long legs. The thick tresses escaping from under his cap showed no sign of thinning and his bright blue eyes still twinkled roguishly when he chose to let them, as he did at that moment. All this distracted from his complexion, which was beginning to border on the florid.

He began confidingly. 'I have been discussing the details of my brother's marriage to Anne Neville, for which we only await the papal dispensation. Now, I have a proposition for you, if that is the right word, and I suspect the queen has told you of it.'

Before sitting down he poured two cups of wine from the flagon on the table between us and placed one beside me. 'I serve you myself because I choose to keep our conversation private,' he remarked as he took his seat. 'I hope you do not object.'

I smiled and lifted the cup. 'I trust my reputation is good enough to combat any suggestion of impropriety in my being alone with the king, your grace,' I said, returning his smile and raising the wine to wet my lips before replacing it on the table, where I intended it should remain untouched during the rest of our tête-à-tête. In fact it was not my reputation that was of concern to me but Edward's, which was notorious when it came to entertaining ladies privately.

He ignored my pleasantry and pursued his own agenda. 'It is five months now since Sir Henry Stafford died and the time approaches to consider your position in society, does it not, my lady?' Edward's smile had been replaced by an expression of almost paternal solemnity. 'Since you were never attainted, you will retain the title of Countess of Richmond until such time as your son marries but that is something to consider later. The Richmond estates reverted to the crown on his father's death and as you know I have since granted them to my brother George of Clarence. However, you still hold possession of the Somerset revenues and I have the responsibility of ensuring that noble widows such as yourself are suitably married, so that their estates are efficiently run. You will understand that I particularly wish to ensure that those who have recently been obliged to renew their allegiance to the crown should confirm their loyalty by making appropriate unions.'

I inclined my head. 'I assure you that I am intensely aware of my duty to the crown, sire,' I said, wondering when he would bite the bone and come to the point. I did not wait long.

'I understand that you are acquainted with Lord Stanley of Lathom,' he remarked, as if it were a matter of little importance.

'We have exchanged pleasantries at court,' I replied, determined not to make it easy for him. 'But he is not here often. I believe he prefers to reside on his estates – in Lancashire, are they not?' The mention of that particular county could be nothing but an irritant to York.

Edward pursed his lips. 'Partly yes, but even more in Cheshire and North Wales and he holds the lordship of the Isle of Man, not that I expect he goes there very often. His ancestors called themselves kings of Man but I have put a stop to that. There can only be one king in England.' To emphasise this point he paused to stretch his lips in a thin smile. 'Anyway, I have arranged for him to meet you. From now on he will be at court because I have appointed him my Steward of the Household. Thus, you will appreciate, he is one of my most powerful nobles, a man who will be a more than suitable husband for you.'

It was my turn to frown, displeased with his assumption that I would instantly approve such a match. 'But not immediately I assume sire.'

Once more the smile did not reach his eyes. 'Not tomorrow Lady Richmond – in a month or two, let us say. You might find his London home an attraction since you will be obliged to relinquish Coldharbour Inn very soon. I have granted the Duke of Exeter a pardon and he will repossess it on Lady Day.'

This was a blow but not an unexpected one, for Coldharbour had come to me during Henry VI's return to the throne but, now that Exeter's attainder had been reversed, repossession of his ancestral London property was inevitable.

I let King Edward take a long pull at his cup of wine before making my response. 'I would not marry again simply to secure a London residence, your grace; nor do I wish to be rushed into a decision.'

As I spoke there was a scratching on the door of the

chamber and Edward immediately called 'Enter!' as if he was expecting the interruption. The rather smug expression he assumed when he rose to greet the new arrival persuaded me that it would be Lord Stanley and I too stood up. It was.

Soon, to discuss our possible marriage, we were walking alone together in the king's private garden, which ran along a terrace on the west wall of Windsor Castle. A weak spring sun warmed the rosemary bushes planted along the crenelated walls, releasing their fragrant aroma.

Lord Stanley walked beside me with the careful, measured step of a man in a long gown not wishing to trip on the hem.

'It is only a short time since the death of your wife, my lord,' I said, keeping my tone conversational. 'Was it a long ordeal she suffered?'

His response, delivered politely, made my heart tighten in my chest. 'My wife did her duty and provided me with a steady succession of children but latterly the babes kept dying and she became very depressed. Somehow, despite a procession of physicians offering remedies, she simply faded away.'

The first Lady Stanley had been a Neville, a family disastrously split between York and Lancaster, and in fact I had seen her, probably on her final visit to Westminster, in the funeral procession for her brothers, the Earl of Warwick and the Marquis of Montagu, both casualties of the same battle at Barnet that had eventually claimed my husband. In her mourning garb, Eleanor Stanley had resembled a very pale wraith.

With this image in mind I said, 'I hope you realise, my

lord, that if we were to marry there would be no more children. I have heard too many doctors pronounce on my barrenness to pray for any miracles of that sort.'

I felt rather than saw him cast me an astonished glance then turn away. 'You are very frank, Lady Richmond,' he said. 'And I will be frank in return. I already have four sons. I am not looking for another heir.'

'Good.' I gave him a tight smile. 'Although I imagine his grace would not have put us in this awkward position were he not aware that there was no requirement of that kind.' We walked several paces in heavy silence before I spoke again. 'I do have a number of wards, however, who are very important to me. I would not wish to abandon them.'

'I can see no reason why you should. In fact my own boys would greatly benefit from a maternal influence and the company of other children. Their own mother, being in fragile health, had become a distant figure in their lives. I have done my best but I fear there is no substitute for the female influence.'

'I must admit that my nestlings, as I call them, keep me from becoming too embroiled in my own concerns. I owe them as much as they owe me.'

'And they must be of comfort to you in the absence of your son. I think Henry Tudor may be one of the reasons his grace has thrown us together in this way, though perhaps not the main one.'

His comment intrigued me. 'Please explain,' I said.

'Edward is still insecure on his throne. He wishes to unite the country behind York and so he gives pardons to those he knows still secretly cleave to the Lancastrian affinity, hoping they will stand by their oaths of loyalty out of gratitude and a wish for peace. But perhaps rightly, he does not fully trust them. He has made me steward of his household because that way he can keep me at his side.' Then he added with a crooked smile, 'And if we are married, he can keep an eye on you as well.'

'Or get you to do so,' I retorted. 'He is the puppet-master. But I have my own agenda too, my lord. I wish to get my son back from Brittany but not without also having his title and estates restored to him. I have the queen's ear on this already. Perhaps I do not need any further support than hers.'

He pursed his lips. 'Like you and I, the queen was reared in a staunch Lancastrian family. She has to tread as carefully as any of us and if she shows too much favour to you he may suspect a conspiracy. Have you thought of that?'

We reached the end of the terrace garden and paused in our walk to study the view. A pair of courtiers could be seen riding out into the park, a man and a woman, conspicuous in the bright-coloured clothing permitted only to people of rank. We watched them disappear into the evergreen undergrowth beneath the bare branches of the great oaks.

My arm swept the vista. 'Even now, in her confinement, the queen will hear of those two riding out together unescorted and it will be the subject of speculation. The court thrives on affairs and conspiracies my lord, and the queen's solar buzzes with scandal. Sir Henry used to say to me that the only safe talk was between the sheets.'

Lord Stanley laughed at that and his sombre, plump-cheeked face was transformed. 'More candour, Lady Richmond! Is that a hint you are in favour of marriage?'

I shot him a sideways glance. 'I am always in favour of

marriage, Lord Stanley, between the right man and woman and in accordance with the degrees of consanguinity. Is it not ordained by God?'

His laughter died and he shrugged. 'So we are led to believe. It is certainly ordained by the king, at least for those of us with any stature in his realm. What will you say to him after this meeting?'

'I would rather know what you, his faithful steward, will say to him.'

The baron expelled air. 'Huh! If we were youngsters I would say, "I asked *you* first." But being a gentleman I will bow to your ladyship's rank and sex. I will say to him that I am willing if she is.'

I shrugged. 'Then I will let the king give you my answer my lord, when I have confided it to him.'

With a sigh of resignation he turned and we made our way back to the spiral stair that led from the garden to the royal apartments. I thought it mere good manners when he stood back to allow me to precede him but as I passed by he stopped me in my tracks. 'No doubt you are aware that I am on the king's council, Lady Richmond. I think you should know that today it was decided to send emissaries to Brittany to negotiate the return of Jasper and Henry Tudor to England. The appointed leader of the mission is the queen's brother, Earl Rivers.'

9

Harri

Château de l'Hérmine, Vannes, Brittany, late spring 1472

THE CITY OF NANTES was often plagued with fog due to its position close to the ocean on the estuary of the Loire and Duke Francis considered it unhealthy for young people. Therefore, in preparation for his first marriage, he had made improvements to his Château de l'Hérmine at Vannes, a flourishing merchant town on the Bay of Morbihan halfway along Brittany's southern coast. He considered it a healthier location to bring up the new ruling dynasty he hoped would preserve the independence of the duchy from France.

Unfortunately the son born to them there died soon after his birth, no more children were conceived and the marriage soured. The duke removed his court back to Nantes, the duchess remained in Vannes; visits between the two castles became fewer and further between, until she died unexpectedly of a fever. The family that now lived at the Château de l'Hermine was that of the duke and his mistress, Madame de Maignelais.

Lord Jasper heard this sorry tale from Duke Francis's man of affairs, Pierre Landais, who had been detailed to escort us to our new home. We rode in cavalcade, with Mistress Jane and Sian in a litter some distance behind, but ahead of the carts that carried the baggage and servants. Pierre was a commoner, the well-educated son of rich cloth merchants and a forceful character of similar age to the duke, who in my uncle's opinion relied on him rather too much. However, he made a lively travelling companion and the two men laughed and exchanged stories freely during our journey. Nor did they trouble to temper the vulgarity of their jesting when joined by Madame de Maignelais, who was taking advantage of our escort to visit her children. Riding behind them, Davy, Evan and I were astonished at the lady's evident enjoyment of their ribald jokes and her responding repartee. They certainly added to our own meagre repertoire.

'I think Madame de Maignelais rather likes Lord Jasper,' Davy commented to me during the second day of the journey. 'She is always putting her hand on his arm and giving him funny looks.'

'I had noticed,' I said gloomily. So had Mistress Jane, of course.

But everyone became cheerful on arrival at Château de l'Hérmine; it was spectacular. There was no mistaking its association with the national emblem of Brittany, for every turret and facade was embellished with small stone figures of ermines in various attitudes, some of them amusing and some of them positively crude, though these were usually the more discreetly located. Once we were settled in, Davy and I spent merry hours hunting down these more risqué carvings and sniggering over their suggestive poses. Along with the beautiful gardens and 'places of exercise and sport' it was evident that this was intended to be a pleasure castle.

We had been allocated the top two floors of one of the corner towers, the ground floor being given over to a guard-house for the adjacent sally gate, which led from the central court into the great outer bailey. It was a moot point whether the sentries posted there were guarding us from danger or spying on our comings and goings. Four chambers were made available to us and I was pleased to see that Mistress Jane appeared much happier now that we were all living together once more and she was sharing Lord Jasper's bed. In contrast, despite the distraction of tennis, archery and comic stone ermines, I grew more and more depressed.

Before leaving Nantes I had learned of my mother's oath of loyalty to the Yorkist King Edward and her re-appointment as lady in waiting to his queen, news that arrived soon after my fifteenth birthday at the end of January and induced a deep melancholy. Uncle Jasper tried to explain the reasons why my mother would have bent her knee once more to York and agreed to serve the commoner queen again, two actions that I thought should have been anathema to one who held such a proud relationship to Lancaster.

'Your mother has responsibility for the lives of her hundreds of tenants and retainers, Harri. She would be devastated to see her estates and the people who inhabit them being handed over, perhaps to an unscrupulous over-lord who would not be concerned for their welfare as she was. She was distraught when your Richmond lands were stripped from her care. The oath of loyalty to York is a move she must have felt obliged to make in order to conserve her

Somerset holdings and in becoming Elizabeth Woodville's lady in waiting she is in a good position to further her efforts to get your Richmond lands back. Also you must bear in mind that she will always be secretly working for our cause and sending funds to support it, as soon as we manage to convince Duke Francis to back us.'

'Back us for what, uncle?' I asked. 'You said yourself that York has destroyed the Lancastrian succession; that the future died at Tewkesbury when the prince was killed.'

Lord Jasper gently refuted this. 'I did not say that, Harri. I said that only we remain to carry the Lancastrian cause forward. That is why we had to flee Yorkist England. Your mother knows that you carry the Lancastrian succession, the royal line that her father and his father and grandfather have passed to you. She will never abandon it; no matter what impression her actions may give. I advise you as she would, to trust in God and take one day at a time.'

Despite how it seemed, he wanted me to believe in my mother's innate loyalty to Lancaster but I could not help feeling that if she was dissembling for my sake it was a lost cause. Lord Jasper might pin gorse flowers in my hat and hail me as a Plantagenet but I was not persuaded that there was any point in pursuing that line of thought. In my opinion by becoming one of them my mother was publicly admitting that the York dynasty was unbeatable and that her future and mine lay in making what progress we could under its aegis. My uncle was a dreamer who could not abandon his loyalty to a Lancastrian succession, even though it no longer existed. How could I point out to him that one fifteen-year-old boy and his landless exiled uncle hardly constituted an affinity?

I tried very hard to do what Lord Jasper said my mother would have advised, take one day at a time and trust in God, but if it had not been for Duke Francis's generous loan of horses to ride out into the windswept hills around Vannes and the exhausting training sessions his Master at Arms put me through, which left me too tired to think, I do not know that I would ever have emerged from the winter gloom that beset me. I tired even of the laughter and teasing of the duke's two boisterous boys, ten-year-old Franc and nine-year-old Antoine. The only people who lifted my mood were Davy and Mistress Jane; Davy because he was almost incapable of being glum and Jane because her feminine perception of the world enabled me see my mother's actions in a more favourable light.

'She is a woman alone, Harri,' she reminded me. 'The last time she married, the king forced her to abandon you into the care of your uncle. As then, she will do whatever she must do now to promote your future. Why should she not pledge allegiance to her enemy and serve his queen if doing so will bring you back to England sooner? She wants you back in her life, with your own estates and in your rightful place close to the throne. A mother who loves her children will go to any lengths to give them the future she believes they deserve.'

The thought that she was doing it for me, her only son, somehow made it easier to bear; I could lay some of the blame at my own door and shoulder my share of guilt. When her next letter came the news it contained did not disturb me as much as it might have done before Jane's wise words.

<u>To my dearly beloved and only son Henry Tudor, Earl
of Richmond greetings,</u>

I write to give you tidings of my marriage to Thomas,
Lord Stanley of Lathom and King of Man. I know you
will wish me God's blessing and pray for the success of
our union, which took place in the Royal Chapel at
Westminster Palace on the twenty-third day of June and
was witnessed by King Edward and Queen Elizabeth.
How I wish you, my much-loved son, could have been
there as witness instead. I pray constantly for your good
health and welfare and receive each of your letters with
boundless pleasure and relief.

From now on I shall be lady of the Stanley seat at
Lathom in Lancashire as well as my own residences in
Lincolnshire and Northamptonshire and the king has
confirmed my possession of Woking Palace, which I know
you enjoyed visiting when you were in England.
Coldharbour Inn has been returned to the Duke of
Exeter, who has taken the king's pardon, but Lord
Stanley has a fine London house in St Paul's Wharf and
has lately been appointed Steward to the Royal
Household, so much of our time will be spent in London
and at Windsor.

The queen conferred on me the privilege of standing
at the font for the new princess, baptised Margaret she
says in my honour, although officially she is named for
the king's sister, the Duchess of Burgundy. Of course she
and the king would have been happier had it been
another prince.

Lord Stanley tells me that an embassy from England

under Lord Rivers is on its way to Brittany and you will be interested to learn that your future is high on the agenda for discussion. I pray constantly for your safe return to England but I have begged the queen to impress on her husband and brother the importance of a full restoration of your Richmond title and estates as well as a pardon. This could take time, in view of the fact that the Richmond estates have been granted to Edward's brother George, Duke of Clarence. However, crucially, the title has not.

This letter will be despatched in the mailbag for the court of Duke Francis and I trust it will be forwarded to you at the Château de l'Hérmine, where I hope you are now comfortably lodged. I have sent gifts and greetings to his grace of Brittany in heartfelt recognition of his kindness and generosity in giving refuge to you, his cousins.

Master Bray continues to set aside a portion of rents and fees from my Somerset estates to be at your disposal and it will be sent to you quarterly by personal courier. I know you and your uncle will not wish to be beholden to the Duke of Brittany any further than has already been necessary.

I keep you daily in my thoughts and prayers and am, as always, your devoted mother,

Margaret, Countess of Richmond and Somerset and Queen of Man.

At Stanley House, London on this the twenty-seventh day of June, 1472

When he read the letter, Lord Jasper laughed as he reached the end, saying, 'I know she finds it irresistible but your mother is reckless to adopt her husband's royal title,' he said. 'The Isle of Man is not officially a kingdom any more and Lord Stanley could incur a considerable royal fine for calling himself its king.'

As he handed the letter back to me, he became serious. 'I wish I could say that Duke Francis keeps me informed of such matters as "an embassy from England", Harri, but alas he has not. Therein may be the reason we are housed so far from his court. Lady Margaret's letter was carefully worded since it was sent care of the Duke. I think she would have imparted news more freely, if the letter had been secure.'

I peered closely at my mother's crest raised in the wax. She had kept the Beaufort portcullis, not adopted the Stanley crest, whatever that might be. 'There is no sign of any tampering with the seal, uncle,' I said. I did not tell him how pleased I was to see she considered herself a Beaufort still, as was I in the maternal line, not a Stanley.

My uncle shrugged. 'Hot wires and skilful hands do not leave telltale signs,' he pointed out, adding, 'but tell me, Harri, how do you feel about having a new stepfather?'

I hesitated before answering. 'Mistress Jane believes everything my mother does is with my interests in mind, so I cannot criticise her for marrying a courtier who is so close to the throne.'

My uncle clearly did not find my reply convincing. 'Hmm. As his Steward, Lord Stanley will certainly have the king's ear and with a seat on the royal council he will be a powerful protector. But let me tell you what little I know of him. He has a reputation for managing to avoid committing himself fully to any particular cause, which delivers the great advantage of keeping him alive and –' he gave me a shrewd look '– he already has four sons, so he has not married your mother to get himself an heir, if that is what is worrying you.'

I felt the blood rush to my cheeks. He had touched on the very subject that troubled me most, the concept of my mother in bed with a grey-bearded stranger. I appreciated that at twenty-nine she was still a relatively young woman but I shrank from this thought, although I had no wish to discuss it with Lord Jasper, or indeed with anyone else. 'No uncle,' I replied, 'what worries me most is the idea of the queen's brother coming to negotiate with the duke for our return to England. Do you think there is any chance that he may be successful? A forced repatriation would not augur well for you, would it?'

Lord Jasper tried to reassure me. 'Duke Francis has vowed to protect us, Harri. I cannot think that Lord Rivers has anything to offer that would induce him to break that vow.'

IO

Margaret

Stanley House, St Paul's Wharf, London, 1472

I LOOKED UP FROM my desk at a knock on the door and
Meg Woodville entered the solar at my call. Judging by
the clothes she wore she must have just returned from a
ride into the fields behind Lincoln's Inn or Smithfield.
Stanley House was on the west side of the City where good
places to ride were more accessible and the older 'nestlings',
such as George Stanley and Nicholas Vaux, had been quick
to take advantage of this. I instructed the Master of Horse
to send men at arms as well as grooms to escort them and
I insisted that if Meg rode out she should be accompanied
by a maid and should not take part in any of the jousting
exercises that the boys might practise. So as she was looking
nervous I guessed that she might have taken part in their
soldierly contests. She was a spirited girl, one who was
always likely to fly in the face of authority – an attitude I
understood but must, nevertheless, quash.

But she had a more serious transgression to confess. 'I

have something to show you, my lady,' she said sheepishly, placing a folded letter on my desk. 'I have been corresponding with Robert Poyntz against the wishes of you and my father. I am not really sorry for the letters but I am frightened by what Robert says my father might do.'

I picked up the letter, frowning, though the confession did not worry me overmuch since Lord Rivers and I had made enquiries about Robert Poyntz and discovered that he was a young man of good breeding and would inherit considerable lands in the West Country. No doubt his pursuit of Meg Woodville was inspired by genuine attraction to a beautiful girl but there was probably also a certain intelligent self-interest involved, given her close relationship to the queen and the fact that Robert Poyntz also had brains to match his good looks. He might expect to be appointed to lucrative offices in due course, but for the present, thanks to his legal training, he had been seconded to Lord Rivers's embassy to Brittany.

I could see from the address that the letter I held in my hand had been included in the royal courier's bag from Nantes and doubtless delivered secretly to Meg by some servant in return for a silver penny or two. It contained everything a maid might relish from an ardent admirer, including an ode of indifferent literary merit addressed to her 'bluebell eyes' and a few amusing stories from a young man's first sortie abroad, although I am glad to say that Robert was discreet and no mention was made of visits to taverns or houses of ill repute. The final paragraph, however, raised the hairs on the back of my neck.

. . . these negotiations drag on interminably and as you know your father does not have a reputation for

patience. The other day in a fit of pique he declared that
the king's instructions were to bring the two Tudors
home 'dead or alive' and, being so frustrated in his
efforts to achieve the latter I fear it cannot be long before
he will find himself unable to resist the former. I think if
Lord Rivers agrees to the Breton demand for a thousand
English archers to reinforce the duchy's defences, Duke
Francis may agree to put the Tudors in a vulnerable
position and turn a blind eye to the consequences.

My blood turned to ice; I saw my only beloved son with his throat cut and his body sealed in a barrel of Breton brandy, for shipment. A king who had achieved the death of all other Lancastrian contenders in order to secure the English throne would not flinch at one more.

Seeing me blanch Meg moved swiftly to the tray of wine and cups laid out for visitors. 'Here, my lady, drink this. You look faint,' she said, offering me a small measure. 'I am sorry to be the bearer of such shocking news.'

I was glad to be sitting down and took a fortifying gulp of the strong red wine. Hand on my beating heart, I said, 'Well, Meg, even though you should not have been corresponding with this squire, it is fortunate that you were and we can warn my son and his uncle of this threat, to put them on their guard.'

She gave me a stricken look. 'Oh but you will not reveal how you found out will you, my lady? I am sure Robert would not be involved in any violent action against the Tudors and I should not want him to suffer my father's wrath.'

For my part, I was far from convinced that Master Poyntz,

a close servant of King Edward, would be able to avoid some sort of involvement in Earl Rivers's nefarious intentions, if indeed there were any, but I would not have said so to Meg.

'I am very pleased and grateful that you brought this matter to my notice, Meg, and I will not reveal my sources. However, your disobedience cannot go unpunished and I insist that you make confession after chapel tomorrow and I will lend you a goat's-hair belt, which you will wear next to your skin for three days to atone for your sins. In addition it should go without saying that I expect your strict obedience from now on.'

Her brow creased in a frown. 'But if I do not reply to this letter Robert will wonder why and become suspicious,' she said unhappily. Then her mutinous nature reasserted itself. 'I will make confession and I will wear the belt but you have promised to keep my secret, my lady, and so you cannot disclose that I have shown you the letter,' she said, unable to keep a faint note of triumph from her voice.

'You are right and I want you to reply, Meg, but I also want you to show me all your correspondence with Master Robert in future – without telling him that you are doing so of course.' I smiled fondly at her and reached out my hand to bring her to my side. 'We need to trust each other, Meg, do we not? Let us kiss on our promises and I will write immediately to warn Henry and Lord Jasper.'

While waiting to hear further from Brittany, I could distract myself by trying to become better acquainted with my four new stepsons – a delicate undertaking. The chief problem was George, the eldest survivor of Eleanor Stanley's brood and therefore Lord Stanley's heir. He was thirteen when his father and I married and he made it obvious to the point of rudeness that he would not accept my maternal guidance. I would have liked to say it was fortunate that he had taken a shine to Meg Woodville because that could have been my pathway to befriending him but actually it added further complications as Meg found his puppy love irritating and made it clear that she preferred the undemanding friendship of Nicholas Vaux. The frequent arguments that arose as a result even caused a fistfight between the two boys, which brought the situation to the notice of Lord Stanley, when George turned up for serving duties at the high table with a blue bruise on his cheek.

'Have you been fighting, my son?' his father asked. The boy kept his eyes fixed on the washbowl he was offering and mumbled something inaudible. 'Speak up lad and look at me when I talk to you. You are a noble page not a common varlet. What is the reason for that bruise?'

The boy peered up briefly and a blush spread under the bruise. 'I took a punch, my lord father.'

'And who gave you the punch, George?' I could hear patience wearing thin in my husband's tone of voice.

The eyes dropped. 'Nicholas Vaux.'

'Why did Master Vaux hit you?'

'We were fighting.'

'Obviously. What were you fighting about?'

George's cheeks blushed a deeper red. 'Nothing really.'

Exasperated, Lord Thomas threw the napkin back over his son's shoulder and water slopped over the edge of the bowl as the boy flinched away, fearing a blow. 'Well, if you are going to get into a fight, George, take my advice and make sure you know exactly what or who it is you are fighting for and what you stand to gain by it; otherwise avoid the action. Now go away.'

Hearing this advice I felt I suddenly understood my new husband better.

'Was that why you avoided the battle of Blore Heath, my lord?' I enquired as servers laid out the dishes for the next course. 'Because you did not think you had anything to gain by it? I have always believed you were demonstrating your true affinity to Lancaster.'

In fact, I had only given Lord Thomas the benefit of the doubt. The battle of Blore Heath had been in the year that George was born. Allied to the Duke of York, the Earl of Salisbury had called for his son-in-law to bring him support before engaging with a Lancastrian army, but had been forced to face the enemy alone when no help came. Although victorious, the engagement subsequently caused Lord Salisbury to be attainted for treason and forced into exile, whereas Lord Stanley had avoided all guilt and punishment.

Thomas held my gaze for several seconds before replying. 'George is my heir. He must learn that leadership depends on reading a situation from every angle. Tenants and retainers must follow without question but the head of a family has to lead and to do that he needs cunning, which can never be learned too young.'

'And what of women, my lord? What if they choose to disobey their leader?'

The question elicited a mirthless laugh. 'Everyone knows that women have no choice except to obey their fathers and husbands.'

I bit back my instinctive protest. I had married Lord

96

Stanley to acquire the security I needed but I still hankered after the brief period I had spent as an independent widow. It was not the marriage debt I minded; Thomas was a considerate husband in that respect, avoiding my bed on the saints' days and fast days I stipulated and not making excessive demands in between; more of a friend than a lover. But I had soon realised that he would need subtler handling than I had thought. Not for nothing did he secretly cling to the empty title King of Man. In that respect we had yet to establish a satisfactory working arrangement for our marriage.

So, I had not told him of my dealings with Meg Woodville or the fortuitous outcome of her correspondence with Robert Poyntz, nor did I intend to.

Meg and I were on tenterhooks until she received another letter from Robert revealing that Henry and Jasper and their companions had been moved from the Château de l'Hérmine in the busy town of Vannes to Château Suscinio, a hunting palace on a remote coastal peninsula. Later, Henry's own letter informed me that the duke had reinforced the garrison there and provided park wardens to patrol the surrounding forest. Surely this was a safer location than Vannes, but having learned of King Edward's instruction to Lord Rivers to bring the Tudors back 'dead or alive', I no longer put any trust in royal promises.

II

Harri

Château Suscinio, Brittany, December 1473

WE WERE OBLIGED TO move out of the main ducal
apartments at Suscinio when Duke Francis announced
that he was coming for Christmas, bringing his duchess.
We had been luxuriously housed for the past year and our
alternative accommodation in the castle's West Tower was
more cramped, to say the least.

This disruption did not trouble me because I was pleased
I would be reunited with the young duchess, whose company
I had missed since moving to Suscinio. Apart from enjoying
each other's company, I had found her a great source of
information, and I knew that my uncle had also felt cut off
without the frequent visits of the duke to his family at
Vannes.

I had not entirely lost touch with the duchess. Her tutors
had continued to teach me, travelling at regular intervals
from Vannes to ensure that I continued my studies. This
had provided opportunities to exchange letters but I missed

the frequent conversations with Duchess Marguerite about what we had read and what was happening in the duchy and, indeed, in England and Wales.

'I was always able to glean news of affairs by talking or corresponding with the people who knew,' Lord Jasper had complained to me soon after arriving at Suscinio. 'Of course we should not look a gift horse in the mouth because this is a comfortable place to live and we have everything we could wish for but I find it hard to be so isolated. Without the gossip of a court and with infrequent letters from England, it is like living in a void.'

I knew what he meant. My mother's correspondence, which was our main source of information, had been irregular since we came here.

'To be fair, my mother has court duties,' I would point out to my uncle. 'Plus a whole new household on her hands, with step-children, in-laws, residences hundreds of miles apart . . .' I was being loyal, defending her. I longed for her letters more than anyone and wondered if some of them were being intercepted and withheld by the duke's agents. It was something I was hoping to raise with him tactfully during his Christmas visit.

From mid December my uncle could have no complaint about lack of activity around the castle. An army of servants and officials arrived to prepare for the ducal party and the cellars began to fill with supplies, basic stocks of flour, rice, sarrasin, salt, sugar, pulses, cheese, dried fruit and winter vegetables, then exotic luxuries and wine. On rough ground beyond the moat huge piles of firewood were heaped ready for roasting deer, boar and any other game provided by the hunting parties the duke and his guests were due to enjoy.

Temporary kitchens were set up nearby in tents, ready for a cohort of cooks to prepare the sauces and side dishes to be served at a series of banquets for evening entertainment.

The afternoon before the ducal party was due to arrive was one of those crisp, bright, sunny days of early winter when the sky was a clear azure and a fresh breeze was blowing in from the sea bringing salty air and the faint smell of fish. It was only a ten-minute walk through stunted bushes and pines to the beach that ringed Suscinio Bay. In the hot days of summer it had been a delight to make excursions there, to splash in the waves and run and play on the wide white sweep. With a makeshift quintain and two mounts from the castle stables, Davy and I had tried to practise our lance work on the hard sand below the tide line but the horses were as ill trained as we were and the results had been disappointing. I yearned for lessons from a skilled jouster, hoping the duke might now consider me old enough to couch a lance at speed.

Jane and Sian were keen to visit the culinary village of tents and asked Davy and me to go with them, since unaccompanied women were not welcomed where food was prepared, kitchens being a fiercely male preserve.

A long fire-pit filled with spindly branches and brush-wood caused Davy to exclaim, 'Those little sticks will not burn for more than half an hour.'

Sian was keen to air her knowledge. 'That is just kindling,' she said. 'They will light that then throw on charcoal and when all the wood is burnt and the charcoal is white-hot they will sling an iron spit over those forked posts with the skinned deer impaled on it. The fat from the roasting meat will keep the fire sizzling.'

Davy grew excited at the prospect of the feast, and the hunting. 'Do you think the duke will let us ride with the hunt, Mother?'

'I expect the duke will invite his friends and family, Davy and I doubt if that includes you,' said Jane. 'But you never know.'

'Surely Uncle Jasper will go, will he not?' I interjected. 'He will be very disappointed if he is not included.'

Jane pulled her woollen shawl more tightly around her and folded her arms. True, the day was drawing in and the breeze was growing colder but I suspected she did not do it for that reason. 'Yes, I expect he will Harri but it is up to the duke. We are all subject to his wishes.'

As she spoke the sound of hoof-beats and jingling harness became audible, approaching along the castle road and within moments, through the trees came a small procession of mounted men at arms with a lone female rider in their midst, who was wearing a spectacular red Florentine patterned cloak and a turban hat of white fur, scattered with sparkling jewels.

'Who is that?' exclaimed Davy, his deep-brown eyes wide.

I did not immediately recognise her but Jane did. 'That, Davy my boy, is Madame Antoinette de Maignelais, the duke's mistress,' she said. 'It would seem that he is sending his "baggage" on in advance.'

I looked at her, surprised by the acid in her tone of voice and the sneering curl of her lips. As a mistress herself I was astonished she should speak so scathingly of another but she returned my glance with a cold one of her own, challenging me to protest.

'I know you have met her, Harri, and I have not been

introduced, but I do not like her,' she said bluntly. 'She is what we Welsh call a harpy. You would be well advised not to trust her.'

I was not at all sure what a harpy was but assumed from Jane's expression that the word was not flattering. I had recently noticed that the harmony between her and Uncle Jasper, established when we first settled in Suscinio, had evaporated and sensed that her sharp tongue might be a symptom of some deeper trouble. The following morning, on the pretext of asking her to repair a seam on one of my doublets, I mentioned her air of malaise.

'I wonder if you are feeling unwell, Mistress Jane? You seem distracted lately.'

At first she frowned at me and I feared I had offended her but then her brow cleared and she gave me one of her impulsive hugs. 'You are a sensitive and intuitive boy, Harri, but I am not unwell, just sad. If I seem distracted it is because Elin and Will are to be married next year and I am bitterly regretting that I will not be at the wedding of my daughter.'

I smiled at her sympathetically. Elin was her eldest daughter, who had been left behind in London with her betrothed's family and she and Will Gardiner had been betrothed for three years. 'Is there no chance that you could travel back to England for the occasion?' I asked. 'After all, it is not you who has been attainted by the Yorkist Parliament.'

A fierce expression disfigured her features. 'The last thing I wish is to leave your uncle to the clutches of La Maignelais!' she cried.

Aha, I thought, now it was out, the real reason for her dolour and the reference to Madame de Maignelais as a 'harpy'. She suspected that the duke's mistress was making eyes at Uncle Jasper. 'I am sure Lord Jasper would not be "clutched", as you put it!' I protested. 'And anyway he loves you, does he not?'

Jane gazed at me pensively for a few moments then shook her head, as if to rid herself of the thoughts she was having. 'You are still too young to understand, Harri, but I am not naive enough to think as you do. I cannot tell you why precisely, only that the ways of men are ancient and unchanging. One day you will find out for yourself. Now, should you not be at your studies? I will return the doublet to your chamber when it's done.'

It was a polite dismissal and I left, still puzzled. For one thing, I wondered where Madame de Maignelais was accommodated in the castle. Surely with his young duchess accompanying him for the Christmas festivities, Duke Francis would not flaunt his mistress in his own apartments, which were only a short spiral stairway below the duchess's? It was when I took the wall-walk from the West Tower to the small turret chamber on the south wall, where Davy, Sian and I pursued our studies, that I encountered La Maignelais, unmistakeable in her bright crimson cloak, emerging from the corner tower nearest the ducal lodging.

She gave me one of her dazzling smiles and as she approached I was assailed by a waft of exotic scent. Beneath the cloak she wore a gown of gleaming burgundy figured in gold and her bright hair was half-hidden beneath a dark gauzy veil that lifted gently in the chill breeze. 'Ah, Henri of Richemont, how fortunate to meet you here, I am looking for your uncle. I have been told he is living in the West Range. You will be able to direct me I hope.'

'You are right, Madame, but at this moment he is meeting with the captain of the guard in the armoury,' I said, hesitating. 'It is not somewhere a lady would usually go.'

Her smile dimmed. 'How annoying. Yet I believe I will risk it. Would you be kind enough to escort me, Henri?'

I decided to comply; study could wait for a short time. 'It is this way, Madame,' I said with a small bow, gesturing back along the wall-walk towards the West Range, which occupied the entire length of that aspect of the castle and was where the duke's guests would soon be housed. A spiral stair led down to ground level and the rooms where soldiers slept and ate and where a large chamber was devoted to the storage of weapons and armour. Halfway down she stopped abruptly ahead of me and turned.

'You are an intelligent young man, Henri, do you think Lord Jasper will be offended if I interrupt his meeting with the captain?' Her habitual air of confidence appeared to have vanished, replaced by a look of indecision. 'He is normally light-hearted in my company and I would not wish to annoy him.'

I found this sudden change in attitude surprising and was uncertain how to respond. 'Perhaps it might be better to speak to him at dinner, Madame. I believe he and the captain usually share weapons practice at this time of day and they will be hot and perspiring. My uncle may not be happy to converse with a lady in such condition.'

Antoinette de Maignelais astonished me then by lifting high her much be-ringed hand in order to caress my face in a way I might have construed as motherly, had it not been accompanied by an air-kiss blown from her plump, red-painted lips. 'What a thoughtful young man you are,

Henri. I will take your advice and approach Lord Jasper in more favourable circumstances.' She pulled her hand back and rubbed her fingers together with a knowing smile. 'I felt the stubble on your chin my lord. You have become a fine young man since I saw you last. It must be frustrating to be cooped up here without female company, other than your uncle's mistress of course.' She came back one step, close to me on the shadowy stairway. I felt her breath on my cheek and her hand on my arm. 'I would not like to think of you wasting your nobility on some sweaty alewife or a laundress stinking of urine. A woman of experience such as myself has much to teach a youth of your vigour and charm. Please remember that, should the fire burn too hot for comfort.'

Before I could respond I felt those cushioned lips pressed briefly but firmly on mine, then she moved past me and disappeared up the stair in a rustle of silk. I took several deep breaths and waited for the involuntary rush of blood to subside before following the heady trail of perfume that clung around the spiral. My tutor found my concentration sadly lacking that morning.

12

Harri

Château Suscinio, Brittany, Christmas 1473 – spring 1474

THE DUKE AND DUCHESS of Brittany rode in from Vannes, he on his great black and white trapped courser and she on a pretty white palfrey, barded in blue. Long before their colourful cavalcade clattered over the wooden planks of the drawbridge and through the gatehouse tunnel we had been made aware of their approach: the merry sound of the pipes, drums and voices of a band of mounted minstrels singing carols preceded them, carried on the crisp air of a bright December day.

Lord Jasper and I stood in the great court with the Master of the Household to greet them. I was flattered, if a little embarrassed, when Duchess Marguerite almost skipped across the court to greet me as soon as she dismounted. 'Henri, Henri!' she cried, kissing me on both cheeks when I straightened up from my formal bow, 'I have sorely missed our lessons together and I hope you have missed me?'

The duchess's stout chaperone almost fell off her horse in her haste to curb her mistress's enthusiasm. 'Mademoiselle! It is not seemly!' she protested, grunting with effort as she bent to rescue her little mistress's long riding skirt from the dusty flagstones.

The duchess slipped me a sly smile, throwing a parting comment over her shoulder as she submitted to being ushered off to make her formal greeting to my uncle. 'I have much to tell you, Henri; we will speak later.'

'I see your nephew is fast learning how to charm the ladies,' I heard the duke remark, nudging my uncle in the ribs. 'Something he has learned from you, Jasper?'

'More likely inherited from his grandfather,' said Lord Jasper, tipping me a roguish wink. 'Owen Tudor was always a popular guest in the ladies' solar, especially when he played his harp.'

'I fear he did not bequeath me his musical talent, your grace,' I confessed, bending my knee to the duke. 'He gave me a harp as a child but my fingers seem to handle reins better than strings.'

'You see we have our own minstrels with us to make merry over the festivities,' Duke Francis declared, glancing at the musicians who were busy unloading spare instruments from the panniers of their pack ponies. 'And reins will be of more use to us than strings. I hope you will both join us at the hunt.'

'Oh yes indeed!' we said in unison. Our eyes met and we smiled with pleasure as we followed Duke Francis into the banqueting hall. Several other noble guests were already waiting beside the trestles laid for dinner, bowing and curtsying as their hosts arrived, but I noticed with some relief that Madame de Maignelais was not among them. I wondered why the duke's mistress had come to Suscinio, if she was not to share in the entertainment of the season. Could she be here without the duke's knowledge or had she been told to wait on his permission to appear?

Enlightenment came the next day because Duke Francis asked me personally if I would make it my business to ride beside his wife during the hunt. 'I know she will enjoy your company, Henri,' he said, 'and I think you will find that her mare keeps up with the field quite satisfactorily. But I rely on you to see that she does not try to jump obstacles that are too high or too challenging.'

Of course I said I would be honoured to escort the duchess, although the responsibility the duke had laid on me was somewhat daunting. How I was to stop a determined fourteen-year-old from putting her mount at an obstacle that was too high, I did not know.

Hunting territory around Château Suscinio reached several miles inland over terrain that ranged from salt-flats to scrub and forest, so there was a wide variety of game available in a landscape that was constantly changing. As deerhounds were running, the bleaching pans around the Bay of Morbihan were soon left behind and we climbed into a dappled world of majestic broad-leafed trees dotted with glades, which had been cleared of undergrowth to encourage the low-growing sweet grasses that deer liked to graze on. In this favourable setting it did not take long for hounds to scent out a magnificent stag and the chase was on. I found it relatively easy to stay with the duchess and we were together when the quarry finally turned at bay in a thicket of blackthorn. Hounds milled and sniffed around it, deterred from attack by the many sharp points of its antlers, and within minutes the duke dismounted and claimed his precedence, dispatching the animal with a well-aimed arrow to the heart. Stragglers rode in and stirrup cups were passed around while the huntsmen gutted the beast and threw the innards to the hounds as a reward.

The duchess turned away in disgust. 'I dislike this part of the hunt,' she said to me. 'Let us move further back where we can talk, Henri.'

We moved out of earshot of the rest, loosening our reins under an ancient oak tree. 'I know La Maignelais is at Suscinio,' she began immediately. 'I have smelled her scent.'

My eyes widened in surprise. 'But you have not seen her?' I asked.

Marguerite took offence. 'Fortunately not, but only she wears that particularly cloying scent. Have you not noticed? It hangs in the air for hours, wherever she has been. It is vastly expensive, like frankincense. I think she believes it makes her irresistible to men.'

I screwed up my nose, remembering my embarrassing encounter on the wall-walk stair. 'I do not find it irresistible,' I said. 'Quite the reverse.'

'Then perhaps you are not yet really a man,' she said dismissively. 'But I know she is here, however much the duke wishes to hide her presence from me.'

'But why would he hide her?' I asked. 'He has never done so before.'

'Because he thinks to deceive me. I have told him I will not be bedded with him until he dismisses La Maignelais from his court.' Her tone was fierce, implacable. 'In the New

Year I will be fifteen and the duke wishes to consummate our marriage but I have agreed to do so only if he sends La Maignelais away – far, far away, never to return.'

I gave her a dubious look. 'You seem very certain that you can achieve this,' I said, 'but the duke is your husband. As his wife you are bound to obey *him* – not the other way around.'

She snapped her fingers, making her mare jerk her head in surprise. 'Pah! He is a gentle man. He will not force me if I am unwilling and besides, he is desperate for an heir – a legitimate son –' her eyes sparked on the word 'legitimate', '– who will preserve the independence of Brittany against the tyrannous French. I know it is my duty to give him one but I will only comply if he sends his mistress away. And so he will. There is not room in the Breton court for more than one duchess.'

When she put it like that, with the light of battle in her eyes, I anticipated that the days of Madame de Maignelais' ascendancy were numbered.

'I am telling you this because you had better warn your uncle,' she said as we re-joined the field. 'The doxy will be looking for a new protector and I would not be surprised if she digs her nails into him.'

I caught sight of my uncle and the duke exchanging light-hearted banter while they waited for the horn to sound, kindred spirits enjoying each other's company. I recalled that La Maignelais had been seeking Uncle Jasper when I encountered her yesterday. I felt my stomach clench as it suddenly occurred to me that 'the doxy', when she kissed me on the stair, might even have been considering me as a future patron, though I was only a few years older than her own sons. Never for one second had I considered taking her up on her offer and would have felt a twinge of pity, had I not been repulsed by the thought of coupling with someone old enough to be my mother.

Not until the Twelfth Night banquet did the subject arise again during another brief encounter with the duchess. I was more than a little inebriated. She whispered to me, 'Have you noticed how the air smells cleaner at Suscinio now, Henri?' A smug little smile accompanied this murmured comment but I understood immediately what it indicated. 'The duke has given La Maignelais her marching orders. Tomorrow I go back to Vannes, celebrate my fifteenth birthday and begin the pampering and primping considered necessary for a bride's bedding. What do you think, Henri? Will I be a good duchess, both in and out of bed?'

I racked my foggy brain for a suitable response. 'Well your grace, I am hardly qualified to comment but I hope you will prove a fruitful wife because there is no doubting that you will be a forthright and fearless one.'

Festive merriment was rocking the rafters of the hall and so her girlish gust of laughter went generally unnoticed and then the duke came to claim her for the first dance. I wandered a little unsteadily to stand among other well-fuelled courtiers, raising my cup to the ducal future.

Lord Jasper came up behind me, watching the duke steer his young bride in a lively saltarello. 'The duchess has become quite a lady now, do you not agree, Harri?' he remarked. 'No longer the little girl who shared your schoolroom.'

I detected a note of censure in his voice, as if he was about to tax me with being too familiar with her, so I decided to pre-empt him. 'Do you know that Madame de Maignelais has left the court, uncle? Did she speak with you before she left?'

I turned in time to see his cheeks go a deeper red than the wine had already made them. There was a pause as the music crescendoed and my uncle, appearing fascinated by the activity on the floor where couples were leaping and twirling in the steps of the latest dance craze from Italy, took a long time to answer. At length he admitted casually, 'Madame de Maignelais did come to see me, yes. I was surprised because until she knocked at my door I was unaware that she was here. She kept out of sight, which is not like her.'

'No indeed,' I agreed, asking recklessly, 'What did she want?'

He gave me a sideways glance. 'She was worried about the future of her young sons and sought my advice.'

'Just your advice, uncle?' I prompted, the wine loosening my tongue. 'Or was she seeking support of a more ... amorous kind? She is still an attractive lady.'

His brow creased. 'She is indeed, but Harri, you are too young to make the insinuation I believe you intend.'

I turned innocent blue eyes on him. 'I make no insinuation, my lord. But I will pass on something the duchess said. Perhaps understandably she considers Madame de Maignelais a dangerous woman who, to use her words, "has designs" on you. I believe Mistress Jane thinks so too.'

Lord Jasper gave a throaty laugh and threw his arm around my shoulders. 'Oh Harri, Harri! You are definitely growing up. But there are still things you should not meddle with. The time will come when both you and the little duchess understand affairs of the heart but that time is not yet.'

I felt my hackles rise and edged abruptly out of his

embrace. His patronising tone had grated on my ears. 'Well uncle, when I do finally grow into understanding them,' I said through gritted teeth, 'forgive me if I do not come to you for advice.'

I did not see his reaction because I turned away and strode off into the crowd, trying not to spoil the effect of my indignant departure by swaying or stumbling. Glancing at the dancers I caught sight of the duchess, elegantly passing from the hand of one gentleman to the next as the saltarello progressed. I thought she had handled her unenviable situation remarkably well, at an age when Lord Jasper considered her too young to 'understand affairs of the heart'. I sent up a silent prayer that her brave ultimatum to the duke would bring about a fruitful and satisfactory conclusion. I also thanked the saints that the absence of La Maignelais meant I would not have to take care to avoid her in future.

The departure of the ducal party after Epiphany left our little group of exiles bored and bereft of stimulation. The winter closed in and kept us confined for much of January and February. There was no indoor tennis court at Suscinio as there had been at the Château de l'Hérmine and apart from our books and games of chess and bowling in the great hall there was little to relieve the tedium of the short days and long nights. Even riding out for exercise was restricted because we could do no more than walk the horses on the icy rutted ground.

In the past year there had been no diplomatic activity between the courts of England and Brittany, lifting the sense of constant jeopardy brought on by the 'dead or alive' threat of which my mother had warned us while Lord Rivers had been on his diplomatic mission. His empty-handed departure along with his substantial retinue had relieved us of the fear of abduction or assassination and the remoteness of the castle of Suscinio combined to make us feel safe.

When spring came Lord Jasper, Evan, Davy and I were delighted to be able to ride down to the beach for some jousting training on the hard sand exposed at low tide. Since Christmas even the captain of the guards at Suscinio had become more relaxed, and was tolerant of our regular expeditions, with our horses and a portable quintain. Each day we scratched out a form of manège on the wet sand and tried to school our borrowed horses in the complicated pivots and swivels that enabled mounted horsemen to fight from the saddle. In truth it was a fairly unrewarding exercise because such training was lost on the immature cobs we had been allocated and they rarely responded in the way a well-bred charger would have as a colt.

The guards who accompanied us to the beach, bored with watching the constant repetition of the exercises we put the horses through, wandered off to exchange gossip with the fishermen who kept their boats pulled up on the sand at one end of the beach, awaiting high tide to assist their launching. Consequently none of us noticed a boatload of men row into the other end of the bay, camouflaged against the dark stone of the cliffs. It was not until half a dozen armed and armoured soldiers sprang down from the dunes behind us that we became aware of the sudden threat.

Had they waited until we were dismounted, taking a break from the manège, we might well have been done for, but as it was, as soon as he caught sight of them Lord Jasper drew his sword, yelled out our agreed alert, 'To Lancaster!' and turned his horse towards the fishing boats. Davy and

I immediately set off after him but Evan, at the far end of our scratched-out school, found himself cut off by the two fleetest attackers, who rapidly closed on him and attempted to grab his horse's reins. Peering over my shoulder as I clapped my heels to my horse's ribs, I saw him deliver several slashing cuts with his sword, which glanced off the helmet of one and the cuirass of the other, when a liveried man at arms, evidently their leader, screamed an order in English.

'Not him you fools – he is only a servant! We are after the Tudors – the greybeard and the young ones!'

PART TWO

13

Margaret

***Lathom Hall, West Derby Hundred, Lancashire, March
1475***

EVERY TIME I PASSED under the Lathom gatehouse I
yearned to turn back south. It was the Stanley family
seat, built by Lord Thomas to be the headquarters of his
estate empire, a great sprawling mansion open to the
prevailing winds that blew in across the Irish Sea from the
northern wastelands. In all seasons icy draughts funnelled
up the stairways and whistled in the passages, yet Lord
Thomas insisted we travel there twice a year.

The day after our arrival, when the baggage waggons were
unpacked and the rooms warmed from freezing, Lord
Thomas called me to his business chamber. I found him
standing in his favourite position, beside the secret peephole,
which gave him a birds-eye view of the heart of the house.
Stags' heads were a prominent part of the Stanley armorial
bearings and plaster versions of them adorned each corner
of the great hall below. Through the peephole in the eye of

one he could both monitor the activities of family and servants as they passed to and fro and vet any strangers. The position of the stag's open mouth also allowed him to eavesdrop on conversations held there. Only his trusted and senior officials knew of this feature and were sworn to keep the secret.

He closed the icon image of St Mark with his winged lion, which formed a shutter over the squint. 'There is a matter I must discuss with you urgently, Margaret,' he said, waving vaguely at an empty chair beside the hearth. 'Sit down.'

I complied in a dignified manner, wondering if the king ever commented on my husband's crude manners.

The graunch of wood on stone made me wince as he dragged the armchair from his desk to join me. 'I have been talking to George,' he said. His woollen gown amply covered his spread thighs as, hands on knees, he leaned forward with a frown. 'The boy has a grievance.'

Lord Thomas's son and heir made a habit of grumbling and so I did not feel any immediate need for anxiety. 'That is not a rare occurrence, my lord.'

A faint smile stirred his forked and grey-streaked beard. 'As you say. Yet on this occasion I wish something to be done. It concerns that Hussey girl you took in ward.'

'Which one do you mean? Connie or Kitty?' I had taken Constance and Katherine Hussey in ward following the sudden death of both their parents from the sweating sickness.

My husband's eyes widened. 'Blessed St Bridget! Are there two of them?'

'Yes, they are sisters. You have met them both but it does not surprise me that you saw no family resemblance.'

Thomas usually took little interest in my assortment of nestlings. 'One is plump and blonde and the other is small and dark.'

He scratched his head. 'I think George said her name was Connie but he made it sound like Tunnie.'

I folded my hands in my lap and sighed. 'Yes, Mother Hubbard told me that George calls her Tunnie. I suppose it is a reference to her buxom figure. I think it is his intention to compare her to a tun of wine.'

This elicited a bark of male laughter. 'Ha! Not very subtle is he? But then neither is she. George says she tells everyone she is going to marry him. Where has she got that ludicrous idea from?'

'Not from me I assure you.' I spread my hands. 'She has a vivid imagination.'

'She has appalling cheek,' he retorted. 'Who is she anyway? If she were a noble heiress I would have heard of her.'

'Well she is an heiress – of sorts. She and her sister share their father's estate but it is not large. Sir Nicholas Hussey was Victualler of the garrison at Calais. They are gentry, not nobility.'

'Then she is aiming well above her rank. Her silly prattling, if it reaches court, could ruin the chances of the match I am in the process of arranging for George. It is your responsibility to shut her mouth, Margaret.'

'She is already fifteen. I suppose I could find her a marriage more fitting to her station.'

'That will take too long. I want her out of our household. You must ask the queen to change her custody.'

I pursed my lips. 'That might prove difficult. As you know,' I said.

I had not been called to royal service since Princess Margaret, the queen's youngest child, had been found dead in her cot one morning. There had been no illness, no apparent reason for her demise and her mother had been distraught, lashing out at all her ladies with her tongue but at me most of all because I shared the child's name and had held her at the font. Elizabeth had even implied that my barrenness made me jealous of others' ability to breed.

Thomas stroked his beard pensively. 'Yes. But you must endeavour to get yourself back in her favour.'

With an effort I quashed my rising indignation. 'I do not see how I can, when I no longer have entry to her chamber. You have the king's ear, my lord. You could speak on my behalf.'

He held my gaze, his grey eyes narrowed. 'If I chose to I could, yes. But that might depend on whether George continues to suffer the imprecations of tubby Tunnie. He is a fourteen-year-old boy. He should be concentrating on his knightly skills, his riding and his book learning, not being embarrassed by the droolings of an adolescent girl. Get rid of her, Margaret!'

I fixed my gaze on his. 'And if I do will you fulfil your wedding vow to persuade the king to permit *my* son's return to England?' Three years I had been married to Lord Stanley, expecting to benefit from his influence at court and yet Henry still languished in Brittany. He had turned seventeen and I began to despair of getting him back.

Lord Thomas's expression hardened. 'I will keep my wedding vow when you fulfil your marriage debt, Margaret. There have been too many weak excuses, my lady – too many "days of abstinence",' he sneered, waving his fingers fussily. 'When you come to my bed with a smile and an embrace I will reckon your vow kept and I will fulfil mine.'

I stood up abruptly, my cheeks flaming. 'Unjust my lord! Before we married you knew I was barren and you accepted it. You said you had sons enough already. The church holds sex to be for procreation and therefore because I cannot conceive, for me it ranks as a sin. You married me for prestige and precedence, not bodily gratification!'

He rose also, one eyebrow raised, his plush lips lifting into a leer. 'You know, Margaret, when you are angry you become quite beautiful,' he said, lifting his hand to caress my cheekbone. 'You should lose control more often.'

Angrily I thrust the hand away, turned on my heel and left the room. As I crossed the great hall I could feel his gaze following me through the stag squint. The back of my head seemed to burn.

As usual my solar was busy with my bevy of young female wards. Meg Woodville, more beautiful than ever at seventeen, was patiently watching young Mary FitzLewis scratch out her letters on a wax tablet; in the oriel window Mother Hubbard supervised the two Hussey girls and eleven-year-old Joan Vaux, who were memorising receipts from my faithful head cook's book, a useful way for them to learn what basic supplies were needed in a household store. A swift glance showed me that Joan and Kitty had written long lists, whereas Connie's slate was virtually empty and she was gazing dreamily through the leaded panes.

I slipped the slate from her loose grasp, making her jump. 'I wish to speak to you, Connie,' I said. 'Come with me to the oratory.'

This little chamber occupied a narrow space between my solar and my bedchamber and contained only a triptych of the Virgin and Saints Margaret and Catherine, set on an altar table with a Prie Dieu placed before it. A small casement gave a view over the hall demesne and the network of ditches, which drained the meadows that would otherwise still be mossy bog – meadows that fed the source of the Stanley wealth, gleaned from the wool of thousands of sheep. The room offered me a retreat from the bustle of the household and while in residence at Lathom Hall I spent considerable periods praying in this oratory. It was also useful for conducting confidential business. There were no squints or spyholes here.

'Do not look so mulish, Connie,' I urged the girl, whose chin was jutting defensively. 'I am not going to scold you, although day-dreaming is never going to teach you how to run your household, when you have one.'

She shrugged. 'You do not have to know about preserves and spices, my lady. You have cooks and cellarers to do all that and so shall I.'

My eyebrows climbed my forehead. 'Indeed? How so? I should be interested to know.'

'When I am married to Master George I shall be mistress of this household, just as you are now. You do not visit dusty cellars and count jars and sacks.'

'Actually, Connie, I do.' I lifted the chatelaine that was attached to my belt and jangled the keys it held. 'I am up before dawn, while you are still sleeping, and I check the spice cupboard and the household accounts every day. But that will not become your duty here at Lathom. What made you think it might?'

She looked wary. 'We are wards of the queen. She sent us to the Stanleys whose heir is unmarried.' Her cheeks flooded. 'I just assumed . . . I am the elder sister!'

I reached for her hand; it lay reluctantly in mine. 'There will be a fine husband for you, Connie, believe me, but it will not be George Stanley.' I peered into her lowered countenance. 'You do want to be married? No one will force you.'

Her gaze lifted abruptly to mine. She looked horrified. 'Oh yes, my lady. I do not want to rot in some convent. Please do not suggest it. That might be fine for Kitty but not for me!'

'Very well but you are young yet.'

'I do not want to be an old maid.' A note of panic crept into her voice. 'I am no longer a child. I know what is expected of me in marriage and I am ready.'

'Yes Connie, I believe you are but Master George most definitely is not! You must stop behaving as if he is your betrothed and leave him alone. If you do that, I will do my best to find you a good match. This is a serious matter. Do you understand?'

Her head was down again, her curly blonde hair swinging over her shoulders from the edge of her white cap. 'Yes madam,' she muttered. 'But I would like to be a *lady*.'

I sighed. 'You are a knight's daughter, Connie. The best noble marriage I could find for you might be to a younger son. You will have to face facts.'

'One of George's brothers?' she asked hopefully.

I shook my head firmly. 'No Connie, all the Stanley boys are too young.'

She suddenly clasped my hand tightly. 'I do not want to

marry an old man. Please do not hitch me to a greybeard, my lady!'

I stepped back, indicating that the meeting was over. 'I will do my best for you, you may be sure of that. But you must do your best for me, learn the household skills you will need, and do not indulge in daydreams of being mistress of this household, which cannot be.'

When she had gone I knelt before the triptych and tried to steer my mind to prayer but the conversation with Thomas hindered concentration. He was right; I had been angered by his apparent change of attitude to our marriage. Hitherto I had believed our union to be conducted on a civilised basis, albeit I was annoyed by his failure to promote Henry's cause with the king. Now he appeared to be censuring me for a minimum of physical contact between us, a situation I had considered an agreed part of our marriage contract. Moreover, unforgivably, he was using my son's plight as a bargaining tool to force me into a more intimate relationship.

For several unproductive minutes I stared at the images on the altarpiece, then I rose abruptly. It was fruitless to ask three virgin saints for help in my marriage dilemma. What could they know of carnal matters? This was a problem I would have to solve myself, without holy intervention.

A page was waiting outside the oratory as I left. He bowed and held out a sealed letter. 'Lord Stanley told me to deliver this to you immediately, my lady. It came with the courier from London.'

My heart leapt at seeing my name and city address penned in Henry's looped handwriting. I had not received word from him in months, not since he had told me of the terrifying abduction attempt on the beach. Coming so soon after my troubling conversation with Thomas, the information his letter conveyed threw me into confusion.

To my dearly beloved and honoured mother, Lady Margaret Stanley, Countess of Richmond, greetings.

Regretfully I have to inform you that circumstances have changed since last I wrote. Lord Jasper and I are no longer housed together and I have been moved to Château Largoët, a stronghold belonging to Jean, Comte de Rieux, Lord Marshal of Brittany, whom the Duke has now designated my guardian. In addition we have been obliged to dismiss our own retainers and are now served and guarded by Bretons, an inconvenience which has swiftly improved my grasp of their language.

Lord Jasper has been placed under the guardianship of the Comte de Rohan at Château Josselin but the worst thing is that he has been obliged to bid a sorrowful farewell to Jane Hywel, who was ordered to leave Brittany with her daughter Sian and brother Evan, my uncle's long-serving squire. We were told the reason for these moves was for our own protection but I do not like to think of Lord Jasper alone and without the friendship of compatriots. Before we parted he confided that Duke Francis was reacting to fresh demands from both France and England to hand over his Tudor 'guests'. He feared another attempt at our abduction or assassination. It must be admitted that splitting us up has made hostile action of that kind twice as difficult and at least we are now far away from any easy access by sea.

I beg you not to be overly concerned on my account as

Davy Owen remains with me and we are housed comfortably in an upper chamber of a newly built tower here at Largoët, constantly guarded and with an armed escort whenever we ride out. Also, tutors from Vannes now come here with books and scholarly tasks, though they are clearly under orders to evade my requests for information from the outside world. Comte Jean, although very pleasant, is also tight-lipped on such matters. I am encouraged to wear my shortsword at all times and he warns me to avoid contact with anyone other than the liveried castle servants and guards.

I hope all this assures you of my safety and that I continue to develop the knowledge and skills I will need to protect and defend my Richmond estates when the time comes for me to return to England. A return that is, as ever, very much in your hands, dearest Mother. I hope you preserve your position at court and still have opportunity to assure the king of my fierce loyalty to England and its crown. I have every confidence in your eventual success in this matter and look forward to the day I kiss your hand in person.

Please convey my high regard to Lord Stanley; meanwhile you are daily in my prayers and I remain, ever and always, your devoted and obedient son,

Henry Tudor

Written at Château Largoët, Brittany, on this the twelfth day of January, 1475

NB. Letters to me come via Jean, Comte de Rieux, Lord Marshal of Brittany

I re-read the letter with growing disquiet, in no way convinced by its reassurances. I was concerned that it had taken a very long time to reach me and realised things could have radically changed for better or worse since its despatch. Despite Henry's attempts to comfort me, there was still a clear risk to my son's life and my chief aim now must be to expedite his safe return to England. This was not a time when I should be out of the queen's favour or testing my husband's will.

14

Harri

Châteaux Largoët and Trédion, Brittany, May 1475

COMTE JEAN WAS TAKING refreshment with several of his knight-retainers in a first-floor chamber of his residence. A handsome nobleman in dull green hunting garb, he was dark-featured and well proportioned, with the muscular frame of a trained soldier. 'Ah Henri, there you are!' he said, laying a friendly hand on my shoulder. I appreciated the way he treated me as an equal and never as a captive or a junior, which he might readily have done.

The count had ridden in while Davy and I were in the forest. Since spring, which came early at Largoët, we had ridden out most days for hours, as leaves sprouted translucent green in the high canopy and wildflowers bloomed in the dappled sunlight beneath. No strangers had yet been sighted in the environs and our Breton escorts had relaxed their guard enough to join in our games of mounted tag through the trees and take part in our impromptu archery competitions. Like all the Largoët men at arms we used the castle horses randomly and seldom rode the same-one twice in a week.

'Could you not ask the count when he comes if we could at least ride one horse regularly, Harri?' Davy suggested after a particularly stubborn gelding had challenged even his vocabulary of curses.

I shrugged. 'I will try but I do not hold out much hope. I suspect the Horse Master might have been told to give us awkward nags so that we are not tempted to make a break for freedom. It is a subtle way of keeping us in check.'

Davy rolled his eyes in surprise. 'Rather a devious ploy is it not?'

'We never know do we? The count is friendly towards us but he has to dance to the duke's tune.' We were out of earshot of the ever-present guards and speaking English but nevertheless I had dropped my voice. 'Maybe we should do a test run.'

'You mean try to escape? Where would we go?' Davy's eyes had begun glittering with excitement.

I hesitated. My remark had come without due thought and I had not really considered a destination, let alone formed any plan, but I chafed against being under constant scrutiny. For a youth approaching manhood such restriction was stifling. 'We could make for the border. Lord Jasper thought King Louis would welcome us, did he not?'

As usual Davy was ever practical. 'That was four years ago. How do we know he has not changed his mind? Also how far are we from France and which way is it?'

I shook my head and ruffled his hair in a big-brotherly way, even though, strange as it always seemed, I was actually his nephew. 'Stop asking questions! It was only a mad idea.'

He made a face. 'No, it was a good idea—'

A page in blue and gold Rieux livery was making his way across the stable yard.

'The count must be here,' Davy crowed. 'Now is your chance Harri!'

The boy bowed. 'My lord asked me to find you, Seigneur Richemont. Please follow me.'

After saying courteously that I looked well, Comte Jean hastened to explain his situation. 'I am not staying here at Largoët. My wife travels with me and she prefers to stay at her castle of Trédion, a few miles away on the other side of the forest. It has been recently renovated and she finds it more comfortable. But I have an invitation for you – not to the hunt but that will come in due course – she wishes to meet you and has urged me to bring you to visit her today, if that will not inconvenience you?'

Anywhere other than Château Largoët was attractive. 'The countess is very kind, sir, but I am not in a fit state of dress to meet a lady. May I have time to change my clothes?'

Comte Jean's handsome face creased in a smile and he turned to his companions. 'The young man wants to impress the countess. You will have competition in my lady's salon!'

There was general laughter and I felt blood rush to my cheeks. I had sudden recall of my mother's solar when I had stayed with her during the old king's readeption. She had been surrounded by her young female wards and their smiles and smothered giggles had rendered me as embarrassed and tongue-tied as a shy thirteen-year-old boy is capable of being. I raced up the steps of the Tour Elven to change, vowing to avoid such gauche conduct on this occasion.

I learned from one of the knights who accompanied us on our short journey that the manor of Trédion had come to the Comte de Rieux through his wife, the heiress Françoise Raquenel, and as we approached I understood her preference for the place. Set in a forest clearing, the residence was more of a mansion than a castle. Only its two towers and wide moat provided any semblance of fortification and its rows of glazed windows were too large and elegantly mullioned to be of any defensive benefit.

'Since the renovations it has become a lady's house,' the knight complained when I voiced my admiration. 'It is too small to house the earl's retinue so we have to lodge at the local inn. It is a house of "refinement".' He made the word sound like a disease.

Despite my resolution, as I passed through the pillared porch I could feel my belly begin to churn. Facing an armoured knight on a thundering courser seemed a much more attractive proposition than entering a lady's bower. I followed a liveried chamberlain up a curved stone staircase, gripping the polished wooden bannister and imagining being suffocated by rustling silks and the scent of roses. Why did the countess wish to meet me? And what on earth would I say to her? Not having had the benefit of a noble mother's guidance on high society behaviour I feared I would make an idiot of myself.

As the chamberlain flung open the gilded doors and I faltered in the entrance a young girl in a bright blue kirtle came up and took my hand. She could not have been more than ten or eleven. 'Are you Monsieur Henri?' she asked, her head cocked to one side in query. 'My Maman said there was a boy of that name coming. I am called La Petite.'

I looked down at her rosebud mouth and huge brown eyes and my nerves vanished. 'Yes, I am Henri. God's greeting to you, Mademoiselle La Petite. That is an unusual name.'

'Oh it is not my name, Monsieur. It is what people call me because I have the same name as my mother – Françoise. I am a La Petite Françoise, you see.'

I raised her small hand to my brow and bowed over it. 'Ah yes, I understand. But I may call you just La Petite?'

The query went unanswered because a waft of flowery perfume alerted me to a presence at her back and a soft, musical voice broke in to say, 'Do not detain our visitor, La Petite. He has come to see your mother.' I straightened up, startled.

I was enchanted by the figure that met my gaze, a simple dark gown, her hair hidden under a linen coif; her beauty was in the faint blush of her cheeks and the gentle curve of her red lips, her smooth brow, her eyes the blue of the French royal flag – these eyes regarded me.

I made her a polite bow. 'Truly Madame, the child does not annoy me. She is charming.'

'His name is Henri,' La Petite announced. 'And her name is Madame de Belleville. She is my governess.'

The lady frowned and took the little hand that I had just relinquished. 'Yes, all of that is right *ma chèrie*, but I think you should let your mother do the introductions. Look, she is waiting.'

Comtesse Françoise de Rieux sat under a fringed canopy bearing the family crest, a blue shield charged with ten gold bezants. There was no mistaking her wealth and rank. She was sumptuously dressed in shimmering green damask, glittering with jewellery, her hair hidden under a black, pleated chaperon hat, set off with a spray of diamonds. On low stools all around her sat half a dozen young ladies clad almost as splendidly as their mistress but in pastel colours and gauzy headdresses. Disconcertingly they were all staring at me with open curiosity.

Summoning my courage I strode forward and bowed deeply before the throne-like chair. 'Madame la Comtesse,' I said – and waited, eyes lowered, bereft of further speech.

'Monsieur Henri,' she responded. 'Or should I address you as the Comte de Richemont?'

I swallowed and raised my gaze. A welcoming smile had transformed her expression from that of *grande dame* to benevolent hostess. I returned it. 'At present I am simply Henry Tudor, Madame. My close friends call me Harri. Only time will tell what other names I shall acquire.'

'The count calls you Henri and so shall I. Now, let me offer you a seat.' A dismissive wave of her hand sent all the inquisitive young ladies off to a far corner, leaving six empty stools. She gestured towards them. 'Select one and bring it closer. I see you have already met my daughter and Madame de Belleville.'

As I placed a stool beside her chair I noticed that the girl and her governess had joined the other ladies. 'La Petite saw to that, Madame,' I said.

'Yes, she is very confident my little girl. Spoiled perhaps but charming I hope. It comes of being an only child.' A shadow crossed her face. 'It is too bad.'

'I am also an only child Madame,' I told her.

She nodded. 'So you are – and long separated from your mother I understand? That is unfortunate. But I hope you are reasonably happy at Largoët. It is something of a *fortress*,' she said this almost with horror. 'How old are you, Henri?'

'I was eighteen at the end of January, Madame.'

'A boy comes of age at twenty-one in England I understand. That is when you should become Comte de Richemont, is that so?'

I began to wonder where this was leading. 'All being well, Madame – but all may not be well. The English king has given the Richmond lands to his brother and holds my title in abeyance.'

She chose to ignore the loss of my estates. 'It is a title much admired in Brittany. It has been held by a succession of our dukes.'

'Yes, I am told the present duke still lists it among his own.'

The countess gazed at me solemnly. 'Duke Francis speaks very favourably of you, Henri. He likes you and has taken great pains to protect you from your enemies and ensure that you receive the education and training necessary to prepare you for nobility. I hope you will remember that, if and when you do come into your inheritance. England and Brittany have always been friends and while the King of France snaps at our border the duke needs all possible allies.'

I felt as if I was treading on eggshells. The Comtesse de Rieux was a very influential lady, one it would be foolish to offend. I gave a polite little laugh. 'I am gratified to hear that Duke Francis is well disposed towards me, Madame but perhaps understandably I am kept ignorant of his state affairs.'

She leant forward and gave me a pat on the arm. 'You are safe here with us, Henri. That is all that matters at present.' She rose and beckoned to her daughter's governess. 'I must spend time now with La Petite. She will be retiring soon. I will ask Madame de Belleville to introduce you to the young ladies of my chamber while I read with her a little.'

I have little recall of the six young ladies. All were pretty and vivacious, chattering away amongst themselves and occasionally asking my opinion; rather I found my gaze regularly straying to the governess, who took little part in the conversation but whenever she spoke her words seemed apposite, and were spoken in her low musical voice, of which I would have liked to hear more. However, I noticed that the others looked at her with blank stares and rapidly changed the subject. For some reason she was cold-shouldered.

In due course the countess finished the fable she was reading to her daughter and summoned the governess to take her away so I took the opportunity to make my own escape too, bowing my way out in their wake having been urged to visit again soon.

'Where do you think I am likely to find the count at this time, Madame?' I inquired of the governess as she and the girl set foot on the magnificent staircase that led to the next floor.

Madame de Belleville turned with an apologetic smile, causing my heart to skip a beat. 'I am afraid I have no idea, Monsieur Henri. This is the first time I have stayed in this house. I can find my way to the nursery, the garden and the countess's solar, that is all.'

La Petite broke in at this point. 'I think my father will be in the Grande Salle with his knights, Monsieur Henri.

They like to drink wine and make a lot of noise. It keeps me awake.'

I pulled a sympathetic face. 'Oh dear! Is your bedchamber above the Grande Salle?' I asked.

She wrinkled her nose. 'No, not really, it is just there. You can hear them already . . .'

She pointed to some tall, elegantly carved double doors off the stair landing, whereupon Madame de Belleville firmly took her hand. 'I hope you find the Count, Monsieur,' she said. 'Come La Petite, the servants will have finished filling your bathtub by now. Roland will be waiting and the water will be getting cold. Say goodnight to Monsieur Henri.'

I watched them disappear up the stairs and wondered who Roland was. Despite the Countess's regret that La Petite was an only child there was clearly another in the Rieux nursery.

15

Margaret

Westminster Palace, London, June 1475

THE KING HAD LED an army of more than twenty thousand men across the Channel to stake his claim to the
French crown, as so many of his predecessors had done
before him. In all the palace departments only a skeleton
staff was left and the Great Court at Westminster was
unusually quiet when I rode through it on my way to the
queen's apartments. Only the Law Courts were busy, still
in session in the Great Hall, and those domestic offices that
continued to function in order to serve the queen and her
daughters, who remained in residence.

I had not been summoned to Queen Elizabeth's solar
since the death of the baby Princess Margaret more than
two years ago and so I had missed all the trumpets and
bells that had greeted the birth of a second royal prince,
baptised Richard and already created Duke of York. I hoped
this fresh summons might indicate that I was back in the
queen's favour, at least enough to enlist her help once more

139

in bringing my son Henry safely back to England. However, any notion of this had to be shelved when I was shown not to the queen's solar but to her bedchamber and greeted at the entrance by her eldest daughter, a whey-faced Princess Elizabeth.

'I am so grateful you have come, Lady Richmond,' the young girl said anxiously. 'The queen is not well and said you would know best what to do. She would not let me send for the king's physician.'

I wondered briefly why a child should be caring for her mother when there ought to be at least two or three ladies in attendance but, putting this thought aside, I hurried straight to the bedside. 'Your grace, my lady, what is it ails you?' The weeping queen was propped up on pillows, clutching a kerchief, her face drawn and blotched. 'Have you the ague?'

Her brow creased in a deep frown and she sniffed loudly. 'Yes I believe I have an ague and I am also with child again. Thank goodness you have come, Margaret. I do not like the king's physicians. They do not understand the female condition and I remember you telling me you consulted a Doctor Caerleon. As usual I have pregnancy sickness and I cannot keep anything down. Do you think he might help me? My head aches terribly and I fear for my baby.' Her eyes closed and she rubbed fiercely at her temples through the white linen coif that covered her hair.

'I am sure Dr Caerleon will come. I will send for him, but of course I cannot say whether he is skilled in matters affecting childbirth,' I said.

The princess spoke over my shoulder in a quiet voice. 'I think my mother wants to be sure that any potion she takes for her headache will not harm the baby, Lady Richmond.

She has been refusing anything but curds and honey but even they soon come back up.'

I turned away from the bed and drew the girl with me out of the queen's earshot. 'I am sure Doctor Caerleon will do his best to help. He is very good at prescribing. I will write a note. Is there a page who could carry a message?'

She nodded. 'I will summon one and fetch pen and paper.'

'Are you alone here Princess? Are there no other ladies or gentlewomen on duty?'

This drew a rueful smile. 'There were but my mother grew fractious at their chatter and sent them all away. She said you were the only one she wanted.'

I raised an eyebrow. 'She was not thinking like that when she sent me away! But at the time she was mourning your little sister Margaret.' I would have added 'and not in full possession of her wits' but thought better of it. 'She is lucky to have such a kind and capable daughter to tend her now.'

The princess shrugged. 'I was with her in sanctuary at Westminster Abbey when my brother Edward was born. I was the only one who could calm her. I do not know why she is like this now. Perhaps you can find out, my lady? She keeps weeping and being sick. Make sure she has a bowl beside her while you write the note and I will go and summon a page.'

As I scratched out a brief message to the doctor I contemplated the young princess's demeanour. In all my experience of supervising young female wards I had never come across a girl as calm and self-contained as this nine-year-old. She could not have been more than five years old at the time of Prince Edward's birth. She appeared mature beyond her years and was clearly endowed with sympathy and intelligence as well as her mother's good looks.

While I was instructing the page on the note's destination I heard the sound of retching and hurried back to the bed to find the queen hunched over a silver bowl. Lavender-scented water was in another bowl on a nearby table and when the queen at last raised her head I was ready with a fragrant napkin, soaked and wrung out. She collapsed back on the pillows and let me wipe her face and remove the bowl. For all the retching there was little to show and I guessed that she must be starving and thirsty.

I had briefly described the queen's symptoms and condition in my note and the doctor arrived with an array of herbs and powders he thought might provide the necessary relief. Having acquired spring water from the palace source he mixed a potion and recommended she drink a good dose and eat some fresh manchet bread, repeating the process at each of the canonical hours if she was not asleep. His gentle voice and deferential manner reassured the queen and he left voicing his intention to attend again the next day. All through this process Princess Elizabeth sat holding her mother's hand, occasionally exchanging snippets of conversation and reassurance. When her mother was sleeping peacefully at last I suggested that she might like to return to her own quarters and be with her sisters.

'Yes, I will go back because Mary will be missing me,' she agreed. 'And Cecily is being awkward. She is six and thinks no one will dare to scold her because the king will punish them.' Princess Elizabeth gave me a despairing look. 'She is selfish and silly.'

I smiled sympathetically, thinking of my own childhood among a clutch of half-siblings who were older than me.

'Sisters can be like that. I had five but only really got on with my sister Edith. Perhaps I should bring my wards' governess with me the next time I come. Mother Hubbard is wonderful with wayward children. But you look tired, Princess. Go and have some supper and sleep. You have been a great help to your mother. I will stay with her now.'

She nodded solemnly. 'Yes, I am tired. Thank you for coming, Lady Richmond. I believe my mother thought you might not answer her call.'

'Did she?' I was surprised. 'I did not know she was in distress, but I am very glad I came.'

The princess astonished me with her parting remark. 'She does not say so but I think she admires you a good deal. Good night, my lady.' With that she made me a small bob and turned to leave.

I could not resist calling after her softly, 'I think she should be very proud of you, Princess.'

That night I dozed in an armchair beside the queen's bed and in the early hours she woke and roused me. 'Why are you still here, Margaret?' she asked drowsily. 'Should you not have returned home to your charges?'

'They are well cared for, your grace,' I assured her. 'But you were not. How are you feeling now?' I picked up the night candle and held it nearer to her face. 'You look much more like yourself.'

She gave me a sideways glance. 'You mean I looked like a witch before?'

'You could never look like a witch,' I said. 'May I give you another dose of your potion? You seem to have kept it down so far.'

Like a naughty child she put out her tongue. 'Blah! It

tastes horrible, but if you think it is doing me good I suppose I should have some.'

I laughed. 'I think it is definitely doing you good, your grace! And therefore it must be doing your baby good as well.' I stood up and stretched, stiff from my awkward position in the chair. 'Doctor Caerleon will be pleased with you.'

Queen Elizabeth blew out her cheeks and expelled air. 'Oh, of course we all want to please the good Doctor Caerleon! Actually, he is quite charming do you not think?' Suddenly her expression clouded over. 'Did you know that Edward left his four-year-old son in charge of the kingdom – only nominally, of course! Evidently Edward does not trust me with the regency. The Great Seal is in Ludlow with the President of the Prince of Wales' Council, instead of being here in London. Where do you suppose the king is now? Still in Calais do you think? Why does he not keep me informed?'

She was growing agitated again and I sought to calm her. 'Perhaps he means not to burden you while you are with child. Anyway, wherever he is, my lady, my husband will not be far away and it may not be long before they are both facing the French on a battlefield. Perhaps we should not dwell on that too much.'

I picked up the night candle and walked across to the table where the flagon of Dr Caerleon's mixture stood, covered by a napkin, a fine pewter beaker beside it, which I filled and carried to the bed.

When I offered it, the queen did not immediately take it. 'You taste it first, Margaret,' she ordered, adding as an afterthought, 'Please.'

I gave her a sharp glance. 'Why so, your grace? Do you think it might be poisoned? I have been the only one here with you.'

'You think I suspect you of poisoning me?' She gave a harsh laugh. 'No, Margaret, I simply want you to know how disgusting it tastes!' She reached for the beaker. 'Oh never mind, just give it to me.'

I held it back and lifted it to my lips. It was, as she said, quite unpleasant on the tongue and I grimaced. 'I see what you mean, my lady. But perhaps it is worth drinking to be back to good health.' I passed the beaker over. 'You have taken three doses already. Had I or Doctor Caerleon intended to poison you, I doubt you would be awake now.'

She drank the rest of the greenish mixture in a few swift gulps, her brown eyes fixed on my face in the flickering candlelight, and shuddered as she handed the cup back. 'Ugh! Is there some of that manchet bread left to take away the taste? Preferably with some butter.'

I shook my head. 'The doctor said no milk and no butter, or anything from a cow, until your stomach has settled. I will fetch bread and water.'

The queen sank back into the pillows. 'Ah! I am on prison rations. The king would never put up with it.'

'The king is not with child, your grace,' I pointed out. 'He does not have to consider a life other than his own.'

'And he does not consider that enough,' she complained. 'Sometimes he eats and drinks so much he is sick. And then he starts again. I am always telling him to take more care of himself.'

I sliced a chunk from the loaf on the table and cut off the crusts, aware that her teeth were not strong. She was rather too fond of comfits in my opinion; or perhaps her nine pregnancies had taken their toll. She ate the bread slowly and washed it down with the water. 'You should call a couple of my other ladies and take some rest, Margaret,' she suggested. 'If one sits in here and one in the anteroom perhaps they cannot chatter together so irritatingly.'

'It will be an hour or two before dawn breaks,' I said. 'I will stay until then and have them summoned when you wake in the morning. Perhaps you will sleep again now that you have something in your stomach.'

As I pulled the covers around her I heard her quiet chuckle. 'You are quite the nurse, Margaret, are you not?'

'I had much practice with my second husband, your grace. May God bless your rest.'

When I finally left the palace the next day, the None bell was chiming from the chapel and I reflected that I had failed to mention Henry's plight in Brittany but at least my relationship with the queen had been re-established. Whether we were friends I could not be sure, any more than I was convinced that she had not suspected me of conspiring to poison her.

16

Harri

Châteaux Largoët and Trédion, Brittany, summer 1475

M Y VISIT TO THE Comtesse de Rieux's solar was the first of many I made to Château Trédion that summer. Apparently La Petite had asked her mother if I could join her rides in the woods with Madame de Belleville. On the next occasion I took Davy with me and of course we had to have our usual escort of Largoët guards with us but La Petite must have complained to her father that she did not like such a crowded ride, because the next time we went I was called in to see the count in his business chamber.

A clerk had been taking dictation and left the room as I entered. 'You seem to have impressed my daughter, Henri,' Comte Jean began, moving around his desk to greet me. 'But before you ride with her today I wish to clarify a few matters.'

I felt a jolt of unease. 'I am at your service my lord,' I said faintly.

'I will not insist that you take your Largoët escort on

these rides, since the ladies do not like to be so vastly outnumbered. However I will require a gentleman's promise that you and your companion will not attempt to leave the Trédion demesne. I am thinking of your safety. Regular reports from the villages are made to my Captain at Largoët and we have not heard of any strangers in the vicinity, so as long as you remain close to the castle precincts and stay within sight of the grooms who accompany my daughter and her governess I am satisfied that you and they will be safe. Do I have your word on that?'

I could see no reason to hesitate. 'You have my word, my lord. I am flattered that your daughter enjoys my company.'

A fierce frown greeted this last remark and the count took a step nearer to fix his gaze intently on mine. 'On the matter of my daughter's favour, Henri, I should tell you that she has for some years been betrothed to the Laval heir, son of a very prominent Breton border family whose estates march with mine. Therefore you should not be tempted into offering her anything other than friendship. I hope that is understood?'

I suppressed a smile because my focus was not on the count's daughter but on her governess. 'I can give you my word on that also, my lord.'

His eyes did not leave mine for several seconds then he gave a brisk nod. 'Good. That is clear then. Now, one more thing; if he is to ride out with my daughter, the future Comte de Richemont cannot be seen on any old jade from the garrison stable. I will arrange for a courser to be brought over from the duke's stable at Vannes, and I will put you through your paces myself when it arrives. If your riding is up to the standard required for such a mount, there will be a chance to compete in an informal joust that I plan to hold here at Trédion later in the summer.'

I could merely have offered my grateful thanks, expressed enthusiasm for the joust and left it at that but I could not see Davy left high and dry on 'any old jade' as the count put it, when I was mounted on a pedigree steed. 'Thank you, my lord, I appreciate your kindness but . . .' I paused, not sure how to proceed.

'Yes?' He sounded tetchy. 'Is that not enough for you?'

'Oh yes indeed sir, very much enough for *me* but there is also Davy – he is a splendid rider, as I hope you will see, and also deserves a decent mount.'

This was testing the count's patience. 'You do know, do you not, Henri, that the cost of your upkeep and that of your companion falls on the duke's exchequer? It is entirely due to his generosity that you are housed and fed according to your rank. Davy, as you call him, is not of your rank.'

I hung my head penitently but there was no point in backing down once I had started. 'That is true at present, my lord, but his father was a knight banneret, he is Lord Jasper's brother and my blood kinsman. He is a Tudor and destined for knighthood. If he were to be asked, I am sure his grace might also consider Davy worthy of a decent mount.'

I thought Count Jean was going to refuse point blank but after a tense pause he went on, 'I would suggest that the future rank of both of you rather hangs in the balance but I will consult the duke on the matter and your kinsman must be content with that.'

I lifted my gaze and saw that he was smiling benignly

at me, as if approving my championship of Davy. 'Thank you, my lord,' I said.

The rides with La Petite and Madame de Belleville began sedately, walking and trotting down forest tracks kept clear for the count's hunts. Duke Francis supplied us both with personal mounts, as I had hoped he would. They were lively and beautifully trained and we both managed to demonstrate our riding ability to the Marshal's satisfaction. My destrier was a dark bay stallion called Bastion, heavier and stronger than Davy's rouncey, a smaller, prettier grey mare called Alouette but he was not disappointed.

'Not at all,' he declared. 'She is nimble and knowing and her mouth is like silk.'

His glowing description made me laugh. 'You are going to ride her, Davy, not make love to her!' I cried.

His retort was crude but apt. 'No, but your stallion might attempt to, Harri. I hope he has good manners. We do not need any horseplay in front of Mademoiselle La Petite Rieux.'

Fortunately Bastion proved to have impeccable manners to match his immaculate paces, treating Alouette like a cheeky younger sister and only attempting the occasional sly kick when he considered her impertinent.

To one side of the castle at Trédion the moat opened out into a lake where water lilies bloomed in pink and white profusion and fat carp swam among them, oblivious to the fact that this apparent paradise was the final stage on their journey to the kitchen. On the far side of the lake, shaded by drooping willows, stood a pavilion built of pale stone with steps leading down to the water. In warm weather these were strewn with silken cushions, when it was the

countess's pleasure to sit there with her young lady companions. At the end of our next ride we stopped to talk to her,
sending the horses back to the stables with the grooms.
Once again I noticed that the court damsels cold-shouldered
the beautiful Madame de Belleville and puzzled over why
this should be. She might favour plainer dress than they
did but she was of similar age, well spoken and clearly of
noble family, and it troubled me that such a gentle woman
should be ostracised in this way. I puzzled over the reason
but it was not something I felt able to mention.

However, one subject I did broach. 'Who is Roland?' I
asked her one day. My question was abrupt but it had taken
courage to ask it because still I could scarcely believe such
a beauty would actually converse with me openly.

Instead of answering she posed a question of her own.
'How did you know about Roland, Monsieur Henri?' Then
she remembered. 'Ah yes, I mentioned him . . .' She rode
on a few paces in silence before relenting. 'Well, you might
as well know, Roland is my son. He is not yet five – too
young to ride or to be allowed the run of the castle.'

'You have a son of four?' I could not disguise my astonishment. She looked no older than me.

'You think me too young?' Her laugh was unexpectedly
throaty, suggesting experience rather than innocence. 'How
gallant of you!'

I felt my cheeks burn. Further queries leapt to my mind,
none of which it seemed appropriate to ask, so I took refuge
in flattery. 'Much too young, Madame! May we meet this
young man? Would he perhaps like to watch Davy and me
practise with our weapons? Most boys like to watch bows
and swords in action.'

The way her cheeks dimpled reinstated her air of innocence. 'As do many girls, I assure you,' she said. 'Where do
you make this practice?'

'At Largoët usually but we could bring our weapons here.'

'Yes, that might be best. Roland would love that.'

'It is agreed then. Next time we will come early and
equipped,' I said. 'And he will see me thrash this young
upstart here.'

Riding beside me, Davy snorted indignantly. 'In your
dreams, Harri! But I will let you make a fool of yourself
while you try!' Prudently he kneed his mare, which quickly
sidled out of reach.

Roland turned out to be a sturdy little boy, just beginning
to shed his baby fat. He had his mother's royal blue eyes,
which shone with anticipation as Davy and I strode up to
him the next day, bare headed in our padded gambesons
and leg armour, carrying swords and shields and mail coifs.

'These are the soldiers I explained about Roland,' Madame
de Belleville told her son, pushing him gently forward. 'They
are going to show you how they practise with their swords
and bows.'

'God give you good day, Roland,' I said, dropping to my
haunches to speak with him face to face. 'Do you want to
be a soldier when you grow up?'

After staring at me for several long moments he blinked
and said, 'No, I am going to be a knight.'

'Oh, good ambition little man!' I rose, laughing. 'He will
go far,' I told his mother. 'We will start our session at the
Pell Post, which he may not think very exciting but later
he can have a try at it, so he should watch carefully.'

The Pell Post warm-up is not the most riveting part of

weapons practice to watch but a lot of fun to perform. The height of a man, the post represented a battlefield opponent, with markings at leg, shoulder and head height. Davy and I took it in turn to shout instructions at each other as to which part of the body to slash at with our blunted swords, shouting loudly as we did so.

Soon the little boy grew excited and begged to be allowed to 'play in the sand', as he put it. I had brought a small wooden sword from Largoët for him to use, and erected a post of his own height. He quickly got the hang of the slashing movements but the thing he most enjoyed was emitting the required shouts and yells as he made them. As a child myself I remembered taking advantage of this freedom to shriek as loudly as possible and often temporarily lost my voice as a result. Judging by his restlessness, Roland did not find the subsequent mock sword-fight Davy and I staged for him quite as exciting as that unexpected freedom to screech. His mother had spent much of the time with her hands over her ears.

Later I remarked to her that Roland seemed to enjoy the Pell Post exercise. She gave me a funny look but I went on, 'Would he like another go, do you think?' I asked.

'He would but I have no wish to hear him scream like that again!'

I grinned. 'I seem to remember enjoying that part of it the most when I was a boy.'

'I think I will prefer watching the joust,' she admitted. 'Will there be heralds and trumpeters and ladies throwing favours?'

'I hardly think so.' I frowned. 'It is an informal competition between men at arms and squires, not a major event.'

'I thought jousting was cavalry training for knights,' she remarked.

'Battle training is becoming more generalised,' I replied, groping in my memory for the latest I had read on military tactics. 'It is true that only dukes and kings tend to keep a standing cavalry. Destriers are expensive beasts and common men at arms cannot afford them.'

'But they are a splendid sight to see!'

Her eager expression carried me away. 'One day I will form my own cavalry, Madame, just to let you watch them charge!' I cried, adding an extravagant flourish of my free hand.

This wild boast inspired a finely arched eyebrow to lift. 'So you expect to become a duke or a king do you, Monsieur Henri? I think I may be very old before I see that day.'

My bubble burst and I crashed to earth, blushing like a schoolboy. 'Well, yes, perhaps we had better begin with the Trédion joust. I hope you will be watching.'

She would definitely be watching, she confirmed. Personally I hoped to have a little more time to practise, my partnership with Bastion being still rather erratic and the governess was unfortunately there at the tiltyard when I suffered a somewhat humiliating training defeat at Davy's hand: he scored a direct hit on my shoulder target, known as the *écranche*, while I had missed his completely.

Afterwards she said solemnly, 'Your horse swerved; I thought you were a little unlucky Monsieur Henri.'

I felt my throat clench at this offer of sympathy coming from such sweet-cherry lips and had to clear it before uttering my next words. 'I wonder if you would consent to call me Harri, Madame? I am not used to being addressed so formally.'

'Harri.' Of course she pronounced it the French way, leaving the H silent. 'Is that a version of Henri?'

'It is the Welsh version but the English also use it.'

She tilted her head in acknowledgement. 'Well, I will call you Harri if you call me Catherine. That would seem fair would it not? We are not so far apart in age after all.'

'Is that so? I am not prepared to guess your age, Madame, having been wrong once already.'

'Not wrong – just gallant.' Her cheeks flushed a deeper shade of pink. 'I am twenty-one.' She glanced about to check for eavesdroppers. 'And I will make another revelation whilst no one else is listening. I am not Madame but Mademoiselle.'

This took me aback. I had been assuming that she was a widow and Roland the son of her deceased husband. The fact that the boy must be illegitimate cast a tragic and mysterious slant on her circumstances and I realised there was much yet to be learned about Catherine de Belleville. Not being sure how to respond, at first I kept quiet, waiting for her to offer further enlightenment but it was not forth-coming. Eventually I broke the silence.

'Then I need not offer any condolences on the death of your husband,' I said with a smile and a shrug. Such feeble teenage humour was probably risking her wrath but it was an attempt to convey the fact that I did not find her news shocking; there were bastards in my own immediate family.

Luckily she saw the funny side. 'No Harri, condolences would be misplaced. Roland's father is very much alive – and that is as far as I will enlighten you.'

17

Margaret

Westminster Palace, London, September 1475

WESTMINSTER PALACE WAS CROWDED and noisy once more. I stood among the queen's guests at one of the windows in the long gallery off the Great Hall, observing the conclusion of King Edward's ceremonial return to London from his military expedition to France. Preceded on foot by a troop of liveried archers and surrounded by his armoured and colourfully caparisoned retinue of knights, Edward the Fourth was acknowledging the cheers of the crowd massed in the Great Court from the considerable height of his gorgeously-trapped black charger. It was a fine sight but the weather had not favoured him with sunshine to glint off his golden crown and despite fresh straw laid on the cobbles, steady rainfall and a long procession of foot and hoof prints had churned the streets to a malodorous bog, deterring Londoners from coming out in their thousands as they usually did for their monarch. Or perhaps the meagre turnout was due to the fact that King Edward was returning not from a glorious battlefield victory but from a negotiated peace. While it filled the royal coffers with French gold it had done little for England's military reputation.

'His grace looks well, does he not?' Elizabeth turned to address her ladies, making the sign of the cross. 'I thank God and his Holy Saints that my beloved Edward and his loyal troops have returned without serious casualties and a treasury of gold and trophies to enrich the kingdom!'

Naturally there was a general murmur of approval, but more generally there was much closet comparing and contrasting of this ignominious peace with King Henry the Fifth's glorious victory at Agincourt, when his six thousand men had defeated thirty thousand Frenchmen. The outcome of this Yorkist king's French invasion was very different. The much-vaunted alliance with Burgundy, sealed by Duke Charles's marriage to King Edward's sister Margaret six years before, had foundered badly when the duke failed to bring the promised army to support his brother-in-law in France, arriving with only his personal retinue. And Duke Francis, a third party to the alliance, had not sent any troops at all from Brittany, being too fearful that the French might storm his vulnerable border behind his back. As a result, finding himself more or less abandoned in the middle of France, Edward had been faced with the prospect of confronting a French horde with only the twenty thousand men he had brought from England. I imagined him thanking all his favourite saints when Louis of France lived up to his reputation for avoiding war at all costs. Doing so had indeed cost him a fortune.

However, I estimated that by paying Edward seventy-five thousand crowns to take his army back over the Channel uncontested, King Louis had saved millions by avoiding the vast expense of war and at the same time purchased lucrative years of peace and free trade between the two countries. Not only that but he had persuaded the disgruntled English king to abandon his truce with Brittany and Burgundy, which had been threatening France's western and northern borders for years. He might be temporarily low in funds but Louis the Eleventh was not called the Universal Spider for nothing.

'Oh look, my lady; Robert Poyntz is riding in the front rank of the king's squires. He has a fine new jacket. Does he not look splendid?' Meg Woodville murmured excitedly in my ear as she caught sight of her beloved in the procession. I knew that she welcomed the unexpected peace because not only had it brought Robert home safe and sound but also her father Earl Rivers, thus advancing the prospect of her marriage. I felt a stab of regret, knowing that when it happened I would lose the companionship of my favourite trainbearer. However, to acknowledge her delight I thrust my hand back and secretly squeezed hers, hidden by the stiff folds of our gleaming court skirts. It was six months since Robert had left for France and at Meg's tender age such a long separation had been hard to bear.

'There will no doubt be a number of weddings to celebrate, now that so many young men have returned with weighty purses,' remarked the queen, causing me to wonder if she could have heard her niece's whispered comment. Elizabeth was notoriously sharp of hearing. 'And more than one birth during the next year no doubt.' I saw her lay a hand on her own belly as she said this. It would not be long before her next child was born.

'We all look forward to a safe delivery for your grace,' I said, feeling Meg lift my train as I turned to follow the queen from the gallery and down the length of the great hall towards the royal dais. When the prominent members of the cavalcade had dismounted and processed inside for a formal welcome, I would be greeting my own husband, who had led five hundred Stanley retainers to France behind the king. Somewhat to my surprise I felt a frisson of anticipation at the prospect of seeing him again.

After some lengthy speeches, a celebration banquet of numerous courses went on into the night. By the time our torchlit barge deposited us at St Paul's Wharf it had stopped raining but the steep lane that led up to Stanley House was running with filthy water, which soaked the hem of my costly court robes and meant that another pair of expensive Cordovan leather shoes would have to be given to the poor. Young Meg was almost asleep on her feet. I felt her stumbles jerk my train several times, so that when we had passed through the gatehouse and into the hall where Mistress Hubbard met us, I pulled it gently from the girl's clenched hands and suggested the governess take her immediately to bed.

'Meg had a long talk with her father at the banquet,' I told Mother Hubbard quietly, 'but I could not get any real sense of what they discussed. You might probe a little in the morning. Earl Rivers will be paying us a visit tomorrow and it would be nice to be prepared.'

Thomas's face appeared thinner than I remembered, his beard a little greyer. He looked tired and drawn. He stood by the hearth, dismissed the waiting servant, threw a fresh log on the fire, poured fragrant spiced wine from a silver jug and handed me a cup. We stood close together, sipping and feeling the comforting liquid heating our blood as a not-so-fragrant steam began to rise from our damp clothes.

'I have missed you, Margaret,' he said at length with a wry smile, raising his cup to me. 'No one else speaks to me with your honesty and truth.'

I returned his salute. 'Are they not the qualities that should exist between husband and wife?'

'Indeed they are. So give me your opinion of this. After the French peace treaty was signed at Picquigny, King Louis offered me a thousand-crown reward "for successfully steering your king" – those were his very words. I told him that I could not accept his money; that the counsel I gave my sovereign was not for sale.'

I frowned. 'Was that wise? How did he respond?'

'He said it was not a payment, it was a gift.'

'Jasper always said Louis was a slippery customer.'

'Jasper was right. I left Picquigny without the money but at Comines, where we rested on the way to Calais, Edward held a victory party. When I stumbled to my chamber, somewhat the worse for drink I confess, I found a coffer full of gold had been delivered to my duty squire. He said he had accepted it because the courier wore the royal livery of France. It was from King Louis.'

'Could you not send it back?' I asked, sensing his anger.

He shrugged. 'By then I had discussed it with other members of the Privy Council. They had all had these rewards, as they called them. Some had refused at first, but now I was the only one holding out. I decided then that if it was good enough for the king and his council, it had to be good enough for me.'

'So you have been hoodwinked, lured into King Louis's spidery web, Thomas. What will you use the money for? That will demonstrate whether you are prepared to dance to the French king's tune.'

He gazed at me thoughtfully. 'I thought you might advise me, Margaret. You support many worthy causes. Please suggest one for this unexpected beneficence.'

I hesitated. Thomas was not a generous giver of alms, although I knew he paid for a succession of bright young men from his northern holdings to receive a good education. However, as he usually employed their talents in some capacity afterwards there was a certain amount of self-interest in those bursaries. On this occasion some more munificent gesture was required. 'I think you should donate it to a religious institution of your choice, Thomas. Perhaps you could found a chantry at Burscough Abbey near Lathom, where your parents are buried and where you may wish to rest yourself. You work so hard in this life but you do not give enough thought to your soul.'

Eyes fixed on me, he drew a long draught of his wine then nodded. 'You are right. I will take your advice and some good may come of King Louis's craven palm greasing. I might even specify that masses be said for his soul.'

I smiled but shook my head. 'There is no need to go that far, my lord. It is your own soul and the souls of your family that should have the prayers.'

He bent to refresh his cup from the jug. 'An event occurring on our return voyage will be of interest to you,' he remarked. 'By some mischance the Duke of Exeter went missing in the Channel. He embarked at Calais but he never disembarked at Dover. King Edward ordered an inquiry but there was no evidence of foul play and no body was found in a search of the route. He has simply disappeared.'

I was far from upset by this news but very intrigued. 'I believe my lord of Exeter was known to drink rather too freely. Maybe he stumbled on deck and fell over the side?'

Thomas met this suggestion with a wicked grin. 'That was the inquiry's conclusion, which King Edward readily accepted – a little too readily some might say. As you know Exeter had only been released from the Tower on the understanding that he bring a large force of men on the expedition and display his loyalty to York on the battlefield. Perhaps he failed to please Edward quite enough – who knows?'

I swirled the wine in my cup and watched it settle. 'Exeter was a direct descendant of John of Gaunt,' I mused. 'A Lancastrian claimant to the throne.'

'Yes, through the female line, like your son Henry. It is a dangerous position to be in, it would seem.' There was a warning note in Thomas's voice.

I glanced up sharply. 'We *must* get him home, Thomas!'

'You are right. Where we can protect him.'

Instinctively we drew together. Thomas relieved me of my cup and placed it on the tray, then he took me gently in his arms. 'The best way to do that is to work with the king and queen. You know that, Margaret.'

I sighed. 'Elizabeth has asked me to attend her lying-in and I have accepted. It means I will be obliged to stay at the palace when she begins her confinement next week.'

'Well, at least you will be able to plead Henry's loyalty while you are there. And I will do so with the king.' He bent and kissed me, his ardour unmistakable despite his apparent weariness. 'But it does not give us much time to refresh our own marital bond. Shall it be your chamber or mine?'

The following day when Earl Rivers paid his visit to Meg he came to my solar afterwards. My immediate thought was that, compared to the devil-may-care courtier of yore, he looked a distinctly troubled man.

'I am making a pilgrimage to Rome, Lady Margaret,' he declared without preamble. 'I leave within a week, which means Meg's marriage will have to wait until after my return. Predictably she is in tears about it but this journey is a matter of urgency and conscience. King Edward has granted me leave of absence from court, as I will also carry out certain missions for him with the Holy See. I know I can rely on you to reassure Meg that I still have her interests at heart and will attend to the matter of her marriage on my return. Meanwhile Master Poyntz remains in the king's service and continues his studies at the Inns of Court. He has my permission to visit Meg whenever you are able to receive him. I know you will see that they are well chaperoned.'

The earl had not taken the chair I offered him and paced to and fro as he spoke. I peered closely at him, detecting significant changes in his complexion and demeanour. 'She will be well cared for as usual my lord,' I said, 'and I am delighted to have her companionship a while longer. When do you expect to return from Rome?'

'I hope to be there by Advent and return before Easter.' He paused in his pacing to stare at me. 'I see you are wondering why I should have this sudden need to make a pilgrimage so soon after my return from France? I assure you it has nothing to do with the king's expedition but I can tell you no more, except that the older I get the more I sense the turn of Fortune's Wheel and the need to atone for my sins.'

'I understand those feelings well and seek to expiate my sins by regularly wearing a hair belt next to my skin. It is a keen reminder of one's fallibility.'

He grimaced. 'I have been wearing a hair tunic under my chemise for a fortnight now, Lady Margaret. We have more in common than we knew. But forgive me; I must take my leave. There is much to occupy the little time I have before I embark for Calais.'

He left me with questions burning in my mind. I concluded that he was a man in deep personal distress, with an urgent need to atone for some mortal sin recently committed; a man who also owed everything to his brother-in-law the king. I wondered how far his gratitude might have been stretched and, more specifically, in which ship he had crossed the Channel from France two weeks ago?

18

Harri

Château Trédion, Brittany, September 1475

After daily tiltyard practice with Davy and any of the count's squires and knights that we could persuade to take part, I felt I was as ready as I ever would be for the Trédion joust, scheduled for the last week of the de Rieuxs' stay at the château. My confidence was boosted further by the fact that Catherine de Belleville had promised to favour me if I managed to reach the final of the competition.

She and I had spent an increasing amount of time together as the summer progressed and my initial awe and admiration of her beauty had blossomed into genuine enjoyment of her company, which invariably included that of La Petite and frequently Roland also. Davy always joined in the rides but often, when Catherine suggested a walk around the lake or a picnic in the garden with the children he made an excuse. I was not sure whether it was the children or the governess whose company he found testing. Perhaps it was simply a matter of the three-year difference in our ages. At fifteen

Davy was still a boy, albeit a very strong one and blessed with prodigious skill at arms, whereas at eighteen I considered myself a man, endowed with a deep voice, a stubbled chin and carnal urges that led me to confession more and more frequently. Although I continued with my academic studies they became of secondary importance to the pursuit of jousting excellence and spending time with Catherine, during which, inevitably, I fell in love. Or in fact and in hindsight, I fell headlong into total infatuation, but being naive and inexperienced I had little notion of how to follow where my inclinations were leading. Being hampered by the presence of children and the warnings of my confessor, I made a great deal more progress in jousting than I did in romancing.

After our picnics, La Petite was very happy playing games with Roland, leaving the two of us time to talk and although at first she was reticent, having exhausted her questions about my family and childhood, Catherine at last opened up about her own.

'My mother is Guillaumette of Luxembourg,' she explained, 'a daughter of one of the many branches of that ducal family. She and the countess served the queen together at the French court whenever it came to the Loire until she married at the age of fifteen. She was sixteen when she gave birth to my brother Robert, who is now the Comte de Rouci.' She looked at me quizzically and frowned, detecting my distraction, possibly because I was looking intently at her and my imagination was working overtime seeing her natural beauty hidden beneath a modest white linen chemise and a dark blue bodice. 'I hope you are listening carefully, Harri, because it is a little complicated.'

'I am all ears,' I said hastily. 'And I am guessing that if your brother is already Comte de Rouci then your father must have died.'

She nodded. 'Good, you are following well. My father died when I was two years old and not long afterwards Maman married again, to Gilles, the Seigneur de Belleville, and we all went to live at his castle in Anjou, south of Nantes. It was lovely there and my mother was happy and soon had another child, my half-sister Philippe, who we call Pippa.'

'I have a question,' I cut in, forcing my attention away from its rousing fantasies. 'Why does La Petite call you Madame de Belleville, if your father was Comte de Rouci? Should you not be Catherine de Rouci?'

'I told you it was complicated,' she said a little crossly. 'As I was only two when my mother married again her husband suggested I take his name and when the Comtesse de Rieux took me as governess she insisted I be called Madame by her daughter, because of course I brought Roland with me.'

I sat up abruptly. 'That was a big leap in your story, Catherine. Between the ages of two and twenty you grew into a beautiful woman and became a mother. But why did you not marry Roland's father?' I knew I was in danger of offending her but this question had puzzled me ever since she revealed Roland's illegitimacy and it was an irresistible opportunity to probe further.

As soon as I saw the blood flood her cheeks I regretted my crass curiosity but at that very moment there was a shriek from one of the parterre gardens nearby and she jumped to her feet, calling, 'Roland! What is wrong? Where are you?'

I joined her rush towards the source of the cries and there was Roland, standing in the middle of a patch of stinging nettles. Having stepped unwittingly into it, he had thrashed around trying to get out of the nettle patch and unfortunately plenty of naked skin was exposed to the plants' poisonous hairs. It was little wonder the boy was screaming. Catherine swept him up and carried him back to the picnic cloth, making soothing noises and kissing the worst eruptions of the rash.

'Where there are nettles there will be docks,' I called to her. 'I will find some to rub on the stings.'

By now La Petite had emerged from the hiding place where Roland was supposed to find her and she and I began energetically to rub the dock leaves over the red rash blooming all over the little boy's legs and arms while Catherine found him a sweetmeat to hush the strident yells. From then on she chose to supervise the children's games more carefully, at the same time giving me the distinct impression that any further talk of her family history was off limits and the subject of Roland's father a closed book. It did not, of course, stop me regarding her with the kind of youthful yearning that I am afraid did not adhere to the rules of courtly love. Not that they had come within the curriculum of my academic education.

From then on I concentrated on making sure that my horse Bastion was in peak condition and his tack and bardings were polished bright. He had been delivered to me complete with protective armour and trappings patterned with the Brittany ermine crest, so I would be competing in Duke Francis's colours. I found this prospect daunting but Comte Jean pointed out that no equipment would fit Bastion like that which had been made for him and anyway I was, in effect, the duke's ward. 'His grace would not have sanctioned providing you with of one of his chargers if he had not considered you worthy of bearing his livery, Henri. I am sure you will do him proud.'

The event took place over two days and on the second Duke Francis decided to honour it with his presence. Comte Jean must have known he was coming because beside the tiltyard a colourful, tented pavilion was erected, which on the first day housed the countess and her ladies, including La Petite and Catherine, and on the second was embellished with a large ducal banner and rows of fluttering pennants displaying the Breton ermine badge. The duke and duchess had taken their seats in the pavilion in time for the first joust, a knockout competition, the winner of each pass moving on to the next round. I had not realised Duke Francis and Duchess Marguerite were there until I rode into the tiltyard for my first joust; the knowledge did not improve the state of my nerves.

I was quite well placed on the scoreboard after the first day, which had consisted of bouts between pairs of contestants on foot, using a variety of weapons, and was judged by the count and his master at arms, but I was irked that Davy had ended up one place above me. However, I hoped at least my ability with the lance might lift me in the rankings, as well as the superior speed and weight of my charger. I would be mortified if I failed at the first pass, knowing that Duke Francis was watching, but even above that was the paramount incentive of receiving Catherine's favour if I qualified for the final joust.

I fought down my jitters, fearing they would be transmitted

to Bastion, but to my surprise the banners and trumpets and the cheers of the onlookers seemed to inspire the stallion. From the moment he entered the tiltyard, his head and tail rose high with equine pride and his performance ascended to a level he had never shown in practice sessions. Obviously, unlike me, Bastion was an experienced jouster and an exhibitionist. From pass to winning pass the horse seemed to do everything, except to aim a steady lance, without my guidance. There was no need to use my spurs or twitch my reins or even voice a command. He kept himself straight on the line of the barrier, judged when to increase the pace and even made a tactical toss of his head just before the instant of impact to distract my opponent's aim. I merely had to lower the lance from vertical at precisely the right moment and aim to hit my opponent's *écranche*.

Jousting lances had special tips that shattered on impact, proving a hit but causing as little injury or damage as possible. To ensure there was no foul play, even at a 'friendly' joust like ours, a marshal inspected each lance before the pass. Of course it remained a risky sport but that was part of its attraction to the knights and nobles who practised it.

Just as Davy had acted as my squire for my first pass, I acted as his, and sympathised when he took a direct hit from an opponent a few years older and more forcefully mounted. In view of his relative youth, it had probably been inevitable that he would encounter unequal opposition, but at least he had experienced the satisfaction of besting several more senior contestants on the first day of the competition and to give him his due he accepted his trouncing with cheerful resignation, acting as my squire eagerly and diligently through the rest of the competition.

'We are going to get you to the final, Harri!' he cried each time he handed me my lance. 'Go and murder him.'

The wonderful Bastion even tolerated Davy's boyish enthusiasm with an air of patient forbearance, and had anyone suggested it I would cheerfully have agreed that my horse deserved all the credit for my astonishing progress. At each successive pass, the horse and Davy together buoyed me up to keep believing that victory was possible and before the final pass even Comte Jean came to the preparation tent to check my attire and offer advice.

'Sir Yves is one of my best cavalry knights, Henri,' he told me. 'He is also the tallest and heaviest. If he smashes his lance into your shoulder you will know all about it – you may even be unseated – but the final is best of three passes and when you have picked yourself up you will have another opportunity. I advise you to watch exactly how he approaches. He has a barrel chest and he leans well back against the cantle but in that position he can, unless he's careful, get the hand-guard of his lance stuck on his own *écranche*, which will pull it offline. Bastion's sly toss of the head might just make that happen.'

'Was Bastion trained to do that, my lord?' I asked. 'He is an amazing ride.'

'He was well trained by me, Henri, but that trick is all his own idea. He must like you or he would not do it. You are a quiet and gentle rider and the stallion needs that. It was Duke Francis who thought the two of you would go well together.'

For the final joust, instead of going immediately into the first pass we were required to parade up to the pavilion on a flourish of trumpets and present ourselves to the noble occupants. The count had warned me of the 'Goliath' size of my opponent and, as we presented ourselves, it was glaringly obvious that his horse was also heavier and a good hand taller than mine. When the duke's herald introduced us to the spectators the watching crowd clearly supported Sir Yves, the local contender, and cheered him loudly as he raised his gauntleted fist in acknowledgement. They barely managed a faint ripple of applause when my name was called but I was almost unaware of this because Catherine approached from the back of the pavilion, looking glorious in a gleaming green gown and gauzy headdress, and held out the promised favour, a red silk kerchief. My cheeks must have matched this for colour as I leaned from Bastion to accept it. A roar then arose from the crowd which I considered to be all for her. I cantered around the tiltyard, the kerchief flying from my raised fist like a battle standard. Reining in at my station, I tucked it carefully between my pauldron and the mail shirt I wore beneath my armour, leaving one bright red corner fluttering free. I wanted everyone to see that I had the favour of a beautiful lady but I did not want it lost or damaged during the joust.

The first pass was a disaster. Sir Yves scored a direct strike on my *écranche* and while I did just manage to remain in the saddle, my shoulder felt as if a cannonball had hit it. I had no recollection of what happened to my lance but it was not in my hand when Bastion drew to a halt at the other end of the tiltyard. Davy came rushing up with a replacement.

'What happened?' I asked in a daze.

'His whole lance shattered and knocked yours from your hand. Are you all right?' Davy's face was full of concern.

'Bend down, there is a splinter caught in your helmet. God be thanked it did not enter your visor.'

I leaned out of the saddle and felt the blood rush to my head. Suddenly my memory came dizzily back. Exactly as the count had predicted, Sir Yves had adopted an exaggeratedly laid-back position in his saddle, which had caused his lance to exert exceptional force on my *écranche* and split down its whole length. Davy opened the visor of my helmet and extracted the splinter and I took the opportunity to speak into the stallion's ear.

'I need a bigger shake of your head, boy. Show him the whites of your eyes and make him jerk offline. Do it for your master, if not for me.'

Simply saying the words boosted my failing confidence. I straightened up and slammed my visor shut as Davy pushed the new lance into my hand. The starting banner was raised and dropped and the stallion began to trot towards the barrier, breaking into a canter as he drew nearer and then into full gallop. Through the slit in my helm I could see his ears twitching and between them the advancing Sir Yves, already reclining back against the cantle of his saddle. As we both lowered our lances I shouted, 'Now, Bastion!' and the horse raised his head above the line of my lance and into that of Sir Yves's eye. His lance seemed to leap sideways as mine hit his *écranche* and slid off, the tip disintegrating. To my intense relief there was no violent crunch on my left shoulder, just a satisfying thud reverberating up my right arm. The pass was mine.

I took off my gauntlet to run my hand up my horse's neck and scratch under the chamfron, a caress he loved. 'What a brilliant beast you are, Bastion!' I yelled above the noise of the crowd. 'Thank you.'

'Well done, Harri!' Davy rushed up with the fresh lance and checked my girth, dodging an irritable kick from the stallion for his pains. 'Your pardon, Bastion – well done to you too. What is your trick for the last pass?'

'We do not have one, Davy,' I shouted, turning Bastion to face the barrier again before dropping the reins to pull on my gauntlet. 'It is in God's hands.'

'No Harri,' he declared, thrusting the new lance into my grasp. 'It is in *your* hand. Go and murder him!'

So I picked up the reins and we did. Not murder him – Davy always did exaggerate – but perhaps Saint Martin, patron of horses and horsemen, favoured our efforts because when my opponent leaned back against the cantle it suddenly buckled and he very nearly fell off his horse, only righting himself by sheer will-power. Meanwhile his lance snagged on the edge of his *écranche* and before he could free it he rode straight into the tip of mine. At such an unexpected victory my immediate instinct was to pull out the red kerchief and do another circuit of the tiltyard with Catherine's favour held aloft. This time I acknowledged the cheers for myself and savoured her look of pride and delight as I cantered past the pavilion.

Duchess Marguerite presented me with the beautiful embossed-leather jousting saddle, which the count had provided as the victor's prize, but it was the duke who made the most extraordinary announcement in his closing speech.

'It is my great pleasure that this friendly joust has been won by a young and unexpected contender in Henri Tudor. What is more, having seen him riding my charger, I now have the honour and pleasure of giving the horse to him, in order that the winning partnership may continue to flourish. May God and Saint Martin favour their future together!'

'I think it would be best if you leave Bastion here at Trédion, rather than take him back to Largoët, Henri,' the count suggested over the private dinner he gave for me in order to celebrate my win. The duke and duchess were also there, as well as my opponent Sir Yves and the countess and La Petite but to my disappointment Catherine de Belleville had not been invited. I had found no opportunity to speak with her and thank her properly for the favour. 'The grooms and facilities here are more suitable for such a valuable stallion and it is not so far for you to come a few times a week to ride him.'

I was overwhelmed by the generosity of the man who was, after all, effectively my gaoler and wondered if I would have to bring my escort of guards every time I came. 'That is very kind of you, my lord. Bastion will welcome the luxury of your stables and I would certainly appreciate the use of the riding school for training, but will you not be using it yourself?'

Comte Jean shook his head. 'Not for the next few months. My wife and I are leaving soon to follow the duke and duchess to Rennes and Nantes. Perhaps you would be prepared to put my own destrier through his paces as well now and again? It pays dividends to keep them up to scratch.'

'It would be my privilege, sir,' I agreed. 'Will you be able to show me his paces before you leave?'

'Without a doubt,' he said. 'Tomorrow afternoon would be a good time, since you are staying here tonight.'

I had been allocated one of the guest chambers and provided with suitable clothes to wear, once I had shed the sweat-stained chemise and hose I had worn under my armour. Since it came from Comte Jean's garderobe, the doublet was a little long but it was made of beautiful cream damask and trimmed with minerva, a great deal more elegant than anything I had in my own apparel chest.

'You look very handsome, Henri,' Duchess Marguerite told me as we gathered before the meal. 'No wonder you have attracted the attention of the beautiful Madame de Belleville.'

Detecting a hint of affront, I hastened to reaffirm my undying admiration of the duchess, mimicking Lord Jasper and wishing he were present to share my moment of triumph. 'Ah, but no one outshines you, your grace,' I said and indeed it was close to the truth. In the year since our last meeting the young duchess had changed considerably. Gone were the girlish caps and kirtles; now she was unmistakeably the grand lady, in an elaborately figured yellow silk gown with crimson sleeves and a sophisticated hooded headdress. And with the gorgeous apparel came a new and authoritative attitude.

She took my compliment as a matter of course, immediately pursuing a topic she knew would grab my attention. 'Have you heard that Madame de Maignelais died not long after she left court? I believe it was at her home at Cholet in Anjou. Her two sons are still there.'

I was shocked. 'No Madame, I had not heard this. Was she ill or injured?'

She gave a dismissive shrug of the shoulders. 'We had no details of her death but she must have been forty or more – old enough to be my grandmother.' This claim was preposterously inaccurate and anyway hardly seemed pertinent, but in a lower voice she added, 'At least your Uncle Jasper was sensible enough to turn the harpy down.'

I could not let that pass. 'There was never any question of her going to Château Josselin with him. Even so, I am sure he would not have wished her dead,' I said.

A sly smile lit her face. 'Well, I have not seen the duke pining for her. Does he not look sleek and happy?'

'Married life suits you both then, Madame,' I ventured. Nevertheless, I thought, there is no sign yet of the much-needed heir.

When I retired after dinner and compared the stark tower room I occupied at Largoët with the sumptuous luxury of the Trédion chamber in which I was to sleep, it almost overwhelmed me. It came home to me that, were I not a penniless exiled hostage, this was the style of accommodation I might have been occupying in England. Wine and wafers had been left in polished vessels and the bed's painted tester depicted the castle and its flower-studded lake, complete with an image of La Petite as a water nymph in a floaty white dress. I poured myself a gold-rimmed cupful of the blood red wine and reclined on the heaped pillows to review the extraordinary sequence of events that had brought me there. Had I not won the joust, I would be back in the tower at Largoët with Davy.

My battered shoulder ached fiercely, reminding me how fortunate I had been even to survive the contest with the experienced and bulky Sir Yves. I was grateful to Duke Francis for the gift of Bastion and to Comte Jean for his advice and hospitality, but also I felt swamped and confused by their generosity. I would have liked to banish my discomfort of mind and body in sleep but I felt as if I were balanced on a knife-edge, neither free nor captive, man nor boy – fêted as a winner but beholden to and restrained by my two patron-gaolers. Like a falcon I yearned to fly at will, but like a goose my wings remained constantly clipped. Sleep did not come. In frustration I sat up and downed the wine in hectic gulps, hoping it might tip me quickly into Lethe.

Had it done so I might not have heard the faint creak of the door-hinge, alerting me to the fact that I had neglected to secure the bolt. My instinctive reaction was to reach for my shortsword, already discarded on the bed but when the door was pushed ajar, Catherine slid soundlessly through the gap, her finger on her lips. She was wearing a blue chamber robe and her fair hair lay loose about her shoulders. I cannot describe the surge of joy I felt at seeing her. I abandoned the sword and, now loosened by the wine, all my fears and anxieties vanished – together with my inhibitions.

I ran across the room and drew her into an impetuous embrace. 'God has sent me an angel!' I murmured, pressing my lips to her hair and inhaling the intoxicating fragrance of her body. It did not occur to me that she might resist. Just the fact that she was here told me all I needed to know. I reached out behind her and slipped the bolt home.

'I could not go to sleep before I had rewarded my hero,' she murmured, her arms winding around my neck. 'You were magnificent today, Harri. A true knight in shining armour!'

Before I could respond her lips were on mine and I felt the world dissolve into a spinning vortex centred on that kiss. I am ashamed to admit that my knees suddenly failed to support me and I think she must have helped me stumble with her towards the bed. However, the rest of my body proved more responsive than ever. The gift she undoubtedly wished me to receive I accepted with willing ardour. I had been showered with compliments and prizes that day but Catherine, as well as giving, took from me, and what she took was the greatest prize of all.

19

Margaret

Westminster Palace and Stanley House, London, October 1475

'THE QUEEN HAS ASKED me to grant you an audience.' King Edward spoke from the throne in his Great Chamber, while I knelt at the foot of the stepped dais. 'Her grace tells me in a letter from her confinement that you and she have been discussing the return of your son Henry to England.' He made an impatient gesture. 'Please rise, Lady Stanley.'

When I obeyed, I felt as if my feet stood on hot coals and I had to force myself to remain still and calm. We were much of an age, the king and I, but I was never entirely comfortable in his company, especially alone with him as I was then, apart from the chamberlain at the door, who was deaf and blind to his monarch's voice and actions.

'The queen is gracious to mention it to you, sire,' I began, keeping my eyes fixed on his, knowing that if his gaze began to shift I would have lost his attention. Edward's temperament was becoming notoriously mercurial. 'It is more than four years since Jasper Tudor took Henry to Brittany. My son is eighteen now, old enough to comprehend the importance of loyalty and honour.'

He scratched his nose thoughtfully. 'My contacts at the Duke of Brittany's court tell me that he is also well-read and a fine horseman and that he recently won a jousting competition. These are the signs of a promising nobleman. Is he also fair in looks?'

I swallowed hard; by 'contacts' I presumed he meant spies. Talking about Henry always brought a lump to my throat but it was important not to show Edward any sign of weakness. Exploiting human frailties had always been his strong suit. 'He was only thirteen when last I saw him in the flesh and a beautiful boy, in my eyes. I recently had a travelling artist draw his portrait and send it to me, sire. The portrait shows a fine youth of fair complexion and open gaze. I believe he has not yet reached his father's stature, which was over six foot, but he still has growing years ahead of him. I doubt he will reach your grace's exceptional height though.'

At this point Edward deigned to quit his throne and descend to speak more confidentially with me. 'What concerns me more, Lady Margaret, is this – if he returns to England will he kneel and swear fealty to me and remain loyal as you have done? The queen praises your service to her and speaks of your compassion and discretion. She even suggests a possible marriage between our daughter Elizabeth and your son, if he were to be granted his father's Richmond title. As you know I place great faith in my wife's perception of character and worth.'

And in creating Woodville family ties to bind your Lancastrian nobles to your Yorkist throne, I thought, face straight, bowing my head in acknowledgement. 'Such a union would greatly honour our line, my liege,' I told him.

When the queen and I had discussed the idea of such a marriage I had naturally expressed enthusiasm, especially as Princess Elizabeth was only nine years old. Who knew what might happen before any such marriage could be consummated?

Edward narrowed his eyes and gave me a piercing look of appraisal, then with a brief nod he returned to his throne to deliver his final message. 'I am sending another embassy to Brittany to restore the friendship between our realms, which was weakened by the Treaty of Picquigny. Bishop Stillington of Bath and Wells will lead it and he will also have my authority to negotiate with Duke Francis over the matter of Henry's release from his custody. I am sure the mention of a possible betrothal between your son and my daughter will persuade the duke that England means no harm to Henry, whom he is said to hold in high regard. I wish you good day, Lady Stanley.'

With that he signalled to the chamberlain at the entrance that this audience was over. The door was thrown open and I curtsied and took my leave. My mind was swithering between elation and suspicion. Had he actually offered a marriage with his daughter, or was he merely dangling it like a carrot before a donkey?

To consult my husband on this important matter, I managed to get leave of absence from Elizabeth's confinement for one day and night and rushed to Stanley House. 'How much is Edward to be trusted in this matter,

Thomas?' I asked. 'And how deeply is Bishop Stillington in Edward's pocket?'

Thomas stroked his beard thoughtfully. 'Neither question is easy to answer, Margaret. What is trust? For instance, the queen cannot trust her husband to remain faithful; however, the bishop *can* be trusted to give Edward absolution whenever he entertains his mistresses.'

I gave a snort of indifference. 'Huh! I have in fact dared to ask the queen how she can bear knowing that while she is in confinement Jane Shore is taking her place in the king's bed and she maintains that she is grateful for the relief from marital duties. However, I am certain that if Edward were to stop granting her the most valuable custodies and properties and supporting her blatant promotion of her family it would be another matter. As for the bishop, Queen Elizabeth believes Stillington knows something that Edward does not want bruited abroad – perhaps about one of his dalliances – and needs to keep him sweet.' I made a fleeting sign of the cross.

Thomas frowned fiercely. 'Perhaps, but sending the bishop to Brittany may have something to do with removing him from the Duke of Clarence's orbit – these two have been much in each other's company of late. However earnestly Clarence begged forgiveness and swore public fealty after his support of Warwick's rebellion, Edward has no reason to believe that he can trust his brother not to plot against the throne again.'

It was my turn to knit my brow. 'But none of this bothers me unless it bodes ill for Henry. Do you think it does?'

'I cannot see how. Surely even Edward is not going to expect a bishop to endanger his immortal soul by bringing harm to a promising young man, especially one with Henry's connections. No, bluntly the only way Stillington might be of some assistance to Edward is by unknowingly harbouring men in his entourage who are prepared to do the king's dirty work, should he have designs on Henry's life and there is no reason to think that he does, is there?'

I flung myself into a chair in a very unladylike manner. 'I suppose not, especially when he has also thrown up the possibility of a marriage between Henry and Princess Elizabeth.'

Thomas suddenly stared at me, frowning. 'What did you say?' he snapped.

'Both the king and queen seem amenable to the idea of Henry marrying Princess Elizabeth when he returns to England,' I repeated. 'It is an offer worth considering.'

He made a disgusted noise. 'Bah! It is an offer worth nothing! You would not know it, Margaret, because it has not been made public, but another condition of the French peace treaty is a betrothal between the Dauphin of France and Princess Elizabeth of York.'

I stared back at him, my heart thudding. 'The man is worse than devious! When it comes to Henry he is deadly.' I rubbed at my temples, angrily pulled off the wired head-dress, scattering hairpins onto the floor: so, the royal proposition of marriage was an entirely empty one!

And I could not forget Earl Rivers's urgent need to make a pilgrimage to Rome – to expiate a mortal sin? – and the coincidence I had since discovered of his presence on the very ship from which the Duke of Exeter had suddenly disappeared. A successful method of getting rid of a rival could be used more than once and Henry would be very vulnerable on a voyage from Brittany to England, alone among Edward's agents. 'I cannot even warn Henry of this. It is so frustrating that my letters have to go via the duke's court.'

It was then that Thomas came up with an excellent idea. 'How about getting Meg Woodville's young squire into the Bishop's entourage? He went on Earl Rivers's embassy to Brittany so his presence would not arouse suspicion. At the very least he could keep us informed of the progress of the talks.'

I ceased distractedly pulling my hair free and threw out my hands to grasp at this straw. 'Yes Thomas! That is the answer. Can you put that into effect?'

He gave me a smug look. 'I do not see why not. I am sure Poyntz will appreciate the nomination and Stillington will be grateful for a useful legal junior now that he is no longer Lord Chancellor.'

I smiled my thanks. 'And if Master Robert is in Brittany I will not have to worry about preserving Meg's honour while her father is away. We can kill two birds with one stone.'

'Let us hope there is no question of any killing, Margaret,' said my husband, coming up behind me. 'That is what we are trying to prevent.' I felt his fingers plunge into my loosened hair and closed my eyes as he began to gently massage my scalp. Sometimes Thomas knew exactly how to calm me down.

I had retired to my bedchamber to put on a fresh coif and veil when a knock at the door brought Meg, who informed me that Lady Vaux was waiting in the great hall. My friend's daughter Joan was still living with me but her son Nicholas was now sharing George Stanley's education in estate management at Lathom. Kate had not visited for some months because she remained a faithful companion to the captive former queen, Marguerite of Anjou, who had been transferred to the custody of her former lady-in-waiting Alice Chaucer, Dowager Duchess of Suffolk, and moved from the Tower to the relative comfort of Wallingford Castle, a secure stronghold further up the River Thames, towards Oxford.

By the hall fire we exchanged fond embraces and I ushered Kate straight up to my solar to find Joan. I left mother and daughter together while I went to the chapel to hear Mass and seek the solace of prayer against all the anxieties over Henry that beset me. On my return I ordered a light repast to be served to us in my solar and sent Joan off with the other nestlings to take their dinner with the rest of the household. When the meal arrived I had it laid out and immediately dismissed the servants.

'You are pale, Kate, and Joan looked upset. What has happened?' I asked, pouring wine and thinking that she looked older than she should. 'Nicholas is not ill or injured?'

'No, no, I receive nothing but good reports from Nicholas. He seems to love it at Lathom. In due course he will be able to administer the Vaux manors, thanks to you.' Kate ignored the wine and played absently with a hunk of bread. Usually neat, she was dishevelled, her hair escaping from her chaperon hat and her gown splattered with mud. 'If I am pale it is because I have ridden hard from Wallingford, that is all. I am so glad to find you here, Margaret. I need your advice.'

'It is pure chance that I am here because I have been immured in the queen's confinement chamber for the past three weeks and I am ordered back there tomorrow. She will give birth any day now. What is it you need advice about?'

'Queen Marguerite.' Even though we were alone she let her voice drop when she said the name. There was only one queen in England and her name was not Marguerite. 'Are you aware that part of the treaty of Picquigny concerned a ransom for her? At last!'

I was astonished. There had been so much more in that dubious treaty than had initially been clear. 'No, I was not aware of that. What is the ransom?'

'King Louis paid King Edward fifty thousand crowns for her release. It does not seem much for an anointed queen does it?'

'No, but I should think King Louis considered it more than enough and King Edward will be glad to have it. When is she to be released?'

A shadow passed over Kate's face. 'In the New Year and that is my problem. She has begged me to go with her back to France. She says she cannot do without me.'

'Oh Kate, you have made yourself indispensable.' I put my hand over hers. 'And you do not want to go, is that it?'

Her face was anguished. 'I do not want to leave my children. I have hardly seen them since the queen became a prisoner and now she wants me to leave them altogether and go back to Anjou. It might as well be forever and it will not be a comfortable life, for she has no money and nor does her father. Having paid her ransom King Louis will grant her no more than a pittance. But Margaret, we grew up together. I have been in her service since before she was betrothed to King Henry. No one knows her like I do and no one else will go with her to France. How can I let her go alone?'

I did not reply immediately. I understood as much as anyone the anguish she felt, to live apart from her children. 'I know you well, Kate, and in all truth I do not think you will be able to refuse her. At least you can be certain that I will protect them and their interests in your absence. We can never know what the Almighty has in store for us, but tell me, if you had to make a guess, of you and Marguerite, who do you think might outlive the other?'

She looked horrified. 'Oh no Margaret! I cannot possibly answer that. Marguerite has had such a troubled life, which has taken a terrible toll on her health. Losing Prince Edward nearly killed her. Yet she still has a strong will and an even stronger faith.'

I nodded. Her loyal response was no less than I had expected. However, although Kate was much the same age as Marguerite, she was a robust woman who had also weathered many storms in life. Had I been asked the same question I would have predicted that she would make much older bones than her once-royal mistress. Certainly she deserved to see her children married and settled. 'I can understand now why Joan looked so upset when I returned from Mass but she is like you and will conquer any trials that confront her. I pray that God will protect and reward you for the sacrifice you have been asked to make, Kate. Because you will make it, of that I am sure.'

This was greeted with a rueful smile. 'I think I knew that is what you would say, but I had to hear it from your lips.'

I leaned in and kissed her cheek. 'We could be sisters, you and I. Remember that as long as I live there will always be somewhere you can call home.'

20

Harri

Château Trédion, Brittany, autumn 1475 – summer 1476

DAVY AND I HAD come to be considered more or less part of the Rieux household, free to ride between Largoët and Trédion alone. But it was not loyalty to the count or the privilege of training and riding Bastion that kept me from making a break for freedom – it was Catherine de Belleville. As long as the warm weather persisted, our assignations after dark in the lakeside summerhouse fuelled the passion that had been ignited on the night after the joust. When winter came our trysts were less frequent, not from lack of desire but due to Catherine's fear of discovery.

'I do not want to lose my position, Henri,' she told me on our last night beside the lake. 'It would be such a shame. Roland loves it here, the countess has been so kind and La Petite is fond of me I think.'

I stroked the softness of her thigh and noticed the goosing of her skin. 'She is not the only one who loves you, Catherine,' I murmured, then, 'but it is too cold for you out here now.

What about the library? We could say we are studying Aristotle or something.'

I loved hearing her throaty laugh. 'No one would believe that I was studying Ari— whoever you said! I do not have the benefit of a man's education.'

I felt rather foolish for making the suggestion. 'Well, how about *The Romance of the Rose*? Plenty of women read that I believe. And men have been known to study it at universities. It does not matter what we say we are reading because we will not read it anyway. I can think of far, far better things to do in the privacy of a library than read books.'

To illustrate my point, I caressed her stomach and under her shift, my hand moved up to her breast. 'Very well,' she said, arching her back. 'I will contrive to seek permission to use the library. But strictly for studying purposes you under- stand.' I received a sideways glance and the smile that accompanied it was gloriously enigmatic.

At Trédion we were successful at keeping our romance a secret because La Petite and Roland were easily deceived - but Davy was another matter. 'You do not fool me in the least, Harri,' he informed me one frosty February morning while we were taking the two chargers for careful exercise over the frozen ground. 'I know you and Madame de Belleville are not studying books when you stay overnight and, so you say, sleep in Bastion's stable. For a start the head groom would never permit it.'

'Why, have you spoken to him?' I felt a frisson of alarm at the thought of him making not very subtle enquiries around the stables.

'No, of course I have not!' Davy was indignant. 'At least

not about that. On the other hand I hope you realise that this mad affair of yours can only bring trouble.'

I sighed with relief. 'You wait, Davy,' I said. 'It is not a mad affair. You have no idea how enthralling and glorious love can be. It fills your mind and sets your heart racing.'

'Oh really?' he retorted. 'You are right that I have no idea, Harri – but I have a notion that as well as mind and heart, another organ altogether is involved. I cannot say I blame you. La Belleville is a walking temptation, but she does have a shadowy past, otherwise how come there is a Roland?'

I had still not had the courage to quiz my lover further on that topic but I was enraged by his derogatory attitude towards Catherine and I retaliated. 'I wonder how many people ask, "How come there is a Davy?" At least Roland knows who his mother is.'

Seeing him go bright red, I instantly wished I had not said it but the words were out and could not be retracted. It was not that other people had never said anything similar. It was because this time the sneer was from my tongue, normally his champion. Although he was known to be Owen Tudor's son, only Mistress Jane and Lord Jasper knew the identity of Davy's mother and they had told no one.

'Sometimes, Harri, you are a bastard, even if your parents were married!' he cried and set off at a canter, recklessly risking Alouette's legs on the frosty ground.

I let him go, not daring to bring harm to Bastion and musing darkly on what he had said. It was true that Catherine and I sometimes used the excuse of studying in the Trédion library during the early nightfall of winter, when the children had gone to bed and Davy had ridden back to Largoët. The book we actually chose to abandon in favour of more amorous pastimes was the countess's copy of *The Treasure of the City of Ladies* by Christine de Pisan and when I did read it later in life I learned that it advised its readers to pursue chastity, virtue and restraint. However, there had been little that was chaste, virtuous or restrained about our activities shut in among the books while the candles burned low and the fire died to embers. After our lovemaking on the evening following Davy's angry reaction to my stupid remark about Roland at least knowing his mother, I cradled Catherine in my arms, summoned my courage and asked her again about her boy's father.

I felt her body tense but she did not move away. 'You already know that to all intents and purposes he does not have one,' she said and the bitter note in her voice upset me.

'You mean that you do not trust me to know?' We were both lying motionless now, close physically but suddenly emotionally far apart. I turned on my elbow to look at her but she would not meet my eyes and I saw a tear run down her cheek. 'What is it Catherine? Is the truth so hard to bear?'

She shuddered and the tears flowed more freely. 'Yes Harri, it is a burden I will carry all my life and it weighs more heavily every time I look at poor little Roland.'

'Perhaps it will help, sharing it,' I said gently. The heat of the fire was waning but I did not think that was why she shivered. 'Were you raped Catherine?' It seemed the only explanation.

The silence grew profound between us then, fraught with tension. I could sense it building in her, through flesh and bone. She was so slim and with my arms around her I could feel her blood pulsing and her heart pumping. To lessen her distress I wanted to draw the story out of her with a kiss but her usually soft mouth was clenched into a tight line, the lips almost invisible as she fought her demons. When she finally spoke it was a riddle: 'Before we lay together, Harri, you were a boy – a virgin. Now you are a man, yet I think no one would call it rape.'

'I do not understand. What we have shared together has never been rape. It has been joy and pleasure and delight.'

'Oh, I am not comparing our experience with what happened with *him*!' She stressed the word with some venom before continuing. 'But I did not ask you, not in so many words. I wanted to make love with you and I assumed you would want it and that is how it was with Roland's father, only the other way round. Because he wanted it, he just assumed that I did too and I was too young, too innocent and too scared, to tell him I did not.'

'Who was he, Catherine, this rapist, this violator, this devil?' I did not want to frighten her by raising my voice but the pressure to shout my indignation was almost impossible to contain.

'My stepfather.' The words were spoken so quietly that I almost did not hear them. Then she turned at last and the dam of her emotion burst. 'My mother's husband – the man I had been calling Papa, whose name I took because my mother thought he would protect and care for me. When I was fifteen, I would wake in my bed to find him on top of me, he would smile and whisper into my ear, all kinds of words that I did not understand, he smelled of wine, he asked me if I liked it and I said nothing. I wanted to shout for help but I did not dare and I was too ashamed to tell anyone. The fact that there is Roland speaks for itself.' She buried her head in my shoulder.

For several minutes we lay without speech. I held her close and remained quiet while my mind raced, I wanted to know what had happened when it became obvious she was pregnant, had her mother believed her story, had her stepfather faced justice of any kind? And yet a cowardly part of me did *not* want to know any of this, did not want anything to spoil the thrill of being in love, wanted rather to brush all Catherine's sad past away and continue as we had been doing, living in the ecstasy of the moment, careless of the consequences.

She looked up then, as if my irresponsible self had communicated its secret wish, and she brushed her tears away with her hand. 'There. Now that you know the terrible truth, Harri, let us forget it. It is in the past. We should not waste our precious time together contemplating sad things, here we are, alive and in love . . .' She rose nimbly to her feet and reached for her kirtle, pulling it over her head with a luminous smile.

Her bright blue eyes glistened with sudden mischief. 'Please lace me up like the gentleman you are – who unlaced me in the first place. And then, if my lover pleases, we can sneak up to my chamber, you have not been there before.'

Catherine and I were able to continue our sweet and reckless affair into the summer. Then the count and countess arrived once more for their break from court life. The castle filled with people, making it difficult to arrange our secret meetings. Also I was included in the fraternity of Comte Jean's retinue of knights and squires, who hunted, dined and caroused together; he commanded my company.

'Come now, Henri,' he cried, when I hung back from too much drinking. 'What age are you, nineteen? Twenty? It is time to live, work and play like a man! Besides, the duke is soon to start talks with King Edward's embassy and if they are successful we will be losing your company. You will return to England to enter your earldom. Ah – you may not know all this.' Seeing my astonishment at this pronouncement, he signalled a servant to refill my cup and put a brotherly arm around my shoulder. 'The embassy arrived a month ago but the duke has not been well and so negotiations are only just getting underway.'

'God's mercy, my lord! Who is leading the embassy?' I stared at him open mouthed, in a state of shock at the momentous information he had thrown at me like a carelessly tossed ball.

Comte Jean grimaced. 'A dithery old bishop called Stillington and what with the duke's illness and the bishop's indecisiveness I should think it may be months before anything is settled. So at least we should have the summer to hunt and enjoy ourselves.'

I turned away, careless of appearing rude. It irked me that he appeared to think this embassy only a slight matter. I had been a captive for five years, frustrated by the restraints placed on me and frequently in fear of my life and all he thought I would care about was going hunting.

I was grateful not to be invited to occupy one of the luxurious Trédion guest chambers again, as it meant I could return to Largoët and discuss the news of the embassy with Davy.

He was in a grumpy mood. 'I know you have to attend the count's revels, Harri, while I train with the Largoët louts,' he complained. 'Is there any chance I might be invited to the hunt tomorrow?'

'Just come with me Davy and I will make sure you are,' I told him. 'But listen, I have news. The count tells me an embassy has come from King Edward's court to negotiate my return to England.'

'I thought we did not call him king,' Davy reminded me. 'Although who else might be considered England's sovereign I do not know.'

'There are several contenders, of whom, thanks to my mother, I am one,' I said without enthusiasm. 'Which is a good reason why, much as I might wish to claim my title and estates, I should not trust any approach from the man who presently calls himself king. Or should I? What do you think?'

Davy rolled his eyes. 'You are asking me for advice? The motherless bastard from nowhere!'

I slammed one fist into the other and sighed. 'No Davy, I am asking the only person I *can* trust in present circumstances. I am genuinely sorry I called you motherless. I could have bitten my tongue off after I said it. Please will you call off the dogs?'

He pursed his lips, considering, then gave me one of his cheeky grins, put his fingers to his lips and let forth a piercing whistle. 'There, the hounds are in the kennel.' Then his expression darkened. 'Now – do I believe you should trust the man who ordered my father's execution? What do you think!' It was not a question.

I scowled, blinking at the way his cheerful whistle became a bitter snarl. 'When you put it that way I recall other deaths that may be laid at Edward's door, my royal uncle King

Henry being chief among them. You are right, I should not trust him and what is more, if my mother were here I believe she would give me the same advice.'

Only a week later a lone rider came to Largoët at dusk, asking for me. At first I did not recognise the visitor waiting in the guardroom, but his name when he gave it sent my memory in a flash to Raglan Castle in Wales, where he and I had shared a schoolroom. Robert Poyntz; we were both wards of the wealthy Yorkist William Herbert, who had been Lord Jasper's arch enemy and benefitted from his attainted estates. I was six years Robert's junior and regarded him with awe; he wielded a full-size sword and could pierce the ring with his lance. I knew he was subsequently enrolled at the Inns of Court and appointed a royal squire, now it seemed he was a qualified lawyer and a member of the English embassy negotiating my future.

'Is there somewhere we can talk privately?' he asked, once we had reacquainted ourselves. The guardroom was full of soldiers coming on and going off duty, laughing and joking, slamming weapons into racks and discarding protective clothing. It was not a place for a confidential conversation. Yet I was not certain the captain, discreetly hovering nearby, would agree to me having a private meeting with a visiting Englishman.

'You must be hungry after your journey, Robert,' I replied. 'Why do we not go to the great hall where supper will be served soon?' I dropped my voice to add, 'We can find a quiet corner there for a few minutes before the meal.'

This seemed to satisfy both Robert and the captain and we made our way from the gatehouse across the busy bailey towards the torchlit hall. As we walked Robert reached furtively into the front of his jacket and pulled out a folded parchment. 'I will give you this now Henry, while no one is looking,' he murmured. 'It is an uncensored letter from your mother. Tuck it away and read it later when you are alone.'

With a leap of the heart, I slipped the letter into the purse on my belt while he continued in a voice that would carry to listening ears. 'I have been to Brittany once before. I was with Earl Rivers's embassy a few years ago and visited Nantes and Vannes but never ventured into the countryside between.'

In the great hall servants were setting out the trestles but we tucked ourselves into a window embrasure, where we hoped to keep our murmured conversation private.

'The count told me that Duke Francis has been ill, which has delayed your negotiations,' I prompted him.

'Indeed it has,' Robert confirmed. 'And now the duke has handed responsibility over to his Treasurer, Pierre Landais, a forceful negotiator, who likes to move things on, swiftly, while haste is not in our venerable leader's vocabulary. Bishop Stillington is an odd choice for an ambassador. I heard it suggested that the king wanted to get him away from the Duke of Clarence. It is hard to believe that the bumbling old prelate has been plotting with the king's brother, but Edward sees traitors behind every tapestry.'

'As one of his body squires, Robert, would you not know if he was right to do so?'

The squire eyed me sideways and took a swift glance around. 'I pick up his soiled linen and carry his *billets-doux* to his doxys, Henry. How would I know anything about plots and schemes?'

'The Comte de Rieux implied that King Edward wants me back in England—' But he laid a hand on my sleeve and cut in.

'First let me tell you something, Henry. Four years ago during Earl Rivers's embassy it was I who got word to your mother of Edward's instruction to bring you and Lord Jasper home "dead or alive". And judging by the considerable purse of gold he has sent to Duke Francis this time, I have no reason to believe that he thinks of you any differently now.' Bizarrely he smiled broadly as he said this, I presumed in an effort to convince any interested observer that we were having an amusing conversation about old times.

Reciprocating in kind, I clapped him on the shoulder and laughed aloud while I digested his dire warning. 'Ha! You do not surprise me. But although I have no plans to trust his apparent good intent, the real question is, will the bumbling bishop manage to change the duke's mind? Up to now Duke Francis has always assured my uncle and me that he will protect us. He keeps us apart to make abduction or assassination doubly difficult. But if he changes his mind . . .' I was tempted to draw my finger across my throat but decided the action could be misinterpreted and scratched under my chin instead. 'Would you be able to get word to me, Robert, if you discover that he has done so?'

The squire opened his mouth to reply but at this point the Master of the Household banged his staff of office on the high table and invited all comers to the board and we were obliged to bring our semi-private conversation to a halt in order to find a place. During the meal we talked like old friends should and by the end of it I felt as if we were, even after I discovered that Robert Poyntz was betrothed to one of my mother's wards whose name, worryingly, was Meg Woodville. By allying himself to the queen's family but also playing courier for my mother he was cleverly hedging his bets and although I found this rather ignoble, I admired the courage it took.

However, while we were seated among strangers he stuck rigidly to his public persona of loyal squire to the king. 'When Edward first took the crown, we were all torn in our loyalties,' he declared for all to hear, 'but now that we have a strong king with two sons as his heirs, it is time to settle our differences and make the most of a peaceful and well-ruled England. So when you do get back and claim your birthright Henry, let your mother be your example of successful pragmatism in the face of necessity.'

While nodding acceptance of his advice, I wondered if the Inns of Court had only taught Robert Poyntz the intricacies of justice, or whether his tutors might have covered subterfuge and diplomacy as well. When I finally got back to my chamber and broke the seal on my mother's letter I quickly discovered exactly what he meant about her pragmatism.

To my well-beloved son Henry, rightful Earl of Richmond, greetings,

At last I have found a courier I can trust to bring you a letter for your eyes only. However, Robert Poyntz does not know that before the Stillington embassy was given its briefing, King Edward called me privately to an audience, not only to offer you a pardon but also the possibility of a marriage with his daughter, Elizabeth of

York, which of course I had no choice but to greet with enthusiasm. However, although you may find the idea of betrothal to a ten-year-old princess who promises to be a beautiful and intelligent young woman attractive, I warn you that it would be a grave mistake to believe her father's intentions trustworthy or honourable. I have discovered that Princess Elizabeth was secretly contracted to marry the French Dauphin as part of last year's peace treaty with France and so it is entirely certain that the marriage offer to you is a ploy to persuade the Duke of Brittany to sanction your return to England. Should it succeed I urge you to resist such a move with all possible strength and guile.

It is highly significant that the Duke of Exeter, like you a Lancastrian claimant to the throne, failed to complete his return journey across the Channel after Edward's French expedition. His drowned corpse was recently found on a beach near Dover. Also you should note that the Stillington negotiations do not include your uncle. That is because Lord Jasper does not have a claim to the throne and it is clearly the few remaining Lancastrian claimants that Edward aims to eradicate. It may appear that he intends to do this by bringing you into the York family through marriage but as he cannot trust his own blood brother George of Clarence, I doubt that even marriage to his daughter would remove you from suspicion. The more Edward offers the hand of friendship and even a family alliance, the more he is not to be trusted, especially when a channel crossing is involved.

These warnings come with the endorsement of the

*king's own steward, your stepfather Lord Stanley and
the everlasting love of your mother,*
  Margaret, Countess of Richmond.

*Written at Stanley House, this twentieth day of July,
1476.*

*P S: Edward's wife was delivered of another girl last
November, baptised Anne. Indicative of his great desire
for yet another son to further protect his dynasty,
Elizabeth is already with child once more – their eighth.
It is hard not to envy their fertility and requires much
prayer on my part for acceptance of God's will. But I
have you, my only beloved son and greatest hope for the
future.*

In capital letters at the bottom of the parchment, were
inscribed the word:

STAY ALIVE AND BURN THIS LETTER.

21

Harri

Château Trédion, late summer 1476

THE COUNT AND COUNTESS left Château Trédion at the
end of August, while I still waited nervously for news
of the English embassy's negotiations with Pierre Landais.
As this waiting was torture, I hoped that the departure of
the Rieux household and their guests might mean that
Catherine and I could resume our secret trysts. I longed
for her loving to take my mind off my restricted present
and uncertain future and to my delight very soon I found
a note from her hidden in Bastion's feed bucket, telling me
she would be waiting in the summer house at the far end
of the lake.

The sun had set and a thin sliver of a new moon was
rising, its reflection caught in the still surface of the water
between the lily flowers, closed now into tight buds with
the dying of the light. I went to her, my heart pounding
with expectation and desire, fell to my knees and clasped
her to me, but to my chagrin felt no familiar response.

'Something is wrong,' I said anxiously, slipping round onto the stone bench beside her. Although she was wrapped in a shawl against the evening chill, she was shivering. 'What is it Catherine?'

'I suppose you could call it the inevitable, Henri,' she responded. 'I am pregnant.'

'Oh.' In my blissful infatuation I had only fleetingly considered this possibility but now it hit me like a hammer and I was instantly reduced to the callow, unprepared youth that I truly was – dumbstruck, confounded, unable to find the right words. 'Are you sure?'

She gave a derisive snort. 'Of course I am sure. I have known for months but I never thought you would greet the news with such enthusiasm,' she said, displaying a cynicism I had never heard from her before.

I hung my head and watched my hands writhing in my lap, fingers clenching and unclenching. 'I do not know what to say, Catherine. Part of me thrills at the idea of becoming a father, especially to a child of yours, yet regretfully I am in no position to be one.'

'You think I do not know that – that I have not known it throughout the time we have been lovers? Do not fret, Henri, I am not expecting you to marry me.' She turned to me then. 'After all it was I who seduced you, not the other way around.' Pulling one of my hands free she placed it on her stomach. 'There, perhaps you can feel the baby kick.'

I felt the change in her body, the swell of her belly since the last time we had lain together, but I shrank from the thought of feeling the physical presence of the child and to my relief there was no discernible movement. 'No one was seduced,' I said, removing my hand and watching her eyes crinkle in a smile. 'I was unable to resist you. Anyone would be.'

'But I knew what I was doing,' she murmured, leaning forward to kiss me gently on the lips. 'And you did not.'

Her words brought home the invidious position in which I found myself – a captive exile without free will and menaced by a long, drawn-out negotiation, which might possibly decide whether I lived or died. Mad thoughts of escape crossed my mind. I could take Catherine up on Bastion and make a romantic dash for the border but neither of us knew the way and where would we go if we crossed it?

'I can read your mind, Henri,' Catherine said, shaking her head. 'And you are not thinking straight. I will not go anywhere without Roland and we would soon be caught. They will not let you escape and besides you have an earldom to claim. You are in a state of confusion but I have had time to plan.'

'Plan what, Catherine?' My words emerged on a croak and I hastily cleared my throat.

'I will tell the countess that I wish to go home and that she will be obliged to find another governess for La Petite. She may guess the reason but I doubt if she will ask. She knows the story behind Roland's birth and it was generous of her to take us both in when my situation became impossible at home. I hope she will send a coach for Roland and me.'

I was alarmed. 'If your place at home was impossible then, how will it be different now?'

'I have heard from my mother. My stepfather has taken a court post. He will be at the French king's command. The family will travel wherever he is sent.'

'But you cannot be alone!' I cried. 'Who will look after you?'

'My old nurse; she has seen my mother through four births and me through one. Another will not trouble her.' She turned to look at me then. 'I do not want to leave you, Henri, but I am sure you see that it will be best this way. Besides you will probably be leaving soon yourself. We were never destined to be together forever.'

I had no argument to offer. 'When will you have to go? I mean how long before . . .' I faltered on the words.

'Before the child is born? I am not certain – three months, possibly four. I will write to the countess and say I shall not leave until a replacement governess is arranged for La Petite. I have some old-fashioned houpelande gowns that will hide my belly for a while yet.'

On a sudden urge I dropped to my knees before her again and took both her hands in mine. 'I feel enormous guilt that you should have to go through this alone, Catherine.'

She stroked my face. 'Poor Henri, it is a surprise to you, but I am already used to the idea. But there is something I have not told you. Please, sit down again and listen. I think you will be interested.'

Reluctantly I returned dejectedly to the bench. My mind felt numb but as I heard what she had to say it began to whirl.

'My stepfather – Roland's father – is the son of Jean Harpedanne de Belleville, a former Master of the French Royal Household, who married Marguerite de Valois. Her mother was Odette de Champdivers, who was the long-term mistress of King Charles the Sixth of France, known as Charles the Mad because he had periods of mania, which only Odette could handle. I believe therefore, Henri, that you and Roland are second cousins. Was the sixth King Charles not also your father's grandfather? Legitimately, I mean – your grandmother Queen Catherine's brother?'

I counted back the generations in my head. 'Yes, I believe so. My father and my uncle Jasper and I seem to be related to half the royal families of Europe. But Catherine, tell me exactly where you will be living; we must write to each other and surely one day I will be free to visit you and to meet our son or daughter.' It seemed bizarre to be talking with such anxious sincerity to the woman who for the past year had made my senses sing and my heart race. I wanted to kiss all the problems away but I could see from her business-like expression that her priorities had changed. I was in a state of shock but she had already moved on.

That night Bastion went lame and the horse-master sent a message to say that he needed stable rest, so I had no cause to go to Trédion and therefore no opportunity to meet Catherine. I fretted for a week before receiving word that the stallion's injured leg had recovered and after I had given him some light exercise in the riding school I went straight to the Trédion mansion to ask for La Petite and Madame de Belleville but the little girl came down the grand stair alone to meet me.

'Madame asks you to forgive her, Henri,' La Petite said solemnly. 'She is not feeling well but gave me this for you.' She handed over a small, sealed square of parchment. Catherine's note was brief and, to my torn feelings, agonisingly formal:

To Monsieur Henri,

Alas, I am not fit to meet you and doubt I will be before I leave for Château de Belleville. If you would like Roland to come and say goodbye, please send La Petite to fetch him. He will miss you and the games you played with him so do not be surprised if he weeps. He will be six next month so tell him that big boys do not cry.

I hope you will not.

Catherine de Belleville.

When I looked up at La Petite I noticed that her eyes were red-rimmed, as if she had been crying.

'What ails her?' I asked, fearing some serious mishap either to Catherine or the child she carried. 'You look as if you have been crying.'

The girl's bottom lip began to tremble and I feared the tears might flow again but she sniffed hard and gained control. 'Madame is leaving me. A carriage is coming for her tomorrow and she and Roland will return to their home in Anjou. I do not know why. I believe it is my fault.'

'I am sure it is not your fault. Perhaps she is homesick for her mother. Who will look after you now?'

'I do not know. Madame says another lady is coming. I do not want another governess. I like Madame de Belleville.'

'And so do I. We are both very sad she is leaving. Please will you bring Roland down to see me, as she suggests?'

As she had predicted, Roland cried when I said goodbye and I squatted down to hug him.

'I want you to remember my name, Roland,' I told him, thumbing the tears from his cheeks. 'Can you remember Henri Tudor? Look, I will write it for you on this piece of paper and you can keep it in your purse.' I wrote my name clearly in capital letters in a corner of Catherine's letter, tore it carefully and folded it, before placing it in the little pouch he wore on his belt, which already held his treasures, including I noticed a splinter from a broken lance-tip.

'That is from your lance, Henri,' he said proudly, overcoming a crack in his voice. 'I asked Davy to save it for me, when you won the joust.'

Coughing to clear the lump in my throat, I said, 'You will learn to joust one day, and then you will be able to protect your Maman. I am very sad to say goodbye to you and to her, but remember to tell her I did not cry and nor did you, because we are big boys.'

Two days later I woke to hear Davy exclaiming loudly from the window of our tower room. 'Jesu Harri – an army has arrived! The place is crawling with men at arms.'

22

Margaret

Eltham Palace, London, October 1476

THE ROYAL HOUSEHOLD HAD come to Eltham Palace for the autumn hunting and I was delighted that in spite of being four months pregnant Queen Elizabeth insisted on joining in the hawking parties.

'I will partake in some gentle sport,' she told the king on the afternoon of our arrival, as we gathered in an ante-chamber before dinner, which was to be in the new Great Hall. 'I will not indulge in any wild chases, rather my ladies and I will amble quietly beside the woods and fly our merlins and goshawks. If this is yet another son, it will give him a taste for the hunt while still in the womb. You and your young squires can gallop after stags. We shall quietly observe birds of prey hunting, and come back rosy-cheeked, with healthy appetites for feasting and dancing after dark.'

'Take Bessie with you, then,' Edward ordered. 'She needs to practise her hawking skills if she is to go to France next year.'

I saw the queen blench and bite her lip. He had touched on two sore points: calling Princess Elizabeth 'Bessie' was one and the other was referring to the promise he had made that she would be sent to France when she was twelve. Although Queen Elizabeth was secretly pleased to think that her eldest daughter might become Queen of France, she had not been consulted before King Edward had agreed to the betrothal as part of the peace treaty he had signed the previous year. She did *not* consider it necessary for the princess to spend years away from her family in France, while she waited for the Dauphin Prince Charles to be old enough to marry. However she let that bone of contention lie and complained instead about her husband's pet name for his eldest child.

'I do wish you would not call Elizabeth Bessie, my lord,' she said irritably. 'It sounds so common – like a milkmaid or an alewife.'

Edward laughed out loud. 'Ha ha! Bessie could never be mistaken for either, Elizabeth! I call her that because you are my Elizabeth. It is confusing otherwise. Would you rather I called her Beth or Lizzie?'

The queen shuddered. 'No my lord, I would not.'

The princess's sweet voice spoke up from behind her mother's chair. 'I do not mind being called Bessie,' she said mildly, 'as long as it is only by the family. I would not wish to be addressed in court as Princess Bessie.'

'No one would dare to call you that!' the queen cried, aghast.

'They would not,' agreed the king. He smiled fondly at his beautiful daughter, standing neat and trim in her red damask kirtle and cream silk veil, held in place by a silver circlet set with garnets. 'Anyway, as soon as King Louis starts sending your maintenance, you will be addressed as the Dauphine, Bessie – except by me of course.' He clapped his hands to his stomach and groaned. 'Holy Michael, I am hungry! Whatever are we waiting for?'

The timing of meals was the responsibility of Lord Stanley who was organising this one in his capacity as Steward of the Household but he had confided to me that he expected the first court meal in the vast new Great Hall at Eltham to suffer the odd hitch, just as any new venture might suffer teething problems. King Edward, however, liked things to function seamlessly and entirely at his convenience and he paced off to harangue the Lord Chamberlain. 'I am famished, Will,' he thundered, striding across the room to where his great friend, Lord Hastings, was laughing with some of the Knights of the Body. 'Why in the name of Jude are we waiting so long for our dinner? Where is the steward?'

The queen rolled her eyes at me. 'My lord hates waiting for anything, especially his dinner. But do you know, Lady Margaret, I think he might have to wait years for any sign of that maintenance payment from the Spider King. But this may not matter; we should see your Henry back with us soon. Long before my little Elizabeth can be called Dauphine.' She beckoned me nearer and turned to draw her daughter forward and murmur in her ear, 'Would you not rather marry Lady Margaret's clever son and be Countess of Richmond, Elizabeth? Henry Tudor is a handsome young man of good education, you would not have to suffer a dim-witted boy for a husband and you would not have to go to France, far away from your friends and family.'

The princess's brow knitted and she paused for thought

before replying, 'I will marry according to the king's wishes, my lady.' This she said dutifully but then, with a look in her eye that reminded me vividly of her father, she added, 'But should not the daughter of a king aim to be a queen, rather than merely a countess?'

I caught her glance with a nod and a little smile. 'Your ambition is admirable, princess,' I said. 'I always encourage it in my wards – both the girls and the boys.'

At that moment we were finally called to take our places for dinner and processed into the Great Hall, already crowded with domestic servants and lower-order members of the Household. It was the first time I had seen the new roof carpentry, which had been shrouded in scaffolding on my last visit. Now it was revealed in all its elaborate hammer-beam glory, looking very like its larger cousin in the Great Hall at Westminster. King Edward walked first through the privy door onto the dais and almost fell over Scogan, the court fool, who was lying on the floor waving his legs and hands in the air and making a tapping noise with his teeth. The king aimed a light kick and caught the jester in the ribs, silencing the tapping and making him scramble hastily to his feet.

'Riddle me, Scogan, do not scuttle me!' roared the king. 'What were you lying low for?'

'Riddle me this, lord king,' said the fool, waving his bells. He was a skinny longshanks of a man with a straggly beard and shaggy grey locks protruding from under his red and yellow jester's cap. I always did my best to avoid him because I abhorred his smutty jokes and silly riddles. 'What sits on a barrel, runs with ale and augurs death? The answer will tell you what I am when I lie under your feet.'

'Out of my way fool!' King Edward pushed him aside and strode to his seat at the high table. 'Do not let a riddle keep a man from his dinner.'

'I know the answer,' I heard Princess Elizabeth whisper to the queen. 'He is a death-watch beetle fallen from the new roof. The riddle is a joke and a warning, for a barrel has a tap, which runs with ale and the death-watch beetle taps on wood when a death is coming.'

'And the riddle is nonsense,' said her mother, crossing herself. 'Scogan is not called a fool for nothing.'

The jester made a rude gesture behind the queen's back and settled himself at the rear of the king's carved chair, leaning on the legs and jangling his riddle-stick. On his way to his seat, Lord Hastings made a passing comment, which had the king snorting with laughter. 'Make sure it is your *bells* you are playing with down there behind the king's chair, fool!'

As dishes were paraded to the high table, a liveried courier approached the dais with a letter. With a flick of his wrist, Edward signalled a hovering page to fetch it and quickly broke the seal. 'It is from my brother Clarence,' he told the queen and passed it to her. 'You read it, my lady, and tell me what it says. Scrawl like that makes my head ache.'

Elizabeth frowned over the florid script for several moments before raising her head. 'The Duchess of Clarence has been delivered of another son,' she announced. 'He has been baptised Richard.'

Edward speared a small bird with his knife. 'George will be pleased,' he said with a nod. 'And he diplomatically names him after our younger brother, hoping to heal the rift between them over the Warwick inheritance. Well, we might have peace in the family now that the House of York has two young Edwards and two young Richards. If our next child is a boy, Elizabeth, we had better name him after George, otherwise he will fall into another of his sulks and no good can come of that.'

23

Harri

Château de l'Hérmine, Vannes, Brittany, autumn 1476

Davy's 'army' at Largoët had turned out to be an over-sized escort to take us to Vannes. Once there we were escorted to Pierre Landais' office, which was in the old fortified donjon of the Château de l'Hérmine, where the Treasury was housed. Alarmingly this was also the building where prisoners were locked up while awaiting trial. My one shred of comfort was that our swords were not taken from us, but this was hardly relevant since we were surrounded by a dozen armed and armoured men.

Treasurer Landais made an affable greeting and dismissed his clerks with a peremptory wave of the hand, but after they left he frowned at Davy. 'You kept an English servant with you, Monsieur Tudor,' he said in his deceptively silky voice. 'Were they not all sent home?'

Angered by the way, unlike the duke, he failed to recognise my title, I did not offer the polite gesture of removing my hat or offering any form of courtesy. 'Davy Owen is not my servant,' I snapped, 'he is my relative and my companion. Why have you brought me here without the permission of the Marshal de Rieux? The duke made him my guardian, not you.'

Visibly irritated, the Treasurer controlled his response with effort. 'Things have changed,' he said, tight lipped, and indicated the only other chair apart from the one behind his desk. 'Please take a seat.'

I did not move. 'Since you offer only one, we prefer to stand. Exactly how have things changed, Monsieur Landais?'

Landais shrugged and slowly and deliberately took his own seat. 'The French king is once more threatening our border and so to reinforce our defence Duke Francis has been obliged to make a new alliance with King Edward, who has sent men and funds. In return Brittany has agreed to your repatriation to England. That is how things have changed.'

With an effort I prevented myself from shouting my protest and instead delivered it through clenched teeth. 'The duke has agreed to my repatriation? Or have you agreed, Monsieur Landais, without actually asking him?'

'*Brittany* has agreed, Monsieur Tudor,' he repeated. 'Here is a copy of the treaty.' He swivelled a document lying on his desk, so that I could read it. 'As you will see, it is signed on King Edward's behalf by Bishop Stillington.'

I leaned forward, my eyes moving straight to the signatures beside the seals. 'Ah, I see that it is not signed by the duke at all but by you. I cannot agree therefore that it is legal.'

'The duke has designated me his deputy during his indisposition. I have his written permission to sign on his behalf, having of course consulted him, as far as it is possible.'

The smooth tone of his justification only served to increase my ire. 'And how far was it possible Monsieur Landais?' I asked coldly. 'I would like to know how seriously ill the duke actually is, suspecting that if he had been consulted he would not have agreed to you signing this document.' I spun the parchment around and shoved it back to him. 'Duke Francis has assured us that he would reject any attempt to repatriate us. I do not believe he would go back on that promise. Does his illness affect his mental capacity? If so, why is a relative not appointed to act as regent for him, rather than a common servant?'

I surprised myself with my icy fury and I obviously also surprised the Treasurer for he snatched up the document and began to roll it with brisk efficiency. 'The treaty is signed and sealed, Monsieur Tudor. There is no more to be said. Ships are headed to St Malo to take you and the bishop's embassy back to England as soon as final details are agreed. Meanwhile accommodation has been arranged for you in the palace and my men will escort you there now.'

'Just a moment!' Relieved that we were not to be marched directly to a ship, I raised my hand peremptorily. I said haughtily, 'I trust my uncle will be joining me here in Vannes?' I had received no news of Lord Jasper for several weeks and was very conscious of my mother mentioning in her letter that the Stillington negotiations were not due to include him.

'Your uncle will arrive from Josselin tomorrow but he will not be returning to England with you. Now, I am a very busy man, as you will appreciate . . .' Pierre Landais stood up and rang a bell on his desk, which was immediately answered by one of his clerks. 'Monsieur Tudor is leaving. Please alert the escort.'

Lord Jasper was admitted to my chamber the following day, and his appearance worried me. It had rained hard on his journey from Josselin; he looked thin, damp and dishevelled and the old brigandine he wore was threadbare. Jasper Tudor had always played the bold, confident soldier, even during the blackest days of Lancastrian losses. Now he looked weary and defeated.

'I hear you are to return to England, Harri,' he said glumly, as we embraced each other. The door remained open and two armed men stood on either side, trying to look as if they were not listening to every word that was said within.

I ignored them. 'No uncle, I am *being* returned to England. It is not a journey of choice.'

He nodded. 'I suspected that. I am told I will not even be permitted to accompany you to St Malo.'

I narrowed my eyes. 'Treasurer Landais is wielding his temporary powers over-zealously. For safety's sake I always lock myself in my chamber at night but I have never before been locked in from the outside like a common prisoner. The duke's promise to us of security in Brittany has become a joke, but not at his behest, I believe.'

Lord Jasper let Davy pull off his heavy brigandine and slumped into a chair. 'Francis has been ill for some time. It is a chronic malady, I fear.'

'You are better informed than I am,' I observed. 'And did you hear about the death of Madame Maignelais?'

My uncle looked downcast. 'I did. It was a shock. I know

she was lonely and frightened when she left the duke's court. I pray that she did not take her own life and risk her immortal soul.'

I glanced at the door, where the two guards still stood alert but I could see no reason why I should not close it and so I did. They made no protest; nevertheless I dropped my voice. 'I have a confession to make uncle. I have been involved with a lady.' I related the story of my relationship with Catherine de Belleville, while Davy added asides in a caustic undertone. Lord Jasper appeared far from shocked and even smiled occasionally so that I was moved to ask, 'Do you think often of Mistress Jane?'

'Indeed I do, Harri,' he admitted. 'I have received several letters from her. Our daughter Elin is now married and a mother but I fear I may never lay eyes on my grandson.'

'And I fear that I shall never see *my* child,' I confessed, watching his surprise darken into a frown. 'Yes, there is a child, due quite soon.'

'You did not offer her marriage though, did you?' It was a demand rather than a question, as if he feared the answer.

'Regrettably I am in no position to do so, uncle,' I said. 'I pray for them both but if I am forcibly put on a ship to England I fear I will be abandoning them forever. That is why I am telling you.'

'Do not despair yet. I have sent word to my friend Jean de Quélennec, the Admiral of Brittany, who has long been one of Duke Francis's closest councillors. He is on a pilgrimage to Saint Iago de Compostella but he is returning in haste to remind the duke of his promise to you. It all depends on how fast he can travel. He is not so young any more.'

'That was good of you, uncle.' We were still speaking in undertones. 'But I do not know if there is much time to spare. Treasurer Landis speaks of my departure for St Malo in days rather than weeks.'

Lord Jasper meant well but I did not hold out much hope of help from his Admiral friend. I had already decided my best option was to escape, but also that it would be wise to wait until I was in St Malo, where I might bribe some amenable sea captain to take me to friendly territory.

'By the way, did you ever encounter a French courtier called Gilles de Harpedanne, the Seigneur de Belleville?' He shook his head but I pressed my point. 'His mother was a lady called Marguerite de Valois. Does that name ring any bells?'

My uncle looked amused. 'Ah, yes indeed. King Louis told me about her. She was a by-blow of our grandfather, King Charles the Sixth and, as such, half-sister to Charles the Seventh, who managed to marry her off to his Master of Household but I have forgotten his name. What has this to do with me, Harri?'

I told him how Catherine's stepfather had forced himself on her and fathered her son Roland. 'So that makes him a descendant of your grandfather.'

He was unimpressed. 'Many bastards flock around a throne, Harri, and royal blood is much diluted by the time it has descended through four generations.'

I considered this for a few seconds before responding. 'Well, I will remember young Roland de Belleville, if only because he will be half-brother to my own child.' I refrained from reminding him that it was because I was a fourth-generation descendant of King Edward the Third of England, with a Lancastrian claim to the throne, that my return to my own country was so fraught with danger.

Days passed and I was not taken to St Malo to board a ship for England. Bishop Stillington extended his rambling negotiations well into the autumn, stretching Treasurer Landais's patience almost to breaking point. I had not been able to meet Duke Francis and I was told that Duchess Marguerite was too advanced into her first pregnancy to travel. She awaited the birth in Nantes, where I sent a letter wishing her well and telling her that she would be in my prayers. No reply reached me.

Davy and I were kept under close guard, permitted only regular arms practice together and daily visits to the palace chapel for Mass, but obliged to spend hours of our time confined in our chamber with only books and visits from Lord Jasper to keep us occupied. Finally however, towards the end of November, Davy and I set off from Château de l'Hermine, surrounded by fifty English men at arms, heading north for St Malo.

Our farewell to Lord Jasper was emotional and heartfelt. I had confided my escape plan to my uncle and he had approved it and given me ten gold crowns to add to my fund, which I realised he could probably ill afford but for which I was profoundly grateful. So much depended on where we were housed when we reached St Malo and how closely we were guarded, to say nothing of whether we could manage to obtain a passage before the hue and cry caught up with us. However, after weeks confined within stone walls it was a relief just to ride out of Vannes and feel the wind on my face and a horse beneath me.

'Apparently the Malouins despise English merchantmen,'

Davy informed me as we lugged our saddlebags up the tower stair of a sprawling merchant's house located on St Malo's high-walled promontory, between the busy harbour and its cathedral. 'It is because most of their ships are not armed and make easy targets. The St Malo captains hunt them down and threaten them with their guns to extract a ransom for their cargoes – "coursing" they call it. That is why they're known as corsairs and also why they are so rich.'

'Yes, so I have heard,' I replied grumpily. 'And we are stupid English to haul our bags up all these stairs.' There was heavy gold in our saddlebags and we had not wanted to arouse suspicion among our guards by letting them even lift them.

'Still, at least from up here we'll have a good view of the harbour. We can assess which ship looks the most likely. We need one with guns to deter any pursuers.'

'Sssh.' I put a warning finger over my lips and leaned around the spiral to see if we were being followed up the stair, but there was no one. Not being certain how to go about it myself, I had been wondering if I might trust Robert Poyntz enough to ask him to negotiate a passage for us. Then we could run straight from house to ship and hope quickly to put clear water between us and any pursuers.

As we threw our bags down in the top floor chamber we heard heavy footsteps on the stair and a pot-bellied soldier, breathing hard and wearing a sergeant's armband, rapped on the doorjamb. His jacket bore Edward's sun-in-splendour badge. 'Message for Master Tudor,' he growled, thrusting a sealed letter at me. 'Also I am to tell you that there are guards on every exit so do not get any mad ideas about leaving. Food and drink will be brought to you presently.'

'How soon is presently?' Davy demanded, hungry as ever.

I inspected the letter, feeling my heart begin to thump. It was not addressed in Catherine's hand but it bore the de Belleville seal.

24

Harri

The merchant's house, St Malo, Brittany, November 1476

<u>*To Henri Tudor from Agnes Terreblanche, servant to*</u>
<u>*Madame Catherine de Belleville.*</u>

Sir, I write at the request of my mistress, who wished
you to know that after great travail and pain she was
delivered prematurely of a stillborn son on the twenty-
eighth day of October, the Feast of Saint Jude, patron of
lost causes. The moment of her delivery caused her to cry
out to the saint to save her son, whom she would have
wished to give the name Henri, but for the fact that his
soul fled to purgatory before the priest could baptise him.

Before my young mistress fell into a swoon she bid me
send notice of the birth to you through the court of Duke
Francis of Brittany. Woefully she never regained her
senses and the lifeblood flowed from her. She received the
last rites and died in grace on the feast of All Saints,
with whom she must assuredly now be counted.

Her son Roland remains here under my care at the Château de Belleville in Anjou and I await instructions from Comte Gilles de Belleville as to his future maintenance.

<u>Dictated by Agnes Terreblanche in the Château de Belleville on this the first day of November.</u>

The letter utterly confounded me. I could scarcely finish reading it before my knees buckled and I collapsed onto one of the low cot-beds, which had been provided for Davy and me.

'Jesu Harri, what ails you?' Davy cried, rushing to my side. 'Has someone died? Let me see that.' He prised the letter from my hand and must have scanned it fast because he was quick to react to its news. 'Oh – what a tragedy! I know I warned you about her but I never expected it to end like this. I am so sorry, Harri.'

I felt his hand on my shoulder but I shrugged it off and buried my head deeper in the bedclothes. I could not stem my sobs, but neither could I share my grief with anyone else, even Davy. I felt that I alone was responsible for two dead souls. If I had only had the courage to ignore my obligations to family and church and found some way to marry Catherine this would never have happened. The weight of blame lay on me like lead ingots. It was hours before I could either move or speak.

When a meal came Davy tried to get me to eat but I refused and turned my face to the wall. Catherine's beautiful countenance hovered behind my swollen eyelids and I felt as if food and drink would choke me. She would never eat again.

I heard Davy's report when he came back from reconnoitring the layout of our tower prison but gave him no sign that I had.

'There are guards on the ground floor entrance and more guards on the main gate but I cannot see any sign of them in the garden below our window. However it is three floors up and although the casement opens we have no rope. I do not see how we are to escape without eliminating at least one set of guards. Do you hear me, Harri? I know you are grieving but we have work to do if we are going to get out of here.'

My tears had ceased out of pure drought but the pain had not diminished and the notion of turning my mind to escape seemed utterly futile. Distraught, I had discarded any idea of seeking a way out. When night fell, I welcomed the blanket of darkness as a friend.

Meanwhile, events occurred which radically affected our situation. In St Malo the wind, which had been set fair for a Channel crossing, suddenly turned and increased in velocity preventing any vessel leaving harbour. Meanwhile Lord Jasper's friend Admiral de Quélennec completed his hasty journey from Santiago de Compostella and was admitted to the bedside of Duke Francis.

I was summoned to meet the bishop but Davy said I was ill and could not leave my bed. Luckily it was Robert Poyntz who brought the summons and revealed the reason for it. 'The delay has angered the bishop and he will suspect Henry's illness is a ruse.'

'He will recover soon, it is only a slight fever,' Davy said clearly and then urged Robert into the room, closing the door behind him. His voice dropped to a murmur. 'But I can tell you that he was hoping you might obtain a rope for us to leave by the window – and perhaps distract the guards on the main gate? I think you will not be surprised to hear that Harri has no intention of willingly boarding that ship to England.'

'Certainly his lady mother would not wish him to,' Robert agreed. 'She had expected the Duke of Brittany to refuse his release. I will do my best. Tell Henry to rid himself of that fever and we will aim for your escape tomorrow. The wind may not stay in the northeast for long. Where will you go?'

'The idea is to find a ship to take us to Wales or Ireland. We have money and contacts.'

'Good, I will come back with the rope,' he said, and was gone.

I growled at Davy, 'I told you I have no wish now to escape. Let fate do with me what it will.'

'I am not listening to that defeatist talk,' he snapped. 'You are not in your right mind. Fate has much more in store for you, Harri Tudor, than a watery grave or an encounter with Edward's executioner. If you owe the Belleville anything it is to get on with your life, not brood over her death in the mistaken belief that it is entirely your fault. As far as I am aware it takes two to make a child and I did not notice her turning you away.'

I had not heard Davy speak so angrily since I had queried his lack of a mother and his words were a wake-up call, even though it took some time for it to sink in and I did not immediately respond. However, when the next meal arrived I took my share of the meat and ale and by the time Robert returned with the rope hidden under his jacket I was on my feet and forcing my brain to function. The letter about Catherine's death was up my sleeve but no longer entirely occupying my mind.

'There will be a diversion at the outer gate as you requested,' Robert said, 'so when the cathedral bell sounds for Mass shin down to the garden and make a run for it. You should find the gate unmanned. If not, you have your swords and you know how to use them. May the Almighty steer your way.'

His last words came into my head later as the cathedral bell rang over our heads. The rope descent was relatively easy, even with our gold-laden saddlebags but strolling casually across the garden in order not to attract attention, was a nerve-jangling exercise and the sudden release into the front courtyard of a dozen horses from the stables was a huge surprise. How Robert had managed it I do not know but it certainly alerted the guards who, not realising who we were, came running towards us yelling for help to get them rounded up. Needless to say we ignored this request and disappeared through the gate at a swift pace, breaking into a run as soon as we reached the street beyond. Our intention had been to head straight for the harbour but we became disorientated and on a street leading to the cathedral square we paused in the shadow of an overhanging gable to take our bearings. Shouts louder than those we had ignored in the gateway reached us, as a posse of men at arms appeared from the direction we had come, men who wore Edward's sun-in-splendour badge.

'Forget the harbour, Davy,' I yelled, hauling on his arm, 'make for the cathedral!'

'Why? What are you doing?' he protested, trying to look

over his shoulder at our pursuers and tug away from my grip at the same time.

'Going for sanctuary. Robert begged the Almighty to steer my way and this is the way He is steering it. Stop struggling – this will work for us. We can find a ship later.'

The nave of the cathedral was crowded with people waiting for Mass but we managed to duck and dive our way through to the front where priests and acolytes were gathering in the chancel to deliver the bread and wine. Watched in complete surprise by the clergy, we staggered up the steps to the altar and fell to our knees, panting from exertion.

I pulled my sword from its sheath and laid it on the holy table at the foot of a gleaming crucifix. As Davy followed suit I declared loudly to the priest standing nearest to me and wearing the richest robes, 'In the name of Almighty God, Christ His Son and the Holy Spirit we claim sanctuary from our enemies.'

'Who are your enemies?' he asked with creditable calm, moving up to confront us. 'And who are you?'

'I am Henry Tudor, Earl of Richmond and my enemies are the armed English soldiers entering the cathedral as we speak.' I made the sign of the cross and pointed down the nave to the open west door, where sunbeams streaming in from the clerestory glinted off the polished helmets and pole-arms of half a dozen liveried guards.

The sound of their heavily booted feet caused a clamour of protest in the body of the church and the priest swung round, following my pointing finger, then he spoke with the high intonation that all clergy seemed to acquire with their ordination and which carried clearly over the heads of the assembled worshippers. 'Halt Englishmen! Come no further into God's house! You offend the Almighty's laws with your weapons of war.'

His single voice might have had no effect on the hardened soldiers but the congregation picked up the priest's words and, as if under orders, they linked arms and surrounded the intruders, blocking their way and shouting their Breton dislike of strangers. 'Out Englishmen! You offend God's house. Out! Out! Out!'

The priest took advantage of the hiatus to take our arms and pull us towards a door at the side of the chancel. 'Come,' he said, 'you have claimed God's protection but you will be safer out of sight.' He led us swiftly up a spiral stair which ascended the cathedral bell tower and out onto the crenelated parapet surrounding the steeple. 'Stay here and I will lock the door below and keep the key. I am Father William, the Dean of the cathedral; no one will come up here except me and I will return as soon as the Englishmen have been ejected and I have said Mass. Then we will talk.'

He disappeared back down the stair and Davy and I looked at each other in amazement, still trying to digest what had happened. Then I peered over the parapet and exclaimed, 'Jesu Davy, look at this!'

Below in the cathedral square a squad of thirty or more men at arms were gathered, shouldering their pikes and putting the fear of God into me. How desperate was Edward to get me back to England? I thought, and would a few clergy and an angry crowd of worshippers be enough to deter his men from coming to get me? There were no crucifixes or saintly images on the steeple tower but I made the sign of the cross and sent up a fervent prayer to the Mother of God to intercede on my behalf. If ever I had needed divine protection, surely it was now.

Then, unbelievably, into the square at the head of a column of Breton men at arms rode Pierre Landais, the jangle of harness and the clatter of hooves echoing up to our bird's-eye viewpoint. The two contingents faced each other, one mounted, one on foot and I thought, 'They will soon join forces and no mere Dean of St Vincent's Cathedral will be able to resist their demand to hand me over.' But I had underestimated the power of the Virgin Mary. When Treasurer Landais dismounted and climbed the cathedral steps to address the men he did not give the order to arrest me as I expected but explained that his grace the Duke of Brittany had recovered from his malady and issued an order revoking the Stillington agreement.

'I am here on the duke's behalf to return Henry Tudor to the protection of Brittany. In addition all English envoys and troops are required to return to their own country as soon as favourable winds prevail. Meanwhile your orders are to leave the square and remain in your quarters until conditions allow your departure.'

Landais turned on his heel and strode into the cathedral, leaving his Breton detachment to herd the muttering English soldiers out of the square. At the same time their comrades were unceremoniously ejected from the church and ran to catch them up.

'God's blood, Davy! Uncle Jasper's old Admiral must have worked his magic,' I shouted gleefully. 'We are off Edward's hook!' The change in my mood was instant. I tucked my arm in the crook of Davy's elbow and urged him into a jig along the narrow parapet. It was as if the weight of the world had been lifted off my shoulders and for a few minutes Catherine's death and the loss of our little son vanished from my thoughts.

Fortunately perhaps, by the time the Dean made his reappearance I had sobered up. 'I imagine you heard Monsieur Landais from up here,' he said. 'The Treasurer has told me your story, Henri, and I now realise that your claim to sanctuary was as valid as I took it to be in the first place.'

'Thank you, Father,' I said, uncertain how to correctly address a dean. 'But I am puzzled why only last week Treasurer Landais was content to hand me over to the English and now is ready to fight them if they try to take me.'

Father William nodded. 'You are right to be puzzled but the truth is that we are all liegemen. My Lord is God Himself, Landais's overlord is Duke Francis; we are bound to them by oath. Landais assumed he was doing the duke's will when he accepted English money and men to defend the duchy's border for what he considered the relatively minor exchange of your return to England. It took an old friend of the duke's to show him that God's will was not being done by allowing that to happen and that he was breaking his vow to protect you and your uncle. He sent Landais at the gallop to St Malo to fetch you back and he waits below to take you to Vannes. So although you have escaped the English you are not exactly free. You remain in the duke's custody. As I said, we are all liegemen but some of us are bound more tightly than others.'

I was in no hurry to meet up with Pierre Landais again. Impressed by the Dean's obvious sympathy with my predicament, I was inspired to make him a request. 'Before you take me to Monsieur Landais, would you hear my confession, Father? I have lately received news of great significance to me and my mind is much troubled by it.'

The Dean smiled gently. 'I have sensed the anguish in you, my son. Let us descend the stair to my vestry and I will hear your confession before we meet the Treasurer. Pray that the Lord will grant you absolution.'

Interval

Henry and Margaret

Correspondence: 1476 – 1478

<u>To my dearly beloved son Henry Tudor, rightful Earl of
Richmond, greetings,</u>

You can imagine my relief when word reached me that
you had not perished on a ship bound for England but
remain in Brittany. I thank the Almighty for answering
my daily prayers for your safety, which I believe at
present rests in Brittany.

   Soon after Christmas I shall be attending the queen
in her confinement and so there will be little
opportunity for delivering correspondence to a safe
courier.

   This letter will reach you via very reliable hands, one
Christopher Urswicke. He also carries money for your
maintenance. I think you will find him an interesting
character, one of Lord Stanley's protégés from Lancashire,
an adventurous man and, surprisingly, an ordained

*priest. He can be entirely relied on to render Lord
Stanley and his family true and loyal service.*

*He will act as our courier and in time I am hoping you
will trust him to act as your confessor as well. I fear you
are lacking the services of a reliable priest in whom you
can confide. He is privy to all my hopes and aims. He will
bring your reply, and he will carry any other letters you
wish to be delivered speedily and securely.*

*Look on him as a gift from your devoted and
concerned Mother,*

Margaret R.

*Written at Stanley House, this 22nd day of December
1476.*

⌘

*To my dearly loved and honoured Mother, Margaret,
Countess of Richmond, greetings.*

*Thank you for sending Christopher Urswicke, I like him
very much and believe he deserves your high opinion. He
was a lively visitor and an excellent raconteur.
Unfortunately we were not at Château Largoët when he
arrived. Davy Owen and I had travelled to spend the
Festive Season with the duke and his family at their
palace in Nantes, where much to our contentment we
also found Lord Jasper, who has remained with us since,
for which we are thankful.*

*I spent some of the money you so kindly sent us on
gifts for the duke, who has now recovered from the*

*recurring illness that plagues him from time to time. I
did not see the duchess, who was in confinement,
awaiting the birth of her first child, but I also bought
gifts for her and the baby.*

*After we left Nantes we heard that Duchess
Marguerite had been delivered of a daughter called
Anne, born towards the end of January. I fear she will
be greatly disappointed the babe was not a male heir.*

*You made no further mention in your letter of the
possibility of my marriage to Elizabeth of York, which I
take to imply that any such idea has been shelved.*

*You are right, it is safer for me in Brittany. I find it
hard to contemplate returning to England and bending
the knee to York, while the brothers squabble over
Warwick's legacy and the Woodvilles feast on lucrative
offices, custodies and marriages. The English court is
regarded in Europe as an example of overweening greed
and self-aggrandisement. I confess that I can only
admire the way you and Lord Stanley avoid the caltrops
strewn in the path of anyone with a modicum of power
or influence at King Edward's court.*

*Christopher Urswicke accompanied us to Suscinio
before returning to England. He said he would spread
the word among those who still cling secretly to
Lancaster that this is the place to come if life becomes
impossible in England. We remain here with a
substantial garrison to guard us. Among the soldiers it is
a standing joke that Suscinio should be renamed
'Château Tudor'!*

*I thank you earnestly for sending us the priest and
look forward to his return, for I believe a regular*

correspondence brings us ever closer together as mother and son.

My dearest lady Mother, I pray that you continue in good health and peace of mind and I remain ever your obedient and devoted Son,

HR

<u>*Written at Château Suscinio this twenty-fifth day of January 1477*</u>

⌘

<u>*To my beloved son Henry Tudor, rightful Earl of Richmond, greetings,*</u>

Christopher Urswicke has told me about you, my only child, my now adult son – I have received a clear impression of you, with your keen eye, easy manner and sharp mind. It has been a revelation. I am both proud and very humbly thankful at the same time. Now I feel I know more intimately the man to whom I gave birth and the son for whom I have such love and ambition. How eagerly I look forward to the day we shall be reunited.

However, I think it fortunate that you are not at the English court at present. There has been a terrible, and I believe final falling-out between King Edward and his brother George, Duke of Clarence, whose reputation as a drunkard and a troublemaker cannot be denied; already he is twice a forsworn rebel, twice forgiven, and now he rages afresh against the king's rule.

I have not written before of events leading to this damaging row. It started at the turn of the year when his duchess Isabel died from complications of childbirth and their baby son Richard died ten days later, on New Year's Day. A terrible double blow and the court mourned with him as he buried his wife and babe. It was seen as a gesture of sympathy when the king and queen chose to name their new baby son George after his uncle when he was born in February.

As you will now begin to see, rather it was a sad irony, because only weeks after his bereavement, George of Clarence began negotiations to marry again, with the most eligible bride in Europe, Mary, heiress daughter of Duke Charles of Burgundy who was killed in battle in January of this year. It was a marriage supported and encouraged by the Dowager Duchess, Mary's stepmother, Margaret of York, but not by King Edward, who refused permission, an action supported by the younger York brother, Richard of Gloucester.

George accused them of blighting his life, stormed away from court and had the king's horoscope cast by astrologers, which all courtiers know is a treasonous offence. King Edward had him arrested and put in the Tower and the astrologers tortured and executed.

Now it has emerged that Clarence had accused one of his late wife's gentlewomen of poisoning her mistress out of spite and had the poor woman dragged from her home into a courtroom in Coventry, tried for the murder of his wife, and hanged, all in a day. Inevitably rumour spread that he did this in response to the gossip that he had poisoned her himself, in order to pursue his suit for

Duchess Mary of Burgundy.

As I write George of Clarence is still in the Tower and it is obvious that the king does not know what to do with him. The Duke of Gloucester has come down from his northern stronghold to confer on the subject and Lord Stanley says there have been angry exchanges between these two in meetings of the royal council. The House of York is self-destructing.

Edward's inexplicable answer to the problem is to arrange a marriage between his second son, Richard, Duke of York, who is four years old, and Anne Mowbray, who is five and sole heiress to the Duke of Norfolk, who died suddenly last year. Edward seems to believe that the celebrations surrounding two children being married in Westminster, accompanied by glorious processions and tournaments, will divert public attention from Clarence's presence in the Tower.

It is impossible to fathom the mind of the king – but if he is truly contemplating having his own brother executed it is a tragedy, and one that I do not believe can be glossed over, nor one from which his prestige can recover. But the House of York is resilient, and as I write he reigns still.

Christopher takes ship tomorrow so I must sign off now with my greatest affection and constant prayers for your protection,

Your devoted Mother, MR

Written at Stanley House, London, on this 28th day of October 1477.

⌘

<u>To my honoured and much loved mother Margaret,
Countess of Richmond, greetings.</u>

I was horrified by the events described in your letter of
October last year. As a man without siblings it is
unfathomable that brothers and sisters should be enemies
to the extent of contemplating the execution of one of
their number. Is Edward fearful that George will
attempt to topple him from his throne? Does Richard
grow so powerful that he feels it possible to challenge the
king's rule? I wonder what the Princess Elizabeth and
her sisters make of this situation, or if they have been
protected from the wicked course of it? Most earnestly I
hope there are no ill effects on you or Lord Stanley.

We received a visit last week from Duke Francis, who
was particularly keen to inform us of developments at
the English court. I had to pretend that I knew no
details, beyond whatever gossip has already spread
around Europe. I thought it interesting that the duke
made a point of reminding me how fortunate I have
been to remain here in Brittany, 'bearing in mind the
apparent volatility of King Edward's temper and the
fickleness of his promises'. I think Lord Jasper and I
managed to portray our ignorance and amazement quite
successfully. It would be unfortunate indeed if
Christopher Urswicke's position were to be compromised.
The duke's baby daughter is apparently thriving but her
mother has taken time to recover from the birth and the
fever she developed afterwards. Regrettably she did not
accompany him for I always find her company
stimulating.

Life at Suscinio is calm, not to say tedious. It is a beautiful place to live, but very confined in view of the abduction attempt when last we were here. We are so carefully guarded that it is almost suffocating but thankfully Christopher Urswicke is recognised and welcomed. I wonder if there is any possibility that he might be able to carry a book or two? Château Suscinio is more of a hunting lodge than a palace; there is no library here. Any reading material you have found worthwhile would be greatly appreciated, dear lady mother. We all thank you very warmly for the welcome purse received on his last visit. On this occasion I asked him to hear my confession, which he did with remarkable insight and compassion. I will recommend Davy and Uncle Jasper to take advantage of his services on his next visit.

Your letters are very important to us and to me in particular. But I yearn for the sight of your face and the satisfaction of returning to my father's heritage and my mother's love. We are too long apart, you and I. Let us pray that the chaos at Edward's court subsides and there is once more opportunity to raise the matter of my return.

I am, as always, your loving and appreciative son,
Henry R

Written at Château Suscinio, Brittany, this twentieth day of January 1478

⌘

<u>To my only beloved son Henry Tudor, Earl of
Richmond, greetings,</u>

How I love to write your name in conjunction with the
title which should now, in the year of your majority, be
yours, and which I will always strive to restore to your
possession. However, yet more obstacles have arisen to
hinder this ambition.

By macabre coincidence you were writing your last
letter at exactly the same time as King Edward was
prosecuting his brother, George Duke of Clarence, for
treason in a specially convened Parliament at
Westminster. Since its members had been recruited almost
entirely from the royal household or the crown
administration, it came as no surprise that a guilty
verdict was passed, together with a Bill of Attainder,
which deprived Clarence's children of their inheritance
and with it their place in the succession. He himself was
not present and no defence was offered. Of course I did
not witness this myself but I heard all its terrible detail
from Lord Stanley afterwards. Only days before, London
had been in a state of carnival surrounding the wedding
of the king's four-year-old son Richard to little Anne
Mowbray, the Norfolk heiress. The trial in Parliament
was behind closed doors and news of it is only now
leaking out because of what followed.

It was announced in court at the end of February
that the king's brother had died in the Tower of London
on the eighteenth of the month but no details were
given. Because of the Attainder his titles were not used
and no period of mourning was allotted, the business of

the royal household and administration continued as normal, as if the Duke of Clarence never existed. Custody of his orphaned children, Margaret and Edward, has been granted to the Duke of Gloucester, along with most of his estates. This last is of particular interest to us, my dear son, because Clarence had been in possession of your Richmond estates and now they have passed to his brother Richard. It would have been much more to our advantage if they had returned to the king's gift, for I fear that wresting them from Gloucester will be well nigh impossible, as whenever he comes to court he shows no favour to me but is consistently rude and confrontational.

It is beyond doubt that George did not die a natural death and was executed by some means. A disturbing rumour has surfaced that the method used was extraordinary and barbarous, suggesting that he was drowned in a butt of sweet wine, the very drink that had fuelled his drunken rages. By whatever means his death was achieved it was done without witnesses present, and certainly a drowning would have left his body undamaged, as if death had come through a fatal ague or apoplexy. The king and queen hold court as if nothing untoward has happened but Lord Stanley received information from the north that Gloucester has ordered mourning in his home at Middleham Castle, and is described as 'devastated' by his brother's demise. However, he shows no inclination to refuse the grants offered to him from the Clarence honours, some of which are said, significantly, to pre-date George's death. And in addition I point out to you, but to no one else, that the *whole sorry episode has brought him one step closer to the succession.*

I can write no more and only hope that these events have halted Edward's ambitions to wrest you from Brittany's safe keeping. I have entrusted several books to Christopher Urswicke's care and hope they find you and your companions in good heart and health. I am pleased that you have chosen to confide in and confess to him and trust it brings you comfort in your unhappily prolonged exile.

I send my blessing and am ever your devoted Mother, Margaret R

Written at Stanley House, London, on this fourth day of March 1478.

PART THREE

PART THREE

25

Margaret

Windsor Castle, Berkshire, autumn 1482

ONCE MORE KING EDWARD had invited us to join his
autumn hunting party, this time back at Windsor and
it was on our return from a splendid day's sport, with exhilaration still flushing my cheeks, that I was greeted by one
of my own pages with news of equal pleasure.

'Lady Vaux has asked me to convey her greetings, my
lady. She has been summoned to court to give her account
of the death of the former queen and has news for you. I
am to take you to her if you are willing.'

I followed the page to find my friend happily seated
before a fire in the small but comfortable chamber allocated to her close to the royal steward's apartments where
Lord Stanley and I were lodged. With her was Joan, now
aged nineteen and one of my dearest companions. It was
three years since mother and daughter had been together,
when Kate had made a short visit to England, and I could
see that both had shed tears of joy at their reunion. They

jumped up when I entered and all three of us embraced.

'It is so good to see you, Kate!' I cried. 'Have you come straight from Dover? How was your crossing?'

She smiled and gestured me to take the chair in which she had been sitting. 'Considering it is the gale season, it was a very uneventful journey. I attended Queen Marguerite's funeral in Angers and then sailed from St Malo to Weymouth, the way your Henry would have come, had he not escaped Edward's clutches six years ago.' She took the stool on which Joan had been sitting and the girl perched up on the bed. 'And when I stopped in Nantes to pay my respects at Duke Francis's court, I saw Henry.'

'Oh!' The fact that she had actually seen the son I had not laid eyes on for eleven years set my own tears brimming. 'How was he? What did he look like? Dearest Kate, you are my eyes and ears!'

'Better than that, I have brought you a letter from him and he sends you a gift.' She reached inside her purse and passed me a small package before returning to her seat. 'Henry is a handsome and charming young man, Margaret. His face has not changed that much because he goes clean-shaven and his hair is dark brown and neatly cut to his shoulders. He is tall – not over tall, about six foot, I would say, and he is lithe and graceful with a friendly and easy manner. It is obvious that he is intelligent and well read. He speaks fluent French and English and is very articulate in both. He has some Breton and Welsh also, I understand, and he tells me he reads and writes Latin. Judging by the way they conversed together he certainly has the duke's favour. You would be immensely proud of him.'

Her description had moved me and I blinked back

more tears. 'I *am* immensely proud of him and I thank the Almighty that he escaped that ship from St Malo.' Tucking the package into my sleeve pocket to open in private, I gazed at her solemnly. 'Now Kate, tell me about Queen Marguerite's death. I gather you were obliged to nurse her for some time. What was her malady?'

Joan interjected with indignation. 'My poor lady mother was tied to her bedside for months!'

Kate gave her daughter a look of mild reproof. 'No Joan, it was the queen who was the poor lady. Her ailments were various. She had womanly problems, made much worse by a canker of the gut. It was an unpleasant and lingering death and she suffered greatly. I was privileged to serve her to the end.'

'And did she die at Angers, in her father's palace?' I asked.

'Sadly no; further tribulation came after Duke René died. As part of a deal done with the French king, the county of Anjou was returned to the crown and Marguerite was denied any further access to her father's properties. Up to then we had been lodged in great comfort at Château de Saumur, the beautiful castle on the Loire where Duke René entertained all his distinguished visitors, but she was forced to accept accommodation from one of his faithful servants. We were obliged to live on the charity of his long-serving valet, Francis de Vignolles. Marguerite was mortified, as you can imagine. A Queen of England reduced to residing in a small, unassuming house on a few acres of vineyard, when she had lived in some of the finest castles and palaces in Europe. There is no question that the indignity hastened her death but, looking back, perhaps that was a kindness. And at least she will have a magnificent tomb alongside her parents in the cathedral at Angers and masses said for her soul in perpetuity.'

'Poor Marguerite,' I murmured, making the sign of the cross. 'Life did not treat her well. I hope her soul will rest in peace.'

'Amen to that,' said Kate. At this point there was a knock on the door and she called, 'Enter.'

It was Kitty Hussey, now Kitty Bray, for to my surprise and delight at the age of fourteen she had accepted a proposal of marriage from my long-serving Receiver and Treasurer Reginald Bray, and so the two of them remained in my service, happily pursuing their mutual love of literature and study but disappointingly so far producing no offspring. She made an elegant curtsy; everything about Kitty was elegant, in contrast to her rather brash sister Connie, whom I had successfully married off to a member of the Lovell family and who was now busy producing children and managing a chaotic household in Surrey.

'Forgive me for interrupting ladies but a message has come from the king for Lady Margaret. He commands your presence in his Great Chamber.'

I was startled. Although King Edward and I were socially friendly it was a rare event these days that he requested my company other than at court occasions. 'Was any reason given, Kitty?' I asked. 'Have I time to change?' I was still wearing my hunting apparel.

Kitty smiled and shrugged. 'No urgency was mentioned. May I assist you to change, my lady?'

'Indeed you may,' I replied, rising. 'I will leave you to catch up with Joan, Kate. Perhaps we could attend Mass together in St George's Chapel later. More building work has been done there and the ceiling vaulting is now truly awe-inspiring. You must see it.'

'Of course I must,' said Lady Vaux, 'and I would be grateful for your company to re-introduce me to court life.'

Much though I would have liked to settle down in my chamber to read Henry's letter and open his gift, I knew that the king would not brook much delay and so I set that pleasure aside. Kitty was the deftest of my young ladies and soon had me dressed and coiffed fit for the most stringent critic, which we both knew King Edward to be. With Meg Woodville now married to her Robert, the mother of a son called Anthony after her father, and living at one of the Poyntz manors in Gloucestershire, Kitty had taken over as my trainbearer, being discreet and skilled at handling the cumbersome appendage required for formal court attendance.

In March fourteen-year-old Princess Mary, the royal couple's second child, had died of the spotted fever and was buried in the chapel vault at Windsor alongside her little brother George who had not reached his second birthday, consequently all court dress had been restricted to mourning colours. But the mourning period had recently ended and I was able to wear my most elaborate gold brocade gown and a crimson velvet mantle, the train embroidered with the Beaufort portcullis and Lancastrian white swans with uplifted wings. I was aware that Edward mistrusted the Beaufort blood-ties to the throne but now that all my legitimate male relatives apart from Henry were dead, I stubbornly took it upon myself to display the family crests at court.

In his Great Chamber the king was seated at the head

of an oak table, in animated debate with some of his closest advisers, his Chamberlain Lord Hastings, his Household Controller Sir John Guildford, and of course my husband, his long-serving Royal Steward. I was glad to see that Richard, Duke of Gloucester, who would frequently be seated at his right hand, was absent, as so often these days, away in his northern estates where the king relied on him to keep the Scots and his restless northern nobles under control. Having been granted entry by the chamberlain, I waited patiently near the door for my summons to the table. In due course my husband beckoned me over and signalled a servant to place a seat for me beside him. As I curtsied and sat down King Edward was fulminating about yet another insult he had received from King Louis of France.

Pausing in his tirade, he fixed his blazing blue eyes on me. 'Ah, Lady Stanley, you join us at last. I hear you have been entertaining one of your Lancastrian friends.'

I felt my cheeks flame. 'Lady Vaux invited me to hear about her meeting with my son at the Duke of Brittany's court. At the same time she described to me what I believe she had already recounted to your grace, the painful passing of her childhood friend and mistress, Marguerite of Anjou.'

'Ah yes, an unfortunate end to an unfortunate life.' Edward's lips pursed at the very thought of the woman who had sent her army against him at Tewkesbury and thereby lost her son and her kingdom. 'And how *is* your son, my lady?'

I wondered where this was leading but saw no danger in speaking frankly. 'Fit and well, I am happy to say, sire, and at twenty-five, more than ready to accede to his father's title.'

'Except that his protector Duke Francis seems to think it is *his* title, and my brother Gloucester holds the deeds and estates. The earldom of Richmond comes laden with discord, does it not?'

'Perhaps because of its value and its royal connections, sire,' my husband suggested, attempting to shift the focus from me.

'Which is why the honour cannot be held by a woman, so I cannot grant it to your wife Thomas, however much I would like to reduce Gloucester's holdings in the north. I am persuaded that it was a mistake passing it to him from my treacherous brother Clarence's estate and would welcome an excuse to return it to its rightful heir, which I agree is your son Henry, my lady. But how are we to prise him from the Duke of Brittany's grasp?'

Edward glanced from one counsellor to another, looking for a comment. It was Lord Hastings who broke the tension. 'Perhaps we could kill two birds with one stone, your grace,' he suggested. 'You are rightly angered by the King of France terminating the betrothal between Dauphin Charles and the Princess Elizabeth. The Treaty of Picquigny being now effectively in tatters, would it not infuriate him if the marriage were to be offered to Henry Tudor instead? And might that not also convince Duke Francis that England means no harm to his protégé?'

Edward's brow furrowed as he contemplated this suggestion and turned to me. 'Would it convince the duke this time, Lady Stanley? It failed to do so when Bishop Stillington proposed it. Why should it do so now?'

I swallowed nervously. What none of the men at the table knew was that, having heard of the French king's abrupt termination of the betrothal between his son and Princess Elizabeth, the queen and I had already discussed the possibility of renewing the proposed marriage between Elizabeth and Henry. The last time I had reluctantly agreed to such a marriage I had been backed into a corner, fearing Edward's true motives and praying for the Breton duke's refusal to release Henry, but this time the queen had revealed that the king had a very good motive for granting him both the Richmond title and his daughter's hand in marriage.

Edward was regretting the granting of vast swathes of land and power to his brother Richard, Duke of Gloucester, in the north of the kingdom, which now also included his mother-in-law's vast Beauchamp lands, not forgetting his wife's fortune, gleaned from the attainted Lancastrian earls of Salisbury and Warwick. Thus Richard now held nearly as much wealth and property as the crown. Shaken by the treachery of one brother, Edward had now become wary of the other's power and thought to bind my son to his own dynasty by marriage, thus acquiring a new ally and an excuse to remove the Richmond estates from Gloucester. No one dared to speculate how willingly Gloucester would surrender the valuable Richmond lands but Edward had learned his lesson. With sons to inherit his throne, a king was not wise to let his brother achieve too much power.

However, he was not going to admit all this to me and I was still faced with finding an answer to his question. Why would Duke Francis agree to Henry's repatriation now if he had not done so before? 'Perhaps it will not be the duke's decision, your grace,' I submitted. 'Lady Vaux tells me that Henry has also won the personal admiration of the duke and it may be that my son, having long ago reached his majority, will be invited to decide for himself whether he wishes to accept the terms you are offering.'

Edward's eyes widened in surprise and he let his gaze sweep around his counsellors. 'I believe I hear the loud cluck of an over-proud mother hen, my lords,' he remarked with a smirk. 'What do you think?'

At this disparaging remark my colour flared again, along with my temper and I struggled to keep control, lowering my gaze, my hands bunched into fists beneath the table. With all my powers of concentration I willed my husband to defend me but to no avail, as all the men around the table endorsed their king's cutting dismissal with sycophantic grins and nodding heads.

'Well Lady Stanley,' said the king, pointedly refusing to use my official title of Lady Richmond for the second time and leaning back in his chair, steepling his fingers, his honour satisfied. 'Let us not keep you from your embroidery any longer. We will rely on your husband to inform you of our intentions regarding your son.'

As the door of the king's Great Chamber closed behind me, I took several deep breaths to calm my ire and sent Kitty ahead to the queen's solar to see if Elizabeth would accept a visit from me on a day when I was not on duty.

Whilst dallying in the gallery linking the apartments of the king and queen to wait for her return, I pondered the complexities of my son's repatriation until distracted by the rattle of jewellery and a strong waft of attar of roses. A beautiful woman clad in a low-cut gown of shimmering blue brocade and festooned with glittering gold and jewels, glided past me with a merry wave. The royal guards, who kept an armed watch outside the king's bedchamber, recognised her and Mistress Jane Shore was admitted instantly, while they exchanged knowing looks behind her back. King Edward and his Lord Chamberlain and best friend, William Hastings, shared her favours, I understood. Sometimes I found the ways of men – and certain women – incomprehensible.

Kitty returned with the required permission and we walked sedately down the panelled passageway that presently separated the queen from her husband's waiting mistress. Elizabeth Woodville's beauty had not diminished in the eighteen years since her controversial marriage had rocked the English nobility and shocked the courts of Europe. The repercussions from a commoner becoming Queen Consort of England had been seismic, yet the strain of this was just the beginning of an eventful life that should have aged her considerably: waiting to hear whether her husband had survived a dozen battles, the trauma of his six-month exile and the births of their ten children, coupled with the deaths of three of them. But she seemed barely to have any wrinkles and her elegant figure was still perfect. Only the decay of her teeth revealed the passing of the years and consequently the queen did not laugh these days, even when she was amused. And she was amused when I told her of my encounter with Jane Shore.

'Edward is a man as well as a king,' she observed. 'She is lively and droll and not acquisitive. She could demand titles and land but she refrains. I hope she does not live to regret it.'

'It was one particular title the king wished to discuss with me, your grace,' I told her, accepting the stool that was placed for me beside her chair. 'And I am sure you know which one.'

'Is he going to make another offer to your son, Margaret? I spoke to him about it only yesterday. I hope you did not mention that you and I had discussed it together. He likes to think that plans and policies are all his.'

'I did not, your grace, but he did ask me whether I thought the Duke of Brittany would let Henry go this time.'

'Really? And what did you say?' She bent her head nearer, clearly intrigued, and when I told her she opened her huge grey eyes wide. 'I think Edward would find the idea of a young man having a will of his own rather threatening. He was one such young man himself once of course, or he would never have married me, but a king expects everyone to bow to *his* will. How did he react?'

'As you predicted, my lady, the idea did not appeal to him.'

She must have sensed my affront. 'He gave you a flea in the ear? I suffer such fleabites all the time. He likes to win, Margaret – so let him. As long as it achieves what you want. And you do want your son to marry Princess Elizabeth, do you not?'

'I do indeed, your grace.'

Of course my instant reply in the affirmative was what Queen Elizabeth wanted to hear but in truth my main objective in life was to bring my son back into my life, his own country and his father's estates and I would do anything, appease anyone, lie to anyone but God, to achieve this aim.

When at last I was alone, I opened Henry's small gift – a silver brooch depicting a saint I did not recognise but his letter explained his reason for sending it.

<u>*To my beloved mother Margaret, Countess of Richmond,*</u>
<u>*greetings,*</u>

I have taken advantage of Lady Vaux's presence at the
duke's court to entrust her with a gift for you.

This small token is dedicated to St Armel, a Breton
saint in whom I have come to place great faith. Long
ago Armel (a name derived from the Welsh Arthfael,
or Arthur in English) was a young novice in a South
Wales monastery who fled to Brittany to escape the
yellow fever and ended up in Finis Terre, very close to
where I was cast up eleven years ago. From these
coincidences — Welsh-born boy in exile from his home
and stranded at the world's end — perhaps you already
understand why I single out the saint. But in
addition, you will notice that Armel holds a dragon on
a leash, because when such a beast was terrorising a
Breton village he performed a miracle by taming the
dragon and leading it to the top of a mountain, where
it threw itself off a cliff into a river and disappeared.
A Welsh-born saint who tamed a dragon will surely
bring the Welsh dragon banner of Cadwallader to my
side, should I ever need to fight for my birthright. All
this is why I believe that St Armel will look
favourably on my causes and I urge you to include him
in your prayers and offices.

Meanwhile Lord Jasper, Davy Owen and I are
once more lodged at the Château de l'Hérmine in
Vannes, a livelier and more stimulating place than
Suscinio.

May St Armel bring you his blessing, my beloved

mother, along with my utmost gratitude and loyalty as
your true, obedient and loyal son,
  Henry R

Written at the Duke's Palace in Nantes, this third day of
September 1482.

26

Harri

Château de l'Hérmine, Vannes, Brittany, December 1482

To my beloved son Henry Tudor from his devoted
mother Margaret, Countess of Richmond, greetings.

I write so that you may know King Edward has now
consulted the Archbishop of Canterbury regarding a
papal dispensation to permit your marriage to Princess
Elizabeth. This indicates a new level of validity in
Edward's offer, though the request must yet pass through
the labyrinthine processes of the Holy See.

Already Meg, my one-time ward, and her husband
Robert Poyntz have been blessed with a healthy son at their
manor of Iron Acton in Gloucestershire, where I visited to
stand godmother to Anthony, named for his grandfather,
who also attended. They expect another child already and I
pray again for a safe delivery. In Meg it is good to see what
a careful upbringing in a Godly household can achieve, and
our friend and ally Robert is a worthy beneficiary.

Please inform Lord Jasper, that I have written to Jane Hywel to enquire after his daughters and offered the eldest, Elin, a place in my household if ever she has the opportunity to accept it. I find it helpful and pleasant to have young ladies around me as attendants and can often be of assistance to them and their families. I dearly wish we could spend the Christmas season together and I pray for a time soon to come when we shall do so.

Always your devoted mother and greatest earthly supporter,

Margaret R.

<u>*Written at Stanley House, London, this sixth day of December 1482, the anniversary of your blessed uncle King Henry's birth.*</u>

Post Scriptum: I wear your St Armel brooch and am often asked about it so your special saint's fame is spreading in England.

Strangely when I read of the birth of Robert Poyntz's heir tears came unbidden to my eyes. I forced them back but not so easy to dismiss was the sudden image of Catherine de Belleville and the stillborn son I would never see. I thought of Duke Francis and Duchess Marguerite. The duchess now had two little girls and was expecting another child in the summer – she prayed it would be the desperately needed heir. How envious she would be of Meg Poyntz, producing a boy at the first attempt.

My mother knew nothing of Catherine. After my narrow

escape at St Malo I had told Lord Jasper of the deaths of Catherine and our premature son, and he had embraced me and sympathised but also offered advice.

'Because of King Henry's illness I was never able to seek his permission to marry Jane,' he told me. 'I do not know if he would have given it but I could not offer her marriage without it and it still preys on my conscience. You are in a different position, you have your mother to consider, and the cause you share. I would advise against telling Lady Margaret of your romance and sad loss. Let it steer your own path, Harri, but do not let it spoil your special relationship with your mother.'

'I made a vow, uncle,' I had confessed. 'I shall not marry or take a mistress until I am back in my own country and can do so with honour and the blessing of legitimate children.'

I remember I had found it hard to interpret the expression on Lord Jasper's craggy face, it was a smile and yet there was little amusement in it, and perhaps a trace of cynicism. 'A fine sentiment, Harri,' he had murmured. 'A young man like you should have high ambition and may God reward you for your virtue.'

When I told him the message my mother had asked me to pass on, that his daughter Elin might be taking up a position in my mother's household, a rare smile lit his face. 'I am grateful to your mother. Although she never approved of bringing illegitimate children into the world, Lady Margaret never held the stigma of bastardy against the child.'

However his smile vanished when I told him of my mother's renewed efforts on my behalf. 'I have some hope that on this occasion the offer of a marriage with Princess

Elizabeth is a genuine one, uncle. It may be that this time next year we will both be in England, you and I.'

If anything Lord Jasper's cynicism had magnified ten times since events in St Malo. 'Personally I still would not place too much faith in York's machinations, Harri,' he warned, 'especially on my behalf. I am now convinced that an army and the support of Breton ships is the only way back for us. Many of my lonely hours at Josselin were spent devising ways of confronting Edward on the battlefield. He has defeated me once but he will not do so again.'

'Do you seriously think to regain Richmond and Pembroke at the point of a sword, uncle?' I cried. 'No rebellion against York has ended well, even yours and Warwick's failed eventually – through none of your fault, I acknowledge – but I do not forget that Edward condemned his own brother Clarence to death – drowned like the runt of a litter, in a barrel of sack they say. Suppose we were to lead an invasion, even win a battle? Far from getting our lands back, at best we would end up with our heads on the block. At worst he would have us hung, drawn and quartered as convicted commoners.'

He shook his head and gripped my arm fiercely. The years of isolation and close confinement by guards had stiffened Lord Jasper's resolve and his expression was determined. 'I do not think merely in terms of titles and estates, nephew. And neither do you. I notice you wear that St Armel amulet with its dragon companion and none other. Welsh bards will sing your praises; hundreds, even thousands of men will muster under the dragon banner of Cadwallader. Edward's fear of your return weighs heavier since you have become a man. A man who carries the blood of Lancaster in his veins and has the Welsh dragon at his heel is a constant threat to York. The time may not be yet, Harri, but when the time comes, it is to you that the followers of the dragon will look for leadership. I look towards the crown for you – a Tudor crown.'

I stared at him, thunderstruck. 'You think to put a crown on my head, uncle? No! Even should I want it, there is one who already wears it and four legitimate heirs with claims far greater than mine, three of them only boys. It might be possible to remove a man on the battlefield, but do you suggest we turn child murderers?'

'No Harri, I do not. But I urge you not to ignore your true heritage. Like me your father was only half-brother to King Henry but your mother is a direct descendant of John of Gaunt and she has passed her Lancastrian blood to you. Richmond may be due to you from your father but a claim to the English throne is your mother's legacy. She would not want you to forget it.'

I stared at him for several seconds, my brows knitted. 'I do not forget it, uncle, but England and Wales have suffered many years of discord and war. I do not wish to perpetuate that by inflicting more. I will only fight if I truly believe that God intends me to do so but I would rather be Earl of Richmond in a peaceful country than king of a constantly embattled one. That is why I give serious consideration to a marriage which would unite the blood of Lancaster and York, instead of shedding it.'

Lord Jasper shrugged. 'You must follow your young man's heart, Harri,' he said solemnly, 'and I will follow my grey-beard's sword. But I still hold out hope of a slim chance that one day the sword and the heart will unite.' With a rueful smile he turned away.

This conversation lingered in my mind, long after it had occurred. Nor was Lord Jasper the only one at this time who evinced a keen interest in my future. After a wine-fuelled feast during the Christmas celebrations, Duke Francis took me aside and began to sing my praises with embarrassing enthusiasm.

'When I look at you, Henri, I see the son I always hoped to have,' he gushed, his arm around my neck and his grizzled beard tickling my clean-shaven cheek. When I had first arrived in Brittany the duke had been a man in his prime, dark-haired, handsome and muscular, but the ensuing years had robbed him of his health and good looks. He had become flabby and florid, his buoyant charm worn away by cares and disappointments, still without the male heir he needed to preserve the independence of his duchy from the greedy grasp of France. I could not help pitying the Duchess Marguerite, who remained a proud and spirited young woman, tied to a husband who had lost his vigour and now looked for it at the bottom of a wine jug.

His paean of praise continued. 'A superb horseman, fine archer and champion jouster – what more could a father ask of his son? Your mother will be so proud of you when you are finally reunited. And I have an idea that might bring this about sooner rather than later. We could arrange a marriage between you and my daughter Anne. She is only five but in ten years she will be fifteen and you will only be thirty-five. Younger than I was when I married the duchess. Marguerite tells me that she is certain the child she now carries is a boy but she said that about the last two. However, if it is a boy he will need someone to act as regent for him until he is grown and who better than the Comte de Richemont? But if it is a girl, then as husband to my eldest daughter you would take the title Duke of Brittany and your son will become duke on your death. What do you think, Henri? Does the idea appeal to you?'

Because he was leaning heavily on my shoulders I could make no eye contact and was therefore able to hide my astonishment at the suggestion he had made. He had called me Comte de Richemont but that was an empty title, without land or revenue attached. My own lost Richmond title and estates were held by Richard, Duke of Gloucester, and they were destined to remain with him unless I accepted Edward's dubious offer of marriage to his eldest daughter and risked returning to England to claim them. And now here was another ruler, albeit the worse for drink, making me another offer altogether, one which would tie me to Brittany forever – a fate I could not contemplate. It was not that I favoured Elizabeth of York for her beauty – I had never laid eyes on her – but I had made a vow to God, which depended on me returning to my home soil and establishing a Tudor family on my own estates. It certainly did not involve spending another ten years living on Breton handouts and waiting for my wife to mature.

I gently extricated myself from the duke's embrace and made him what I hoped he considered a grateful bow. 'It is a magnanimous and generous offer my lord but I am sure you agree that we should wait until after the duchess is delivered even to consider it.' I glanced about to search for eavesdroppers but thankfully saw none. 'In fact I believe she would be mortified if she knew you were making such a suggestion.'

Duke Francis touched his nose, his habitual way of indicating secrecy, especially when he had drunk too much wine. 'Between you and me, Henri, just between us, eh?' he said.

27

Margaret

Palace of Westminster, April 1483

THE KING WISHED TO celebrate Easter in St George's
Chapel, where two of his children were buried and
where he loved to hear the resident boys' choir singing
hosannas to Christ's resurrection, their high, pure voices
echoing around the intricate vaulting. Pascal Sunday had
been fine and sunny but cold enough for the royal couple
to don their fabulous sable-lined mantles for the formal
procession down the hill from the royal apartments.

But the following day an icy wind had brought in a
rash of sleet showers, confining the ladies to their solar.
Edward however had insisted on the fishing trip, organised
by some of his household knights, going ahead. It was to
an island below the castle where the river split into two
and formed a pool famous for luring large chub and pike
to the hook. He had returned full of enthusiasm about
the day's catch and shivered his way through several jugs
of hot, spiced wine and a dinner of five courses, declaring

that he was starving and freezing and needed to warm his belly.

'His doctor warns him against over-indulging but he does not listen,' Elizabeth had complained when the ladies retired to enjoy the blazing fire in her private chamber. 'I hope he will not stay drinking too long. I asked Lord Hastings to try and persuade him to go to bed but he is just as bad. Might Lord Stanley prevail on them do you think?'

I was as concerned as she was about her husband's health. It did not go unnoticed that the king had lately taken to stopping halfway up the grand staircase in order to catch his breath, a climb he would have made at the sprint only two years ago. I thought the royal physicians were right to encourage self-restraint but Edward was not a man to be restricted in any way and I confessed I doubted Thomas could have any influence. 'Perhaps he will tire quickly,' I added, hopefully. I did not mention the king's bad cough, which had led me to think this.

Elizabeth shook her head. 'If he wants to enjoy himself Edward does not listen even to his own body.'

Lord Stanley and I were not on the royal barge on our journey back to Westminster the following day – we travelled close behind in our own vessel. The king and queen were wrapped in furs and enclosed with glowing braziers in a cabin hung with tapestries against the cold. On calm pools we could hear Edward's hacking cough, carried to us on the chill wind. Usually Edward stood in the prow of his barge when navigating the flash locks down to Sheen Palace, where we were to spend the night – these were always an exhilarating and enjoyable ride – but on this occasion he remained out of sight and when we docked the king leaned heavily on one of his sturdier body squires for the walk to his apartments, where he remained, there being no sign of him at supper.

The next morning a chair was used to carry him back to the barge and it was not until we reached Westminster Palace that a worried Queen Elizabeth came to consult Lord Stanley.

'I think we should send for the king's surgeon, Thomas,' she said. 'He needs bleeding to reduce the humours.'

'Are you sure, your grace?' Thomas asked. 'He seems very weak. Perhaps the physician might be called first to make a diagnosis?'

'Well, call them both,' she responded tetchily. 'It cannot do any harm, as long as they do not argue.'

The surgeon William Hobbs and the physician Doctor Jacques Fries were duly called to the king's bedside, where his condition showed some improvement after a little blood-letting and the administration of a strong herbal potion. He slept heavily and Thomas and I were able to leave the palace and return to Stanley House, confident that the ague had passed its worst. However, at dawn the following day, Thomas was called back to Westminster Palace for a meeting of the Privy Council.

My husband returned home at dusk and reported that Edward had developed a high fever in the night. 'The king is propped up on pillows to ease the congestion in his lungs and the surgeon and physician argue constantly about what treatment to give him,' he confided. 'But between some exhausting periods of violent coughing he is quite sensible and he has not lost sight of his royal obligations. Indeed, he has summoned his friend Hastings and his stepson, Thomas, Marquess of Dorset. I believe he is going to force them to settle their dangerous squabble by claiming to be on his deathbed. It might be a good ruse.'

I frowned at this. 'Perhaps it is not a ruse, Thomas. Elizabeth must be worried if she is constantly at his bedside. Perhaps Edward really does believe he is dying.'

Lord Thomas pulled a face. 'Bah! He has an ague that is all. He will recover in a matter of days.'

'Have you actually seen the king?' I asked. 'How does he look?'

'He makes a noise when he breathes but I think Elizabeth is making too much fuss. In the king's name she has called another meeting of the Privy Council in order to arrange for the Prince of Wales to be sent for, from Ludlow, so I am again obliged to go to the palace tomorrow, even though I have business of my own to attend to.'

I did not like the sound of all this and made a swift decision. 'I will come with you. If the queen is that worried I should go to her.'

Thomas shrugged. 'As you wish. I suppose there is no harm in showing your concern.'

His own lack of concern about Edward's health worried me. 'The health of the king is important for everyone surely? But speaking selfishly, for us it is particularly so. We are just beginning to believe that very soon Henry will receive his pardon and be able to return to England. A dead king cannot grant a pardon and the Prince of Wales is only twelve years old. Who will rule for him if he becomes king? Who would we have to deal with?'

'Be careful, Margaret.' Thomas put his finger to his lips.

'Remember there is a fine line between worrying about the king's health and plotting his demise. Imagining the king's death is a treasonous offence and walls have ears. By all means comfort and advise the queen in her anxiety but do not speak of the king as dead before he actually is.'

The following day, when Lord Hastings and Elizabeth's oldest son, Lord Dorset, answered their summons, King Edward dismissed all the others around his bed, so that none heard what he said to make the two rivals settle their differences. Whatever they were, he succeeded and the former foes left arm in arm, giving no details as to why or how. Queen Elizabeth immediately rushed back into the king's chamber and I followed. Edward was already in the midst of a fit of coughing, sprawled on the pillows, his face puce with effort. A servant rushed in with a bowl and he immediately reared up, bent over and spat foul bile into it. The room smelled of rotting matter. It reminded me of my last husband's final days.

'You have over-taxed yourself, Edward!' Elizabeth cried, climbing onto the bed beside him in a rustle of skirts and mopping the sweat from his brow with a linen kerchief.

He turned to her, making a visible effort to cease coughing in order to speak. His voice came in a hoarse croak, seared by the poison passed up from his lungs. 'I need to see the Chancellor, Elizabeth,' he said, pausing to gasp air, which rushed in with an alarming rattle. 'Make sure he comes with clerks. I have codicils to add to my will.'

Alarm immediately registered on the queen's face, which she rapidly disguised with a forced smile. 'I will summon him, my lord. But you must rest. The physician will give you some more herbal tonic to ease your throat.' She turned to signal to the black-gowned figure hovering with his flask and spoon. Doctor Jacques moved forward to administer his dose.

Elizabeth slid carefully off the bed, her exit decorous but her expression grim. She made the sign of the cross and clasped her hands under her chin, eyes closed briefly in desperate prayer, before taking my arm and guiding me away from her husband's distress.

'The doctor and surgeon say this cough will pass, Margaret,' she murmured, her lips close to my ear so that others could not hear. 'But listen to him! How can anyone believe that? Only God and the Holy Saints can save Edward's life and we must all pray for him. I would be on my knees at once but now I must attend the meeting of the Privy Council to make sure they send for the Prince of Wales, because our prayers may not be enough. I know my brother Rivers will keep young Edward safe in Ludlow but I am worried that the council will not commission a large enough escort for his journey. I hope Lord Stanley will support me in my demand for a large army. Travel is so dangerous these days and it will become even more so if word gets out of the king's illness. The sooner we get the prince to London the better.'

I thought of Lord Thomas's scepticism about the severity of King Edward's illness and wondered whether he would back Elizabeth's demand for an army to bring her son to London. I suspected he might see it as an excuse to bring troops into London in support of her Woodville affinity. Elizabeth may well have seen Edward's will already and the fact that he wanted the Lord Chancellor to add codicils had obviously alarmed her. There was already no love lost between her and the Duke of Gloucester, and both of them would want to be named as Regent. If the king's condition continued to deteriorate I could see that Thomas was right about a serious battle developing in the Privy Council.

I decided to follow my husband's example and remain uncommitted. 'I cannot join you in the Privy Council meeting madam but I can pray for the king's recovery. Shall I accompany you to the meeting and then be your representative at the chapel altar? Praying is one thing at which I have had much practice. I will leave my trainbearer, Kitty Bray, outside the Privy Chamber to help you when the meeting ends.' Kitty was a particular favourite of Elizabeth's and I knew she would be tactful and intuitive, whichever way things went inside the chamber. She would also keep me informed of events.

By the time I emerged from the chapel in mid afternoon, steps had been taken to mute the palace out of respect for the king's illness. Servants and officials had tied cloths around their shoes to allow them to move quietly about their duties along the passages and staircases near the royal apartments, while thick layers of straw covered the flagstones in the courtyard under the windows to dampen the noise of hooves and wheels. While I had been diligently praying for his recovery, clearly the king's condition had worsened.

Having been admitted to the anteroom of Edward's bedchamber, I found Thomas in earnest discussion with Lord Hastings; as Steward and Chamberlain they were together responsible for the running of the palace and for instigating the emergency procedures. When Thomas broke off his conversation to come and greet me I immediately asked the obvious question. 'Do you now believe that the king is dying, my lord?'

He frowned fiercely. 'I will not believe it until he takes his last breath. However, he has laboriously dictated codicils to his will, between worsening coughing fits, and so I must recognise, as Hastings does, that Edward believes it himself. He is certainly very ill.'

'Elizabeth believes only a miracle will save him,' I said. 'I have been praying for that miracle.'

'Very wise of you,' he murmured, 'because if he goes, everything starts again. All your best-laid plans and hopes for a family reunion go up in smoke and, judging by Elizabeth's performance at the Privy Council meeting, there will be an all-out war for the Regency between the new king's vixenish mother and his power-hungry uncle.'

For the next two days and throughout the nights between, Edward fought on for his life like the soldier he was and I for one found it heart-breaking to witness the deterioration of one who had been such a glorious physical figure of a man. Eventually the doctor and surgeon ceased to call it an ague and managed to agree that it had developed into quinsy, the painful and deadly condition that turned the throat into a furnace and filled the lungs with fluid, making every breath an agony. Elizabeth left his side only to issue orders to her servants, desperately anxious for the safety of her family in a court that she was acutely aware had sworn loyalty to her husband but not to her. As I listened to her dictating letter after letter to those she hoped she could depend on, I saw with sudden enlightenment that she distrusted Richard of Gloucester as much as Lord Thomas did.

To assist my own memory and in order to keep Henry and Lord Jasper informed, in the free time available to me I put pen to paper, to write my own account of events in the form of a letter.

To my dearly beloved son Henry, greetings.

As I write the Yorkist King Edward lies fighting for his life here in the Palace of Westminster. I am sure you will realise as I do what would be the consequences for us of the demise of the man who usurped the throne of our kinsman Henry VI and ordered his death in the Tower of London. It would put an end to any hope that you, my most dear son, might soon return to England and claim your Richmond title and estates. The crown will pass to the head of another Edward but the power will likely be in the hands of a Regent who will not have our best interests at heart. Before his voice failed, Edward dictated codicils privately but none save the two clerks concerned know their content and presently they guard them closely. Queen Elizabeth is praying that the king has adjusted his will to name her as Regent for their son but Lord Stanley is certain it will be the Duke of Gloucester.

At first the king's malady was thought to be merely an ague, caught while out fishing at Windsor but as the days have passed Edward has not proved as robust as his looks and physique might once have indicated. A simple ague has developed into quinsy and fever fills his lungs and causes him to fight for each breath. The doctors have become more pessimistic by the hour. I pray long and daily that Edward will survive to complete the task

*he began for your reinstatement my son but I greatly
fear that now this will not be the case . . .*

Here I broke off from my writing, hearing a loud commotion in the vicinity of our apartment, which is very close
to the royal chambers, and within a few moments Kitty
Bray burst into my chamber, her face flushed and her
demeanour uncharacteristically agitated. 'Forgive me, my
lady but I thought you should know immediately. The king
is dead.'

Her right hand flickered across her breast in the sign of
the cross as she said the fateful words. In the past few days
she had been attending the queen who had taken a liking
to my Receiver General's pretty, discreet wife and asked me
to release her from my service into hers. Since Kitty was a
married woman and no longer my ward I had left the choice
to her and she had acceded to Elizabeth's wish. Thus she
had been in the royal apartments when the death was
revealed.

'Does Lord Stanley know this, Kitty?' I asked. 'Was he
with the king when he died?'

'Yes my lady. He is presently making arrangements for
the knell to be sounded.'

As she spoke the doleful clang of the chapel bell began
to ring out, penetrating the thick palace walls and echoing
through the passages. It was to be the background sound
to the rest of the night and the day that followed, while the
dead king's body was displayed under a gold-tasselled canopy
on a black velvet-covered trestle in the great hall of
Westminster, royally crowned and closely guarded but
covered only by a purple linen decency cloth, to prove to

courtiers and servants who queued to pay their respects that there was no sign of any injury. The bell tolled a mournful accompaniment to the prayers I, and many others, made for the dead man's soul, although I was grimly doubtful that they would hasten the journey through purgatory of such a serial sinner as Edward of York.

28

Harri

Château Suscinio, Brittany, spring 1483

AFTER THE DEATH OF King Edward, my mother's letters began arriving more often and as the days of spring passed through May into June, my astonishment grew at the revelations they contained.

The official announcement of the death reached Nantes in mid April and must have taken Duke Francis and his court completely by surprise. When a king only forty years of age dies suddenly and apparently of 'an ague', as the reports suggested, there is inevitably rumour of foul play, and this suspicion spread through Europe like a forest fire. We were back at Suscinio but even there we heard that Lord Jasper and I were suspected of engineering the death from Brittany, although how, why and through whose offices were details never mentioned. However, as if to illustrate his dismissal of such a ludicrous suggestion, Duke Francis granted new and more generous living allowances to our guardians and a relaxation of our custody terms, which included permission to ride out without restriction and the freedom to send and receive correspondence without censorship. He must have felt that with the death of Edward the threat of our abduction had vanished.

To my relief there had been no follow-up to the duke's tipsy Christmas suggestion of my betrothal to his daughter Anne, although Duchess Marguerite's third child, a boy as she had predicted, was unfortunately born prematurely and did not survive. Lord Jasper and I had been invited to Nantes for Easter but the duchess had not attended and was reported to be suffering greatly from her loss. I had written to her with my condolences but received no reply.

'Will you give up the idea of marrying Elizabeth of York now?' Davy Owen posed this question as we were leading our mounts to the manège at Suscinio, where we gave them their daily training session. We both still possessed the horses Duke Francis had sent to us at Largoët and working the stallion Bastion never failed to remind me poignantly of Catherine de Belleville; her silken favour, given at the Trédion joust, still nestled in the depths of my apparel chest.

'Who knows, Davy. My lady mother writes that the government of England is in chaos. The last I heard was that the Prince of Wales – or King Edward the Fifth I should say – was being brought to London from Ludlow to prepare for his coronation, which is set for the beginning of May. Gloucester is on his way south from York and Lord Hastings is riding to meet him. Heaven knows what schemes they will be cooking up between them. In the Privy Council Queen Elizabeth is contesting the codicil of her husband's will naming Richard, Duke of Gloucester, as the young king's Protector, and it is no secret that Gloucester considers the Woodvilles common upstarts who do not belong among the governing nobility. I do not think anyone will be giving thought to a marriage between me and a York princess, that is certain.'

'Which means we are stuck here for ever then?' Davy sounded thoroughly dejected, plodding along beside Alouette, his head down.

I tried to lighten the mood. 'Oh cheer up, long face! Everything is bound to be up in the air when a king dies but it is just possible events might fall in our favour. Why are you so glum?'

'Because it is just as possible that we will end up staying in Brittany until we are old and grey and as hostages and strangers we have no prospect of advancement. I do not want to remain a penniless squire all my life, Harri. If we were in England I might stand a chance of joining the new king's retinue.'

I chewed my lip, understanding his depression. He was no longer a youth without thought for the future or yearnings for the past, he was a man, a trained soldier, with ambitions and desires, who wanted to make his mark in life and was hampered and frustrated by his restricted circumstances. I had been lucky to have his company for so long but I realised it would be selfish to stand in the way of his progress. 'Well you are not obliged to remain here, Davy,' I reminded him. 'You are not a Tudor. You chose to use the surname Owen, like the good son of a Welshman. There is nothing to stop you returning to England and making your fortune.'

His head lifted instantly on being told he was not a Tudor and I had scarcely finished my speech before he snapped his response. 'What do you mean I am not a Tudor? I am as much a Tudor as you and Lord Jasper! More so in fact because I have no blasted English or French blood in me. So you will not get rid of me like that, Harri. I am going back home when you go back home but let us hurry up and get there before we are both old men. We need a plan.'

'You are right there, Davy. And as soon as we find out who is now ruling England we will set about persuading them to let us back in.'

Like everything in our lives since going into exile however, it was not to prove as simple as that. The next letter from my lady mother made this abundantly clear. It was also obviously written in haste.

To my dearly beloved son, greetings,

Richard of Gloucester has moved more swiftly and alarmingly to establish his position than anyone expected. Already Earl Rivers and his nephew, Queen Elizabeth's son Sir Richard Grey, have been arrested on charges of treason and imprisoned, we know not where. They were escorting the new king to London to prepare him for his coronation on the fourth of May, when a message from Gloucester suggested a meeting as they passed through Northampton. Having let the young king and the rest of his escort travel on, they made a short detour to keep the rendezvous and an apparently convivial dinner together followed. But before dawn Gloucester's armed agents had taken Rivers and Grey by surprise in their beds. Their offence has not been made public and meanwhile Gloucester has taken control of the young king.

As you can imagine Elizabeth is both furious and frantic, raging at her brother Lord Rivers for separating from the main royal escort and putting himself and her son Grey in jeopardy and wondering if she should flee into sanctuary once more at Westminster. She and the Marquess of Dorset have tried to raise a force to confront Gloucester and take the young king back into their care but they cannot find enough support among the lords. Woodville power has rapidly evaporated. Meanwhile Gloucester moves closer, London seethes with unrest and it is only a matter of days until the young king is due to be crowned.

As far as your return is concerned, we may be back where we started but I must despatch this with Urswicke now. I will keep you informed.

Your ever-loving mother, MR

Written at Stanley House, London on this twenty-sixth day of April 1483

I lost no time in taking this letter to Lord Jasper, who in these days spent considerable time in the luxurious steam room off Château Suscinio's ducal apartments, which he happily occupied while his host was not in residence. Hot steam he said worked wonders in relieving the pain of aching joints.

I waited in the duke's private chamber, which was dominated by a vast tester bed hung with curtains patterned in black and white ermine tails, lest he who lay in it should forget that he was ruler of a fiercely independent Brittany. It was heaped with crimson pillows and covered with a gold-embroidered quilt but it was obvious that Lord Jasper did not sleep there because a rather rumpled truckle bed was tucked into a far corner of the room.

'With no one to share it I do not care to sleep in such a large bed, Harri,' he had told me and his forlorn expression had stirred my sympathy. We were three lonely exiles – Lord Jasper, Davy and me – missing our families and friends and without close female companionship. We all needed an aim, a purpose to our lives and it had struck me then that it was my responsibility to provide it. Now fifty-three, my uncle was too old to take the lead and Davy was not ready.

Jasper entered the chamber wrapped in a linen sheet, face flushed from the steam, his once-thick ginger hair sparse on his pate and fading to white. His vulnerability struck me. Usually a figure of indomitable assurance, at that moment he looked irresolute, even elderly.

'Gloucester has shown his hand, uncle,' I said, handing him the letter. 'He and Hastings have control of the young king and Rivers is arrested.'

He nodded briefly. 'I am not surprised. Richard is his father's son, far more so than Edward ever was. His pride would not stomach power falling into an upstart's hands.'

He began to scan the letter but I could see he was becoming cold and brought him his chamber robe, which had been hanging on a clothes pole nearby. 'Here my lord, *you* will catch an ague,' I warned, adding grimly, 'And we know what harm that can do.'

He grunted as he shrugged into the robe, never taking his eyes from my mother's epistle, but I noticed that he held it closer than hitherto. I acted as his dresser, knelt and tied the sash of his robe with a lump in my throat. The roles were reversing, the guided becoming the guide.

'I would not give Rivers and Grey very long to live,' Jasper remarked grimly, folding the letter and handing it back. 'Gloucester will not waste an opportunity to eliminate a Woodville threat.'

'You think he will have them killed?' I asked, disturbed.

'Oh it may be done with a show trial before the axe falls but he will relish being rid of Rivers's influence on his young nephew. And I wager that if the young king's mother has not yet taken sanctuary they will soon enclose her in a convent. History shows there is no one more dangerous than a minor's uncle.'

I raised both eyebrows. 'I have never considered you dangerous, uncle,' I remarked pertinently.

He shot me a humorous glance. 'I never had the power to be, Harri,' he quipped, 'and it is too late now. But I would not be at all surprised if some of Elizabeth Woodville's relatives soon join us in exile.'

My lady mother's next letter did not reach us until the end of May, by which time we had received news from Duke Francis's agents that Edward the Fourth's widow had taken sanctuary at Westminster Abbey with her remaining children. And Jasper's prediction was proved right when Elizabeth's younger brother Sir Edward Woodville, who the dead King Edward had made Admiral of England, had brought two of his ships and their crews over to Brittany and sailed up the Loire to Nantes. To my surprise, Duke Francis had immediately summoned Sir Edward to his court and offered him sanctuary and subsistence.

'The duke would never turn Sir Edward away, Harri,'

Lord Jasper commented. 'Ten years ago he and his brother, Earl Rivers, brought a thousand archers from England, who harried the French so effectively that they were forced to retreat. Besides, apparently on the way here he pirated – although he would say "confiscated" – a large sum of gold from a French merchant ship, which he presented to the duke, so he could hardly refuse him refuge.'

'It is a pity he did not present it to us,' I muttered. 'It might have bought supplies for all the men he has foisted on us.' Some of the crew-members of Sir Edward's ships had chosen to return to England, but a number preferred to stay with their Admiral, and the entire contingent was even now on the way to Suscinio.

'Look at it this way,' Lord Jasper said, 'Sir Edward is a skilled knight and commander and he will drill the men he has brought and enforce discipline. We will have English men at arms at our disposal and it will be pleasant to hear our own language spoken around the castle.'

I had to agree with my uncle's last remark and Sir Edward Woodville, a knight only a little older than me, might make a good co-conspirator. Lately Davy and I had been lamenting our lack of knowledge of England's coast and countryside, and we might learn a great deal from an experienced navigator and soldier, even if his name was Woodville. Nevertheless, I still anticipated his arrival with some trepidation. Since being reunited with Lord Jasper we had been a tight-knit trio, mixing with our Breton guards at meals, on the practice grounds and in the manège but otherwise tending to keep ourselves to ourselves. I feared that the arrival of another Englishman might change the dynamic between us.

Meanwhile Christopher Urswicke had made yet another journey to Suscinio with a confidential letter from my mother, which contained some alarming news.

To my dear and only son Henry Tudor from his Mother, greetings

By now you will no doubt have heard that Queen Elizabeth and her children have once again taken sanctuary at Westminster Abbey, only days before her son, the new king, arrived in London. Gloucester has installed his nephew in the Tower, where kings of England have traditionally lodged prior to their coronation, but the new Regency Council has now postponed the ceremony to the twenty-second of June, declaring that Elizabeth's original date was too soon for proper arrangements to be made.

I saw the young king at Westminster Palace soon after his arrival and he looked well but very bewildered, which is hardly surprising when he must have been expecting to be reunited with his mother, brother and sisters, who of course were all absent. He has his father's red-gold hair and handsome features. Gloucester kept him closely surrounded by his own cronies and so I did not speak with him. Lord Stanley however still holds office as Royal Steward and says that the king is wary and uncommunicative and although Gloucester is kind and deferential towards him, the boy does not appear easy in his uncle's company.

Being mindful of my lord's position, I have not visited Elizabeth in sanctuary but keep in contact

through our mutual physician, Dr Caerleon. He says
that she is extremely distressed, especially since Gloucester
requested that she send the Duke of York out of sanctuary
to keep his brother company in the Tower. Her reply
amply demonstrates her distrust, for she declared that she
would release Prince Richard when her brother Rivers
and son Grey were released from wherever they are
detained. Elizabeth must remember well the arbitrary
execution twelve years ago of her father and brother
John on the orders of the Earl of Warwick. The kingdom
is in the same state of perilous insecurity now, as it was
then.

Written in haste at Stanley House on this sixteenth day
of May 1483

My misgivings about Sir Edward Woodville were misplaced.
Queen Elizabeth's younger brother was a cheerful, friendly,
competitive individual, who also happened to be extremely
good looking and would doubtless have been a lodestone
for the ladies, had there been any females of interest lodged
at Suscinio. After only a few hours together at the practice
ground he was calling me Harri and I was calling him Ned.
At dinner afterwards he admitted he was nervous about
being separated from the two ships he had left moored at
Nantes.

'I was going to leave a skeleton crew aboard, I do not
wish to find that some Breton pirate has stolen them, but
Duke Francis assured me his Admiral of the Fleet would
put a guard on them. Should I trust him on this, Harri?'

I was quick to reassure him. 'The Admiral is a good friend

of Lord Jasper's. His name is Jean de Quélennec and he is one of the duke's closest councillors, and the duke himself you may trust completely. Your ships should be safe.'

'Good.' Sitting at a trestle in the great hall, we were making short work of some bread and cold mutton; with good gulps of his ale, Ned wiped his mouth carelessly on his sleeve and gave me a wink. 'We may need all the ships we can lay our hands on before long. The men that are still with me are all keen to get back to England, as you can imagine – do you have any plans?'

His blunt question put me on the spot. I had only known him a matter of hours and the plans Davy and I had discussed regarding a return to England were as yet rudimentary and would certainly be thought treasonous, should they ever reach the ears of the new Regency Council. Though we knew little of the English coast Davy and I had spent a good deal of time considering ways and means to best invade England. It was always possible that Ned's claim to have fled Portsmouth when he heard of his brother's arrest by Gloucester's men was only a ruse to worm his way into the confidence of Duke Francis and place himself as a spy in our midst. I liked him but as yet I did not trust him.

I returned his grin and made an airy gesture. 'Oh, we always have plans, Ned, but as you know the best laid plans have to be adjusted according to circumstances. Ours went back to square one when we heard of King Edward's death.'

He pursed his lips and scratched his ear. 'Yes, I must admit that did throw an ember into the powder keg. Do you get news from England regularly? It would be useful to know what is happening there now.'

'We have our sources,' I said enigmatically.

'But you do not trust me enough yet to reveal them?' He nodded approvingly and stood up from the board. 'I cannot say I blame you. Shall we go and work off some more frustration? I would like a look at this splendid stallion you were telling me about.'

I was glad I had not revealed the content of my mother's last letter because her next contained even graver news.

To my dear son Henry from his despairing Mother,

My mind and heart are rent by the news I have to tell you. Your stepfather, Lord Stanley, is confined in the Tower, unjustly suspected of conspiring to remove Gloucester from the Regency. As yet he has not been formally charged or committed for trial but I earnestly pray he will not be submitted to torture or coerced into making false confession. Shockingly, the Lord Chamberlain, the late king's closest friend and ally, Lord Hastings, was dragged from the same Council meeting, which was held in the Tower and summarily executed in the courtyard, without benefit of priest or trial. This is tyranny of the worst kind. Bishop Morton was also accused and is in the custody of the Duke of Buckingham. Gloucester sees treachery everywhere and has arrested Mistress Jane Shore for carrying messages between the accused conspirators. All the close friends of the late king are under suspicion, as is the dowager queen. Fortunately Dr Caerleon has carried only verbal messages between Elizabeth and me and so he and I have escaped suspicion.

Written in haste at Stanley House on this fourteenth day of June, 1483

P S fifteenth day of June: God be praised my lord has been released without charge or forfeit. He wisely swore an oath of loyalty to Gloucester and miraculously not only achieved his freedom but also retains all his honours and estates including his office as Steward of the Royal Household. However, poor Jane Shore is sentenced to make a walk of shame through the streets of London in her shift, carrying a penitential taper and must pay a crippling fine but I truly believe both she and your stepfather are lucky to have escaped with their lives. I pray for the soul of Lord Hastings, so unjustly and heinously murdered. The late King Edward must be turning in his grave. MR

A week after receiving this letter we received a message from Duke Francis to inform us that Richard, Duke of Gloucester had caused a sermon to be preached at St Paul's Cross in London, declaring the marriage of the late King Edward and Elizabeth Woodville to be invalid owing to the existence of a previous contract between him and a lady called Eleanor Butler, daughter of the Earl of Shrewsbury. Edward and Elizabeth's children were pronounced illegitimate and their son therefore ineligible to be crowned king. The following day representatives of the Lords and Commons had petitioned Richard to take the throne as the legitimate heir.

Ned Woodville, Davy and I listened open-mouthed as Lord Jasper read this message aloud. 'Can this really be true?' I demanded when his recital drew to a close. 'Where has this evidence of a pre-contract come from? Were witnesses produced? I cannot believe it to be true.'

'It is not true,' cried Ned, puce with anger, 'if it was, why has it not come to light earlier? Edward and Elizabeth were lawfully married by a priest and before witnesses. Their marriage was recognised and judged valid by Parliament and she is a crowned Queen Consort. Where is this woman who is supposed to be Edward's true wife? Conveniently dead. Where is the evidence of this pre-contract? There is none. It is a wicked invention. The truth is that Richard of Gloucester's overweening pride cannot bear to see a boy with Woodville blood wear the crown of England. If we lacked a good reason to invade before, now we have one. Young Edward is the legitimate heir and Gloucester is a traitor, a tyrant and a usurper!'

29

Margaret

**Stanley House and Westminster Abbey, London,
June/July 1483**

THOMAS FOUND ME IN the chapel of our London house
when he returned from Westminster Palace after dark
at the end of June. During those days of turmoil and confusion I was spending more and more of my time at prayer,
yet the more I prayed the less my prayers were answered. I
felt as if the Almighty was determined to test my faith to
the limit, little knowing He had only just begun.

I did not hear my husband enter the chapel, or if I did
I ignored the sound of footsteps, assuming them to be some
supplicant member of the household coming, like me, to
lay his troubles before God and His saints. When someone
knelt beside me on the Prie Dieu reserved for the head of
the household I turned, ready to scold the intruder and was
surprised to see Thomas's bearded profile outlined in the
light of the altar candles against the stone wall of the chancel.

Close to, I was shocked at the pallor of his cheeks, more commonly a healthy pink.

'Blessed Marie my lord, are you ill?' I asked anxiously. Although we were alone, the presence of the Holy Spirit kept my voice at a low pitch.

His voice trembled in reply. 'Not ill, Margaret, but angry. I have come here for guidance.'

'What troubles you, Thomas? Am I at fault?' I feared he might have discovered my secret exchange of messages with the dowager queen.

He made the sign of the cross and stood up, holding out his hand to raise me. 'Not as far as I know. Come, let us sit and talk, here under divine benevolence. First and foremost, I have terrible news to impart.'

I felt a sharp pain knife through my heart. 'Not Henry, Thomas? Dear God, not my son!'

As I swayed to my feet, clutching at his gown in panic, his hand closed on my arm to steady me. 'No, no; as far as I know he is well. This news concerns the Woodvilles.' He led me to the stone bench that ran along the chapel wall, providing seating for the weak and lame. From Blackfriars' Church the Vespers bell began to toll, echoing mournfully across the lane that ran down to the Thames at St Paul's Wharf.

He kept his voice quiet and even. 'Four days ago Earl Rivers and Sir Richard Grey were beheaded at Pontefract Castle.'

'Oh dear Lord Jesu,' I said, my hand fluttering to my chest where my heart had begun to beat at double speed. 'Gloucester?' I asked, faintly.

Thomas nodded. 'Doubtless, although the Duke of

Northumberland was appointed to hold a trial – of sorts. The charge was treason, the jury certainly rigged and the verdict guilty. Sentence of execution took place on the following day.'

'Oh poor Meg Poyntz! She has lost her beloved father and in such an unjust and violent way. And little Mary FitzLewis has lost her husband, to say nothing of Elizabeth who mourns a brother and a son and her royal children who all loved their Uncle Anthony. So many bereaved and for what?'

'For being upstart commoners who reached for the stars and got burnt by the sun. The Woodvilles' comet has lost its tail.'

I made to rise. 'I should go to Mary. She does not know that she is a widow, even before becoming a true wife.'

When Mary reached the canonical age I had agreed to Earl Rivers's offer of marriage in order to protect her lands but stipulated that she should remain with me until I judged her ready to set up a household and consummate the marriage. Child though she still was, I knew she would be devastated by Rivers's death for she adored her dashing spouse, just as she had his daughter Meg, in the schoolroom at Coldharbour.

Thomas laid a hand on my arm. 'Before you go Margaret, I need to ask you something. When I made my oath of loyalty to Richard of Gloucester, he demanded that I vouch for yours as well. It is vitally important now that I am not forsworn because Richard sees conspiracy at every turn. Please assure me that you have had no communication with Elizabeth Woodville or any of her party since she took sanctuary.'

I swallowed hard, staring at him and feeling the eyes of all the saints represented in the chapel focused on me. I did not want to burden Thomas with my actions but how could I lie to him in God's house, under the image of Christ on the Cross?

'I dearly wish you had not vouched for me my lord,' I said softly. 'I have been exchanging messages with Elizabeth regarding the proposed marriage between her daughter and my son through the offices of our mutual physician, Dr Caerleon. But they have all been verbal. There is nothing in writing.'

For a moment I thought he might strike me. His face contused and his right fist clenched but his hand did not rise off his thigh. 'By the Holy Rood, Margaret! – if Richard ever discovers this we are both headed for the Tower and I am a dead man. What have you done? And why did you not tell me?'

'Because you would have reacted just as you have now. How was I to know you were going to vow loyalty to a usurper?'

My voice had risen with indignation and he cast a hasty glance around the chapel, which fortunately remained empty apart from us.

'Sssh,' he snarled through clenched teeth. 'I used the only way I knew to preserve my family's lives and livelihood. Richard has agreed to take the crown, he is in command and if we do not want to be accused of treason we have to swear our loyalty. It is the only way to survive this upheaval, Margaret, believe me. I have spent the last twenty years holding the ground between Lancaster and York, without letting either think that I support anyone but them. In fact the Stanleys are for neither. We are for Stanley. At today's council meeting we approved the arrangements for Richard's coronation, which will test our loyalty even further. As Royal Steward I will be carrying the mace, while you will have the honour of being the queen's trainbearer and at the banquet you will be seated at her left hand.'

I felt the blood drain from my face. 'Thomas I cannot! The world will believe I have abandoned my son and taken up the cause of a tyrant – worse, Henry himself will believe it!'

'Then let them – let him.' Lord Stanley was adamant. 'We have no choice in this, Margaret. Our coronation robes are already being made.'

'You forget that as well as being for Stanley I am first and foremost for Henry,' I insisted. 'My son can never trust the word of a man who uses lies and deception to steal the throne of his own nephew, so how can he ever return to claim his rightful lands and title while Richard of York wears the crown? Queen Elizabeth is right. For our children's sake we have to contest this absurd claim that Edward of York's marriage was not valid and restore the rightful king to his throne. She is already making plans with her followers.'

Thomas lost patience, forsook his warning for quiet and stood up, pacing the figured floor-tiles of the chapel and raising his voice to echo off the ceiling vaults. 'Do you still not understand, madam? Elizabeth is no longer Queen Dowager or even Queen Mother. Her followers are minnows. She commands no power!' He stopped in front of me, glaring into my face to be sure I understood before continuing the dreadful tirade. 'Even her own son, Dorset, has abandoned her and managed to take ship, aiming to join Henry in

Brittany, I presume.' Another glare at me, to be sure I was listening. 'Parliament has accepted the word of our old friend Bishop Stillington of Bath and Wells as witness to the pre-contract of marriage with Eleanor Butler that renders Edward's marriage to Elizabeth Woodville invalid and all their issue illegitimate. Richard of Gloucester is to be crowned king in Westminster Abbey in ten days' time and there are no lords prepared to risk their necks to contest the legality of it.'

I rose to confront him and felt my fiercely guarded control also slip. 'I understand completely, my lord! On the word of a demented old bishop who will say anything in return for a fee or a living, the lords and commons have offered Richard of Gloucester the throne of England. And now, to save our skins, we have to fool him into thinking he has our support but I for one will never cease to consider him anything other than a treasonous tyrant.'

I clasped my hands together and fell to my knees at Thomas's feet. 'As your wife I am sworn to obey you and I will carry the false queen's train and share her coronation cup and make her think I support her husband's throne. But I declare here and now, my lord, in the presence of God and in His holy house, that in my mind and my heart I will never owe my loyalty to Richard of Gloucester as king.'

He took a deep breath and let it out slowly. His burst of temper seemed to have evaporated. 'Then who commands it, Margaret?' he asked.

I made some careful mental calculations before answering. 'War and executions have wrought havoc with the succession and through my father, John, Duke of Somerset, I believe I now possess the most direct Lancastrian bloodline, which

I have passed to my son. And so it is to Henry Tudor that I owe my loyalty and while we both breathe I will never cease to support his claim to the earldom of Richmond and, ultimately, to the English throne.'

Thomas's expression was bleak as he bent to raise me to my feet then he set his lips to my ear to whisper his next words. 'If you discount Stillington's evidence, which I gather you do, there are two boys in the Tower of London who some might say have a far better claim than Henry.'

I heaved a great sigh, my heart like lead in my chest. 'But are they still there, my lord? And if they are I warrant it is only until Richard is safely crowned. One of Elizabeth's sons has already gone to the block under his rule and Doctor Caerleon has described to me her constant fear that Richard means deadly harm to all her sons. That is why Dorset has fled abroad.'

My husband nodded sombrely. 'You may be right, Margaret, about Richard. Meanwhile I thank God that at least you have acknowledged that we must dissemble to survive.'

I wondered if my appointment as Queen Anne's trainbearer might have been intended as some form of penance because her purple-velvet, ermine-trimmed mantle had a twenty-seven-yard train and weighed far more than I could lift. Fortunately eight young damsels supported the sides but even so it tended to drag along the priceless Persian carpets laid along the route, as the procession moved at a snail's pace through the Great Court of the palace, while the soon-to-be-crowned monarchs acknowledged the cheers of a fawning crowd of Londoners. The coronation of King

Richard the Third may have been hastily prepared but it was nevertheless splendidly ostentatious. Every member of the attendant nobility taking part in the procession which escorted the new king and queen from Westminster Hall to the Abbey under golden canopies of state was provided with a gold coronet and a crimson velvet mantle lined with white cloth of gold.

After the anointing, shielded from view by another lavishly embroidered cloth of state supported by a group of high-ranking ladies from which I was grateful to have been excluded, her damsels removed Anne's purple mantle and replaced it with one of cloth of gold for the crowning ceremony. The train of this garment, although shorter, proved considerably heavier. Carrying it under the heat of the summer sun as we made our way back to the Great Hall, where as many as three thousand people were due to witness the coronation banquet, I perspired so much myself that I could feel little sympathy for the glistening brow of the new queen, weighed down by her gold mantle, crown and sceptre. To keep up my strength I mused on the irony that the Earl of Warwick, the self-styled Kingmaker, should have missed this grand occasion when his daughter Anne finally received a crown, he who had turned his coat from York to Lancaster and ultimately given his life in battle attempting to place his Neville blood on the throne.

30

Harri

Château Suscinio, Brittany, September 1483

IN EARLY SEPTEMBER, WHEN three messengers from England had arrived at Suscinio within days of each other, each carrying considerable sums of money and more or less the same message, I realised that the end of my exile might at last be in sight. I also realised that the stakes had risen dramatically, for my lady mother no longer intended that I should return to England merely to claim my earldom.

> *To my very dear and honoured son Henry Tudor, Earl of Richmond, from his mother Margaret, Countess of Richmond, greetings.*
>
> *London is throbbing with rumours that King Edward's two young sons are dead. They have not been seen anywhere in the Tower precincts for weeks. Attempts to rescue them by supporters of the late King Edward have been violently suppressed and the usurper has made no*

attempt to show the boys to the people. It was he who placed them in that fortress and he who is responsible for their health and safety and yet he remains silent as to their whereabouts and makes no effort to demonstrate their continued existence. There is no alternative but to assume that their 'disappearance' has been on his orders. Their mother is distraught as you may imagine.

You do not need me to point out that their removal from the line of succession would move our Lancastrian claim to a pre-eminent position and with the kingdom in crisis it is to you, Henry, that the people will look to restore the realm to order and justice and to God's good grace. Stirred by the rumours, lifelong Yorkists are deserting the usurper and he has had to call an army down from the north to protect his throne. Even his close ally, the Duke of Buckingham, has joined the ranks of those who cannot tolerate his reign.

It is time to load your ships and land with Lord Jasper in Wales, where men of many affinities are ready to rally to the dragon banner. Bishop Morton of Ely is also calling on his tenants to respond and men are committed in Kent, Wiltshire and the West Country. The trumpets will sound on the last day of October. You do not have much time.

I beg that you ignore the news you might hear that I have shown my support for the usurper by attending his poor queen at their coronation. Like many who dissemble at court, Lord Stanley and I are preserving our position but rest assured, my most noble and beloved son, that all my powers and prayers are dedicated to you and to your blood-right to lead the people of England from the *darkness of tyranny into the peace of justice and divine favour. On the day of your crowning I will be the first to pay you homage.*

May God distinguish our cause, MR

I looked up from reading this letter and Hugh Conway, one of Lord Stanley's clerks and the bearer of the letter, dropped to his knee before me. 'As your lady mother's chosen envoy, my lord, may I pledge my own loyalty and offer whatever service you may need to further your expedition,' he said. 'There are many thousands in England who join me in praying that you will lead us in ridding our country of the Yorkist tyrant.'

I frowned at him in bewilderment. 'I would be amazed if there are hundreds in England who know of my existence, Master Conway, let alone thousands ready to fight with me. The name Tudor can hardly be a byword in the inns and alehouses. Please rise. I have done nothing yet to gain my earldom, let alone a throne.'

As the messenger got to his feet, Lord Jasper strode forward. 'I have not yet read the letter, Harri, but judging by the contents of Master Conway's strong-box, Lady Margaret has serious expenditure in mind. Let me be the first to take encouragement from her ambassador and endorse his pledge.' He, too, dropped to his knee and kissed my hand. 'I do not bend to a fellow earl or to my much-loved nephew but to the man who will be the next king of England. In allowing the devil to put his acolyte on the throne, God has sent a sign, which we cannot ignore. I vow my loyalty and every breath in my body to you and to the cause we will pursue together – the destruction of Richard of Gloucester, and the birth of a new dynasty with the reign of King Henry the Seventh!'

There were tears in his eyes as he spoke his vow and his words obviously stirred a chord in Davy and Ned because they moved forward from the window seat where they had been playing cards.

'What is all the fuss about, Harri?' asked Davy as my uncle rose with a grunt and, requesting permission with a raised eyebrow, took the letter from me.

'You should keep up, Davy Owen,' my uncle said sternly. 'We may all be putting to sea before too long.'

'That cannot come too soon for me,' remarked Ned. 'The sooner we kill the hog the better as far as I am concerned.' It was from Ned I had learned that Richard of Gloucester used a silver boar as his personal badge.

'Even if he is replaced by me?'

For a moment my question seemed to stun the Yorkist in him but he recovered himself, grinned and made me a bow. 'There could be no better man, Harri. But you will need a few more supporters than just me, your old uncle and this young upstart.' Davy skilfully dodged his attempted cuff on the ear.

Hugh Conway had listened to this exchange with a puzzled frown. As a former squire of King Edward's household, he recognised Ned. 'Your brother-in-law, the late king, would not have stood for such levity at a time of crisis, Sir Edward. I think you, too, should read Lady Margaret's letter.'

Ned flushed angrily at the implied censure. 'It will be a weird day when I take advice from a servant, whatever-your-name-is!'

I bristled at this. Although an amusing companion, I had

quickly learned that Ned could be full of hubris. 'Nevertheless you should take his advice, Sir Edward,' I told him, adopting formal address. 'Master Conway has brought this letter and a considerable weight of coin all the way from England. He is a man who has my mother's full trust and therefore mine. Besides, the letter contains news particularly abhorrent to anyone bearing the name Woodville. Read it sir! Or if you have not the ability, perhaps my uncle will read it to you.'

Having vented my disapproval, I turned my back. If I was to take men and ships to England to join a rebellion I would certainly need Ned's skill at navigation, but each one of those men would have to understand that a certain level of courtesy was essential between fellow travellers. We were no longer boys to use banter at all times. Perhaps I was just beginning to realise that myself.

Later that week Lord Jasper and I made the journey to Vannes, where Duke Francis was hearing petitions. When we gained an audience on the evening of our arrival I was disappointed to find that Pierre Landais was also in attendance. I had been astonished when he rode to my rescue in St Malo, because he had been the chief instigator of my repatriation to England, but I had been grateful. Nevertheless I did not welcome his presence at this crucial meeting when I intended to ask for the duke's help in staging an invasion. Such a mission would require considerable financial input and Landais had a tight grip on the Breton purse strings. However, again to my surprise, it was the Treasurer who persuaded the duke that my request for ships and men would be a worthwhile investment for Brittany.

'While Master Tudor and his co-conspirators keep King Richard busy at home, your grace, we will not have to fear

English interference in Brittany,' he pointed out. 'He will land his men and then our ships can patrol the Channel and we will win a welcome respite from English pirates harrying our fishermen and merchants.'

'And furthermore, when the present usurper is defeated, there will be a man on the throne of England with much gratitude and goodwill towards Brittany,' Lord Jasper reminded them, putting an avuncular hand on my shoulder. 'Is that not so, my Lord of Richmond?' He placed stern emphasis on the title and shot a gimlet glance at Landais, who had not used it.

Duke Francis took the hint and nodded sagely. 'Lord Jasper is right, Henri. Apart from offering us goodwill in the future, it would be wise to assume your title now, if you mean to lead an invasion force with intent to conquer. For a conquest is what it will be, is it not? And a man who wishes to command the respect of such an army needs to display nobility, as well as military skill.'

Hearing the true nature of my intentions voiced so bluntly gave me a jolt. 'If I do display military skill it is greatly thanks to you, my uncle and the Marshal de Rieux, your grace, but let me assure you that any financial and maritime aid you are prepared to provide will be reimbursed when the usurper is unseated.'

'Of which I have no doubt.' The duke smiled, silencing with a wave of his hand his Treasurer's loud demand that he get this assurance in writing. 'The Henri I know is a man of his word. I will see that at least ten great vessels are placed at your disposal in Paimpol Bay before the middle of October. That will only leave you with the recruitment of enough fighting men and provision of supplies and ordnance, for which I shall pay and require reimbursement. I will not charge for the use of the ships and there is a special gift I would like to present to you personally before you leave. One that I feel is well overdue. That is the honour of knighthood. Before you embark on your hazardous expedition I invite you to the Chapel of St Michael the Archangel in Auray, where I wish to install you as a member of the Breton Order of the Ermine.'

It was when, two weeks later, Duke Francis struck my shoulder with his fist and fastened the gold collar of the Order of the Ermine around my neck that I truly felt the significance of the task I was about to undertake. Until then I had found it hard to believe that the years I had spent in the duchy would ever lead to anything other than a life without purpose or achievement. At times it had been hard to keep up my study and training when contemplating years stretching ahead while I stagnated like a hostage cabbage. In fact, had it not been for my faith in God, the guidance of Lord Jasper and the companionship of Davy Owen, I do not think I could even have begun to fulfil my mother's demands for leadership and action. Along with the encouragement of my family, I owed so much to the friendship and generosity of Duke Francis that I had come to consider him part of it. During our procession from the Order's chapel at Auray back to Vannes I rode beside the duke and made a point of singing the praises of him and his duchy, reminding him of the diffident youth that he, and it, had rescued from drowning in the lonely sea of exile.

His response brought a lump to my throat. 'As you know, Henri, I have two illegitimate sons, but you are to me like the legitimate heir I have not achieved and look likely never to get. It is in that frame of mind that I have knighted you and equipped you to seek your throne but let me tell you it is like cutting my own flesh to send you off on such a dangerous mission. I have no doubt that yours is a worthy cause and that you will find much support when you land in England but none will pray harder for your success than Duchess Marguerite and I. We both look upon you as part of the Breton nation and part of our ducal family and hope that when you sit on the throne of England you will look back with affection on your time with us.'

I reached across the gap between our horses and took his free hand, bowing over it to kiss the soft leather of his riding glove. 'Of that there is no doubt, your grace,' I said with feeling, 'and I will take the Breton Saint Armel with me for protection and intercession. If I am successful I will build a shrine to the saint close to the seat of my government and every time I visit it I will pray for the health and continued prosperity of Brittany and all of its people but especially for you, who showed me how a nation should be ruled.'

While our hands were linked our horses plodded serenely on and for several seconds I studied the duke's face, so much older now than I remembered, lined with pain from his recurring illness, his hair iron-grey and thinning under his velvet hat. He turned our hands and bent to kiss my gloved knuckles in return. I could see tears in his eyes but there was a wide smile on his face. 'Well, we've kept the damned French out of Brittany so far, Henri, and I stopped your enemies in England from taking you back. Now all we have to do is get you onto the throne of England and we will each have a lifelong ally across the Channel. I could not ask for more from the drowned rat that the monks dragged from the sea at Le Conquet!'

I forgave his exaggerated description of our landing in Finis Terre because it was not so far from the truth. Our hands parted and I asked, 'Will you come and see us off at Paimpol, your grace? We could certainly do with your blessing.'

But he shook his head and brushed an escaped tear off his cheek. 'No my dear friend, I cannot do that. I would shame myself by weeping more tears than are in the ocean. You have my blessing when you wear your Ermine collar. May St Michael bring you all the courage you will need.'

'Admiral' Ned had experience in such matters as victualling ships and I left them to him; Lord Jasper took charge of marshalling the Breton mercenaries into a coherent force on the flatlands around Château Suscinio, where they also made camp. Fortunately the weather during September proved warm and dry so the troops were happy enough with their lot, even when they were told they would be making a three-day march across Brittany's Black Mountains to reach their port of embarkation. Despite Ned's protests, Lord Jasper and I resolved not to take horses across the Channel, especially in view of our brush with shipwreck on our journey from Wales. I had no wish to risk Bastion, or any other valuable horse, on the seas we had encountered then and it was decided that, along with another contingent of fighting men I would request mounts to be provided for those who required them from the West Country estates of my lady mother. Despite her recommendation that we land in Wales, Ned and I planned a more direct course across the Channel from Paimpol to Exmouth, a port he knew well and a strategically suitable destination. Edward Courtenay, a scion of the attainted Courtenay earls of Devon, and his cousin Peter, Bishop of Exeter were committed to raising a force in and around that cathedral city, which was only a few miles inland from our chosen port. From there we could march to a rendezvous with Buckingham and continue towards London, wholly expecting the usurper to block our path and give battle.

I had given much thought as to why Henry Stafford, Duke of Buckingham had become involved in the conspiracy. As a child of five years he became the ward of the new king, Edward of York, at the death of his staunchly Lancastrian grandfather, and had been brought up in the royal household. When Elizabeth Woodville became queen she had taken the young duke's wardship and married him to her youngest sister, Catherine. It seemed sensible to consult Ned Woodville on the subject, who was Catherine's older brother, and I caught him before he left for Paimpol, over a flagon of Rennish wine after supper.

'That was a toxic marriage from the start, Harri,' he confided. 'Catherine was only eight and young Stafford eleven and he was a loud-mouthed boy, who told anyone who would listen that he had been foisted with a minion for a wife, a nonentity, a commoner who should never have been matched with a royal duke. Of course he was soon put in his place by King Edward but the damage had been done and Catherine never forgave him.'

I knitted my brows. 'But the marriage was consummated was it not? There are children I believe.'

'Oh yes, my sister is a well-brought up young lady and knows her duty. They have two boys and two girls, the

312

perfect set – but not the perfect union by any means. True, my sister enjoys the trappings of being a duchess, but she avoids being in the same castle as her husband these days, let alone the same bed.'

'So why would Buckingham be joining a rebellion instigated by the dowager queen, who is, after all, a Woodville?'

Ned blew out his cheeks but his look was serious. 'Well, he rarely loses an opportunity to remind people that three of his great grandparents were direct descendants of King Edward the Third. He has a claim to the throne some might consider stronger than yours, Harri, so I would imagine that he sees himself as the leader of this rebellion and believes that he will be the one to take the throne as a result.'

This certainly gave me food for thought. 'Why then are you here supporting me, Ned? Should you not be in England, giving your brother-in-law the benefit of your fighting spirit?'

'I am a Woodville, remember, the hog would have my head off if he caught me in England.' He took a big gulp of the strong red wine and set down his cup. 'Buckingham is a buffoon, Harri,' he went on, with conviction. 'I would not give him the benefit of a kick up the arse. Well, perhaps that is the only thing I might give him.' He grinned at me over his neat beard and fixed his brown eyes on my face. 'If the murdering usurper is to be given his marching orders to hell, the king that replaces him has to be a man of intelligence and spirit who can mend the damage Richard has done to England's soul and reputation. Your blood-claim may not be better than his but your claim on those two counts most definitely is!'

For several seconds I held his gaze, twisting my mouth in deliberation, then raised my cup in salute. 'Not quite an oath of loyalty, Ned, but it will do for now,' I said, and took a ruminative sip. I found it dispiriting, to say the least, to be entering into a rebellion in which it was possible our success in removing one man from the throne would result in conflict over who occupied it next.

Having feared for my life on the only sea voyage I had previously made, even the first stage of the rebellion held its terrors, due to the vagaries of weather in the Channel. The fishing port of Paimpol was tucked in behind one of the most northerly headlands of Brittany and it offered a haven for shipping of all kinds seeking shelter from Channel storms. Many a prayer of thanks had been offered there to the Archangel Michael, protector of soldiers and the Leader of the Army of God against Evil who also gave protection against storms at sea. Michael was also the Order of the Ermine's patron saint. To ensure his approval, we had intended to leave port on the saint's Feast Day, September the twenty-ninth, but shortly before this I had received a letter from the Duke of Buckingham, graciously inviting me to join his rebellion, which was scheduled to break out simultaneously in various areas of southern England on the eighteenth of October. It was the first direct communication I had received from Buckingham and Lord Jasper and I had agreed it would be wise to adhere to his timetable, for fear of jeopardising it by landing too soon and alerting the usurper's coastal watch.

However, just before the agreed date we received news of various rebel outbreaks in England's southern counties including a rising in Devon, where we intended making landfall, and so we set sail a few days early. Our flotilla of twelve ships headed out of Paimpol Bay on a brisk south-westerly breeze, the early morning sun shining, mariners calling cheerfully to each other in the rigging. The wind in the sails sounded to me like a flock of starlings coming to roost, a reassuring, business-like noise, full of confidence and purpose.

In those favourable conditions of wind and sea we could expect a swift crossing but it was a false impression of weather set fair. Within an hour the wind had veered violently to the northeast and a gale howled in behind us, throwing huge waves over the ship's stern and defying our helmsman's efforts safely to turn the bow into its raging onslaught. Freezing rain battered the sails, ripping through the slightest weak spot in any canvas. Davy was with me and, echoing childhood memories of our last sea voyage, our ship was swept westwards, out of control, remaining afloat only by total submission to the hurricane and because there were no islands in mid-Channel to cause a shipwreck.

I knelt, clinging to a stanchion in the aftcastle cabin, praying to my patron saints and to the Virgin of the Sea, who had answered the desperate Ave Marias of Jasper's daughter Sian in similar circumstances twelve years before. Again and again I asked the Almighty why He had delivered us into mortal danger even before we had attempted the perilous task we had set ourselves. Was it His way of telling me that I was presumptuous to even contemplate assuming the throne of a country I had not set foot in for all those years and about which I knew so little? Could He intend to scuttle our venture by sending us all instead to an ignominious and watery grave?

I received no answers to these questions but neither did our ship sink. However, when the storm abated and visibility improved only one other ship of the twelve that had formed our flotilla was in sight. Whether the others were lost or had managed to turn back to the Breton coast it was impossible to know and my only personal consolation was that the other storm-battered vessel proved to be that captained by Lord Jasper. Together we headed for the coastline now visible on the horizon and the sailors from Ned's English ships, who had been spread among all the crews of the flotilla, recognised the long tail of land protruding into the sea as Start Point on the southern tip of Devon. Steering clear of the treacherous rocks surrounding it, we hove to in the lee of the cliffs while temporary repairs were made and Lord Jasper and I held a conference, shouting from one aftcastle to the other.

'We are too far west, Harri,' he yelled. 'Plymouth Sound is the best bet now. We could wait there for a while to see if any of the other ships arrive.'

'My guess is they managed to turn back,' I shouted back. 'We cannot wait too long or we might find ourselves blockaded. I would like to send a recce party onshore for news but we will need to get nearer to a town.'

'Plymouth is the place then but it is risky because the coastguard may be on the lookout for us.'

'It is worth a try though.'

The waters of Plymouth Sound were quiet as dusk fell. We lowered a boat manned by eight mariners detailed to assess the situation onshore, three of them English. I warned them not to land unless they were certain it was safe. The boat was in sight until it entered the walled harbour and we waited on tenterhooks for it to reappear; soon it did, with only five men at the oars, rowing furiously.

When they were winched up the leader came to report, a Breton sailor called Yves, chosen for his quick thinking. 'There were some men on the quayside, my lord. They looked like fishermen and we asked if they had heard anything about an uprising but they said all was quiet and did we want to come ashore? Then four of us jumped onto the quay, including English Wat. I could understand what was said but did not let on and left the talking to him. It seemed there had been an uprising and that Exeter was under siege. Wat asked if they knew anything about the Duke of Buckingham and they said he was on the way to meet the Breton ships here at Plymouth.'

I interrupted. 'But Buckingham was expecting us at Exmouth.'

Yves nodded. 'Just so my lord. I yelled at the lads to get back on the boat but they were not quick enough and by the time I was on board the fake fishermen had put knives to their throats and yelled that they were under arrest. We just rowed for our lives. I am sorry sir, there were not enough of us to take them on.'

'No, you did right, Yves. We must weigh anchor immediately. The other men may be held prisoner but we will get them back.'

With a heavy heart I wrote a note to Lord Jasper with brief details and had it fired over to his ship by one of the crack archers. Although it was almost dark we could not delay departure now. Our part in 'Buckingham's' rebellion – if there had ever been one – was over.

31

Margaret

Stanley House, London, November 1483

THE FIRST TEMPEST WAS the prelude to a series of ever more violent storms that brought unprecedented rainfall in the west, flooded the river Severn and washed away crops and livestock. Descriptions of the death and destruction were horrific, telling of bodies floating in the fields and houses being carried out to sea. The Duke of Buckingham lost most of his rebel army, men deserting to return to their devastated villages and farms, rather than fight in a deluge. Forced into hiding, he was betrayed by a retainer he had believed to be loyal but who could not resist the thousand-pound bounty offered. Taken by the Sheriff of Shropshire to Salisbury, where the usurper Richard had based his headquarters, the duke was quickly tried and found guilty of treason, taken to the marketplace and beheaded in public. Richard refused him a last meeting, unprepared to face the cousin he had so long thought his loyal friend.

It was several weeks before I discovered how close my

beloved son had also come to being the usurper's prisoner and doubtless his next candidate for the block. I truly believe my constant petitions to God and His saints for Henry's protection led him to exercise laudable caution on his arrival at Plymouth, but I could not write to him with praise and consolation because by then I was a prisoner myself. My gaoler was my husband, appointed by the man who still called himself king.

'There will be no more dissembling at court for you, Margaret,' Thomas told me flatly when he returned from what must have been an exhausting audience with Richard soon after his return to Westminster Palace. 'There is to be a Parliament in the New Year which will pass Acts of attainder against all those you conspired with and it is only Richard's desperate need to count on my support that has saved you from being on the list. He knows you were a prime instigator of the rebellion but he let himself be persuaded that you are merely a silly misguided woman and not responsible for your own actions. He berated me for not keeping you under control. I was surprised he was able to resist calling you a witch.'

'He did not hold back from pinning that label on poor Jane Shore,' I observed bitterly, pacing to and fro and trying to conceal my genuine terror of what else he might be about to tell me. 'Richard – the youth who sought so eagerly to charm the ladies – has become as warped as his spine! Oh I know he thinks to hide his disfigurement from the world but Edward used to joke about it, in his cups. "My twisted little brother," he would jeer, "loyal – but deformed!"'

'Be silent Margaret!' Thomas raged. 'I refuse to have gone to the trouble of saving you from the block, only to hear you gabbling treason like a brainless gossip! For Jesu's sake sit down, hold your tongue and *listen* woman!'

Abruptly I stopped my pacing and turned to stare at him. 'He wanted to send me to the block? A woman?'

He grabbed my arm roughly and led me to a chair. 'A very powerful woman, Margaret – and one he knows will go to any lengths for her only son. You and he have that in common at least. Now, sit down and I will tell you what he *has* sentenced you to.'

I listened, head down and wringing my hands, as he outlined my dismal future. I was to be stripped of all my properties and estates, all my servants were to be dismissed and my ranks and privileges revoked. 'And from now on you are committed to my custody, to be known only as my wife. Not Margaret Beaufort, Countess of Richmond but just plain Lady Stanley. I know that will hurt.' He ended on a rueful note.

'How long is this sentence to last, Thomas?' I asked, furious and heartsick at the thought of losing my high-ranking title, my treasured legacy from Edmund Tudor, granted to me by two previous kings.

He gazed down at me, sympathy softening his expression. 'Forever, Margaret. This is a life sentence.'

With my eyes closed, I gave thought to this blunt state-ment for several moments. 'But for whose life, Thomas?' I queried at length. 'Mine or his?'

He bent over me, placed a finger under my chin and lifted my face to his. 'That is in God's hands,' he said and pressed his lips briefly to my unresponsive mouth. 'But I know where my wager would go. Meanwhile let us thank God that the thousands of loyal Stanley supporters in the northwest make me essential to Richard's grip on the throne, so please, for the time being do not jeopardise that – Lady Stanley.'

Another thought occurred to me. 'My servants are to be dismissed you said. What will happen to them? Especially those who have helped me so loyally – Reginald Bray, Richard Guildford, Christopher Urswicke; and my women – Kitty Bray, Mary Rivers, Kate Vaux and her daughter Joan? Where will they all go? How will they all live?'

Thomas took another chair. 'The men will probably sue for pardon or else they will flee to Brittany and join Henry. The women can simply move from your household account to mine. Actually, I think I might recommend your friend Kate to poor Queen Anne as a Lady of the Bedchamber. She has much experience at serving a distressed queen.'

I frowned, temporarily distracted from my own woes. 'Why is Queen Anne distressed? Is she ill?'

He pursed his lips. 'I think Richard tires of her, and she does not look well. He wants her to take the Woodville girls under her wing and she is not keen.'

'The Woodville girls? You mean his nieces – Elizabeth and her sisters? Are they coming out of sanctuary?' Attainted I may have been but I had not lost sight of Elizabeth of York as the ideal wife for Henry; a marriage to join the Houses of Lancaster and York – the ultimate union for peace.

'Richard wants to lure them out. He thinks if they come willingly into his care, people will no longer believe he can be responsible for their brothers' deaths.'

'Ha!' My laugh in response to that was brittle. 'But he sits on the throne! They disappeared on his usurping watch. He *is* responsible. The people are not so gullible surely?'

Thomas shrugged. 'They are easily cowed. They will see the hangings at Tyburn of the commoners involved in the rebellion and they will no longer dare to question the king's actions.'

'I do not feel cowed,' I declared roundly. 'I will never cease to work for Henry's cause. You do know that?'

He sighed and nodded slowly. 'Yes, I do and I know you are desperate to continue exchanging correspondence with Henry but we must be very careful.' He pulled at his beard in the way he always did when pondering. 'Richard genuinely does think all women are feeble and brainless so why do you not use your women to help you? Mary for instance could go and visit Meg Poyntz in Gloucestershire. She is her stepmother after all and no one would see conspiracy in that. And Robert Poyntz is not on the attainted list so he has somehow slipped out of range. He must know merchants in Bristol who will carry messages to Brittany. Lady Vaux could pass on information from the queen's solar and her daughter Joan might take a post as companion to the Woodville girls if they are released. But always bear in mind, Margaret, that I am your gaoler and I must be seen to keep you under strict house arrest at all times. Do not attempt to meet anyone outside or communicate personally with Elizabeth Woodville or you will throw us to the wolves.'

'I have no way of doing so now poor Doctor Caerleon is in the Tower. I hope he is not put to the question.' I knew that other participants in the recent conspiracy had been tortured for information.

'Actually you might be surprised to hear that among my rewards for loyalty, Richard is to make me Constable of England, with access to all royal castles, so you need not fear for the good doctor, Margaret. As long as I remain in favour.'

In an echo of his earlier gesture to me, I rose and crossed to where he sat, took his face between my hands and pressed my lips to his in an eloquent kiss. 'Thank you Thomas,' I said. 'I understand everything. I am your prisoner. And you are my saviour and my inspiration. May God save us both.'

Perversely the shrinking of my life under the regime ordered by the usurper inspired an increase in the mental energy I brought to Henry's cause. I had no way of knowing how he had reacted to the disappointment of the failed uprising, but I wanted urgently to assure him that his supporters in England would not cease to pursue all means of trying again. Therefore, as Thomas had suggested, I took the earliest possible opportunity to speak to Mary FitzLewis, or Lady Rivers, as she insisted on being called. I was permitted daily exercise in the garden at Stanley House and, although my own servants no longer attended me, no one prevented me crossing paths with other members of the household during this time. As Thomas had promised, my lady companions had been taken into his household and were now accommodated in chambers on the opposite side of the central court to mine. At his suggestion they made visits to the garden at the same time as I did but only one at a time and in an erratic order to avert suspicion. Pleased though I was to socialise with the others, I waited impatiently for it to be Mary's turn and wasted no time in broaching the subject uppermost in my mind.

'Although you must still be mourning your husband, Mary, I feel sure you will privately join me in wishing to encourage Lord Henry further in his endeavours,' I said cautiously.

'The failure of the Duke of Buckingham's venture must have set Henry back but I so wish to let him know that there are many people in England who would support him in ridding us of the usurper.'

Mary's pallid countenance was rendered even paler by the deep black of her mourning gown. She fingered a gold reliquary at her breast and glanced around nervously for listening ears before responding. 'I would do anything to remove the murderer of my dear lord from this world, my lady. But I am only one very young woman, with no power or influence. How could I possibly help to achieve that?'

She had stopped in our walk among the hedged knot-gardens but I moved purposefully on. Not wanting to draw attention to the earnestness of our conversation I forced a merry laugh. 'You may have more to offer than you think, Mary. How would you like to make a journey into Gloucestershire to visit Meg?'

Her face lit up and she hurried to catch me up. 'Oh I should very much like to. She has borne two little girls since I last visited her and I would love to see them. Was her husband involved in the recent troubles?'

'He was but do not speak of it abroad. I believe he has achieved a pardon but I do not know what part he played. He holds important posts in Gloucestershire and Bristol and may be irreplaceable. But if you visit them you will discover all this yourself and when you return you can tell me what you hear.'

I had always considered Joan Vaux to be my ward of sharpest intellect but Mary now proved a close second. 'You want me to be your eyes and ears in other words,' she said and I detected a thrill in her voice. 'To spy for you, my lady?'

I laughed again. 'No, no Mary – not spy exactly. As you say, to be my eyes and ears, and perhaps take a few letters to Master Poyntz, to be sent on to Brittany. This would be the greatest thing you could do for me.'

Her smile was brilliant. It banished the signs of grief and pain that had added years to her tender age. 'I would be honoured to serve you in this way, my lady. I would feel that I was, in a small way, avenging my husband's death.'

'It would not be in a small way at all, Mary,' I assured her. 'It would greatly assist me in my efforts to bring my son to his rightful inheritance. But you must promise me to be careful. Say nothing of this to anyone. Lord Stanley will arrange for you to have an escort to Meg's home at Iron Acton as soon as possible. Veil your face when you travel, for your guise as a widow will be very helpful. Men do not like to intrude on the grief of a bereaved lady. Come to the garden again in two days and I will have letters for you to carry. There will not be many for I must ration the paper I have. Who knows when I might be able to obtain more?'

She gave me an eager look. 'I could bring you more, my lady.'

I shook my head with a rueful smile and glanced briefly up at the windows overlooking the garden. I spotted no faces behind the leaded glass. 'It is too risky, Joan. Those who serve me now, if you can call their sullen presence service, are in the usurper's pay. These days spies are everywhere.'

I wrote brief notes to Meg and Robert Poyntz, earnestly seeking their help, but the longest and most important letter was penned to Henry and sealed with my heartfelt prayer for a safe passage. I saw no reason to modify our titles to satisfy the usurper.

To the much beloved and noble Henry, Earl of Richmond, whom God preserve, from his mother Margaret, Countess of Richmond.

Despite the failure of the Duke of Buckingham's attempt to unseat the usurper I beg you not to lose heart, because there remains massive support for you in England. By the time you receive this letter, many of the men involved in that ill-fated endeavour might have made their way to Brittany and will assure you that what I write is true. Even in parts of the north the usurper's popularity is waning and in the southwest and Wales it has sunk beneath the waves that almost took your ship. I thank God daily for your survival. Perhaps He was showing us that autumn is not the season to plan a Channel crossing.

By now you may have heard that many of our supporters are to be attainted for treason in a January Parliament. However, due to Lord Stanley's position as Steward of the Royal Household and his new appointment as Lord High Constable of England, I am not included, which demonstrates how much the usurper needs my lord's power in the northwest and how little he understands the fragility of his fealty. Lord Stanley now holds all my properties and estates and I am committed to his custody, with my servants dismissed, but all this means nothing because it is only temporary, until you, my dauntless son, come again with troops and trumpets.

You should know, also, that Elizabeth of York remains in sanctuary at Westminster, but the usurper hopes to lure her and his other nieces out by promising them dowries and marriages, which would jeopardise our plan to unite the royal Houses of York and Lancaster on your accession to the throne. This new threat to your marriage hopes must surely hasten your arrival once more on English soil.

My brave and honourable son, I pray and scheme every hour for the day you will sail again and, being still persuaded that a landing in Wales would be greatly to your advantage, I urge you to write personally to all your Welsh supporters and command their commitment to your cause.

I am ever your devoted Mother, MR.

Written at Stanley House, this last day of November 1483.

327

32

Harri

Château de l'Hérmine, Vannes, Brittany, 1484

THE JOURNEY BACK TO Brittany was fraught with danger and delays, giving me plenty of time and cause to agonise over the consequences of our fruitless expedition. After suffering yet another storm on leaving Plymouth, both our ships finally made safe harbour at La Hogue in Normandy but I fretted over the other vessels and their crews and passengers, concerned whether they had found shelter or foundered. I also worried about the fate of those men in England who had taken arms against the usurper. How many had died and, if they managed to flee, where had they gone? Would they any longer have respect for the Tudors who had failed so miserably to bring the promised Breton troops to their support? As well as these worries, our own immediate situation was not without danger, because the French might regard our landing in their territory as a Heaven-sent chance to detain us and take their turn at using us as hostages.

But at the end of August the old Spider King, Louis the

Eleventh, had died suddenly, and in the toil of preparing our expedition I had not fully grasped the significance of this. Louis's heir, the eighth King Charles, was only thirteen years old and there was conflict over who would act as Regent in his minority, echoing the discord that had recently thrown England into disarray. However, somehow his older half-sister, Anne de Beaujeu, had managed to gain control over the Regency Council and it was she who, to my relief, granted a safe-conduct for me, Lord Jasper and our retainers to travel overland back to Brittany. One of King Charles's household squires was even sent with money and horses for our journey. The Breton soldiers and sailors, who had found shelter in various other harbours in Normandy, were free to sail their ships back to their home-ports.

During the ride back to Vannes I brooded over what should be our next course of action. Grateful though I was for the safe passage, it occurred to me that if the French no longer thought of us as valuable hostages, then neither did they consider me a worthy contender for England's crown. And if I was now a nonentity, without power or influence, how could I hope to persuade the Duke of Brittany to support another expedition, or rally the disaffected English nobles to unite behind another bid to oust the usurper? As the days passed I grew more and more certain that my future was an empty void.

At the end of our journey, whilst changing our travel-stained apparel at the Château de l'Hérmine, Lord Jasper and I received a summons to the Great Hall. I assumed it would be to meet the duke, an encounter I did not relish, having squandered his gold and almost lost his generously loaned ships.

So although I entered the hall with my head held high, my spirits were in my boots and I could not believe the sight that greeted us. The long, vaulted chamber, normally used for formal ceremonies and banquets, was crowded with men who burst out cheering and waving their fists in salute on my appearance. I glanced back to see if someone important was walking in behind me but then I gathered, in utter astonishment, that the cheers and salutes were aimed at me. Some of the men even dropped to their knees, a gesture I found disturbing, especially in view of my recent melancholy. As I stood there, gazing about in bewilderment, Ned Woodville pushed his way forward, bringing with him a taller and bulkier man wearing a crumpled but costly fur-trimmed doublet and, conspicuously, a tarnished badge of the English Order of the Garter.

Ned said, making a courtly flourish, 'Your loyal followers and supporters greet you, my lord of Richmond. Allow me to introduce one of the most illustrious, Thomas Grey, Marquess of Dorset. He is my nephew though we are much of an age, as are you and Davy Owen, your uncle. I do not believe you can be acquainted.'

The Marquess and I exchanged bows. 'We are not, but of course I know of you, my lord, and of your remarkable military reputation,' I said. 'You are most welcome to Vannes. I hope you and your companions have been comfortably accommodated.'

Dorset made a curious noise in his throat, which I took to express dissatisfaction. 'I have been in hiding for some weeks in England, avoiding the damned usurper's spies and henchmen, and am grievously short of funds. We are camping with Sir Edward at present but I have every confidence that now you are here we might receive some credit from the local burgesses, or even a little of the duke's largesse. It is easy to grow tired of sleeping on a pallet.'

Lord Jasper entered the conversation at this point, clapping Dorset on the shoulder and nodding vigorously. 'Indeed it is, my lord, as most of us have been doing lately. But now that my nephew is back and in command things will begin to get more organised.'

I took the chance to clasp hands warmly with Ned and ask him, 'How come you are back so soon, my friend? And where did you wash up when the storm hit?'

'We managed to heave to and ride it out but getting back to harbour was not easy. There are many stories of danger and adventure to be told in this room, Harri, but first you must address the men. Most of them have yet to hear your voice or gauge your mettle and yet here they are, still full of hope and expectation, despite seeing comrades killed and leaving their families and tenants stranded. Come where you can be seen.'

He led me up to the dais, waving away servants who were setting up a trestle for dinner. Then we both turned to face the mass of men gathered below – waiting expectantly, heads close together in murmuring groups. Still with lowered voice, Ned adopted a formal tone. 'Here is your stage, my lord of Richmond. Now is your chance to rally your troops.' Then he turned and raised his voice to make an announcement to the assembled crowd. 'My lords, knights and gentlemen, he is here – the man who will dethrone the usurper. You see before you Henry Tudor, Earl of Richmond!' And with that he left the dais.

I was rooted to the spot, panic threatening, trying desperately to gather my thoughts. Before me were men of every rank from yeoman to nobility; a few may have been closet Lancastrians but most were Yorkist in allegiance and all were now rebels, outcast from their homeland. They had fled here in search of a figurehead, someone on whom they could pin their ardent hope that the usurper could be brought down and held responsible for the disappearance – probably for the murder – of their true king, Edward the Fifth. Yet I was a Lancastrian, by blood and allegiance, without experience in command or government. If I wanted their support I had to persuade them that I was not only fit to be their leader but also aware of their split loyalties and sensitive to the sacrifices they had already made to try and right the evils being perpetrated from the English throne.

I closed my eyes and sent up a prayer to St Michael for inspiration. An expectant hush fell over the assembled company, making the thumping in my chest sound as loud to me as the drums of war. Yet it had to be a voice of authority and not the echo of my fear that carried to the back of the hall.

I lifted my chin. 'Men of England – and some, I hope, of Wales!' A reassuring cheer arose from a small rear-guard. 'I greet you all with a beating heart; one that has seldom beaten under English skies but which holds them as dear as any denizen. And holds you dear, for all in this room are brothers, not in blood but in allegiance because we pursue a cause both honourable and just. That is, to rid our native land of an evil mind and a tyrannous usurper.'

I was encouraged by some shouts of approval and continued more confidently. 'In the past some of us have fought under opposing banners and may hark back to old enmities. But the present reality is worse than the dynastic struggles of the past, and we must vow to bring it to an end; to move forward to a future that is neither York nor Lancaster but both. If you will march behind my banner to establish a new order and the future peace of the realm, I will undertake to unite York and Lancaster to the satisfaction of all.

'To that end I invite you to join me and my lords of Pembroke and Dorset at Christmastide in the great cathedral of Saint Pierre in Rennes to celebrate our new alliance. I ask that there you make your oath of loyalty not only to a common cause but also to me as one who, by his birth and blood, Almighty God has purposed to occupy the throne of England.

'I in my turn will swear a solemn oath to you that once I wear the crown, I will join my Lancastrian blood with that of York by marrying the Princess Elizabeth. And before I do, it will be my bounden duty to legally erase the stain of bastardy so falsely and wickedly laid upon her and her siblings by the lies and calumny of the usurper, whose life and unlawful reign our allegiance will justly bring to an end.'

As a final gesture I raised my hands and face to Heaven in supplication to the Almighty, whose grace and divine will would be essential to me and all who chose to follow me. 'May God distinguish our cause!'

Ripples of applause had peppered my speech at various points, but there was no rousing ovation. The greatest roar arose at my promise to marry Elizabeth of York. As my lady mother had so astutely advised, the prospect of mingling the blood of the two warring royal houses would do the most to bring Yorkist support to a Lancastrian cause and thus, with God's grace, some peace to our troubled land.

Over the next weeks a growing army of English exiles established a self-supporting community in Vannes, living as lodgers with Breton families or as bands of knights and soldiers in the households of the nobles like Dorset, who had rented houses. Duke Francis generously granted pensions to a number of the higher-ranked exiles and guaranteed credit for them with the local merchants and shopkeepers. Training camps were established for weapons practice, skills were kept honed for battle with regular jousts and archery competitions and Lord Jasper and I appointed a council to debate and organise a timetable of action towards our next expedition. But I could not blame those men whose frustrations occasionally boiled over into quarrels and brawls.

We made a pilgrimage to the cathedral at Rennes and took our solemn oaths, but meanwhile I grew more and more anxious about my mother. I made frequent visits to the house of the merchant to whom the first letter from her house arrest had been delivered but to no avail, until at last and with considerable relief in early May I was able to carry away a communication from her, to read in peace. However, scrawled in haste in my mother's hand, it brought me no reassurance.

Greetings to my beloved son Henry,

My lack of trustworthy servants has made it difficult for me to smuggle letters out. My former lady companions have come under suspicion and been removed from

Stanley House and my lord is much absent. Do not assume that your stepfather is aligned against you; it is more the case that he cannot be outwardly with you. However, he is secretly depositing money at his house in Liverpool in readiness to be brought to you as soon as you indicate need of it for your next expedition, which I pray will be soon for the following reason.

Recently the usurper made a solemn oath in the presence of the court and the Mayor and Aldermen of London to protect Elizabeth Woodville's five daughters. He promises to treat them as his own kin if they will quit sanctuary and place themselves in his care – a dubious contract in view of the 'disappearance' of his two unfortunate nephews. I cannot believe this will allay their mother's fears but the offer to Elizabeth Woodville herself of a home and a pension might be enough to attract them all out of the restrictions of sanctuary where they have languished for many months. In my own confinement I admit I have some sympathy with the notion of release.

My other major concern is the truce just announced between the usurper and the Duke of Brittany. I very much fear this might indicate an imminent danger of you being handed over to England as a gesture of good faith. I wonder if you should continue to trust Duke Francis? For your own safety perhaps you should give serious consideration to crossing the border into France. Do not risk your life and freedom, my dearest son, for the sake of keeping faith with a sick man who may no longer have control of his duchy.

As ever your devoted and anxious mother, MR

335

This letter jolted me into realising that even though she was closely confined, she was better informed than I was. No word had reached me of Brittany's truce with England and this was because the duke had once more retired from public life, due to a recurrence of his malady.

I had asked the Marquess of Dorset to liaise with Pierre Landais about raising men and ships for another expedition across the Channel but he had failed to glean this crucial information at the same time. I taxed him with this in the armoury at the Château de l'Hérmine, as we prepared for our daily arms practice.

'I never got wind of it, Richmond,' Dorset responded glibly. 'To be frank I speak as little as possible to Landais. I find him a cocky bastard and tend only to cover the essentials with him. He says he has his orders from the duke for ships and men for us and I notice that recruiting is going on among the lieges. So we can be assured that our needs are being addressed.'

I bristled at his casual approach but hid my displeasure while Davy pulled my practice gambeson over my head. Once my head was free of the stiff canvas tunic however, I asked, 'Does it not occur to you, my lord, that troops might be recruited to serve more than one purpose?' He and I had not, so far at least, adopted companionable forms of address, I suspected because he was very conscious that his title outranked mine. 'For instance, if the usurper stipulated that the truce will only hold if certain exiles are returned to England, might that not include you as well as Lord Jasper and me? And in order to make the arrests might a force of some size not be needed to outnumber our own men?'

Dorset frowned fiercely. 'But you have said that the duke will never sanction such an exchange.'

I made an exasperated noise. 'Has it perhaps escaped your notice that the duke is ill, my lord? So ill that he is probably unaware of what is going on in the duchy. That was certainly the case eight years ago when I was very nearly forcibly repatriated. When the duke is ill, Brittany may not be the safe haven you and your fellow exiles believe it to be. Landais needs English support against the Breton nobles he has alienated with what they call his upstart greed and attitude. The usurper will be well aware of this and keen to take advantage.'

Dorset's complexion grew pale under the coif he had donned to protect his skull from the pressure of his helm. 'You mean I have been lured here under false pretences? I expected to find what you have found, Richmond, a welcome from a duke who is closely related to the English crown and generous to its unjustly attainted outcasts.'

I nodded patiently. 'Now perhaps you understand why it is important to glean every bit of information and insinuation you can from your meetings with Pierre Landais.' Glancing around in case of listening ears I added, 'I am thinking of sounding out the French Regent about asylum there.'

With unnecessary violence Dorset shoved one hand into a battered practice gauntlet. 'But God's blood, Richmond, the French Regent is a female!' he protested, beckoning impatiently for his squire to offer the second glove. 'No man can trust the word of a woman.'

I picked up my own gauntlets and pulled them on, turning a puzzled gaze on the Marquess. 'I am told you have fourteen children, my lord. If you cannot trust the word of your wife, are you certain they are all yours?'

I heard a smothered snort of amusement from Davy and we walked out of the armoury together, leaving Dorset fulminating as his squire buckled on his sword belt.

The following day my mother's trusted cleric Christopher Urswicke arrived in Vannes with a letter for me from Bishop Morton of Ely. At the same council meeting in the Tower of London from which Lord Hastings had last year been so distressingly dragged to the block, the usurper had accused Morton of treason and it was generally agreed among the exiles that he had only escaped execution because Richard feared to risk his soul by beheading a prelate. The usurper had sent him for house arrest under the nobleman he believed at the time to be his most faithful ally, the Duke of Buckingham, little knowing that instead Morton and the duke would plan his overthrow together. When their insurrection failed, Bishop Morton had fled to Flanders but he maintained his many contacts in the episcopal world and it was one of these who, while attending a conference in Westminster, had gleaned information of Richard's secret agreement with Landais. Being unable to get letters from my mother, Christopher had decided to confer with the Bishop in Bruges and so at Morton's urging, I made a firm decision there and then to make the break for France.

Posting Davy at the door of my chamber, I conferred with Lord Jasper in utmost secrecy, suspecting that if so much as a whisper of my intention reached Pierre Landais, there would be a detachment of guards surrounding us before we could draw a sword.

Christopher Urswicke was also present and while Jasper

scanned Morton's letter, Urswicke put a suggestion to me. 'So that you do not risk a leap in the dark, Lord Henry, the bishop suggested that I go in advance to the French Regent and acquire a promise of asylum for you,' he said. 'I could probably achieve this within ten days as I believe the court is at Langeais on the Loire at this time of year – only a four-day journey from here.'

Jasper had overheard and looked up, his brow creased in surprise. 'Langeais was King Louis's favourite château – it might be four days away for the cavalry, Master Urswicke, but it must be over two hundred miles from here.'

'Only fifty miles a day, Lord Pembroke and I will change horses.'

'Ha! I like your style,' responded my uncle, clapping the cleric on the back. 'You are far from being the usual man of the cloth.'

'I am a true Lancastrian, from the shire itself and I like a good long ride, if that is what you mean, my lord.'

'Well, you can leave tomorrow, if that suits you, Father Christopher,' I told him. 'I shall be interested to hear your opinion of Madame de Beaujeu when we next meet. I have heard she is a woman of great intelligence and guile.'

'She would have to be,' observed Lord Jasper. 'She managed to impress her father the Spider, which was not an easy task I assure you.'

'But something you also achieved during your time at the French court, I believe, uncle and which might be greatly to our advantage when we get there. I have a plan, which involves the Comte de Rieux and I think might deceive Treasurer Landais.'

33

Harri

**Château Trédion and the Brittany Forest,
September 1484**

I RECEIVED A REPLY to my message to Comte Jean; he
would meet us at Château Trédion. He was there alone;
Comtesse Françoise had sadly died three years ago and the
mansion reflected the lack of a chatelaine; where once the
windows had sparkled like diamonds and the rooms had been
fragrant with flowers, it now projected a gloomy, desolate air.
The pavilion on the lake, where I had trysted with Catherine
de Belleville, was overgrown with ivy and the lilies in the
water at the foot of its steps had become clogged with weeds.

Comte Jean however was in ebullient mood, almost
pulling me off my horse and engulfing me in a warm
embrace.

He abandoned me to bow to Lord Jasper as he dismounted
and then also embraced him like an old friend. 'I am
delighted to welcome you to Trédion, my lord. Come. My
house is at your disposal, it was my wife's favourite residence

and I seldom come here now. But we have refreshment and I am anxious to hear your immediate plans.'

In the dusty banqueting hall, it being a Friday, we were served a meal of bread and fish stew – I had attended the sumptuous wedding of La Petite here, to the Seigneur de Châteaubriant; that was not so long ago, but now she too was gone from Trédion.

'You are right to seek asylum in France, Henri,' Comte Jean declared. 'That upstart Landais is a villain. The duke has given him far too much power and wealth and now he is too ill to control him.'

One of his servants came with urgent news from Rennes. The soldiers Pierre Landais had mustered on the pretext that they would form our next expedition force had been mobilised instead to cover roads and bridges giving access to the French border.

'Landais has got wind of your plans, my friends, and intends to block your escape,' the Comte concluded. 'But if you will permit me . . .'

I soon understood why the Comte de Rieux was considered one of Brittany's most capable generals for he had contingency plans for everything in hand. We had arrived in the apparel of knights attending a summer joust, tailored doublets and polished leather boots over bright-coloured hose; we left in coarse brown linen jackets and woollen hose, as worn by stable grooms, and set about ruining the shine on our boots by rubbing them with mud and sand.

We would masquerade as grooms riding horses from one stable to another. We intended to split into two parties, on the grounds that we could move faster and more easily avoid the border patrols. Guided by the servant Jacques, who knew the less-travelled paths, Lord Jasper and Davy were to take a northerly route, aiming to cross the border at Châteaubriant, the home of Comte Jean's daughter Françoise, 'La Petite'. Comte Jean and I would turn south.

'I have hunted in every forest between here and Nantes,' our host informed me. 'I defy any common soldier to follow our tracks and most of the castles on this part of the French border belong either to me or to my daughter's husband so we will not be short of a refuge, should we need one.'

My intention had been to ride Bastion, mostly because I did not want to leave him behind but also because he was fleet of foot and likely to outrun any pursuit but Comte Jean advised against it. 'That handsome stallion of yours will attract attention. But I will see that you and he are reunited, wherever you end up. All you have to do is send me a message and I will arrange it.'

I put my saddlebags on the sturdy bay gelding I was offered, fed Bastion an apple and told him what the Comte had told me, before mounting up and following my leader, who was riding an equally unremarkable horse. It had been hard saying goodbye to Jasper and Davy. We had agreed to rendezvous at Langeais, hoping the French court would still be there but all of us were thinking that it was entirely possible we might not meet again, at least not as free men. I forced the notion to the back of my mind and set it instead to keeping my wits about me. I had been promised forest tracks and it was only a matter of moments before I was completely lost. To me the mighty trees and dense undergrowth seemed like a maze but Comte Jean seemed supremely confident of his direction, occasionally pausing in a clearing to glance up at the sky and gauge the position of the sun.

'At this rate we should cross the River Vilaine before sunset,' he said at one point. 'Do you mind a night under the stars or shall we make a detour up to my manor of Rieux, which is a few miles upstream?'

'I think we should go as far as the horses can manage and then catch what sleep we can, wherever we are,' I replied. 'I will only believe I am safe when I am in France.'

He nodded, pleased with my response. 'I had no doubt of your reply, Henri. The most dangerous part of the journey will be when we get close to Nantes. Somewhere we have to cross the River Erde and there are several places to choose from. It has not rained for some weeks so I am hoping water levels will be low and we can avoid using the bridges at all.'

'Where are you planning I should cross the border?'

'Do not imagine you will cross it alone, Henri. I fully intend to come with you. Then at least if we encounter any opposition they will have to contend with a count and an earl, which may give them pause for thought.'

'We do not exactly look like nobles, my lord,' I pointed out.

'And with that in mind, Henri, perhaps you should start calling me Jean.'

I laughed. 'Perhaps I should – Jean.'

We rode on for as long as the horses could carry us and saw no one except a few foresters and coppicers, who took little notice, except perhaps to raise a hand as we passed. In a grove by a narrow stream, we stopped to let the horses graze and drink, while we ate some of the bread and cheese we had packed in the saddlebags.

'We are nearing the River Vilaine,' Comte Jean said. 'I know of a crossing that we should be able to wade.'

The closer we got to the border the more nervous I became. I could not escape the fact that falling into Landais' net might this time prove fatal. There would be no Admiral de Quélennec to rush to the duke and remind him of his promise to me. 'How long is it since you saw Duke Francis, Jean?'

The Comte had followed my train of thought. 'Too long,' he replied dolefully. 'But I spoke with the duchess in Nantes last month and she said his health was improving.'

'What exactly is his malady?'

'The doctors do not seem sure, he has weakness in his muscles and finds it difficult to walk so he does not like to appear at court. He communicates with Landais in writing but this bypasses the council of nobles and we become progressively more anxious that his mind is disturbed. Landais is taking full advantage of this to pursue his own agenda.'

'Which is to ally the duchy to England's usurper,' I remarked bitterly. 'A regrettable decision.'

We tightened the horses' girths and set off again with the sun sinking behind the trees at our backs. The fertile land in the river valley was given over to fields and farms, with little cover available should we spot any kind of military patrol. When we reached the River Vilaine we found the water was indeed at low level, brown with silt and flowing sluggishly. This far upstream it did not present a formidable obstacle as we headed north along its bank, looking for shallows to ford.

The Comte fretted as we rode, then brightened and said, 'Just under this rocky bluff is the crossing I mentioned – cock's piss, there is company!' We had rounded the rocks and run straight into a small encampment. 'At least they are not soldiers. Let me handle this.'

I hung back near a mangy, hobbled skewbald pony cropping grass beside a dilapidated cart while Jean rode up to a woman who was washing wooden bowls in the river. They exchanged greetings and several remarks in Breton, which I roughly gathered concerned the depth of the river and an invitation to share their site if we wished to camp, which the Comte politely refused. He trotted back to me and muttered, 'Tinkers. We can cross here but the horses may have to swim in the middle. Hoist up your saddlebags and we'll take the plunge. It looks an easy exit on the other side.'

Two ragged children ran out of one well-patched tent to watch us make the crossing and a man wandered down to the river's edge to piss into the water, glaring at us from under a tattered straw hat. The swim was only a few yards but it soaked our hose up to the waist.

'Unfortunate,' Comte Jean remarked tersely.

I thought he meant getting wet, but he went on, 'That pissing rascal could describe us in detail if anyone questioned him.'

'Let us hope they do not,' I grunted. 'I could describe him right down to his cock, if anyone asked me.'

'Ha! He was expressing his opinion of us, Henri!'

'Angry at losing the chance of stealing our horses I'd guess.'

They were frisky after their swim so we let them canter up the wooded hill ahead, grateful to disappear into the cover of the trees. I swore inwardly at the discomfort of wet hose. It was going to be a damp night under the stars.

Comte Jean did not seem bothered by the water that

dripped from his boots. 'We ride until we cannot see the way. Tomorrow it will be a full day's journey to Château Oudon.'

'Oudon,' I echoed. 'Is that one of your castles?'

'It was my wife's,' he confided a little glumly. 'Françoise was the Lady of Malestroit and she inherited considerable lands and properties in her own right. Oudon was one of them but now it belongs to our daughter and will pass out of the Rieux family. However, I am still well known there and the constable will welcome us no matter what time it is when we arrive.'

'Where is it?'

'Happily it stands on a lonely stretch of the Loire above Nantes, where the river forms the border between Brittany and France. All we have to do is cross it to get to Anjou.'

'Is there not likely to be a guard on the Breton side, Jean?'

'There probably would be if there was a bridge but there is not. Nor is there a ford. We will have to find another way to cross. I hope you are prepared to do some more swimming, Henri?'

I gave a rueful smile at this sly dig but made no reply. Jean's mention of Anjou had started an idea running, which I mulled over as we rode into the dark until a half-moon rose. By its light we hobbled the horses and found a sheltered spot to lie down in, with our shortswords beside us, ready to tackle human or animal intruders. Against all my expectations I fell quickly into a deep sleep, only to be woken by a hand clamped over my mouth and a voice growling in my ear. 'Do not make a sound.'

My heart leapt in my chest and I automatically made a silent prayer to the Almighty, thinking it was bandits. Then the hand was removed and Jean's whispering voice became familiar in my ear. 'There is a wild boar, Henri, only yards away. I could not see him clearly but his silhouette looks enormous. He will not bother us if we wait quietly until he goes away.'

It seemed an age before we heard the boar crashing off through the undergrowth, having nosed and munched his way through some wild parsley roots nearby. I sat up and realised daylight was creeping across the tree canopy.

'It is a pity we have no fire and no time,' muttered the Comte. 'I am hungry and very partial to wild boar cooked on a spit in the open air. But we have fifty miles to ride today and Landais's men are doubtless closing in. First however, we need a clear stream to drink from and I think I hear the sound of running water.'

Among the towering trees and the tangled undergrowth a narrow rivulet was running from a hidden spring. Having quenched our thirsts and watered the horses, we mounted up and rode towards the sunrise. On this stage of the journey, through deep forest, we met no opposition and the small streams in our path were easily waded. Jean explained what lay ahead. 'The River Erde cannot be crossed except by bridge or ferry, it is too wide. There are both at a village called Nort and I know the ferryman of old, if it is still the same one. Otherwise we have to risk the bridge, which is bound to be guarded.'

We reached Nort in late afternoon, tired and still hungry. While the horses drank from the river and munched grass on the bank we chewed on the last of our bread and cheese, now stale and hard from the late summer warmth. The Comte left me with the horses while he went off to the ferry crossing, hoping to find his old acquaintance. He returned looking glum. Not only had the old man died but Landais's troops had arrived in Nort to guard the bridge and search every ferry, cart and bag.

I felt the blood drain from my face. 'Is there no other way to cross?' I asked. 'Further upstream for instance?'

He shook his head. 'The river broadens into lakes both up and down stream and my man says all the ferry docks are under surveillance. But it is the old man's son who is now the ferryman and he offered to make a diversion at the bridge, suggesting that we make a break for it while the guards are distracted. It is a risk but it looks like our best option, Henri.'

'What is the distraction?'

Comte Jean shrugged. 'He said it is better I do not know. We are to be ready when the church bell rings for Mass. He added that his daughter can swim like a fish.'

'What does that mean? Is it some kind of code?' I asked irritably. I disliked the whole plan. The ferryman could be in the pay of the guards and his offer of help might be a way for him to collect a reward for delivering me into their hands. But there was no time to hesitate. As I spoke a bell began to ring from the nearby church tower.

The Comte read my mind. 'I have no idea but I knew my ferryman friend well and I trust his son; come on, Henri, mount up. We must be ready to ride!'

As we approached the bridge at a slow walk a shout went up from the water below. 'Ahhh! Jesu save her! My little girl has fallen in! Please someone help! There! There! She is going under! I cannot swim. God Almighty help us!'

To their credit, the two soldiers on guard both ran down

to the bank below to help. We did not wait to see what happened next but kicked our horses into action, guiding them onto the bridge and over it at the trot, threading through people running to the rail to watch the drama in the water. Once on the far bank we broke into a canter to put as much distance as possible between us and the bridge. When we slowed to allow the horses to catch their breath we listened for the sound of following hoof-beats but there were none.

'Well I hope he spoke the truth when he said his daughter could swim,' I said.

34

Harri

Château Oudon and the River Loire, September 1484

Fʀᴏᴍ ᴛʜᴇ Eʀᴅᴇ ɪᴛ was only a two-hour ride at a steady ambling pace to Oudon. The forest had become less dense, scattered with farms and hamlets which we took care to avoid. Château Oudon stood on a rocky promontory where the river of the same name ran into the Loire and it reminded me of Largoët, its donjon being a tall octagonal tower, very like the one Davy and I had inhabited for nearly two years while in the Comte's custody. A strong curtain wall encircled the bailey, which also contained a stone-built great hall, ringed by all the usual domestic buildings belching steam and smoke; kitchen, alehouse, bakery and laundry. Below it on the river-bank a few cottages and workshops clustered by a wooden pier where a few fishing boats were moored.

We had dismounted at the forest edge to give the horses a break and to review the scene. The Comte pointed at the pier and said, 'I spy our way across the river right there. One of those boats will take us over to France.'

'And I see no sign of soldiers,' I remarked with relief.

'They will be upriver in Ancenis to guard a bridge the French call "the key to Brittany", but on this occasion it will not be your key to France. Let us hope sleepy little Oudon will open that door for you without attracting any attention.'

Looking down on the peaceful scene I suddenly felt confident that I would actually get to France and so I asked the Comte the question that had been burning in my mind since he mentioned crossing into Anjou. 'Château Belleville, Jean, it is in Anjou, is it not?'

He gave me a sharp look. 'Yes, but only just, why do you ask?'

Despite my best endeavours to control it, I could feel a blush creeping up my neck and into my face. 'It was the home of Madame de Belleville, who was governess to your daughter when I was living in your custody. Did the Comtesse ever tell you why she had to leave her post?'

'No. She just said she had decided to appoint a new governess. I did not interfere with her rearing of Françoise.'

'But you met Madame de Belleville's little boy?'

'Her son, yes – illegitimate I believe.'

'Indeed. His name was Roland. And you knew that his mother died soon after she left your service?'

'My wife did mention it. Why are you asking all these questions, Henri?'

I drew a deep breath and took the plunge. 'Because Catherine de Belleville died in childbirth and the child was mine – my baby son. They both died.'

There was a pause, while Comte Jean considered this revelation, rubbing thoughtfully at the stubble on his chin.

'Which, sad though it may be, as things stand now is probably just as well. So why are you asking me where Château Belleville is?'

'I feel a certain responsibility for young Roland. If it were not for me his mother would still be alive. He is thirteen years old now and I would like to ensure that he is being raised as Catherine's son should be – as the son of any noblewoman should be, legitimate or not.'

'Is that not his father's responsibility?' Comte Jean did not sound very impressed. 'Do you even know who his father is?'

I nodded. 'I do but I will not reveal the name, except to tell you that coincidentally, through his father, Roland is distantly related to my father and to my uncle Jasper. Therefore he is related to me. This is my first chance to check on his progress and may be the last in a long while . . .'

My companion blew out his cheeks. 'Phew. Well, I have to admire your sentiments in the matter but if you are determined to visit Château Belleville we will need to keep you on the right side of the French border or you may find yourself inadvertently back in Brittany.' He gathered the reins and swung himself into the saddle, as did I, and we rode on to the castle.

With the help of his wife, the constable did all and more to make us comfortable, feeding us a hot meal, unsurprisingly of fish soup and fresh bread and even supplying us with clean clothes to wear the next day from his own apparel chest; plain, coloured doublets with neat lacings, linen chemises and fine woollen hose, for which we paid him well. A servant took our boots away to polish them up again and when Comte Jean explained our mission the constable sent another out to find the man he thought might be of most help.

'He is a fisherman from the village but not only does he know the river and the sandbanks, he knows exactly where the border is at all times. Small parts of the duchy eat into French territory south of the Loire and he smuggles salt from the coast so that the fishermen can preserve their catch. He does not want to stray over the border inadvertently on such occasions. His name is Perret – Jean Perret. I think you will like him.'

I did like him but not instantly, a dark-haired, black-bearded young man of few words. At first I took his reticence for rudeness but his eyes began to gleam with interest as the Comte explained our mission. 'Do you know Château Belleville?' I asked him.

He made a dry spitting noise, his lip curling. 'I know the Seigneur de Belleville, my lord, it is he that taxes salt so high and would ruin us. If you intend dealing with him I am not your man.'

'On the contrary, I hope to avoid him at all costs. There is only one person I wish to contact at Château de Belleville and that is a boy of thirteen, whose name is Roland. Would you be able to guide me there? If the boy is not there we shall turn around and make our way to Château Langeais.'

'If it rains I might take you there by boat, my lord, but right now the Loire is too shallow.'

Comte Jean broke in. 'Can we row across from here, Perret?' he asked anxiously. 'We are not keen on swimming, even on horseback.'

The fisherman grinned and his swarthy features lightened considerably. 'I understand that. I will row us across and get other men to swim the horses over. But it will cost money.'

'And there will be all the more for you if you swear not to reveal any of our plans to these other men,' I told him.

He held out his hand. 'Give me something to swear on and I will do it now.'

I pulled at the chain that hung around my neck and dragged out the amulet I always wore. 'Swear on your Breton Saint Armel and there will be a gold crown for you now and one more when you deliver me to Langeais.'

Two gold crowns was a fortune to a fisherman and so the deal was done. It would be safer for the river crossing to be completed before dawn and with this in mind we arranged an early rendezvous with Perret. The constable departed to organise suitable mounts for us from the castle stable and his wife showed Comte Jean and I to a clean and comfortable bed.

The crossing was completed as dawn light crept across the eastern sky. As I stepped onto French soil I turned anxiously to look across the Loire for pursuers. There were none on the water and we had been swept upriver and out of sight of Oudon by the incoming tide, so if there were any frustrated Breton soldiers standing on the opposite bank, they could no longer see us, nor we them. I felt a surge of relief, like a bird released after thirteen years from its cage. But elation was tempered by the knowledge that I would never truly find freedom until I set foot on the land that bred me and furthermore I knew once I did I would have to fight for my life to remain there.

Unaware of my thoughts, Comte Jean clapped me on the shoulder. 'What does freedom feel like, Henri?' he asked.

'Ask me when I land in England or Wales,' I told him

soberly. 'I still have to ask France for asylum and abide by whatever rules they set for me to stay. You and Perret are a good deal freer than me but at least I no longer have a hostile army hot on my heels. I just hope my uncle and Davy have made it over the border.'

He tried to reassure me. 'I feel sure they will have, they had the shorter trip to the border – but the longer ride to Langeais. Once we have made the detour to Château Belleville, with any luck you should all reach the French court at about the same time.'

The horses had swum more directly across the flow and were steaming gently in the rising sun when delivered to us. They looked like three serviceable military cobs, strong enough to carry an armoured man at a steady pace for a whole day. Comte Jean, Perret and I retrieved our saddles and saddlebags from the boat and began tacking them up. One of the horses had been led so there were only two riders to pocket the silver deniers I offered them and take up the oars to row themselves back to Oudon.

'We should head south before we turn west,' said our guide, swinging into his saddle. 'That will avoid most of the towns.'

'Lead the way, Perret,' said the Comte cheerfully. 'We are in your hands.'

He could afford to be cheerful about it, I thought, falling into line. I was still not confident of Perret's reliability. It was possible that he knew someone in authority on this side of the border who would pay him more to turn me over than I had offered, or Pierre Landais might have put a bounty on my head that we knew nothing about and he would lead us blindly back into Brittany to claim it. In my darker moments on that ride I wondered if there would ever come a time when I felt entirely secure. However, my gloomy thoughts proved needless and we rode up to Château Belleville well before dusk.

Plaster was crumbling off the castle's stonework and neglect had allowed vegetation to grow up the peeling walls of the main residence. It had the air of a castle suspended in time, like in the folk tales told around great hall fires in winter. I particularly remembered one called 'Perceforêt', about a beautiful princess in an ivy-clad tower who slept for a hundred years and yet had two children by a passing prince, who secretly married and bedded her while she slumbered on. I had never understood why the servants and retainers around the fire enjoyed this macabre tale so much and later compared it with the circumstances Catherine de Belleville had described surrounding the conception of her son.

Comte Jean broke into my reverie. 'It looks deserted. Are you sure this is where you will find the boy, Henri?'

'From the sight of it I actually hope not, Jean,' I replied. 'But if we do find him I intend to remove him immediately.'

I noticed the Comte's deep frown and warning glance but chose to ignore them. He could worry all he liked about charges of abduction but if Catherine's son had been left to rot in this crumbling pile I felt honour bound to provide him with a life more fitted to his birth. With fierce determination I kicked my tired horse on towards the castle entrance, where we confronted ironbound gates that were clearly well bolted against any entry. A splintered wooden handle hung from a rusty chain and I made its attached bell ring half a dozen times before detecting any movement from within.

A tremulous and elderly female voice called from within. 'Who is there?'

Comte Jean and I exchanged surprised glances. 'My name is Henri Tudor,' I called back. 'I seek a goodwife by the name of Agnes Terreblanche.'

There was no reply but there came the screech of bolts being drawn reluctantly back, an eerie sound in the gathering gloom. With much grunting, a small sallyport was pulled open enough to allow a wrinkled old woman to emerge wearing a limp linen coif over her straggly grey hair and a shapeless brown gown cinched at the waist with a leather belt, from which hung a chatelaine, heavily weighted with keys of various sizes.

I dismounted to speak to her. 'Give you good evening, goodwife. Are you Madame Terreblanche by any chance?'

A hoarse cackle greeted this address. 'No one has called me Madame for many years, Monsieur, but yes, I am she. And you are Henri Tudor you say?'

'Yes. Do you remember writing to me after your young mistress died? I thank you for that letter.'

My gratitude elicited another cackle. 'I cannot write. The priest wrote it for me. Why have you come here? Mademoiselle Catherine is dead. She told me all about you but there is nothing for you here.'

'I wish to speak with her son Roland. Is he still here?'

As soon as she heard the boy's name she looked shifty and turned her head away. 'Why do you want to know? He is nothing to you.'

'On the contrary, goodwife, he means a great deal to me as Catherine's son. If he is here I would like to see him.'

'What if he does not want to see you?'

357

'So he is here. May we come in? We are weary, it is getting dark and our horses need feeding and watering.'

I could see by her expression that she was fighting a natural urge to offer hospitality to benighted travellers but we were never to know if those feelings won because another voice called from inside the gate, 'Is all well, Agnes? Who is it?'

I dodged around the old woman and pushed the sallyport further open. 'Roland, is that you? It is Henri Tudor. Do you remember me?' It was eight years since we parted at Trédion and he had been barely five years old but when I stepped over the threshold he was standing just inside the gate with a shy smile on his face.

On his belt he still wore the little leather purse his mother had given him and he patted it eagerly. 'You wrote your name for me and put it in here. I look at it often,' he said. 'My mother would not have wished me to forget you.'

'But I hardly recognise you, Roland!' I responded. 'You have grown tall and your hair is darker.'

'I am thirteen,' he said proudly. 'Old enough to leave home.'

I looked around me. 'It does not look to be a very comfortable home but may we stable our horses for the night and find somewhere to sleep? We are all weary and hungry.'

He made a face. 'If Agnes will let you. She is the chatelaine.'

'Are there only the two of you here?'

'And a couple of guards but they always go to the village tavern in the evening and come home drunk. Ah, it seems you are to be admitted, Monsieur Henri.'

The old woman had stepped back through the sallyport

and started laboriously pulling back the huge iron bolts of the main gate. We both went to help her. When it finally opened, the horses clattered into a weed-ridden courtyard.

'Does the Seigneur never come here now, Roland?' I asked, kicking at a clump of ragwort growing through a crack in the flagstones.

Roland scowled, his brow knitting fiercely. 'Never. I am glad. The last time he came he beat me.'

I turned, frowning. 'Why did he beat you Roland?'

He did not answer. Instead he muttered, 'The stables are down here,' and led the way through an archway into a second courtyard containing a range of lean-to buildings, which included a row of timber-framed stalls.

'Thank Jesu for this,' Jean said, 'I thought we were destined to sleep rough again. See if you can wheedle food and a bed of some sort out of the old hag, Henri.'

'Who is he?' Roland whispered, coming close to help me unsaddle my horse.

'Do you not recognise him? It is the Comte de Rieux, La Petite's father. You remember her, do you not?'

A look of alarm crossed his face. 'Does he know who I am?'

'Yes but if you find him some food and a bed for the night he will not bite you.' I ruffled his hair and smiled reassuringly. 'Are such things available in this ramshackle pile?'

'There are plenty of beds in the house but they have no linen. And I can wring a chicken's neck for your supper. Will that do?'

'Admirably Roland, thank you, but two chickens would be better. We can pay for them to be replaced.'

Roland made for the stable door. 'I will tell Agnes,' he said, 'and stoke up the fire.'

We ate in the kitchen, around the great scrubbed slab of oak that was the cook's table, except that there was no cook and it was Roland who turned the spit that held the chickens, which Agnes had plucked. She also raided the Seigneur's cellar and produced a cask of very reasonable wine. Over the meal we made arrangements for Roland to join me on my journey to Langeais. Having learned that Gilles de Belleville had not made a visit to his home for three years and only sent occasional funds to Agnes for upkeep, I decided that Catherine's son would fare better if I took him with me, wherever I ended up. The boy was touchingly enthusiastic about such a change and Agnes offered little opposition to the idea. I think she realised that she was getting on in years and Roland would fare better in the train of a young man who could show him places and teach him skills that would serve him.

'We are going to the king's court, Roland,' I reminded him, eyeing his faded brown hood, baggy green tunic and torn hose. 'Do you have any apparel with a touch more style?'

The boy blushed and admitted he did not. 'I grew out of everything and after my mother died there was no one to buy me new clothes. These are hand-me-downs the priest found among the donations to the foundling home.'

I smiled. 'Never mind, every town has a second-hand clothes dealer. We will buy you something better on the way to Langeais.'

After the meal Agnes showed us where we could lay our heads, handing us lighted tapers and leading us through the dank passages of the empty mansion to a series of musty bedchambers. I took the opportunity to speak with her privately about the traumatic birth of my baby son.

'Did Catherine suffer greatly?' I asked, knowing the question to be naive but needing to hear the answer.

The old woman looked at me pityingly. 'Every mother suffers pain in birthing a child, Monsieur Henri, and she only had me to help her. In the end I had to call the priest because I did not want the babe to be unshriven. She fought so long to give him life and he barely breathed long enough for the holy water to touch his forehead. And then she bled. Oh, how she bled and I could not stop it.'

Tears began to creep down her cheeks, glistening in the light of the tallow candle that dripped and spat in her shaking hand. I took it from her, struggling to suppress my own tears and asking hopefully, 'God took her quickly then?'

Agnes wiped her eyes with the drooping sleeve of her dress, nodding. 'Yes, Monsieur. The priest gave her the last rites and she slipped away. I knew she had gone when the bleeding stopped. She looked so peaceful then – but the bedclothes and mattress had to be burned.'

While clearly relevant to the old chatelaine, this final dreadful detail proved my undoing. I hastily put both candlesticks down to pull my kerchief from the purse on my belt and was supremely glad that Roland had not accompanied us into the mansion.

In the morning as the boy tucked his minimal belongings into my saddlebags, I inwardly cursed the man who had sired and abandoned him. I promised myself that if our paths ever crossed I would expose Gilles Harpedanne, Seigneur de Belleville, for the scoundrel he was.

Since there had been no rain to swell the Loire, it was decided that Perret and I would take the Oudon horses on to Langeais, while the Comte returned directly to Brittany to pursue his own affairs. I had packed pen, ink and paper in my saddlebags and I gave Jean the letter I had written overnight to Duke Francis, apologising for leaving his duchy without permission and thanking him for his generosity and kindness in sheltering me for so long. Then I found myself adding:

When I come into my kingdom, as I pray the Lord God will judge me worthy to do, I vow to repay everything you have invested in me and to forge a treaty of friendship and alliance between our two realms. But I must ask your grace for one last favour; that you allow the men who have followed me to your shores and sworn allegiance to me as their leader and future monarch, to leave Brittany and join me in France. When that is accomplished they will no longer be a drain on your resources and all will remember you and your family with profound gratitude.

In a ramshackle tack room beside the stables, we found an abandoned pillion seat and attached it to Perret's saddle. Gentle probing revealed that Roland had not even been taught to ride, so there was no point in acquiring a third mount and the sturdy cob the fisherman rode would easily carry the additional weight of a skinny boy. We took our leave of Comte Jean just outside the village of Belleville where the road forked. He was going north to Nantes and we were heading east.

'It is entirely due to you that I have reached France safely, Jean,' I said, dismounting to say farewell.

He grinned and shook his head, slipping from his own saddle. 'A man can do too much hunting; I rather enjoyed being the quarry for a change.' He took my shoulders in a friendly grip. 'Let me know when you are settled and I will send Bastion to you.'

'Perhaps you might bring him yourself,' I suggested. 'Do you not visit the French court occasionally?'

He looked doubtful. 'Possibly, but first I have a certain Pierre Landais to deal with. I and many other Breton nobles think that this time the man has gone too far in taking matters into his own hands.'

'In that case the Treasurer had better watch his step,' I said. 'It is a foolish man who gets on the wrong side of Jean de Rieux!'

We exchanged a warm embrace and he looked me solemnly in the eye. 'Do not forget me when you are king of England, Henri,' he said.

PART FOUR

35

Margaret

Stanley House, St Paul's Wharf, London, October 1484

I HAD BEEN COOPED up in Stanley House for a year, confined to my chamber, the chapel and the privy garden, with only the presence of a few taciturn females in the pay of the usurper to render me grudging service and constant surveillance. I called them my stooges. My only relief from their dreary company came when Lord Thomas made his visits, which occurred less and less frequently as Richard grew increasingly suspicious of the loyalty of his nobles and insisted on his household officials remaining at his side. Since he moved constantly about the kingdom, checking on his garrisons, appointing commissioners of array and gathering information from his network of spies, the court often did not return to London for weeks at a time.

With Dr Caerleon still a prisoner I was no longer able to communicate directly with the dowager queen, who remained in sanctuary and the only information I received about her and her daughters was through the biased gossip of the stooges. Had I believed them, I would have despaired of Elizabeth Woodville's apparently docile acceptance of the usurper's disparagement of her marriage, the disinheritance of her children and most unlikely of all, the mysterious disappearance of her two young sons. If there was one thing I knew from my husband, now High Constable of England as well as Steward of the Household, it was that if young Edward and Richard of York were still alive, they were no longer anywhere in the Tower of London and if their mother was showing signs of co-operating with the usurper, as the stooges took great pleasure in informing me, it was for the same reason as the rest of us, to save her skin and the future of her remaining children.

The situation worried me particularly because I also knew that when my son took the throne he would need his avowed union with the Princess Elizabeth in order to secure the support of her father's affinity and if Henry did not act soon her uncle, having robbed her of her royal status, would marry her off to some nonentity. I was desperate for news from France.

It came unexpectedly when Thomas slipped into my bedchamber just as I was about to extinguish my night candle, his finger on his lips as he closed the door with stealthy care. 'The dragon is sleeping,' he whispered, approaching the bed. 'Let us pray she does not wake.'

By the dragon he meant the female guard who always slept in the ante-room, ostensibly for my protection but actually to ensure I did not leave my room at night. 'It is permitted for you to enter my bedchamber, Thomas,' I whispered as he shed the damp cloak he wore over his furred robe. 'Richard has not yet dared to come between husband and wife.'

He kicked off his boots and climbed onto the bed. 'I do not want any of his spies to know I am here. I am supposed to be visiting the Tower.'

'How did you enter the house? The gatekeeper must have seen you arrive.' I reached out and pulled the curtains closed on my side of the bed, indicating that he should do the same. 'It will stop our voices carrying.' Nevertheless I spoke softly.

He complied and then patted his purse. 'I still have my own man on the gate and just to make sure I slipped him a groat.'

'All this subterfuge is so irritating. We are getting too old for midnight trysts. When will it ever end, Thomas?'

He leaned across and kissed me – a kiss of re-acquaintance rather than passion. 'Soon, if your son makes good use of the man I am about to send him.'

'Who is that?'

He looked smug – there was no other word for it. 'The Earl of Oxford.'

'John de Vere? Surely he is still a prisoner in Calais.'

'Not for much longer. His gaolers are about to turn coat.'

I sat bolt upright. 'How is that? They are Richard's men surely.'

He shook his head. 'Not any more. Oxford is being held at Hammes Castle in the Calais Pale and Richard is sending one of his trusties across the Channel with orders to bring him and the commander of Hammes, James Blount, back to England. What the usurper does not know is that I have warned Blount that Richard no longer trusts him. I have advised him to leave Hammes and join Henry and to take Oxford with him.'

'But will he believe you, Thomas?' I asked sceptically. 'It is only your word against Richard's.'

'He will believe me because my messenger is a man called John Riseley who is a tenant of John Fortescue, who holds the gate at the Calais garrison. Fortescue is also going to turn coat and take half the garrison with him. Not only will Henry receive a troop of thirty good fighting men but in John de Vere, Earl of Oxford, one of England's finest front-line commanders. It will boost his confidence considerably Margaret, to say nothing of reducing Richard's military superiority.'

I looked at him for a steady minute. 'You have risked a great deal to achieve this, Thomas. Are you certain Richard does not suspect you?'

He took a deep breath and let it out slowly. 'One can never be certain with Richard, but Henry has no battlefield experience and he needs someone like John de Vere. Richard has been fighting wars since he was sixteen. If everything goes according to plan we will have supplied Henry with a general who will unquestionably help him win his battle for the throne of England. I only hope your boy is worth it.'

'When you meet Henry, Thomas, you will know that he is.' It was my turn to kiss him, an embrace that held the passion of gratitude.

Having suffered for weeks without trustworthy word from the outside world, only days later I received another visitor. Lady Vaux showed the gatekeeper a letter from Queen Anne, which spirited her past him and even past the resident dragon and into my private oratory while I was at prayer. When she came to stand quietly behind me I could smell the camomile she always used on her hair.

'Kate! Oh Kate, it is so good to see you!' Those who accused me of bearing a constant air of solemn piety would not have thought so then, as I flung my arms around my oldest friend. 'How have you gained entrance? I am so constrained these days.'

She laughed and kissed my cheeks. 'I have friends in high places – did you not know?'

As she told me of Queen Anne's letter, I led her to the window seat, where I often sat to gaze longingly over the rooftops of London. The cushioned recess was just wide enough for two small women to sit together, provided their skirts were not too full. Among its distorted diamond-shaped panes was one of stained glass, a tiny image of St Margaret with her dragon, which Lord Thomas had put there to mark our marriage. At first I had thought it a wry comment on our barren union but now I knew it had been a pledge of protection.

'Your visit is the high point of my present life,' I said. 'I sometimes resort to communing with the jackdaws through this window. They nest in the eaves of St Mary's Church across the lane and at least they are friendly and do not tell tales.'

Kate studied me closely in the bright daylight. 'You look tired, Margaret. Have you been sleeping badly?'

I gave her a crooked smile. 'Thomas makes clandestine visits. I hope you have good news for me.'

She made a balancing movement with her hand. 'That depends on your point of view. Queen Anne is dying. She has a wasting disease and coughs blood. She never really recovered from Prince Edward's death in the spring.'

I made the sign of the cross. 'The boy was never strong they say. Poor lady, I prayed for her then and will again. So once more you will see a queen into the grave, Kate.'

It was her turn to cross herself. 'It is in God's hands. We none of us know when our call will come. But Anne seems resigned to it – even happy – expecting to be reunited with her son. She said something very strange though. I think she had taken a little too much of her potion.'

'In what way strange?' I asked.

'She made no secret of the fact that she would not welcome Elizabeth's daughters into her household but Richard brought them to court anyway. He is anxious that they attend the Christmas festivities so that people can see they have accepted him as their king. The other day Anne told me that she had ordered young Elizabeth a costly gown to wear that was just like one of hers. "We can wear them together at court," she said. "So that Richard can see what she will look like as a queen."'

I felt my heart miss a beat. 'What did she mean, Kate?' My voice seemed to flutter like a candle flame in a draught.

Her shoulders lifted. 'I really do not know. As I said, I think she had swallowed too much poppy syrup. She is not always quite herself.'

'There are many who believe the princess should be queen if her brothers are dead. That is why Henry has vowed to marry her if he should take the throne.'

'Yes, I am aware of that. That is why I am telling you this. But I do not know whether Anne had that in mind and thought to taunt Richard with it or if she believes he wants to marry her himself and this is her way of telling him she knows.'

'An uncle marry his niece? Surely not! That would be incest – no pope would grant dispensation.'

'You are right. And I do not believe he has any such intention. Anne's action is born of jealousy, coupled with a sick woman's fevered imagination.'

'It is a dangerous notion though. Will Anne even be well enough to attend the Christmas festivities?'

'Again, it is in God's hands.'

I stood up. 'I must write of this to Henry. Will you wait while I compose a letter, Kate? You are my only way of getting it out of the house. If you deliver it to Lord Thomas he will find a courier for it.'

'Of course I will but do it quickly, Margaret, because I should be back at the palace soon.'

I found pen and ink and wrote my letter.

To Henry Tudor, Earl of Richmond, from his mother Margaret, Countess of Richmond

To my alarm I have heard from my good friend Lady Vaux, gentlewoman to the usurper's queen, that there is some suggestion that he might approach the Pope for a dispensation to marry his niece, Elizabeth of York. Remarkably, the idea comes from Queen Anne herself, who is still alive but very sickly and cannot live more than a few months. Lady Vaux thinks it the wild fancy of a sick woman and I think it very unlikely that such a dispensation would be granted, but it does further indicate a need for haste on your part. Elizabeth is young, beautiful and from fertile York stock. Any man, especially a king, would be well served by such a wife. Come soon and claim her as you claim your throne my dearest son.

   In haste to catch the moment,
   Your devoted Mother
   MR

Written at Stanley House, the twentieth day of October 1484.

36

Henry

IT WAS ANNE DE Beaujeu who had first addressed me formally as King of England and from the day we met I realised that if I was to receive any help from the French crown it would be she who granted it. Ever since she became Regent, French courtiers had taken to calling her Madame la Grande. Even during its summer residence at Château Langeais the court she dominated in her young brother's stead was impressive and she herself was a magnificent presence; tall and imposing with an erect stance and prominent brown eyes. She was not beautiful but striking, in looks and personality.

It was thanks to the political tutoring of her father, Louis the Eleventh, that after his death, when she was only twenty-two, Anne had outsmarted her cousin Louis of Orleans, won the vote of a specially-convened meeting of the French Estates General and effectively become governor of France. So although her younger brother, King Charles the Eighth was, according to French tradition, at fourteen officially of age to rule, in fact he merely signed laws and edicts devised by his appointed guardian. Luckily for him, unlike his unfortunate counterpart in England, his older relative and protector was no scheming usurper.

Wearing a blue court robe lavishly embroidered with the gold *fleur de lys* of France, Anne stood close to the young king's throne at one end of a great chamber hung with glorious Flemish tapestries. Magnificently clad courtiers crowded the walls and alcoves, taking care to leave a central pathway open, which led directly to the royal presence. Royally crowned and clad the young king sat enthroned, with his feet swinging free of the ground, seeming swamped by the lavish curtains of his throne, in deep blue velvet trimmed with a gold fringe. I whispered to Roland to slip into the crowd as the chamberlain announced me in ringing tones. '*Le Chevalier de l'Hérmine, Henri Tudore!*'

Observing the tailored elegance of the men in the room, I was glad I had polished up my Order of the Ermine collar and fervently wished I had been able to purchase a more stylish outfit than the grey silk doublet that had been the only garment of any distinction at the second hand clothing shop where I had taken Roland on our journey from Belleville. Now, during my prominent promenade to the throne, every eye in the room scrutinising my appearance, I felt it was sadly wanting but my discomfort vanished when I went on one knee before King Charles. The boy king was roused from his ennui when his sister immediately moved forward and signalled me to rise, studying my face with her piercing eyes.

'It is not right that a king should kneel to a king,' she

said, her vice loud enough to be heard around the room. 'France has no truck with the regicide usurper who falsely occupies the throne of England. As far as we are concerned you, Henri Tudore, are the rightful King of England and we heartily welcome you to the court of King Charles.'

This caused a buzz of interest among the courtiers and her accolade was applauded by the boy king, who piped up in a voice yet to break, 'Yes, welcome to my court *Majesté*!' But then he retired once more into the depths of his throne.

Tactfully Madame la Grande made no reference to my sartorial shortfall but her next move was to offer me maintenance funds, 'To clothe yourself and your retinue, Monseigneur.'

'That is a most generous proposal, Madame,' I said with an appreciative bow, 'but I fear I must entreat funding for vastly more important and costly matters than my own adornment.'

'Of course, *Majesté*. We intend to see that you are well supplied with all you need to secure your kingdom. You did right when you crossed the border into the France of Charles the Eighth. May I ask how many men you expect to follow you from Brittany?'

I gave a noncommittal lift of the shoulders. 'There are around five hundred in Vannes, Madame, but I cannot be sure that any will be permitted to leave. It depends who holds the reins in the duchy.'

The lady frowned and lowered her voice. 'Indeed. But I think this time Pierre Landais may have over-reached. My informants tell me there is much unrest among the lieges. An appeal for your followers to be permitted to join you will be addressed directly to Duke Francis and sent under the seal of the French crown.'

I was expressing my thanks when the king leaned forward again from the deep seat of his throne. 'I saw you enter with a young companion, *Majesté*,' he said. 'Is he a relation of yours?'

I bent low in order to address him more easily. 'A very distant one your grace, and perhaps, indirectly, your relative also. His name is Roland de Belleville.'

'I would like to meet him. Have him approach.'

This last was directed at his sister who looked at me apologetically. 'Charles rarely speaks with anyone of his own age during court proceedings. Would your companion be willing to be presented to the king?'

'He would be honoured, your grace – Madame,' I agreed, nodding to them both.

As Anne de Beaujeu sent a page to seek out Roland I spent anxious moments wondering how he would behave towards the king. Roland had not been reared among the high echelons of society and might fail to pay the required amount of respect to a king who was of his own age. However, something of his mother's elegant manners must have rubbed off during his early childhood because he exercised a surprising amount of deference and clearly did not give offence. King Charles soon called for a stool to be placed beside him so that they might converse more comfortably together.

Understandably Anne de Beaujeu was curious. 'Exactly what is Roland's relationship to you and my brother – and by the same inference – to me?' she inquired. 'I had not realised that you and I were related.'

I could not avoid giving her the truth. 'It goes back to your great grandfather Madame, King Charles the Sixth. As was common knowledge at the time, he had a mistress called Odette de Champdivers and in due course her daughter Marguerite was acknowledged as his half-sister by King Charles the Seventh. He then arranged her marriage to his Chamberlain, Comte Jean Harpedanne de Belleville and before he died he sired two sons. The younger of these, Gilles Harpe danne de Belleville, is I believe an official of your court.'

Madame Anne frowned before acknowledging this fact through pursed lips. 'A minor one, yes. He commands one of the king's fortresses on the Spanish border but I must tell you that he will go no further in my brother's admin-istration. At least not while I control it.'

I took this as a hint that she held the man in question in the same low regard as I did. 'That is of some relief to me, Madame,' I admitted. 'Personally I hope never to encounter him but nevertheless he is young Roland's father. Regrettably, his wife's daughter by a previous marriage was the boy's mother but she has sadly died.'

Judging by the way her prominent eyes widened at these revelations, I had piqued Anne de Beaujeu's interest consid-erably but there was no time for her to react, due to a sudden stir at the entrance. My heart leaped at the announcement made and the sight of Lord Jasper and Davy Owen making their way through the crowd of courtiers.

They, too, had made an effort to dress for the occasion but, like me, had fallen short of the splendour of this court. I stood back to let them make their obeisance to the king and watched as they exchanged greetings with him and his sister, admitting that while they had encountered no trouble crossing the border into France, they had missed their way several times en route across country to Langeais. During this encounter I noted that young Roland had deferentially faded into the background.

Anne de Beaujeu drew us all behind the throne to allow our reunion embraces, remarking as we drew apart, 'I can see the family likeness between you three. A Tudor straightness in the nose and the set of the mouth I think.'

'Or might the nose not be a Valois trait Madame?' Lord Jasper suggested. 'Your father was my first cousin after all.' A veiled reference I deduced to Louis the Eleventh's famously substantial nose, a feature repeated to a lesser extent in his daughter's countenance.

'Even more reason for us to support each other's schemes and intentions, Messeigneurs. But tell me, where are you all to lodge, now that you are reunited?' She turned to me. 'Will you allow me to instruct my Maître d'Hôtel to have rooms prepared for you here, *Majesté*?'

After this encouraging introduction, our relationship with the French king and his sister continued from strength to strength, leading us to share their autumn progress from royal castle to royal castle, firstly by barge along the Loire, then overland to Montargis where we celebrated Christmas and then northwards, again by barge, down the Seine to Paris, which we reached in early February. It was because Anne de Beaujeu took me under her wing during this time that I learned a great deal about the French system of court administration and royal prerogative.

France was changing from an ancient feudal system, when nobles had often failed to deliver their quota of revenue to the crown, to a more royally focused government where the crown levied taxes directly from the duchies and counties, without reference to the elected representatives of the Three Estates: the Parliaments of the Nobility, the Church and the People. In this respect King Louis the Eleventh had been lucky, for a general dearth of male heirs among the nobility had allowed him to exploit the French Salic law disallowing female inheritance and to take extensive territory back to the crown from some powerful families. However, although the crown had become richer and more powerful as a result, it also meant that unrest was spreading in the Estates.

In Brittany a stricken Duke Francis had received my letter personally from the hands of Comte Jean and immediately countermanded the restrictions Pierre Landais had placed on the five hundred English exiles living in and around Vannes. True to her word, Anne de Beaujeu not only sent letters of safe-passage to the leaders but also money, horses and guides to facilitate their journey into France. She made one caveat however.

'While King Charles would welcome any nobles and knights you nominate to join your entourage here at court *Majesté*, we would prefer the bulk of your English followers to remain together in the city of Sens. There is plenty of accommodation there for your countrymen to make themselves comfortable and the French crown will pay for their lodgings. I hope this arrangement will content you.'

I lost no time in expressing my gratitude and took early advantage of the offer of a barge to travel by river to Sens and to welcome the long column of English exiles. However, I soon hastened back to Paris when I learned that the escapees from Hammes and Calais were on their way there. I brought the Marquess of Dorset, Sir Edward Woodville and several other knights on the barge with me.

When in Paris, King Charles and his guardians chose to stay at Château Vincennes, a magnificent fortified palace situated in the midst of an ancient hunting forest that stretched from the Bastille fortress on the eastern Paris wall to the river Marne, where Anne de Beaujeu considered the air to be better for the young king's health. So it was to Vincennes that the Earl of Oxford and his fellow escapees were directed to present themselves and where Lord Jasper and I went to meet them. On the second floor of the castle's massive square donjon a somewhat reduced French court had gathered in the King's Chamber, a large room reached by a broad spiral staircase where recently glazed windows afforded sweeping views over the seemingly endless forest canopy. In a room of such regal proportions King Charles's velvet-draped throne looked almost inadequate.

John de Vere, Earl of Oxford swept in with a substantial entourage: his friend and fellow prisoner Viscount Beaumont and several other knights and their squires, all wearing body armour and long boots, as if they had just galloped in from a battlefield, which in many ways they had. For while making their escape from Hammes Castle just ahead of the arrival of Richard's agents, Oxford and his defecting gaoler, James Blount, had left a substantial garrison behind, both to defend the castle from attack and to protect Sir James's young wife, who was heavily pregnant and unable to flee with him. For several days they had waited over the French border until a messenger came to tell them of the child's safe delivery, adding the grim news that the castle was now under siege by a force sent from the Calais garrison. The usurper had been swift to order retaliation for the audacious departure of his appointed officers.

'Naturally we felt honour-bound to return to Hammes to raise the siege and retrieve mother and baby.' The earl looked pale but remarkably fit and well, considering his ten years of confinement and announced this with a suitable flourish, making it clear that there were more revelations to come. The young king was not the only one who listened spellbound as the dramatic story of the rescue and relief of Hammes unfolded.

'This man here –' Oxford laid a hand on the shoulder of the figure beside him '– is James Blount, until recently commander of Hammes Castle. Knowing that the men sent to fetch me also carried a false charge of treason for him, he had no choice but to abandon his post. His wife would have come with him but she was very close to her time and begged him to leave her, promising to bring his child to him whenever she was able. She knew that for him to stay would be his death sentence. So we crossed the marsh into France by moonlight and took some like-minded members of the garrison with us; those who chose to leave the sovereignty of the usurper and declare for King Henry instead.'

At this point King Charles spoke up and gestured in my direction. 'Your king is here,' he said dramatically. 'You may do so now.'

Immediately the three Englishmen, the Earl of Oxford, Viscount Beaumont and James Blount, turned from the French king to bend the knee to me. There was applause as one by one they placed their hands between mine and pledged their allegiance.

No matter how many times I received these oaths of allegiance they never failed to move me, I felt a gratitude that was genuine, greater than me, signifying a powerful bond. 'With all my heart I thank you, my lords and brothers in arms,' I said, feeling uplifted, 'and I salute your chivalry and courage. Our cause is greatly strengthened by your presence and I will be honoured to have the advice and counsel of such experienced commanders.'

I paused, my thoughts of the future and what these men and I would do, but came hurriedly back to the present. 'I pray that all is well with your brave wife, Master Blount. Please continue your story, my lord Oxford, which I sense is incomplete.'

There was a further ripple of encouraging applause from the courtiers and Oxford eagerly complied. 'Indeed, Mistress Blount is as stalwart a soldier as any among us,' he declared. 'Not only did she encourage the remaining garrison to resist the siege but within hours of its start, with cannonballs pounding the walls, gave birth to a healthy baby girl. Taking advantage of the winter freeze, we crossed the marsh at speed and succeeded in surprising the siege force from behind, putting them to the rout and taking back the castle.'

There was a pause as loud clapping greeted this chivalrous but potentially foolhardy move on the part of men who had risked their lives and their freedom. It was Anne de Beaujeu who interjected first. 'I trust you have brought the lady and the child to Paris with you, my lord, and they are safely and warmly housed.'

Bowing his thanks, James Blount replied, 'They will be

in Paris later today, Madame. They are following in a litter, escorted by the defecting members of my garrison.'

The Marquess of Dorset strolled up to join us, sporting as usual his tarnished badge of the Order of the Garter. Askance, Lord Oxford cried, 'Jesu Dorset it is you. You look older and have you no squire to polish that badge, or just no respect for such an honour?'

'Well!' exclaimed the Marquess, offended. 'At least I do not take Christ's name in vain in the very room where Lancaster's conquering hero died.'

'He was not just Lancaster's hero!' retorted Oxford, nostrils flaring. 'The great Henry the Fifth was England's hero and its most glorious king! In his death these walls witnessed one of the greatest tragedies of the century.'

'Some might say that the greater tragedy was when his father usurped the throne of the second Richard,' persisted Dorset, grimly turning the blade.

Oxford's face grew a deeper crimson. 'In God's name Dorset, what are you doing here? Should you not be crawling back to your Yorkist pretender and begging for mercy?'

I rolled my eyes at this and steered the furious Oxford away from his antagonist. 'Much as I value the enthusiasm with which you embrace our cause, my lord,' I murmured in his ear, 'I would rather Dorset stayed with us than took our plans and schemes across the sea to Richard.'

'But you surely cannot trust him?' The earl was still indignant.

I led him further into a corner of the room and put my lips close to his ear. 'I do not trust him, my lord, but I keep my eye on him. His correspondence is vetted and the

Channel is wide. You have my word that he will not cross it before I do.'

The earl caught my determined glare and appeared mollified. 'Good,' he said. 'I have ten years to catch up on. If you will trust me, your grace, I look forward to hearing your plans and training our fighting men in battle strategy.'

There was no hesitation in my answer. 'As far as military matters are concerned, my lord of Oxford, of all those who have lately joined my cause you are the man in whom I will place most trust.'

37

Henry

THE HÔTEL DU ROI, where we had made our Paris base, was part of what had once been a sprawling complex of royal residences established along the right bank of the Seine and known as the Hôtel de Saint Pol. In its heyday, during the long reign of Charles the Sixth, one extensive curtain wall had enclosed separate mansions for the households of the king, the queen and the dauphin, magnificent stables for the royal horses, kitchens, kennels, mews, laundries, smithies, a large menagerie of exotic animals, orchards and ornamental gardens for feasts and ceremonies. Sadly, later in his reign it had become his prison as the king succumbed to increasing periods of insanity and the palace gradually became derelict. Only the mansion in which we were housed had been refurbished by his son Charles the Seventh and therefore remained habitable.

The day following Oxford's arrival, the French king and his sister made an unexpected visit, bringing a large entourage so that servants had to be hastily despatched to city bakeries, ale-houses and cook-shops to acquire sufficient refreshments. While a meal was being prepared we spent an entertaining hour on the Rue de St Antoine watching King Charles and several squires of his age and stage, including his young friend Roland de Belleville, display their weapon and jousting skills and it was my first opportunity to see how readily Catherine de Belleville's son had taken to knightly pursuits.

However, the true purpose of Anne de Beaujeu's visit was to discuss the preparation of my expedition, which was done over a midday meal in strict privacy, with only our closest advisers present. As we gathered, I saw among the French contingent a man I recognised vaguely from my Brittany days, who was greeted by Lord Jasper as an old friend. He was presented to me as Philibert de Chandée, an extraordinary soldier of Savoy with an open, blue-eyed gaze that conveyed candour and humour and a hint of ruthlessness but at that moment Anne de Beaujeu approached, anxious to start our meeting.

'I see you have met our Monsieur de Chandée, my lord king, but I regret we cannot stay long,' she informed me in her business-like way. 'May we take our places? We have much business to conduct.'

King Charles was not present at this meeting, being fêted by the squires and younger knights with food, games and minstrelsy in the hôtel's great hall, but all the proposals would be made in his name and it would be his seal and signature on the documents, which made the decisions final.

When we were seated around the board, French on one side, English on the other, Madame de Beaujeu opened proceedings. 'It is the king's wish that sufficient funds be made available to King Henry's expedition to pay a French army of at least two thousand men. The French government will supply ships to transport them and their ordnance to a landing place of your choice across the Sleeve and Admiral Guillaume de Casenove will command the fleet. All French troops will be under the command of Monsieur Philibert de Chandée, who will be responsible for their discipline, their conditions and their repatriation. It is not proposed that horses be transported, so arrangements will need to be made for acquiring mounts from your English and Welsh allies. The French Royal Ordnance will supply artillery at the king's discretion. All this is to be done in a spirit of co-operation and with the intention of forming a firm alliance between our two countries following the successful conclusion of the expedition.'

There was a long pause while the Earl of Oxford, who was seated next to me, leaned in to murmur in my ear, 'Is it a condition of this deal that we should be dictated to by a woman, your grace? And by a Frenchwoman at that? Command of your troops and your ships should surely be up to you and your generals.'

I made a sign to show that I had heard him but did not react directly. Oxford was a soldier, a man with set views and no fear of confrontation. If and when it came to a battle I had every intention of giving the aggressive earl command of my army's advance guard, but I had decided that it would not be until much nearer the time that I would make such dispositions known.

In fact I was wary of discussing any details of strategy until we had made a safe crossing, being concerned that recent events in England might prompt leaks and disloyalties from certain members of our company, one of whom was sitting very close by.

Meanwhile Anne de Beaujeu stared at me expectantly, awaiting a response. I leaned in to select a choice cut of meat from the dish before me and placed it on the white bread trencher covering my silver platter. Red juices seeped into the smooth slice, like blood into a bandage, perhaps presaging violent clashes, but I had no intention of causing offence by questioning Madame la Grande's announcements.

'My gratitude for the French king's generosity runs deep, Madame,' I said at length, meeting her intense gaze. 'And it will not be forgotten when I wear the crown of England. Careful accounts will be kept of all costs and interest incurred and all loans will be repaid. The service of your countrymen, from commanders to common soldiers, is greatly appreciated and will be for many years to come. Particularly welcome is the addition of artillery, although I would suggest it should be of the lighter variety, since it may have to be transported across some distance after landing.'

Having listened carefully to my words, Anne de Beaujeu found nothing in them to offend, so took her cup and raised it in salute. As I lifted mine in reply, beside me Lord Oxford began to clap and gradually applause spread along our side of the board – a brief but heart-warming burst of approval, which lifted my spirits. However, the reluctance of Thomas Grey, Marquess of Dorset, to join in was too obvious to ignore. Something had to be done.

Ned Woodville had showed me a letter he had received from his sister, Edward the Fourth's bereaved and besmirched queen Elizabeth Woodville. One paragraph in particular had set alarm bells ringing loudly.

> *Thomas will explain to you why I finally yielded to Richard's promises regarding the future of my daughters. They are all his wards now and flourish at his court and he wants me to persuade the rest of my family to come back to England, take his pardon and display their acceptance of his reign to the world. I find I can no longer resist his demands. I am tired brother, tired and grieving and desperate to know the truth of what happened to my boys. I could do nothing for anyone while I was confined in Sanctuary and now I have at least persuaded Thomas to flee the Tudor net. Talk to him, listen to him and come with him Edward, I beg you.*

Early the following morning, Ned came to me again. 'Thomas has gone, Harri,' he said. 'I went to his chamber at dawn and found it deserted. Something he said to me last night made me suspicious – I believe he is planning to take ship from Flanders. He has contacts in Bruges.'

'I am glad you were not tempted to go with him,' I said.

'And bend the knee to the murderer of my nephews? I think grief has robbed my sister of her wits. With your permission I will join the search party.'

I reached out to stay his immediate departure. 'I know about Bruges, Ned. Richmond Herald told me he had carried letters there for Dorset. I have organised a posse of loyal men and yesterday I snatched some private words with King Charles and his sister, who agreed to put their seals on a free pass for them.'

This had been a precaution, which at the time had eased my sense of looming jeopardy, and now the jeopardy was real.

I went on, 'Dorset is misled, Ned. I cannot trust him but wish him no harm. The posse has orders to detain him and bring him back to Paris. That is all. He knows too much. I simply cannot let him fall into the usurper's hands.'

He nodded. 'I know. I will see that he is well guarded when we bring him back.'

Lord Jasper and I were in Rouen when Ned Woodville brought news, to my huge relief, that Dorset had been apprehended just on the French side of the Flemish border.

'He was staying at a small inn at a village called Lihors,' he told us, 'but his trail was not hard to follow. He only had his valet with him so when he looked out of the inn window and saw our troop in your livery he took his hand off his sword hilt. We escorted him back to Paris and I came straight here to report to you. At present he is under house arrest at the Hotel du Roi and I hope I never have to take the field beside him.'

'Have no fear Ned, Lord Dorset will never be trusted to fight under my standard,' I assured him.

We were in Rouen with the French king and his sister to lobby a meeting of the Normandy Estates for further financial support for our expedition and as we rode through the city to a welcome banquet I had been fascinated by the city's famous Great Clock, located high in the tower of the curfew bell outside the ducal palace. It had an intricate wrought-iron mechanism and as we passed, the bell sounded noon and the arrow of the clock's hand pointed directly to Heaven, embellished with the figure of a sheep, to indicate Rouen's chief source of wealth. I wondered whether any of England's cities yet boasted such a marvellous contraption.

Seated beside Anne de Beaujeu, I asked after its origin. 'I do not know exactly,' she admitted, 'but I believe it is very old. Certainly the bell would have rung out in joy at the birth of Edward of York, because his father governed Normandy for your Lancastrian King Henry at the time. Did you ever meet King Edward?'

'Happily I did not,' I replied flatly. 'Had I done so I fear it might have been to hear him pronounce my sentence of death.'

'And yet I gather you intend to marry his daughter, Elizabeth.'

'I have vowed to marry Elizabeth of York, yes Madame. I believe only a union between the Houses of York and Lancaster can bring an end to the terrible conflict England has suffered these many years.'

'She and her sisters are now living at the usurper's court I understand. A little unseemly perhaps, since his queen has lately died?'

I stared at her aghast. 'I had not heard of Queen Anne's death. It must have occurred quite recently.'

'A week or so ago but the news only reached us this morning. You seem surprised but I thought she had been ill for some time.' Anne busied herself washing her hands in the silver bowl of water offered by a page. 'Does this affect your plans, Henri?'

I took my turn at hand washing, using the time to compose myself. 'I hope not, Madame. However there are rumours that Richard wishes to marry Elizabeth himself, ostensibly for the same reason I do, because she is her father's heir and commands the loyalty of many.'

'But surely she is his niece! The Pope does not grant dispensations for such a minimal degree of separation. Not to mention the fact that he is the man responsible for – let us call it "the disappearance" – of her brothers.'

'Let us call it murder, Madame! In my view there can be no doubt.' I gave a harsh sigh. 'And he is unlikely to give her any choice in the matter. It is more urgent than ever that I take an army to confront him.'

Her eyes suddenly glittered with excitement and to my astonishment I felt her hand on my thigh beneath the cloth. 'I do so admire a man of ambition, Henri and nothing stirs the senses like a shared exploit, do you not agree?' Her grip tightened on the muscles of my leg. 'Marie! Even though you are a king, I believe you must train every day.'

With some difficulty I edged out of her grasp. 'It is a knight's duty Madame,' I said. 'I think every thigh in this room is probably as taut as a bowstring, except perhaps the Archbishop's.' I cast a knowing glance down the board to where the young and newly installed Archbishop of Rouen was chewing the breast off a quail with gusto.

To my relief Anne laughed and lifted her hand above the board to pick up her cup. 'But I wager he relishes a breast as much as any man – of a bird I mean of course. To your health, Henri!'

38

Margaret

THE DEATH OF QUEEN Anne had given rise to rumours of poison and witchcraft, like those that had followed the death of the Duke of Clarence's wife seven years before, stirring the king's wrath. Much of it did not reach me but Thomas occasionally made swift visits to Stanley House and in the privacy of the bedchamber, out of the earshot of Richard's 'stooges', was able to transmit true and full details of the usurper's dilemma. We sat in the window recess, which was as far from the entrance as possible.

'I have spoken to your friend Lady Vaux,' he said quietly. 'She is in no doubt that the queen's demise was from natural causes, unless Richard found someone to administer a slow and undetectable poison and make it look like death from the wasting disease,' he said, pouring us both wine from a jug.

My voice stayed low. 'Richard's soul is destined for Hell, whether he killed her or not.'

Thomas changed the subject. 'You may be pleased to hear that your friend has been granted a pension from the crown of twenty pounds a year but she remains at court for the time being as chaperone to the former princesses, and her daughter Joan stays with her as companion to the two older girls.'

At this point I gave way to some reprehensible self-pity. 'How I wish they could both be here with me, Thomas! I feel so useless. All I can do is pray for my relatives and friends. I have no idea where my son is, or if he is even alive! Is there any news at court about Henry?'

'No, but I have some good news for you, Margaret; not directly about Henry but about his intended bride. To squelch the speculation that he murdered his queen in order to marry Elizabeth of York, Richard is sending her away. I am ordered to assemble an escort and take her and her sisters to his Yorkshire stronghold of Sheriff Hutton. Richard has arranged a marriage—' Seeing my horrified expression he hastened to add, 'No – not for Elizabeth – perhaps he still plans to keep her for himself – but for Cecily. I am to take her onward to Upshall, on the North York moors, to marry Ralph Scrope, the younger brother of Lord Scrope of Masham.'

My face must have expressed the horror I felt. I did not have a great deal of time for Princess Cecily, who in contrast to her elder sister struck me as wilful and selfish; but this was a sad fate for a girl who had been brought up to antici-pate marriage to the heir to the Scottish throne, being sent to marry a low-status younger son in a peel castle on the edge of a wind-blasted moor. 'What on earth can the poor girl have done to deserve that?' I almost shouted and had to smother my exclamation in a cough. 'I know she can be difficult but marriage to a nobody who lives in a remote tower, which is probably buried in snow all winter, is practically a death sentence.'

Thomas shrugged. 'Perhaps Richard likes her as little as you do and wants to be rid of her. She may be jealous of Elizabeth but in a way she has brought the marriage on herself, behaving at court like a resentful, spoilt brat.'

My indignation was not assuaged, but then my husband gave me one of his enigmatic smiles. 'You never know, some unlikely unions forge a relationship that might almost be called love.'

'And some do not, Thomas,' I said, returning the smile. 'For Cecily's I predict the latter.'

One afternoon, less than a week later, the sound of multiple hooves on the central courtyard heralded a significant arrival. I was taking my morning exercise in the knot garden, shadowed as usual by my companion stooge and was astonished to see Lord Thomas bow two ladies through the entrance archway. To my delight it was Princess Elizabeth, followed by Joan Vaux. Except for Lord Thomas of course, who kissed me, we ladies all greeted each other with small curtsies, mindful of the stooge's eagle eyes. It was two years since I had shared her mother's solar with Elizabeth and months since I had seen Joan and I would have liked to add additional embraces as well.

'We are to stay here overnight, my lady, before departing for Sheriff Hutton,' Lord Stanley said loudly. 'I await the arrival of an additional troop of men at arms to strengthen the escort. I hope that will not overstretch your domestic arrangements.'

'It will not, my lord,' I said. 'There are always guest chambers ready, but how many horses and men will be requiring accommodation?'

'None. They can lodge at the Tower and return in the morning. There are some advantages to being Constable of England.' With his back to the stooge he cast his eyes towards the archway and added, 'Perhaps you might send your servant to the kitchen for refreshments. I cannot speak for the ladies but I have not yet dined today.'

I smiled inwardly, thinking how little my unwanted lady companion would appreciate being described as a servant, while I asked her politely to inform the cook of Lord Stanley's request. As soon as she disappeared I relaxed formalities and took Elizabeth and Joan's hands in mine. 'I cannot tell you how much it pleases me to see you both and to greet you properly, princess,' I said, dropping her a deep curtsy as if she had never been reduced from the ranks of royalty. 'So much time has passed since your father's death and I long to hear how your lady mother is coping with all the grief and insults she has been forced to endure. Where are Cecily and the younger girls? I thought you were all going to Sheriff Hutton.'

Elizabeth exchanged glances with Lord Stanley, who stepped in to explain. 'They are still at Westminster Palace and will be joining us tomorrow. Lady Elizabeth expressed a wish to speak with you before leaving London and I thought this the easiest way to make it possible.' He dug in his sleeve pocket, withdrew a small phial of liquid and handed it to me. 'I have acquired something that will give your night guard a sound sleep and you will have time to confer in safety after dark.'

The princess watched me tuck the phial away in my bodice. 'I do not want to compromise you, Lady Margaret,' she said with a nervous cough, 'but I thought you should hear what I have to say from my own mouth. It concerns your son Henry, that is why.'

Thomas started to explain further but bit back the words when he noticed the stooge reappear through the archway. She must have quickly passed on the message to a genuine servant and the garden was no longer a safe place for us to speak freely.

I had always suspected that the overnight stooge made free use of the bedchamber wine flagon and the proof of it greeted me when I peeped through the door after evening prayers and found her fast asleep in the anteroom already. So I made my way swiftly to the arranged meeting place in the guest wing of the house. In candlelight Princess Elizabeth looked almost ethereally beautiful, sitting writing at a table, having in the summer heat removed her outer gown and headdress and combed out her long, red-gold hair. As it was nearly midsummer the shutters were not yet closed and a luminous sunset, visible through the open window, filled the room with a rosy glow. Joan Vaux was busy in a corner shaking out discarded clothes and brushing off dusty riding boots. As it was too warm for a fire, the hearth stood empty.

Elizabeth pushed back her chair and came to greet me as I entered on soft soles. 'I saw no one to challenge me on the way here,' I told her. 'And my stooge is sleeping like a baby.'

She offered me a seat across the small table and went to a sideboard to fetch a tray of wine and sweetmeats. I gazed at her as she returned, a nineteen-year-old beauty who had experienced more than her fair share of grief, deceit and loss. 'May I ask who you are writing to?' I said accepting a cup and a sugared plum.

'My mother,' she replied, sitting down. 'It may be my last chance to write uncensored for some time. One can never predict the future.' She pushed the half-written page aside and put down the tray. 'Do you really believe, for instance, that your son Henry can take the throne from my uncle Richard?'

I did not hurry to reply, wondering what she hoped to hear. Did she want me to give her an emphatic yes because she would rather marry Henry, or was she, as some rumours suggested, attracted to the older, more familiar father-figure offered by the usurper?

'Yes, I do,' I said at length. 'Do you believe that your uncle Richard has petitioned the Pope for dispensation to marry you? And if so, that he will get it?'

'I say no to both those questions, my lady,' she replied. 'But I will also say that he would like to marry me. And not just for the reason your Henry wishes to.'

'Which is?'

She shrugged. 'Because I am York and he is Lancaster, and I have more claim to the throne than he does.'

'Is that not also why Richard wants to marry you?'

'It is one of the reasons yes.' She smiled and her teeth were pearly white. 'It is all about dynasty, is it not?'

'Royal marriage is always about dynasty,' I agreed. 'Do you think that is wrong?'

Her eyes widened. 'Oh no. I have been brought up to expect to further a dynasty. Does Henry wish to father one?'

'I have not asked him but I imagine he does. What he wants from a marriage with you is to bring an end to the conflict in this kingdom. I think both are laudable ambitions.'

'And are they your ambitions as well, my lady?' She took a sip from her cup and I followed suit. It was not wine but small ale. She must have requested it especially, as we usually provided wine to visitors. I took another sip. I was thirsty but not for strong drink.

'At present I am hardly in a position to have any ambition for myself,' I pointed out. 'Mine is all for my son.'

'Do you think I would come to love him?' Her grey eyes held mine in a candid gaze.

At last she was showing signs of her youth I realised, considering my answer carefully. Had I wanted love as a young girl? I thought I had found it with my first husband and perhaps that was why I now expended so much effort on the product of it. But I had been so young; much younger than her. 'Yes princess, I genuinely think you might.' Her gaze broke away and her cheeks flushed, as if she was surprised by my answer. 'Is that what you want?' I asked gently.

She suddenly became business-like and changed the subject. 'This is not what I wanted to discuss,' she declared. 'You said that you believed your son could take the throne from King Richard. So now I ask, how could I help that to happen?'

I was momentarily stunned. 'You mean you want him to do so?'

'Yes.' She nodded emphatically and her expression became dynamic. 'Yes I do. I loved my little brothers. I believe Edward would have made an excellent king; he was clever and charming and within only a few years would have become an intelligent and just ruler. But he was not given the chance. It is a crime and a sin and I want the man responsible to be held to account. And I believe that man to be my uncle Richard. Oh, he may not have actually killed the boys himself but he was in charge of the kingdom. He should have kept them safe, not let them become victims of his or anyone else's ambition. He does not deserve to sit on the throne that should be Edward's.'

I took a deep breath. This vehemence on her part was totally unexpected. 'And you believe that Henry does deserve to?'

'There is no one else,' she said simply. 'This terrible civil conflict between York and Lancaster has cut the tree of Edward the Third to pieces. I have looked at the roll in the Westminster palace library on which it is inscribed and I have wept. I would demand to take the throne myself if I thought I could muster the means to do so but I am a woman and no nobleman I know would or could ask his affinity to follow a female into battle. My mother discovered that to her cost when my father died. But I want to bring something of what my brother would have brought to the throne and I believe you and Henry Tudor and Lord Stanley and all their followers can help me to do it.'

It was at this point that Lord Stanley arrived, looking unusually flustered. 'I have been delayed by a message from the king,' he said straight away, without even making a bow of greeting. 'I am clearly under suspicion. The court is in Nottingham and I wrote requesting leave to go to Lathom after delivering the princesses to their destinations. He has given me permission to be absent from court as long as I am recruiting, which of course I said I was. But he demands that George take my place at his side as a sign of my good intent.' He drew up a chair and sat down. 'He does not say it in so many words but he is taking my son and heir hostage and I am going to have to let him.'

39

Henry

Honfleur on the Seine Estuary, Normandy, July 1485

FORTUNATELY SOON AFTER I had arrived in Paris a young English cleric called Richard Foxe, who had been attending the University, had come to offer his services and I soon realised that he not only shared my fierce opposition to his throne-stealing namesake but also possessed prodigious skill in both letters and figures. So it was not long before he became my unofficial Chancellor and Secretary, seeming to relish the workload, which increased daily as records needed to be kept of personnel, correspondence and funds, plus notes and minutes taken of agreements and meetings. Not only did I value his skills, I also began to appreciate his sound advice, even if it did not always mirror my own direction of thought. When the French king and his sister had returned to Paris in June, the last offer she made was a royal loan of forty thousand livres, for which I of course expressed heartfelt thanks. However, it was not made in writing and when I relayed the information to Richard Foxe for recording, he was sceptical.

'I should not spend it, my liege, until you see either a written pledge or the coffers full of coin,' he suggested. 'I do not believe Madame la Grande can have had time to acquire the endorsement of the Regency Council and it is a very large sum for her to pledge without their consent.'

'But it will hire another two thousand men, Master Foxe,' I protested. 'And Lord Jasper is champing at the bit to commission them. Also we could buy hand-gonnes for our French infantry, who have only crossbows so far. If we wait too long to order them they will not be ready in time for them to practise.'

He shrugged. 'You will need to show the pledge in writing in order to obtain both men and guns, my liege. Unless you are a crowned king they cannot be hired or purchased without proof of funds.'

'Perhaps not but they can be located. Are you really so doubtful that this is a genuine offer? I have faith in Madame de Beaujeu's integrity.'

Foxe made a small gesture of submission. 'Of course it is your wager to call, sire. I merely give my opinion.'

I chose to sit on the fence. 'We will wait two weeks before making any further move,' I said. 'Thank you for your candour Master Foxe.'

At the beginning of July we moved down the Seine to the port of Honfleur and as I walked with my entourage through the narrow streets to the inn hired as our headquarters, I realised with trepidation that such a port could provide fatally easy access to any assassin sent by the usurper from England to put an abrupt end to my life. We already knew that he had a comprehensive spy network he could call on for 'special duties' and I appointed a personal guard from my most trusted followers to protect me.

Otherwise the port was ideal for our purpose, tucked away from the fierce Channel winds and providing a haven large enough to moor a flotilla of sea-going vessels. The bulk of our recruits could be transported by barge down the Seine straight to their ships, along with the necessary food and drink, weapons, artillery and ammunition, saving the town from becoming clogged with carts and overwhelmed by thousands of men at arms. Of course this plan relied on the arrival of the promised ships before the men and supplies completed their journey from Sens, but a week after our arrival in Honfleur there was still no sign of them, or of Anne de Beaujeu's promised loan of forty thousand livres.

There were tense meetings with my council, when I found it increasingly difficult to persuade them that we had to trust King Charles and continue to pursue arrangements for the expedition. Even Lord Jasper, usually the most optimistic among us, became fretful and joined my daily visits to the Church of St Etienne on the harbourside. I regretted the absence of Christopher Urswicke, who had made a risky trip to England, to hear my anxious confession, my growing fear that I was misleading thousands of men into trusting my ability to rule their country, when I could not even organise an invasion force. He at least might have given me the comfort of absolution.

Christopher's sudden return from England took us all by surprise. Most of my advisers were with me, gathered in conference when he came in, bringing his sumpter's panniers and dumping them on the floor of the taproom, which doubled as a council chamber. The coffers he pulled from them came as welcome financial relief.

He knelt to kiss my ring and I motioned him to rise. 'You would be extremely welcome Christopher, even without what I anticipate is in those coffers,' I said, indicating a space on the end of a nearby bench. 'Pease sit and take refreshment. We have missed your ministry and sound advice.'

'I bring funds from Lord Stanley and your grace's mother. I collected them from their house in Liverpool and took ship from there. Luckily it was a swift voyage, without incident.'

I beckoned to Davy Owen, who moved forward from the back of the room. 'Could you see that these coffers go to Master Foxe please, Davy? I believe he will be in the strong room as usual.' When I saw the effort the squire had to make to lift the coffers I realised the strength of the sturdy priest. 'Get Roland to help you,' I suggested. 'And ask Master Foxe to join us as soon as he has counted the contents. Then we can set about paying some bills around the town.'

'I have other news that might please you, my lord,' Christopher said, straddling the bench and accepting a tankard of ale from one of the other squires.

'If you saw my mother it would please me greatly to hear that she is well,' I probed.

He shook his head. 'I was not permitted into her company I fear. However Lord Stanley told me that she is well, but fractious.'

I smiled grimly. 'That does not surprise me. House arrest may not be incarceration but it is still hard and she has borne it for fifteen months. When did you see Lord Stanley?'

'He met me in Liverpool and he looked a worried man. There was much talk of the usurper at the taverns I stopped at on the journey from London and I gathered that he is mustering in anticipation of an invasion so he knows of your preparations. He must have spies here in France.'

'Oh, he has plenty and not just spies! He would rather be rid of me than fight me. I do not move these days without my personal guard. Where is he based? Did you manage to glean that information? It will affect where we make our landing. The last thing we need is the usurper's army lined up on the shore to greet us.'

'He has been in or around Nottingham since June,' Christopher revealed. 'And his commissioners of array are recruiting all over the country. But let me tell you my other news, my liege, about the ships.'

'By all means tell me,' I encouraged.

'The captain of the ferryboat from Le Havre pointed out a large number of sails on the far horizon. He thought they must be corsairs or pirates.'

I frowned, feeling my heart begin to flutter with anticipation. 'Could they be the ships King Charles promised?'

'Well if they're headed to Honfleur they should be close enough by now to see their ensigns from here. Shall we find a viewpoint?'

Our inn was close to the town wall and we swiftly made for the fortified gate that guarded the road to Caen. From its battlements there was a view down the estuary and, to my growing excitement, ships of various tonnages were converging from both east and west. The width of my smile probably rivalled the estuary mouth. I felt as if I had been granted absolution.

We made our way down to the quay to watch the first vessels drop anchor. The flagship, considerably larger than any I had seen before, particularly attracted Lord Jasper's interest. 'It is called a carrack – the newest form of ocean-going vessel,' he enthused, 'and belongs no doubt to the admiral we were told would command the flotilla. What was his name Harri?'

'Guillaume de Casenove. Madame de Beaujeu told me he was a good friend of her father King Louis, who turned him from a corsair with an infamous reputation into a French admiral and put him in charge of policing this side of the Channel.'

Jasper gave a bark of laughter. 'Ha! Yes, he sounds like quite a character. He must be a greybeard by now though.'

'Well I shall make sure to be on his ship. It looks as if it could outrun any other.'

Counting the smaller ships sailing into the bay behind the big carrack, a quick calculation revealed deck space for three thousand men, but we had field guns and supplies to carry as well.

The admiral disembarked and made his way to the inn for refreshment and strategic discussions. 'Have no fear that you will be short of transport, my lord king,' he assured me when I asked whether more ships would be coming. 'Your friend Jean de Rieux has organised another flotilla from Brittany. They will be here very soon.'

'That is welcome news, my lord admiral. Our men and supplies are only two days away and I have sent to the Louvre for the guns King Charles promised. Do you have any skill divining the weather? If it is favourable in ten days' time, then that is when we will depart.'

'And where exactly is our destination?' he asked.

'That is still a secret.' We were sitting in the tap room, which was busy with men talking in hushed groups and servants coming and going; eyes and ears, of which I could never be entirely sure. 'There is no point in letting the usurper know in advance.'

He scrutinised me fiercely with his sun-faded gaze. 'You have stayed alive so far but you are right to be extra vigilant here in Honfleur; there are too many dark alleyways and Godless men. My ship is guarded at all times and safely out in the haven. You could bring your bodyguard with you and stay on board until we leave.'

His offer was a good one but I could not accept. 'It is a fine idea sir but I prefer to stay with my men. We have much to arrange and it would be time-consuming for them to come to the ship to communicate with me.'

He shrugged, gave a brisk nod and raised his cup. 'I salute you Henri le Roi,' he declared. 'I hope you will at least let me sail you personally to your kingdom.'

I returned his salute. 'Now that is an offer I will gratefully accept.'

Davy Owen and Roland de Belleville had been acting as my body squires for several months but I decided that evening to send Davy to Wales, to stir up the landholders there. 'It is not enough to just send letters,' I told him. 'The Comte de Rieux has shown me that recruiting is done best through personal contact.'

Davy looked dubious. 'I will go if you wish of course, Harri, but I only have faint memories of any of the Welsh gentry,' he said.

'Yes but your father was Owen Tudor. That name is

enough. This matter is urgent, Davy. There is a ship in the harbour which is heading for Tenby tomorrow and I need you to be on it.'

Roland was busy unlacing my hose and took me by surprise when he suddenly spoke up. 'I do not wish to abandon you, Monsieur Henri, but could I not be of more use to Davy? I would like to go with him if he would accept my company and you would permit it.'

I frowned, remaining silent as I studied the boy's beard-less face, full of eager expectation as he tugged the hose from my feet. Gossip surrounding his birth and his connec-tion to me had faded gradually among my household and he had kept laudably quiet about it himself. He was just another young squire, fiercely protected by Davy if anyone tried to bully him.

'What do you think, Davy?' I asked his mentor. 'Would Roland be a help or a hindrance?'

Davy grinned at the boy and gave him a soft cuff on the ear. 'He would be a nuisance of course but at least he can look after the horses.' He shot me a sharp glance. 'We will be able to acquire horses when we reach Wales, will we not?'

I laughed, pleased at an outcome I had not anticipated but which seemed exactly right. 'I do not expect you to tramp around Wales on foot like bards and minstrels, Davy. Besides there is not enough time. Master Foxe has instruc-tions to provide you with funds to purchase mounts and to maintain you on your travels. I expect you to meet me with the promise of hundreds of recruits soon after our landing, which will be in South Wales, but keep that to yourselves. I will not tell you exactly where yet but word will reach you, have no fear.'

Two days later the Breton ships sailed in, bringing sacks of sarrasin flour, wheels of hard cheese and a troop of armed recruits from the duchy's ports and fishing villages. Having welcomed the commander at the quayside and left him for the present to his tasks, Lord Jasper and I decided to visit the Church of St Catherine to give thanks. 'The very place to thank God for the magnificent flotilla we now have at our disposal,' said Jasper.

It was the church the sailors frequented, because it had been built by the town's shipbuilders and resembled an upturned hull.

I had noticed its unusual design but it was located in a rough quarter, amidst narrow, crowded streets, where taverns and brothels served the needs of sailors from many different countries; the kind of area I usually avoided. However, as it was only a matter of days before we would take to the open sea ourselves, I was keen to offer prayers and thanks in a church dedicated to preserving the lives of mariners and the ships they sailed in.

We left my bodyguard with their clattering sword-belts and nailed boots outside and entered together, leaving them with orders to search any subsequent visitors for weapons. The church's likeness to a ship was more marked inside than out, the bare, arched ribs of the roof resembling the inner hull of a cog or caravel. The usual rows of candles burned beneath holy statues set in niches and a pair of young, cassocked priests turned silently from tending the flames, recognised us as nobility and bowed, content to let us approach the altar and kneel on the steps before the carved and painted image of Christ on the Cross.

The smell of hot candlewax, wood and preserving oil

calmed my jangling nerves and, our prayers done, the sense of peace and the undoubted presence of God followed me back down the nave, where I pressed a gold crown into the senior priest's palm as an offering. Jasper hung back to tell him how impressed he was with the architecture and I wandered idly into the porch alone – except that I was not alone.

With the outside door closed, the porch was dark and an assailant came hurtling out of nowhere and caught me from behind, one arm and leg pinning my left arm and sword to my side and the other slashing a knife blade upwards towards my throat. I jabbed it away with my other arm and dug my elbow sharply into his ribcage but he was not to be shifted. 'This is from King Richard!' his voice snarled in my ear as I saw the knife glint close to my face where a stray beam of light penetrated a crack in the timber-work. I grabbed at his wrist and sunk my chin into my chest to protect my throat but the blade still edged towards my face. Whoever he was, he was extremely strong. Where the hell was Jasper, I thought desperately, staggering forward to try and shake him off and kicking back with my right foot. I should have yelled for help but instead my mind screamed silent curses and prayers. Jesu save me! Blessed Saint Armel – not now, not yet!

Salvation came in a burst of light as the outside door flew open and a figure surged in, black and anonymous against the glare. 'Monsieur Henri!' he cried and hurled himself at the two of us screeching like a demon. If my assailant was strong, this man was even stronger, for the knife was wrenched from the attacker's hand and used instead to slice at his forearm, revealing the sharpness of the blade in a spurt of bright red blood, which surged through the coarse cloth of his sleeve, accompanied by a yell of pain and anger. The weight fell off my back and I pulled away, turning to catch a glimpse of my would-be murderer's face, his mouth contorted with fury and both his hands reaching for my rescuer's throat. My own hand went straight to my shortsword, but my intention to run him through was pre-empted by Lord Jasper who hurtled in from the church wielding his own poniard, which he plunged into my attacker's back. At the same time my burly rescuer had thrust the knife he held into his chest. The would-be assassin crumpled to the floor, leaving Lord Jasper and my rescuer facing each other over his body, each hesitating over whether to strike again.

'Hold uncle!' I had recognised the other man. 'He is a friend. His name is Jean Perret. He has just saved my life.'

At this point several of my guards arrived, alerted by the yells from inside the porch and the priest rushed in from the church, crying out in alarm at the sight of the blood, the blades and the huddled body on the floor.

'It is all right, Father,' said Lord Jasper, calmly wiping his dagger on the dead man's jacket and slipping it back into its sheath. 'There is no need to deliver divine unction. This man is the devil's spawn and is headed straight to Hell. He has just tried to murder the king of England.'

40

Henry

Aboard the Poulain de Dieppe, *August 1485*

ADMIRAL DE CASENOVE'S BIG carrack had an unusual name, *Poulain de Dieppe*, and I remarked on it, gesturing up at the gilded words as we were rowed under its stern.

'I had the ship built at my own expense – here in Honfleur as it happens – and so I gave it its name,' declared the Admiral stoutly. 'A *poulain* is a young horse, a colt, and I called it that because it goes like the wind. *Poulain de Dieppe* because Dieppe, on the coast of Normandy, is where I was born and where I learned to sail.'

I nodded, satisfied. 'It is a good name for a fast ship. I only hope we do not lose all the others in the flotilla as we did in a storm on my last expedition.'

His laugh was characteristically boisterous. 'Ha, ha! That would not suit you at all, would it my lord? Because you have not told them where they are heading. But do not worry, the weather is set fair and we shall not lose sight of the other ships. We will all arrive at the mouth of your Milford Haven together.'

'Yes, we will sir, because I have called a meeting of all the captains here on your ship at dawn tomorrow. That is when I will tell them our destination and no one will return to shore before we sail. I want no chance of the usurper learning of our destination and sending ships and troops to intercept us. How long do you think it will take us to get there?' I had revealed our landing place to the Admiral the previous night and he had immediately left my chamber to consult his charts.

'If we were sailing alone with present conditions prevailing, it would take us a mere three days but these little cogs and caravels do not carry so much sail and cannot therefore travel as fast.' He waved expansively at the thirty smaller ships moored in lines across the haven, already loaded with guns and supplies and crowded with men talking and laughing and making music out on the open decks as the sun kissed the sea to the west. 'Keeping together and the wind remaining steady, we should all reach your beachhead within the week.'

'And when we do, how long do you estimate it will take us to unload the cargo and men?'

The Admiral gave me a sly smile. 'You have chosen a good time of year to sail, my lord king, and I will choose a good time to arrive. According to my calculations the tide will be ebbing there at sunset and in the hour before low water we can run the cogs up onto the beach. You say there is plenty of sand in front of the cliffs?'

'So my uncle assures me and he knows the place but we must be able to get the guns and carts up the cliff path before the tide flows.'

'We can unload straight onto the beach, guns first,' said the Admiral. 'They can be lowered by winches straight onto their cradles and wheeled away. Carts can be dropped off too and then arms and provisions lowered into them by the same method. The men can simply climb down the ladders, taking their weapons with them. The only people who will need to disembark by boat are those on board the *Poulain de Dieppe*, which is too large and heavy to re-float; that is you and your retainers, *Majesté*. All should be ashore before dark and we can re-float on the incoming tide at moonrise.'

'You make it sound simple Admiral but I remember vividly our arrival in Brittany, when we were driven onto the sand by storm waves and thought we would hit the cliffs or smash on the rocks,' I recollected. 'I pray the Almighty will not show us His wrath like that again.'

'Who can tell what He has in store but all the auguries are good.' The Admiral sniffed experimentally. 'The breeze sends me portents of prolonged fair weather – not good conditions for pirating! We liked it rough and murky so we could pounce on the merchantmen out of the fog.' His hearty laugh rang out as rope ladders snaked down from the deck above, to be caught by the oarsmen. 'Now, may it please you to climb aboard?'

A plentiful and tasty farewell feast had been prepared on the carrack and it was a lively party that filled the Admiral's cabin that evening. Occupying the entire top deck of the aftcastle, this spacious and panelled room was a far cry from the cramped little shelter on the fishing boat *Marie Gwyn*, in which our small band of exiles had huddled during our storm-tossed escape from Wales fourteen years before. I missed Davy's company; he would have understood how the memories of that hazardous voyage into the unknown came flooding back to me.

Around the table in that lamp-lit cabin sat the men of my personal entourage, chosen partly according to rank and family relationship and partly from my assessment of their potential as trustworthy soldiers and advisers. Lord Jasper was pre-eminent among them and either side of him Philibert de Chandée and my mother's half-brother John, Viscount Welles, the heir to her late stepfather's attainted estates in Lincolnshire. Given their renowned military skills, the Earl of Oxford and his boon companion Viscount Beaumont were also obvious choices, along with the men who had enabled their escape from Hammes Castle, James Blount and John Fortescue, and I could not leave out Edward Courtenay, heir to the attainted Earl of Devon, or the ebullient Ned Woodville. All these men looked to be restored to their family estates when the usurper was dethroned. The unreliable Marquess of Dorset had been left in France, in the courtly custody of King Charles and his sister, as a convenient hostage for repayment of the loans I had received from the French exchequer.

I had appointed two worthy men to replace Davy and Roland as my chamber squires, William Brandon and his younger brother Tom, who had fled their Suffolk home to join me in Paris, and my chosen Master of Ordnance was Richard Guildford, who had served King Edward before fleeing the usurper's reign. Finally and crucially, I could not do without my financial and spiritual supports, the clerics Richard Foxe and Christopher Urswicke.

Thus, including myself and the Admiral, we were sixteen buccaneers, bravely ignoring the fact that we were embarking on a do-or-die mission, while eating what was probably our last decent meal for some time and bolstering our spirits by singing sea-shanties to music played with gusto on fiddle and pipes by two of the ship's crew. The only man who clearly felt no qualms about the weeks ahead was the ageing but swashbuckling Guillaume de Casenove, who had only to navigate thirty ships to a remote Welsh beach, watch men, supplies and guns unloaded, then sail blithely back to France, probably to live out his life peacefully on the proceeds of his considerable remuneration and the profits of his pirating days.

In the past my best-laid plans to claim my birthright had been destroyed by elements beyond my control and so, as the *Poulain de Dieppe* sailed out of the Seine estuary the following morning, leading the flotilla like a hart before his herd of hinds, I stood in the prow of the ship feeling the balmy summer breeze trying to lift the hat from my head and praying to Saint Armel for heavenly intercession.

'There is so much more at stake than when the *Marie Gwyn* took us away from our country,' I confided to the saint on whom I had become so reliant, fingering my amulet, now nearly featureless from wear. 'Let God not find me so proud and arrogant that He sends another storm to punish me, for there are many good men sworn to my cause who would be blamelessly lost. And if the Almighty spares me to take the throne of England, I vow to build a chapel to Our Lady, that all men will wonder at.'

I was so lost in prayer and reflection that I did not hear footsteps behind me and jumped at the sound of my uncle's voice. 'Your council is waiting, Harri.'

When I turned, my doleful expression clearly surprised

him for he reached out a hand to grip my arm. 'What troubles you, nephew? You seem weighed down with woe when you should be celebrating; we are going home!'

'I am full of trepidation, uncle,' I admitted. 'Two years ago I fled to France from Brittany with only the clothes on my back and an enemy at my heels. Now I am embarking on what strikes me as a preposterous mission – to claim the throne of England. Thousands of men will risk their lives in order to put a crown on the head of a man who is a stranger in the country he aims to lead. I come armed with men and guns to prove my right to rule over a nation that barely knows my name. Do you wonder I am swamped with doubt? Does my blood truly flow with Lancastrian resolve; the boldness of Bolingbroke, the valour of his son of Monmouth, or even the conviction of *his* saintly son of Windsor?'

I thought Lord Jasper's grip would crunch my upper arm into splinters. Gone was his air of easy charm, supplanted by heightened colour and a gimlet gaze. 'May God forgive you, Harri Tudor! Your lady mother would be ashamed of you. It is too late to question your right or your ability to rule. There are five hundred Englishmen on this ship alone, who have put their trust in you to oust the devil's acolyte and bring peace to their country, under a fair and just ruler. To say nothing of the Frenchies and Scots and Bretons, and the Welshmen to come, who have sworn to put their weapons at your disposal. By right of your mother's bloodline, they believe you are the one God has chosen to bring this about, and do it you will!'

At last he released me from his terrier grip and took a step back but his expression remained implacable. 'I believe in you, your lady mother believes in you and many Englishmen you have yet to meet are relying on you to lead them to confront the tyrant. They see you as their only possible future. Besides, when you land it is entirely possible that Richard will be so cowed by reports of the multitude that has rushed to your standard that he will take fright and flee to the skirts of his sister Margaret in Flanders, just as his brother Edward once did.'

This last scenario struck me as so unlikely that I found rumbles of laughter taking the place of the trembling in my belly. 'Ha! I have heard wishful thinking before uncle but that caps it all! Richard of Gloucester has declared to Englishmen that I am the bastard aggressor who will seize their property, a heinous enemy whose soldiers will burn their crops and rape their wives and daughters. To flee from that would commit him to history as a coward and a liar.' I rubbed ruefully at my aching muscle. 'Incidentally, I pity the men who cross weapons with you, my lord; your sword arm is powerful!'

Jasper tugged a little guiltily at his beard and grunted in amusement. 'Hm! I may have been a little over-forceful there Harri but for a moment I thought the faeries had substituted a changeling for the real Henry Tudor. Now, as we walk back to the Admiral's lair perhaps you will tell me why you have called this meeting?'

'The landing on our native soil should be marked in some memorable way and I have made a list of men I intend to dub knights,' I began, stepping carefully over a coiled rope. 'Philibert de Chandée is one of them. You know more of the rules of chivalry than I do. Would there be any objection to my dubbing a Frenchman, do you think?'

'I can see no problem and such recognition might help him to control his more exuberant recruits,' he replied. 'He expects to have a hard job with some of them but he says a long march should sort them out.'

'Especially those who are dragging the guns,' I agreed. 'It will not be an easy task over the high places.'

'It will be worth it though. There are scores of cannon in the Tower of London and Richard will have a huge battery. Who else is on your list?'

We halted at the bottom of the ladder that led up to the Admiral's cabin. 'I have asked William Brandon to carry my standard. He is a strong man and a fine rider but it does mean that in the field he would be without a free hand to wield a weapon. It is an honour not everyone would be glad to bear and such sacrifice deserves a knighthood I believe.'

Lord Jasper nodded decisively. 'Unquestionably. His father is a knight, as I remember, and Will is the eldest son. It would be appropriate. How many are on the list?'

'Twelve so far, a good number but there may be others who occur to me during the voyage. Let me know of any you would recommend.'

'I will.' At the door to the great cabin he stood aside with a courtly smile and bowed. 'After you, my lord king.'

After my battle with doubt, the seven days it took the flotilla to reach the entrance to Milford Haven were among the calmest of my life, both in terms of weather and my own mood. Perhaps it was in answer to my fervent prayers, or due to the regular masses held on deck by Bishop Courtenay of Exeter that the Almighty sent us perfect winds and moderate seas to carry us to the coast of Pembrokeshire without incident. The Bishop had fled his diocese in full armour after the failure of the storm-hit rebellion two years before and the daily appearance of this soldier prelate with his mace, cope and mitre, seemed to impress and encourage the band of exiles, who otherwise used the open deck to hone their fitness and practice their weapons skills.

Many of our followers had been none the wiser when Lord Jasper told them we had chosen to land at the mouth of Milford Haven. The location was as far away as possible from the usurper's heartland and within the boundaries of the earldom of Pembroke, on lands that had been granted to my uncle by his half-brother, King Henry the Sixth. During his time as earl, Lord Jasper had made alliances with many of the surrounding gentry and expected to attract substantial military support from them. Also his contacts had informed him that although the usurper had increased the garrison at Pembroke Castle, which stood at the eastern elbow of the long and winding Haven, for some reason he had reduced the garrison at Dale, at its western mouth, to a minimum.

'Perhaps he assumes that we are unlikely to land such a distance away, the crossing from France to southern England being both shorter and less risky,' my uncle had concluded. 'But he forgets what advantage this gives us. We will gather support as we march through the Principality and muster with our northern Welsh allies in the March.'

Being acquainted with the geography of England and Wales only on paper, I felt unable to assess Lord Jasper's proposed campaign in any detail but I had been much encouraged once the Earl of Oxford had vetted and thoroughly approved of my uncle's dispositions. My confidence was further boosted by a message from Davy Owen just before we sailed indicating that Rhys ap Thomas, the usurper's appointed Lieutenant in South Wales, had hinted through a close relative that he might turn coat. Lord Jasper had been jubilant. 'If Rhys joins us Richard's knees will surely tremble!' he had crowed.

Even so, all these plans depended on making a safe landing and that depended on Admiral de Casenove successfully steering our flotilla of ships through the treacherous waters between Land's End and the scattered Isles of Scilly, where many a vessel had come to grief. At this crucial point his pirate days served him, and us, in good stead. For several years he had played cat and mouse with unwary merchant ships in those tricky seas and made detailed charts of the random, barely-submerged rocks to be avoided. Nor did we encounter any of the usurper's naval patrols, indicating that they must be concentrating on England's southern shore.

All our ships made safe passage, rounding the famous headland like a flock of eager seagulls and sailing towards the Welsh coast unopposed on a brisk southerly wind. When the shout 'Land Ho!' went up from the crow's nest it was only a blurry line on the horizon, but it stirred emotions in me that I had not expected. Sudden images of the white walls of Pembroke Castle and the rolling hills around Raglan flashed through my mind, inspiring bittersweet recollections of childhood.

I found Lord Jasper up on the poop-deck, keeping his back to the mariner on the whipstaff and I could tell from the way his throat was working that he too was fighting his emotions. I laid my arm companionably around his shoulders and he turned his head. Our misty eyes met.

I cleared my throat. 'It may not look much from here,

uncle, but it was once all yours, and will be again if God should favour us.'

'The land of your birth, Harri,' he said. 'May it welcome you with open arms.'

'And with men at arms I hope,' I responded dryly.

41

Henry

Mill Bay, Pembrokeshire, the landing, 7th August 1485

ILLUMINATED BY THE DYING sun, the cliffs around Mill Bay were dramatically layered in shades of rose pink and blood red rocks, shot with random ribbons of white limestone and yellow clay. Storm, wind and waves had created an artwork of nature's diverse colours and sculpted shapes reminiscent of heraldic beasts from the fallen boulders at the base of the cliffs. I chose one with a bear-like outline to lift me high enough for the sun's rays to catch my face before it slipped below St Ann's Head, the northern gatepost of Milford Haven.

I had a good view of the teeming bustle of activity in the bay. A haphazard row of cogs lay at slight angles, their timbers still gently swept by the receding tide, their prows nudging the dark red sand into small heaps ahead of them. Ladders leaned against the lower gunwales, busy with men coming and going, and winches were slung over the bulwarks, their ropes straining under heavy loads. At the back of the bay, teams of men were hauling guns and carts up the steep path that led to a rough farm track; others were piling sacks of meal, rolling barrels of ale and wine, stacking bundles of arrows and chests of artillery ammunition above the high tideline, ready for collection. Richard Foxe's clerks were counting items and ticking them off on their tallies and Lord Jasper was making his way from the skiff that had just transported him from the *Poulain de Dieppe* to join the crowd of knights and squires gathering around the base of my natural podium. A select group of them were lined up at the front, their armour glowing in the sun's rays reflecting off mine.

I raised my arms and waited for quiet. My first words had been carefully chosen from the Book of Psalms.

'*Judica me, Deus, et discerne causam meam.* Judge me O God and favour my cause. These are the first words of psalm forty-three and an appropriate and memorable prayer for any soldier embarking on a great endeavour, as I am – as we all are. The psalmist goes on to beg the Almighty to deliver him from the deceitful and unjust man, another prayer we can all repeat as we set off to confront a man who truly deserves to be unseated from the throne of an honest and godly nation.'

There was a murmur of approval. The bear-rock having fulfilled its purpose as a pulpit, I leaped down and strode up to the line of polished and expectant candidates for knighthood.

Standing before them, I said, 'I salute the land of my birth,' dropping to my knees and bending to kiss the sand. Rising again I added, 'I invite you to do the same, salute this land that has provided us with a secure and secret

427

landing.' As one, they did so and remained kneeling in a gleaming line of chivalry.

Lord Jasper and Lord Oxford fell in behind me, ready to act as sponsors and behind them came two squires carrying sets of polished new spurs. The conferring of knight-hood was a solemn ritual, but I proceeded down the line of kneeling men with dignified haste, aware that the daylight was fading fast. I named them clearly one after another, striking each on the shoulder with my gauntleted fist. There were fourteen, starting with the two attainted noblemen, Lord John Welles and Lord Edward Courtenay, followed by the Commander of the French mercenaries, Philibert de Chandée and the heroes of Hammes, James Blount and John Fortescue. A clutch of other worthy squires followed, including at Jasper's suggestion Charles Somerset, the illegitimate and only son of my mother's cousin, Henry Beaufort, the last Somerset duke who, like my grandfather Owen Tudor, had been beheaded without trial by Yorkists following a skirmish on the Northumbrian moors. They were a loyal and varied group, all now linked in the brother-hood of knights.

Each new knight rose and the two earls kneeled and fastened the spurs on his heels. It was as I came to the last man in the line that I noticed a commotion on the cliff path. Two determined figures struggled to make their way down, to the rowdy disapproval of a team of men who were straining to haul a cannon up it. Even in the gathering dusk I recog-nised Davy Owen and Roland de Belleville. On an impulse I decided to delay dubbing the last kneeling squire. It was William Brandon and I gestured him to rise, murmuring a reassurance that it was only a temporary postponement. Then

I beckoned his brother Tom over to give him an errand, on which he hurried away.

Meanwhile I congratulated each of the new knights and left Lord Jasper to make a closing announcement. 'Let those of you who have attended this ceremony spread word among the company that these men have received the honour of knighthood from the hands of the king and must command the respect which their rank deserves.'

Meanwhile Davy and Roland had made their way through the bustle on the beach and finally reached us, bending the knee in formal greeting. 'What news do you have for me Davy?' I asked anxiously.

'My news is good – and bad, your grace,' he admitted. He was unshaven and hollow-eyed, like a man who had not slept for a week but Roland seemed cheerful and alert, gazing around excitedly at the hive of activity.

'What is the bad news?' I demanded.

'Rhys ap Thomas holds back. He has mustered a large force at Carew Castle but he will not publicly commit it. I fear he means to go to the usurper, sire.'

This was a severe blow and I did not conceal my disappointment. 'The Devil take him if he does!' I glanced at Lord Jasper, who looked as glum as I felt. 'Is that a guess, Davy, or do you have inside knowledge? Did you meet with Rhys?'

The squire shook his head. 'We went to Carew but were not admitted. The castle was crawling with men. I only have what I could glean from tavern gossip. The general consensus was that Rhys was sticking to York.'

I swore under my breath then drew myself up and glanced around. All the new knights had heard what Davy had said and I knew Rhys's absence would spread gloom around the campfires tonight. It was not a good start. 'More fool him. He will regret it if he does. Now, tell us your good news.'

Davy's face grew brighter. 'Your cousins Maredudd and Evan are recruiting hard in Gwynedd. They expect to bring five hundred men to the muster. A hundred more are promised in Haverford and John Wogan of Picton has brought a good number there already, about seventy I think. Oh, and the garrison at Dale have opened the gates and invited us to camp in the castle demesne.' He could not suppress a wide grin. 'I swear the captain went pea-green when I told him four thousand armed men were on the ships.'

'Has he sent out a messenger though?' growled Lord Jasper. 'To get word to the usurper?'

'Not to my knowledge,' said the squire. 'He is falling over himself to be helpful. Offered beds to the officers – I suppose that means you, my lords.'

I gave a sceptical grunt. 'Huh! I will feel safer in a tent among my own men,' I said. Over his shoulder I spotted Tom Brandon coming back from his errand, carrying a pair of spurs in one hand and a long pole in the other. 'But you have arrived just in time, Davy. You do not look like a squire who has held vigil, bathed and made your confession but we are in battle order and I invite you, travel-stained and weary though you are, to kneel with William here and receive the honour of knighthood.'

He stared at me, dazed. 'Knighthood? Here and now, at this very moment? From you, Harri?'

'Yes Davy, from me – from your king. I take it you are not going to refuse?'

Will Brandon saw his confusion and spoke encouragingly.

'Perhaps I am more prepared than you Davy. If his grace permits, I could receive the accolade first and become your sponsor afterwards. Then we will be true brothers in arms.'

Lord Jasper moved forward to remove Davy's sword from its sheath. 'And as you and I are already brothers, I will be the other sponsor. I will return this when you are a knight. Kneel down now, it grows dark and the king is waiting.'

Both squires knelt and I gave Will the accolade first, striking him so firmly on the shoulder that I saw the blow vibrate through his body but he did not wince or react. When he stood up Lord Jasper knelt to fasten the spurs and I reached out to take the pole from Tom. A brightly coloured cloth was wrapped tightly around its upper section. 'I appoint you, Sir William Brandon, standard-bearer to the king. This banner will be your sword in the field. May you defend it well.'

He took it from me, bowing his close-cropped head solemnly. 'In battle it will never leave my grip, sire, unless in death.'

I nodded approval and moved on to Davy, who pre-empted my administration of the accolade by putting up his hands as if in prayer and making the oath of fealty. 'I promise that in the future I will be faithful to my king, never cause him harm and observe my homage to him against all persons.'

Touched by this unexpected pronouncement I realised that due to our close friendship, he had never before actually sworn fealty to me as his king. I bent to enclose his hands in mine. 'I accept your vow, David Owen; I return your faith and hereby dub you knight.' The force of my blow took him by surprise but I believed it right that the act should be a memorable one.

Davy stood up and allowed Lord Jasper to return his sword to him, raising his arm to let it slide into its sheath. Will knelt before him to fasten on his new spurs while his eyes sought mine, solemn and soulful. In his gaze I saw pride, curiosity and a hint of disbelief; it stirred a memory from our youth of a foolish jibe I had made about him having no mother, words that I knew had deeply hurt him at the time. Quietly, so that my voice did not carry to the others, I said, 'You are not the only baseborn knight I have made today, Davy. I hope one day your mother will find out and be proud. You have been my rock and my friend ever since we were children. I trust no one more than you. If we knew who she was and where she was, I would write and tell her how much you deserve to be Sir David Owen.'

His Adam's apple jerked in his throat and when he spoke his voice was hoarse. 'One day perhaps, Harri . . . but not before we have all used our swords to make you king.' Will Brandon had completed his sponsor's task and Davy bent to lend a considerate hand to bring him to his feet. 'The exception is our standard bearer here, who will have only your banner to defend himself and must be hailed as the bravest of us all.'

Will shook his head in denial. 'I think that tribute should go to King Henry, Davy. It is he who is to lead us all to victory.'

I gave him a wry smile and turned again to Davy. 'Which reminds me Sir David, did you manage to acquire some horses during your mission?'

I had momentarily forgotten Davy's sense of humour. He put his palm to his forehead in a gesture of exaggerated despair. '*Mea culpa!* I completely forgot the horses!' Then he shot me a wicked glance under his brow. 'Of course I remembered the horses, Harri! There are mounts for you and your entourage waiting at Haverford, courtesy of Wogan of Picton. I cannot vouch for their magnificence but I guarantee they will be strong and nimble.'

'Good Welsh mountain ponies – excellent! Well done.' I put my hand on his shoulder and we turned towards the beach. The tide was at its furthest ebb and the flat stretch of hard red sand was now fully exposed, cluttered with stranded ships and off-loaded carts, which had yet to be filled with tents and provisions. However, to my concern there were still at least ten ships out in the bay, awaiting their turn. Lord Jasper came to my side to make a suggestion.

'If the garrison is now no threat, perhaps we should send the rest of the ships round to Dale beach. The light will last longer on the other side of the headland and if we are camping at the castle it is a shorter distance from the shore.'

I nodded in relief. 'A good idea, my lord, please give the order. Roland, can you find the victualler and tell him I want rations of ale and flour issued before the campfires are lit? The men will need bread to break their fast before they march at first light. We must get to Haverford by noon.'

42

Henry

The march through Wales, August 1485

LORD JASPER WAS APPREHENSIVE about the reception we would receive from the nearest town but to our surprise the scurriers reported that the gates of Haverford were open, with men already gathered in the marketplace carrying their weapons, ready to march out and join us. It was while he was organising their formal recruitment that Lord Jasper was approached by a soldier called Arnold Butler, a relative of Rhys ap Thomas by marriage, and the man who had warned Davy Owen of Rhys's reluctance to desert the usurper.

Arnold explained that this was due to a demand that he send his five-year-old son and heir to court in Nottingham as a guarantee of his loyalty. He had refused but was now wary of showing his hand. With nigh on two thousand men committed to his standard he was holed up twenty miles away in Carew Castle playing cat and mouse. I toyed with the idea of making a detour to confront him personally but decided my own troops might desert me if I left them.

We took delivery of the promised horses at Haverford, although 'horses' was an exaggeration, as the sturdy steeds were the size of those I had learned to ride on as a boy, while a ward of the Herberts at Raglan Castle. At least that experience had taught me that although they were small, Welsh ponies had more stamina than their taller kin and legs as strong as an ox's. Nevertheless, mounting my little flecked grey did make me hanker somewhat for Bastion. However, all thoughts of that kind vanished, as we tackled the Preseli Mountains north of Haverford, which gave us our first taste of the craggy terrain that my uncle had warned me typified the landscape of central and north Wales. The sturdy grey showed me exactly why Welsh fighting men favoured their native equine breed, coping nimbly with the steep slopes and rocky hazards underfoot.

In addition to providing us with a trouble-free Channel crossing, the recent fair weather and lack of rain had caused the usually fast-flowing streams of this mountainous region to shrink, so although we encountered many small water-ways, they were trickles rather than streams. Nevertheless hauling carts and cannons over such uneven hillsides was exhausting and the infantry, especially the French artillery-men, were much in need of rest and recovery by the time we reached the busy port of Cardigan. The small royal garrison kept the castle gates firmly shut against us but the shops and taverns in the walled town readily supplied the soldiers' needs and my entourage found comfortable lodgings at an inn.

Over a hearty meal, the commanders debated the next stage of our journey and opinions split between two possible routes. The consensus was tending towards turning east and following the valleys of the rivers Teifi and Tywi via Carmarthen and Llandovy. However Lord Jasper was adamantly against this because it would bring us to the border with England in the centre of a York heartland and the scene of a disastrous defeat he had suffered at the hands of Edward of York over twenty years before. I would have been inclined to support Jasper's reluctance but the matter was settled outright when scouts reported that a large force had been spotted marching towards us on that very route.

Lord Oxford left his dinner half-eaten and immediately rushed to put his crack troops on standby and the thought that heading east might have led us straight into the enemy's net caused an instant change of heart and made the northern route via the River Dyfi the obvious choice, despite warnings that we would encounter mountainous terrain even more challenging than any we had so far tackled.

I was in my chamber writing letters by candlelight when I was drawn to the window by a commotion outside. In the courtyard of the inn numerous men with pole-weapons were milling about and for an alarming moment I thought enemy troops had stormed the town, but quickly realised that the standard they held aloft was the twin of the red dragon of Cadwallader, king of Gwynedd, which I had chosen for myself.

There was an impatient rapping on my door and Tom Brandon opened it cautiously, admitting a stocky man in armour, carrying his helmet and bearing the dark hair and beard of the Celts. Striding purposefully into the room he went on one knee before me and spoke in Welsh. 'I am

Richard ap Gruffydd, lord king, and come at the urging of my ally, Rhys ap Thomas of Carew, to put my men and those of my friend John Morgan at your disposal.'

I had been practising my rusty Welsh with some local recruits during our ride and made an effort to reply in kind. 'You are very welcome, Richard ap Gruffydd, and I see you already ride under Cadwallader's dragon. But I am surprised you come at Rhys's urging. I heard he was holding to York, perhaps under some coercion.'

'He takes the road into England to fulfil his obligation as Lieutenant of the Principality but there is no guarantee that he will fight under the white boar. I bring the dragon standard to you in his stead to ensure it is there when Richmond and Gloucester clash.'

'But will the dragon have the benefit of his support?'

The dark Welshman raised his shoulders and hands in an enigmatic gesture. 'It will have my thirty men and John Morgan's twenty, that is all I can say. Will you come and address my troop, sire? They would be delighted to hear the Son of Prophecy speak to them in Welsh.'

The label 'Son of Prophecy' had dogged me all my life. Employed by the bards, who sang of a Welshman descended from the early Kings of Britain who would rise to rule a united kingdom, I did not hold with the notion because it smacked of blasphemy, echoing 'Son of God' and implying prophetic powers.

I prevaricated. 'I have urgent letters to write, Richard ap Gruffydd, but I will send a clerk to register your troop. We move further north tomorrow. I wish you a very good night.'

He was making his exit, looking disappointed, when Roland arrived to report that the scouts had made no sighting of troops approaching Cardigan from the east. 'Lord Oxford has stood the elite ranks down and Lord Jasper believes the Welsh sent from Carew were mistaken for William Herbert's Yorkist vanguard.' He indicated the door, which had just closed behind Richard ap Gruffydd. 'Was he one of them, your grace?'

I nodded. 'He was and he gave me the impression that Rhys sent him as an ambassador. He may yet raise his ravens alongside the red dragon.'

I turned back to my correspondence but was surprised when Roland drew nearer and fell to his knees. 'May I fight with you when the time comes, Monsieur Henri?' His hands were clasped together in entreaty and his eyes shone with fervour. 'Sir Davy says I have developed excellent weapons skills and I have studied the rules of chivalry. I long to serve you and share in your glorious victory. Do not leave me with the baggage train I beg you!'

I gazed down at him fondly. 'How old are you Roland?' I asked. 'And do not lie to me, boy!'

'I am fourteen, sire.' He hung his head. 'I know you think that too young but I have grown tall and I am strong.'

'That is true but that does not make you ready for battle. You already serve me well as a body squire but I will not permit you to take arms against my enemies at your age. If we should be ambushed on the march you may need to use the skills Davy says you have but there is a difference between an unavoidable skirmish and a set battle. I do not wish you to ask me this again, is that clear?'

Crestfallen, he nodded dumbly and his head drooped. I leaned towards him to reinforce my point. 'War is a serious business, Roland. It is life and death and the outcome is never predictable. You will honour me with your obedience in this matter.'

'Yes, Monsieur Henri.' He scrambled to his feet and retreated. I knew there were tears in his eyes but there was nothing more to say. His mother had already died for my mistake. I would not be responsible for her son's death as well.

After we left Cardigan the weather turned. Not that it rained incessantly, as I knew it could in these mountainous parts, but the clouds dropped low and from time to time a soft drizzle fogged our armour and turned our mail shirts to rust. We all longed for the sun to reappear and dry us off, and the only crumb of comfort was that it was humid and we did not shiver. Nor did we meet any opposition, which both Lord Oxford and I found surprising but which Lord Jasper took in his stride.

'You do not know the Welsh people as well as I do, Harri,' he scolded me. 'Some may support you with men and supplies and some may not but few will draw weapons against a fellow Welshman unless there is a family vendetta. In North Wales our name counts for a great deal. I have heard that a sizeable force has been raised in Anglesey and Gwynedd ready for our muster in the March. Our cousins have been busy.'

Nevertheless, when we reached the Dyfi valley we took the advice of the scouts that the north bank was the safer route, even though it would mean crossing the river again before we tackled the high mountain pass over its watershed. Our mile-long column followed a drove road, which gradually drew us up into the foothills, to a ford close to a confluence with Afon Twymyn, which translated as Fever

River. Fortunately there had not been enough rain to churn it to a fever and the ford was only inches deep.

The footsoldiers took a rest while the gun-crews tackled the ford and Lord Jasper and I took the opportunity to visit a celebrated bard, who lived nearby in a long stone farmhouse. 'Dafydd Lloyd is one of the bards who has sung Tudor praises, Harri,' he told me. 'He is not just a poet but also a prophet. You should ask him if success awaits you.' Once again I had taken my uncle's advice.

The bard was a vision from the tales of King Arthur – a thin old man with a wizened face and white hair and beard, who looked as if he had weathered a hundred winters. But his eyes were bright beneath his snowy brows and he greeted us with almost boyish glee, kissing my hand.

'Forgive me if I do not kneel to such a distinguished guest, my lord,' he said. 'If I did you would have to haul me up again.' His voice sounded like the river flowing outside, rattling the pebbles on its bed. 'God is good indeed to have allowed me to live long enough to lay eyes on the Son of Prophecy.'

His fingers felt dry and papery, as if they might crumple under mine. 'I have come to ask if you can foretell the outcome of my mission, Bardd Dafydd,' I said. 'They tell me you are a seer.'

He did not let go of my hand but pulled me through a low door into a dim and cluttered room that looked more like a sorcerer's lair than a poet's den; he was stooped with age but Jasper and I had to duck under the lintel and crouch to avoid the heavy oak beams supporting the low ceiling. A small, unglazed window let in light that fell on the table in front of it, the sheets of paper littering it perhaps blown by a gust of wind, the spidery writing spun about in all directions. Shelves along the inner wall contained rows of crocks and jars – undoubtedly the source of the pungent smell that permeated the room; as if he had been mixing spells and potions. I gazed at them with interest. 'But I see you are also an apothecary.'

The old man cackled, causing a cough that lasted long moments until he struck his chest alarmingly, bringing the wheeze to an abrupt halt. 'No sir, not an apothecary but I study the elements, to see what happens if certain elements are put together. Sometimes they tell me things immediately and sometimes I have to wait for them to release their information.'

Lord Jasper and I exchanged dubious glances. 'Is that how you see into the future – through these "elements"?' I asked.

The bard's head seemed to wobble on his neck as he nodded. 'Sometimes. But I do not need them to see your future, my lord. It shines from your eyes and it is good.' His gaze fixed on mine despite the wobble. 'You are the Son of Prophecy and your head will be crowned with gold, as the ancients predicted. You are Welsh-born and you have come to bring order out of chaos.'

'But will I be with the angels when my head is "crowned with gold", Dafydd?'

He gave me a near-toothless smile. 'You are witty sir and test my words but they are honest and I speak truth. Your head will be on your shoulders when it is crowned, the shoulders of a king united with his people to banish anarchy, and you will be hailed king.'

I digested this for a time before probing further. 'And will my reign be a worthy one?'

This time he shook his head. 'I cannot see that far but I do know that it will be fruitful and that your wife will bear you sons. That is all I can tell you.'

At this point a woman entered with a tray of refreshments and placed it on the table. 'This is my wife Mared, sire. She has borne me sons.'

Thin and white-haired like her husband, the woman curtsied politely. 'But he cannot prophesy any more sons from this source, my lord.' Her laugh came like a hen's cackle as she hurried out.

The old seer waited for her to close the door. 'When we heard you were coming up the valley I asked Mared what I should say if you came to consult me,' he said.

'And what did she advise?' I inquired, intrigued.

'She said I should tell you that you will be victorious.'

'Is she also a seer then?'

'No my lord, she is a practical woman. She pointed out that if you failed you would not be alive to come back and chastise me and if you were victorious you would reward my prophecy.'

Jasper and I both laughed. 'A practical woman indeed! And you are what you say, Bardd Dafydd, an honest man who deserves his reward.' I drew from my purse a silver shilling and laid it on his table. 'If your forecast is right this one will multiply.'

The bard poured three cups of mead from the jug on the tray. Its fragrance overcame the pungent smells wafting from the shelves. 'Let us drink to that, lord king,' he said, passing us each a cup.

When we caught up with the marching force, the French gunners had completed their crossing of the Dyfi and were pushing on along a well-trodden stock track, climbing steadily towards a row of peaks, which the Welsh called the Mynydd Rhiw-Saeson, or the Mountains of the Englishmen, a name that offered a hint that we were at last heading in the right direction.

By this time I estimated that the usurper must have received news of our whereabouts and would be mustering the troops he had put on standby, laying plans to intercept us. When we reached a stream somewhat ominously called Nant yr Eira or Snowy Water, I prayed that the high pass we were approaching would not too much delay our entry into England and the planned rendezvous with our supporters from North Wales and the English counties of Cheshire and Shropshire. And crucially, that they would include the army of Rhys ap Thomas. Would he bring his two thousand men to my dragon or take them to Richard's boar?

43

Margaret

Lathom Hall, West Derby Hundred, Lancashire, 12th August 1485

THE LETTER TOOK ONLY two days to reach me. It felt as if the son I had not set eyes on for fourteen years was suddenly very close. Henry wrote from Cardigan. It was not a place to which I had ever been but I wondered if, by now, he might even be in England.

Although I had never liked Thomas's estate at Lathom I preferred being under house arrest here than in London. Being confined in the city had been frustrating; there was so much life and activity outside the walls, which I could hear and smell and sometimes see from my window but which I was denied, being even forbidden to attend Mass at St Paul's, only a short walk away. For once I was glad to be here.

'You will be safer than in London,' Thomas said when we arrived. 'Richard is angry and gathering more hostages like my George. There are several youths in his train now, sons of nobles who cannot believe their luck, being invited to share the king's apparently insatiable lust for hunting. They do not know that their lives depend on their fathers showing unquestioning loyalty to their host.'

'Which you, too, must do from now on, Thomas; George is the future of the Stanley family.' I forced these words out in my capacity as a dutiful wife and stepmother but they were like dust in my mouth. I knew Henry was expecting military support from his stepfather, who had already sent him substantial financial help.

Thomas gave me an unfathomable look. 'George already has a thriving baby son and tells me his wife expects another child early next year.' George had married an heiress and taken her lands and title as Lord Strange. 'But you and Henry must understand that I will have to play my cards very close to my chest.'

At Lathom my stooges were less stringent and had actually handed me Henry's letter from Cardigan unmolested. On the same day I was told that Reginald Bray had arrived and I hurried from my chamber to the great hall to greet him before anyone realised that he was one of the forbidden visitors. 'It is good to see you again Master Bray,' I said formally, conscious that there were servants in the room. With Thomas in control of my finances and estates, the Receiver and I had not met together for nearly two years. 'Had you expected to find Lord Stanley here?'

He smiled. 'No my lady, it is you I came to see.'

'In that case we had better sit down.' I gestured towards a cushioned window embrasure and beckoned to one of the servants. 'Have you travelled far? May I offer you refreshment?'

'Thank you. I have ridden from Knowsley, where Lord

Stanley and his brother have been mustering their men in obedience to King Richard's commission of array.' Reginald waited while I gave my instructions to the servant and watched him depart before continuing in a hushed tone. 'As you are only too aware they are obliged to obey the king's call to arms, having fear for the life of Lord Strange, but as yet there has been no indication of where the king will go. At present he is still in Nottingham.'

I did not know how frank to be with him, uncertain where Reginald's loyalties lay. While the Stanley brothers remained publicly uncommitted, so too I presumed did their retainers and Reginald Bray was significant among them. 'I wonder, have you heard lately from my son?' I probed.

'Yes my lady, that is primarily why I am here. I received notice that he expects me to attend him armed and ready.' As he spoke he retrieved a closely folded piece of paper from his purse. 'I have endeavoured to keep the summons secreted for obvious reasons.'

He passed it to me but I did not immediately open it because the servant returned with refreshments and I waited while he poured wine and left again before unfolding the letter. It was not in Henry's handwriting but had been copied somewhat crudely, sealed in wax with a dragon image and bore a curt message.

By the King
We will and pray you and upon your allegiance charge
and command you that in all haste you assemble your
folks and servants and with them so assembled and
defensively arrayed for war, you come to us for our aid
and assistance in this our enterprise for the recovery of

the crown of our realm of England. If you fail us in this
you will invoke our gravest displeasure and answer to us
at your peril.
    Henry R.

I looked up. Reginald was studying me gravely. 'That is not a request, my lady, it is an order.'

I frowned deeply and spoke sharply. 'Yes Reginald, and you are a Lancastrian. It is an order from your king. How will you respond?'

He pursed his lips. 'I fear that my quill is mightier than my sword but I will do what you expect me to do, my lady, which is support your son.'

'But I am certain your tenants and servants keep up their weapons skills, as all gentlemen's households are required to do, Master Bray. Have you discovered whether Lord Stanley and Sir William are of similar mind?'

He shook his head. 'I have not but I wager that you know Lord Stanley's mind, if not his brother's.'

I avoided comment on that. 'All I can tell you is that Henry has called a muster in the Welsh March. He should be on a hill called Long Mountain outside Pool on the Welsh border tomorrow and at Shrewsbury the next day. If I were a man I would be on my horse right now, riding to his side.' I sighed heavily.

'But if you were a man you could not have borne the child who is going to win back the crown of England for Lancaster,' he pointed out. 'Does your informant give any indication of the size of his force, my lady?'

I shook my head. 'All I know is that he left France with a flotilla of ships and that if they were all full it would imply up to four thousand men. And others have been joining as they marched through Wales. I do not know how many. What will be the size of Richard's force do you think?'

The Receiver assumed an air of professional calculation. 'He has his own elite retinue – perhaps five hundred knights and squires – and then there are his tenants from the north and those of his noble allies from Northumberland and Durham, probably five thousand altogether, and the Duke of Norfolk's trusted forces, maybe three thousand. Apparently Richard has been sending out orders of array even more demanding than Henry's so there may be others who turn up on the day. I would imagine he will have upward of ten or twelve thousand, especially if you include the Stanleys.' He paused. 'Would you include the Stanleys?'

I shrugged, thoroughly disliking his total, with or without my husband's family contingent. 'They will be there but on which side I would not like to guess. Perhaps they will sit on the fence. They have done in the past.'

'I think they will have to commit to one side or the other this time and we must pray that it is Henry's. But if I and my small force are to get to your son in time I must take my leave.' He emptied his cup, rose and bent over my hand. 'It may all depend on how many have joined Henry's army from Wales and how well the French mercenaries fight, my lady. Let that be the focus of your prayers.'

'May God be with you Reginald,' I said, 'and with Henry. Please give him my blessing.'

44

Henry

Long Mountain on the Welsh March, 13th August 1485

LORD JASPER WAS RIGHT; from the Long Mountain you could see for miles in every direction. We had lookouts posted at both ends of the ancient Roman road that ran north south along its two-mile crest and at the top of the steep tracks that led up to the summit from the east and west. The various companies that made up my growing army had set up their camps on the rough common grazing covering its conveniently flat top. It resembled a tournament camp, with coloured pennants fluttering from every tent-post, announcing the identity and allegiance of the occupants. Outside the large central tent, in which my council met and my bed was assembled at night, stood a twenty-foot flagpole and from it a giant version of my green and white standard flew in a brisk breeze, displaying the cross of St George and the red, fire-breathing dragon of Cadwallader. The scouts confirmed that it could be seen from a distance of several miles in every direction and it had already drawn supporters in gratifying numbers.

We had moved up the mountain the previous afternoon, having skirted Powis Castle, the seat of Lord John Grey, who had mustered his troop and already marched off to join forces with the usurper. His huge red sandstone fortification, which might have offered a serious threat, had stood aloof on its mound as we passed, its gates shut fast and its battlements bare. In a break of discipline, some of the French mercenaries had taken the opportunity to round up a few cattle from the pastures outside its walls and herd them up to their camp and the smell of roasting beef filled the air. Lord Jasper led out a small troop to remonstrate with Philibert de Chandée but the French commander claimed spoils of war and declared that his men were sending supplies of freshly butchered joints to all parts of the mountain in a gesture of fair play. Eventually, as we were holding our daily strategy meeting, a few well-roasted cuts reached the council tent and any thought of disciplinary action faded from the agenda.

'Let us consider it a legitimate raid on the enemy's supplies,' remarked Lord Oxford, swallowing his last juicy morsel and smacking his lips. 'After all the French deserve it, having hauled those guns of theirs over the mountain pass. All credit to them, for we will undoubtedly need their fire-power.'

The following morning our meat supplies were more lawfully boosted by the arrival of a band of well-armed men from the lush pastures of the upper Conwy valley, herding a mob of sheep and a herd of fat cattle and oxen. Their leader was a cheerful squire called Rhys the Mighty, a man who, to judge by his broad chest and considerable height, was the product of his own good husbandry. However, heartily welcome though he was with his sturdy troop of men and his four-footed larder, he was not the Rhys I was most hoping to see.

Scouts had come in with reports that Rhys ap Thomas had left Brecon Castle several days before, heading north with two thousand men, but so far they had not come into our lookout's view and I feared they might have turned east to join the usurper's force, now mustering around Nottingham in the heart of England.

The men were breaking camp and I was concluding my early morning briefing with the troop captains when a soldier came running and threw himself at my feet. 'My lord king,' he panted, 'the southern lookout reports a large force approaching, flying the three ravens. That is Rhys ap Thomas's coat of arms!'

My uncle and Lord Oxford were sitting to my left and right and we all rose as one. 'We must go out to meet him on the road,' I said. 'He will want to discuss terms. Send for the horses.'

Ten minutes later, already armoured and mounted themselves, Davy Owen and Will and Tom Brandon led our three ponies up from the horse lines. Will had furnished himself with my dragon standard, being unwilling to let me stray far from its heraldic significance. They had also rounded up the Richmond Herald, Roger Machado, resplendent in his brightly coloured tabard, and anticipated the need for one of Richard Foxe's clerks, who rode pillion behind Tom with his scrip and writing table slung around his neck. After weaving our way through the dismantling camps, we began the steep descent and because of the thick vegetation, it was not until we emerged onto even ground at the mountain's foot that we sighted a sizeable army approaching. Being always mindful of security, for a dread moment I wondered if I had been foolish to venture out of camp without my bodyguard.

Rhys ap Thomas rode at the head of his column, followed closely by his own mounted retinue and then his infantry, strung out four abreast along the ancient roadway, which at this point ran parallel with the deep ditch known as Offa's Dyke that marked the border with England. As we drew near he signalled a halt and the footsoldiers immediately sat down and pulled out their leather water bottles.

Having frequently blessed my sure-footed little grey when we were tackling treacherous terrain, I now found myself regretting I was not mounted on a horse a little more suited to my royal status. Although not a tall man, Rhys sat in full armour, at least a foot above me, astride a magnificent bay charger trapped in black and white and harnessed in red leather. In the brisk breeze his standard fluttered above his head; a silver shield with a black chevron separating three black ravens; simple but unmistakeable.

'It is good to welcome you back to the land of your birth, my lord,' he said in Welsh.

Everything about him exuded the wealth Richard had heaped on him to keep the Welsh peace; too much wealth in my opinion. I also noted that he hailed me as lord and not king. He considered us equals. I replied in English. 'The welcome has been warm indeed, Master Rhys. But the generosity of the Welsh is well known.'

His dark brows knitted. 'I was told you spoke in your native tongue.' Again he spoke in Welsh, determined to demonstrate his status as *uchelwr* – a member of what passed for Welsh nobility.

'I speak several languages, sir, but I come to take the crown of England from the head of an Englishman on the soil of England. I think it pertinent to conduct my business in English. Under my rule the Welsh would conduct their own business in Welsh but do their trading in English coin. I wish the two countries to be wealthy, united, and powerful together.'

'And who would rule in Wales then?' He had switched to English and I detected that we had reached the nub of the matter. He wanted assurance that he would still have jurisdiction over his considerable territory if he pledged loyalty to me as king.

'I would rule sir, through very able and well-paid Welsh officers – a Lieutenant of the King I believe you are called at present and I see no reason to alter that. But nimble as my steed has been in carrying me over the mountains, I am not comfortable shouting up at you. Let us ride to our camp and discuss this face to face.'

'I have a better idea,' said the *uchelwr*. 'Why do we not ride together and discuss it on horseback?' He snapped his fingers and a groom appeared from the line of men at arms behind him leading a fine white horse, as splendidly saddled and trapped as his own but in the colours of my standard; green, white and red. 'I heard that you brought no horses from France. I would be honoured if you would accept this gift from your loyal Welsh supporters.'

There was silence while I digested this offer. It had caught me off guard, before I had time to decide whether or not I could trust this flamboyant Welshman, who clearly commanded the loyalty of a large number of followers. His showy style tended to irritate rather than impress but it had been agreed that we would rely on mounts acquired after we had crossed the Channel and this white horse would certainly convey me in better style than the plucky little flecked grey on which I was presently mounted. To refuse it out of pride would gain me nothing and almost certainly lose me the support of a vital ally.

I signalled to Tom to come forward and dismounted, handing the reins to him and inclining my head to Rhys. 'A very generous gift, for which I thank you, sir.' The groom dropped down from his own horse, unclipped the lead rein and offered me his cupped hands to mount. I shook my head. 'I am wearing spurs. I do not wish to injure you. Please step away.' I laid hands on the high pommel of the saddle and swung myself up into it, swiftly gathering up the reins to gain control as the horse shied in protest. 'Steady boy,' I said, laying a soothing hand on his neck. 'What is his name?' I asked the groom in Welsh.

'Gwyn Eyrir, my lord.'

'Ah, White Eagle. Very appropriate.' With a little persuasion the stallion settled, responding to my shifted weight and gentle pressure on the bit. 'He is very handsome,' I told the donor, smiling at him now that we were eye to eye.

'He will carry you well,' Rhys said, clearly pleased with my reaction. 'He needs a strong master.'

When we rode back up to the campsite, most of the tents had been struck but Tom and Davy managed to move a trestle off one of the carts and find a jug of ale and some cold ribs from the previous night's sheep-roast, which Rhys and I and my uncle and Lord Oxford consumed while we thrashed out a new plan of action. We now had the makings of a decent-sized army with which to confront the usurper.

Rhys told us that when he had been made Lieutenant of South Wales he had sent a written oath of loyalty to Richard, from which the Bishop of St David's had since absolved him. Putting two and two together, I concluded that the usurper's demand that Rhys send him his only son, a mere five-year-old, as a token of his faith, had greatly offended the proud Welshman.

'A man's word is his bond, is it not, Harri?' he maintained, gulping down another draught of strong ale. 'If you say you will appoint me Lieutenant of South Wales and I give you my vow of fealty we are both bound to keep our word.'

'I believe we are in agreement,' I said, turning my chair so that it faced out from the board. 'I have said my piece so now it is your turn.' I held out my hands, ready to take his between my palms.

To the surprise of us both, Lord Jasper intervened, his expression unusually stern. 'I am old enough to be your father Rhys ap Thomas, and I knew him well, so I feel it my duty to remind you that you are making an oath to your king, not to any Tom, Dick or Harri. Have a care how you address him in future. I have not heard him invite you to use his given name, even in private.'

I said nothing but smiled briefly at my indignant uncle, loving him for his unconditional support. My hands were still extended, waiting for Rhys to make his vow of allegiance. He glared at Lord Jasper and then at me but both of us were now straight-faced and steely-eyed. At last he almost fell off his chair onto his knees and placed his hands between mine.

'I Rhys ap Thomas am your liegeman in life and limb and will remain so until death, or else God smite me now.'

It was said at speed and in Welsh. I waited for several moments, casting my eyes to the heavens, almost expecting the Almighty to send a bolt of lightning, but nothing happened.

'Business concluded then,' I said briskly. Rhys re-seated himself. 'And now to military matters,' I went on. 'How would your men feel about going under the command of my uncle here? Many of them will know him from his days at Pembroke, when your father and grandfather formed a truce with him, which held with some success I believe.'

I could see that Rhys was impressed with this snippet of his family history but any further tactical debate was inter-rupted by Roland who ran up to tell me that another company of soldiers was marching up the western track with supply carts and more spare horses and what he called '*beaucoup de moutons*'.

Lord Jasper rose hurriedly. 'I have been waiting for my cousins to arrive; your cousins too, Harri, with their friends from Gwynedd and Anglesey – more good Welsh fighting men for my command. Will you come and greet them?'

When we reached the west road, the leaders of the new contingent were just arriving at the top of the forested slope. Although it was some years since I had laid eyes on him, I instantly recognised Evan ap Hywel, the man who had been squire to my uncle in power and exile.

On seeing Lord Jasper, Evan abandoned his horse and rushed to throw himself at my uncle's feet, only to be hauled up and crushed in a bear hug. There were tears in both their eyes when they finally broke away and stood back. 'How good it is to see you, Evan!' cried my uncle. 'And the years have treated you well – much better than me.'

The squire's bronze beard was streaked with grey and his

hair, once brown and curly, had faded to white at the temples. He looked considerably older to me but then so did Lord Jasper, whose hair and beard were now the colour of pale sand mixed with silver, instead of the bright ginger they had once been. Both cousins had the weathered complexions of much time spent in sun and rain.

Evan laughed. 'I will not see forty again my lord but at least I am not plagued with farmer's hip like my older brothers. Maredudd sends his deep regret that because of this infirmity he cannot join your muster but he hopes the fine horse he sends will carry you to London. Half the sheep are his as well and leading his troop of archers is his eldest son, Hywel.'

Jasper's left eyebrow rose in surprise. 'Maredudd named his firstborn for his father? That was magnanimous of him.'

I knew the story. My uncle's cousin, Hywel the elder, had turned his coat to York and died fighting against his eldest son, Maredudd, and Jasper and his father Owen. At the time the family rift had been terrible, with their other brother Dewi also adopting the Yorkist cause.

Evan shrugged. 'Hot blood cools when there is work to do, my lord.'

I moved forward, holding out my hand in welcome. 'I thank you warmly for your support cousin. It is greatly appreciated.'

The squire shot a doubtful glance at Uncle Jasper, who nodded encouragement and gestured him on. 'Do you not recognise Harri, Evan?' he said.

The squire took me by surprise when he dropped to his knee and kissed my ring. 'I am yours to command, your grace,' he said, head bowed.

'It is good to see you again, Evan. I will always remember that it was you who taught me that mail must be polished every night to stop it rusting. It is the task every squire abhors but cannot avoid.'

He looked up at me then with a wide grin. 'We used to toss a coin to see who would polish your uncle's mail shirt.'

I nodded ruefully. 'Yes, and it was surprising how often you seemed to win! But please rise; I am sure Lord Jasper is anxious to meet your brother's son and inspect this horse you speak of. It will be good to ride into Shrewsbury on a knight's horse, will it not uncle?'

A young man came forward leading a very decent-looking chestnut courser. 'Shrewsbury? Is that where we are headed now?' he asked. 'Will they open the gates to us, my lord?'

'We will find out when we get there. One thing is certain; the usurper will block our way to London so I hope your men have sharp weapons, Evan, and a good supply of arrows. And tell them to keep their mail polished. We will be needing it soon.'

45

Henry

Shrewsbury to Merevale Abbey, English Midlands, 16th–19th August 1485

RICHMOND HERALD, ROGER MACHADO, spent a busy few days after we left the Long Mountain riding at speed to Shrewsbury with my standard bearer Sir William Brandon, to establish whether we would be welcome to pass through the town. Meanwhile the main army marched in good order to establish a bridgehead over the Severn at Montfort, in case Shrewsbury did not welcome us. Then Herald and Brandon rode back to camp with the not-unexpected response.

Roger Machado reported, 'Although the shopkeepers and innkeepers are keen to profit from our soldiers, the burgesses are protective of their homes and particularly of their wives and daughters. Several of the elders were on English expeditions to France and told terrible stories of what French troops got up to when they overran towns and villages in Normandy. They do not want two thousand Frenchies roaming loose in their streets.'

'I cannot say I blame them,' muttered Lord Jasper, not much enamoured of our French recruits. 'Their discipline is dreadful. If it were not for their artillery I would send them home.'

'We definitely cannot afford to do that,' I said firmly. 'For one thing, Oxford is enthusiastic about the fighting potential of their infantry. But this rejection is frustrating. We could just accept it and take the long way round, or we could exert some pressure. How long would it take you to get to Stafford, Roger?'

'A lengthy day I think, your grace. Then another for the return journey.' The herald looked dubious. 'Can you afford to wait that long?'

'No but the scouts tell me that Sir William Stanley has been recruiting there. If he was to send an emissary to Shrewsbury overnight, I believe a word from him might shift opinion. I will write a letter for Sir William, but you may also have to be persuasive, Roger. I am not yet certain we can rely on the Stanleys' support. I will tell Sir William that tomorrow I will go Shrewsbury and personally reassure the bailiffs that we will march straight through the town, making no stops and respecting the oaths of loyalty that have been made to the usurper. If all this does not work then we will have to take the long route.'

There was a flat stretch of heath near our camp at Montford and the following day Lord Oxford and Philibert de Chandée took the opportunity to drill the French infantry in the arrowhead formation, which Sir Philibert swore would outfox Richard's vanguard. Meanwhile Lord Jasper and I rode to Shrewsbury in our most regal apparel and with an imposing retinue of knights.

The town was famous for its location on a loop of the Severn, which protected it on three sides. Defending the narrow neck of land that formed the fourth side was the distinctive red sandstone castle of the Earls of Shrewsbury but the present earl was a minor and the town was run by a committee of bailiffs, the chief of whom came to meet us, secured behind the lowered portcullis in the ancient tower gatehouse that defended the Welsh Bridge.

Bailiff Thomas Mitton stuck stubbornly to his refusal to admit us. 'I made an oath to God that I would not allow any man calling himself king, other than good King Richard himself, to enter the town except over my belly. I cannot be forsworn my lords.'

Observing Master Mitton's very large belly, I seriously wondered whether I would actually be able to step over it but I waved imperiously at the turreted and battlemented gatehouse, which reached several floors above his head with a long, barricaded tunnel archway beneath, leading into the town. 'If you were to lie on the floor of this magnificent building, Master Mitton, and I was to step carefully over you, the public would not witness your discomfort and you would be fulfilling the terms of your vow. Thus I would gain entrance to your town and you would not be forsworn. Furthermore I give you a guarantee that my army will march in tight formation through the streets without stopping or causing damage. We will return tomorrow, when we trust the gate will be open. Should this fail to be the case you will answer to us at your peril. Good day Bailiff Mitton.'

Having made my grand pronouncement I gave a signal to my retinue, wheeled my white horse and set off at a canter. Further down the road, as we slowed to a trot, Lord Jasper drew level with me. 'For a moment back there I almost broke into applause,' he said with a grin. 'Never have I witnessed you acting so regally.'

I did not smile back. 'I need the practice, uncle,' I said. 'I hope it works.'

Whether it was due to my confrontation with Thomas Mitton or Sir William Stanley conveying his opinion on the matter, the portcullis of the Gatehouse Tower was raised the next morning when I led the long column of my army up to the Welsh Bridge. I had to bite back a laugh when I saw the bailiff lying prone on the cobblestones in the gloom of the long tunnel and feared I might trip myself up or rip the fabric of his gown with my spurs, as I stepped over the mound of his belly. However, such a mishap was avoided and I offered him my hand to help him rise, for which I received profuse thanks and multiple bows after he had made the sign of the cross and sent a grateful prayer to the Almighty for relieving him of his votive obligation.

Each of the troop captains, especially the Frenchmen, had been ordered to impress on their men the strict necessity for restraint in their conduct and Lord Oxford, riding at the head of the procession, set a good pace in order to make it difficult for a soldier to make even a swift disappearance into a tavern on the way through the town's crowded streets. The innkeepers of Shrewsbury would not thank Master Mitton for depriving them of lucrative takings on this day.

Word had spread of our coming and people pressed themselves against the walls under the overhangs of the fine timbered houses to let us pass. There were few shouts of protest and some cheers of encouragement and several small groups armed with bows and battleaxes fell in with the marching column to bolster our numbers. In just over an hour all six thousand of our men had crossed the bridge, traversed the centre of the town and passed through the land gate guarded by its massive red stone castle, out onto the old Roman road called Watling Street, which led eventually to London.

To my treasured and only son Henry, Rightful King of England, from his devoted Lady Mother, Margaret, Countess of Richmond, loving greetings,

I was so grateful to receive your letter from Cardigan, proving that you were once more back on home soil. I sense that the day is now fast approaching when you will confront the usurper and rid our country of his tyrannical and illegal rule. My dearly beloved son, that will be the day for which you were born; that memorable day which, despite the trauma we both suffered and by God's will survived, I have always considered to be the happiest of my life. Never, in all the years in which, by war and mischance, we have been parted, have I doubted that the Almighty would one day bring you to your rightful inheritance, originally as Earl of Richmond and now as King of England.

Regrettably I cannot be with you on the battlefield but I will pray constantly for your victory. There is absolute certainty in my mind that God will favour your cause and send you and your host of loyal supporters a glorious triumph over the usurper.

Signed: Margaret R, proud mother to the King.

Written at Lathom House this seventeenth day of August, 1485

463

On the dusty road towards Lichfield I read the letter several times, savouring the love and fierce ambition it expressed. It had been delivered by a courier who told us that Lord Stanley had left the town with his army only that morning, already aware of our approach, thus making it very clear to me that he had no wish to be seen in our vicinity. Scurriers searching ahead came back with reports of a force of three thousand men, an impressive number indeed for one magnate to be able to call to arms. It made me realise the extent of my stepfather's power and why Richard was desperate to ensure that he fought on his side and not on mine.

Lichfield had a unique and ancient cathedral, unusually endowed with three steeples. So precious was this cathedral to the folk of the town that they had built fortifications around it in the form of walls and ditches, as if it were a fortress. Initially we found the city gates closed but unexpectedly, as we approached they swung open to us, banners were waved from the walls and blank shots were fired from guns on the gatehouse battlements, causing us to flinch and the horses to shy and skitter. Then to my surprise and delight, the citizens came out to accompany us into the streets with songs and sweetmeats. Our time there was short but won us many friends and not a few eager recruits and I dared to hope that the welcome we received had something to do with the fact that Lord Stanley had been there before us. The captain of the town garrison even offered to lend us some of the guns ranged along Lichfield's extensive ramparts.

However, while the troops were enjoying the hospitality of the inns and alehouses, a scout came to report that Richard had mobilised his army and was marching south out of Nottingham, in full royal regalia with his army ranged around him in battle order. Our man estimated that as many as twelve thousand men – footsoldiers and cavalry – were trampling the crops and pastures, heading for Leicester on a path to cut us off.

Sitting with the rest of my high command in an upper room of an inn by the town wall, I felt a sudden wave of panic and turned to Lord Jasper. 'Twelve thousand men, uncle! We cannot face that without the Stanleys. Nor can we retreat back to Wales. It is too far. I need to think. I need to pray. I cannot do that with troops all around me. Is there an abbey or a priory around here where I might safely retreat for a while?'

Jasper's head moved nearer to mine and under his breath he warned, 'It could be a mistake to leave the men, Harri, even for a night. They will think you have abandoned them. You are their lynchpin. If you are not here they will disperse – just melt away. I have seen it happen.'

'We can go after dark and return at dawn; just take my bodyguard and leave Lord Oxford in command. They will trust what he tells them. This is important, uncle. We are going to face a mighty force and I cannot do it without God's help. You know what I am like. I need to put myself in the hands of the Almighty, to lay my fears before Him and receive His holy blessing. Without it I will crumble.'

He frowned, his expression perplexed and troubled. 'There is a cathedral up the street. You could lay your prayers on the altar there.'

I shut my eyes and shook my head. It felt huge and tight, as if it might burst. 'Christopher Urswicke will know of somewhere I can go. Send for him, please.'

I blessed Christopher with all my heart, for it was from

him I learned of Merevale Abbey. 'I have stayed there on my wanderings for Lord Stanley,' he told me. 'It is an old Cistercian foundation, once considerable but now on the decline. Only about ten monks remain, although it has a large church and accommodation for at least fifty. I know the abbot would welcome you with open arms because he is a secret Lancastrian. The abbey owns a lot of land on either side of the Roman road and employs tenant farmers and lay brothers to work it but the buildings are quiet at night and there is a beautiful chapel at the gatehouse, where you could be at peace in God's presence. If you wish I will accompany you and introduce you to the abbot.'

I could feel my panic receding as he spoke. 'Is it close enough for you to ride there and make a request for my overnight retreat? I will come after dusk with Lord Jasper and my bodyguard. We will be leaving Lichfield within the hour for Tamworth where the troops will camp for the night. I am told it is only six miles away. I will hear the scouts' reports and then leave at dusk. Only return to me if Merevale is unwilling to receive us.'

Christopher nodded. 'It is only a half-hour ride from Tamworth to Merevale. I am sure the monks will receive you, your grace, and you will find all the quiet contemplation you need to prepare for the momentous task ahead.'

The camp at Tamworth was strung out in lush pastures along the River Tame, providing a plentiful supply of water for men and beasts. As evening approached Lord Jasper and I rode slowly between the fires, sniffing the tantalising aroma of roasting meat and acknowledging the shouts and waves of the various different companies. Their cheerful greetings and soldierly banter both encouraged and amused, distracting me from the dark clouds of doubt that hovered along the fringes of my mind. The fortitude and endurance of these tough squires and yeomen and even the stoicism of the French mercenaries impressed me greatly. Carrying heavy packs and weapons, they had marched and climbed more than two hundred miles in twelve days, some of them hauling heavy guns, and there had been remarkably few desertions. Even now, when they knew that the inevitable battle was nigh, they remained stoical and even cheerful. I had ridden out to encourage them and found instead that they had inspired me.

The red dragon was flying from the town bridge when we encountered a small group of knights and squires, who had slipped away from a five-hundred-strong contingent that was marching from the south to join the usurper's army. Sir Thomas Bourchier and Walter Hungerford appeared to be the leaders of this breakaway group and they both eagerly swore their allegiance to me before marshalling their men and taking them off to register with the clerks and liaise with Lord Oxford. They numbered less than five and twenty altogether but this small addition to our numbers gave my spirits a further boost. Even better, also with them was Robert Poyntz, the squire who had assisted my escape from custody in St Malo all those years ago. He, too, swore allegiance on bended knee and expressed his admiration for my courage.

'There are many men of courage in my army Robert, and you are now one of them. But I have not had an opportunity to thank you for your service in St Malo, when I was threatened with repatriation to England. Without your help I would not have escaped,' I told him.

'It shall be my privilege to serve you in any capacity for which you consider me worthy, your grace,' he responded. 'And I pray for your success in the battle to come.'

'I think it will not be long now, Robert. Exactly where and when were you summoned to attend the usurper?'

He looked a little surprised by such a direct question but answered readily enough. 'I received the latest royal command this morning to join his army at Leicester but by then I had also received a note from Lord Stanley telling me of your whereabouts. I believe that since my departure, there must have been some correspondence between my wife and your lady mother.'

I mulled this very interesting information over as Lord Jasper and I rode away from the camp later. Night had fallen and my bodyguard kept me closely surrounded as we trotted along the Roman road, heading south out of Tamworth. In order not to attract attention, we wore plain half armour with no distinguishing livery or badges and were mounted on small Welsh ponies, for the scouts had warned us that there were posses of enemy troops already patrolling the area. As yet the moon had not risen and the shadows were deep but the straightness of the road made our journey uncomplicated.

Robert's words had given me much food for thought. Why should my stepfather have assisted Robert Poyntz to locate my army if he did not intend to join forces with me himself? Lord Stanley and his brother were certainly maintaining a close proximity even if, for fear of the usurper's spies, we had never actually met.

Christopher Urswicke had given us detailed landmarks to identify which track led to the abbey but clouds had gathered to obscure the rising moon, making it difficult to discern one tree from another, so it was fortunate that he had decided to come out and wait for us at the junction in order to lead us in. 'The monks were at Vespers when I left but they will be out by now and the abbot waits to welcome you to Merevale, your grace,' he said, letting his mount fall in beside my pony. 'He will be at the gate to meet you.'

In his pale Cistercian habit, the abbot made a ghostly figure as we rode up to the open abbey gate. He was a tall, thin man with an ascetic face, which belied the sweetness of his smile. With his hands hidden under his scapula, he made me a deep bow. 'We are honoured to receive you, my lord and you are welcome to the hospitality of our house, such as it is. May I offer you refreshment after your ride?'

'I thank you Father,' I replied, dismounting and leading my pony through the gate. 'I would be grateful for a bowl or a plate of whatever your brothers have eaten but I would rather not join them in the Refectory. I urgently need the quiet of the Lord's house to pray, so perhaps I may eat and drink in the porch or vestry of your gatehouse chapel, which I am told is a place of quiet sanctity, where I can be solitary.'

Lord Jasper also stepped down from his mount. 'I will accompany my nephew and would appreciate the same refreshment and if there is somewhere nearby that we may sleep for a few hours, that would fulfil all our needs.'

Christopher Urswicke came forward. 'If I may my lord Abbot, I will show his grace and my lord of Pembroke to the chapel and make sure there is a guard on the door, wherever they are. Also you did indicate to me that they would be welcome to bring their army to your harvested fields tomorrow, if they so wish.'

The abbot nodded. 'I did so, and they are welcome. The Hospitaller has prepared beds in the infirmary, which at present I am happy to say is empty.'

I found myself growing impatient to pursue my intended purpose in coming to Merevale. 'I fear that if battle is imminent in the vicinity it will not long remain so, Master Abbot, but thank you for the offer of a campsite. Perhaps tomorrow I may send my marshals to survey it. Now, if you will excuse me, I would like to place my endeavours before the Almighty.'

We heard the bolts slammed home on the abbey gates as Lord Jasper, Christopher and I crossed a grassy court to the hunched shape of a small chapel. To my right I could see candlelight flickering in the arched windows of a much larger church, situated within the abbey precinct. Shadows passed across the stained glass as monks and lay brothers moved from their Vespers Office to their evening meal. I did not envy them their great church and on entering the chapel made my way straight through the nave into the chancel, through a finely carved oak screen. Its images of famous saints inspired me to reach for the worn emblem of St Armel I wore on a chain around my neck. Proceeding towards the altar, I drew my sword from its sheath and reverently laid it on the embroidered cloth, at the foot of the simple polished silver crucifix. I could tell that Christopher had prepared the way for me because altar candles had been lit to either side and a cushion had been placed on the altar step. Not pausing to remove my half armour I knelt and began my orisons.

With my fingers pressed around St Armel's silver image I rehearsed his story in my mind as a way of conjuring his intercession; it followed so closely my own journey through life. A youth who fled his native Wales, narrowly escaped shipwreck to find sanctuary in Brittany, developed a talent for soldiery and diplomacy, found a patron in the French king, tamed a dragon and helped a prince in battle to reclaim his rightful place on the throne of his country by replacing a usurper.

As I prayed I became spellbound by the light of the candles flickering at the edge of my vision and closed my eyes in order to concentrate. Then something made me open them again and raise my gaze to the mullioned window in the wall above the altar. There, between the curved quatre-foil transoms at the top of the lancet-shaped frame I could see vivid images of Saint Armel and his symbols, a mace, a leashed dragon and a ship tossed by violent waves. They were set within the transoms in bright reds and greens and browns and blues, while the saint's long tunic was a blinding white. I stared up at the images for perhaps half a minute before I was forced to blink. Instantly the illumination disappeared and the plain glazed window receded once more into the gloom beyond the flickering glow of the candles.

I felt my tense muscles relax and the tide of my anxiety recede. St Armel had revealed himself and I knew him to be my strength and support.

46

Henry

Merevale Abbey, Warwickshire, 21st August 1485

'I COME TO TELL you, sire, that the tyrant's army is only seven miles distant. I have seen his tents on a hill above Redemoor Plain. He has chosen the perfect lookout point from which to spot an advancing enemy.'

I frowned at the sturdy, compact figure in half armour kneeling at my side, his helm tucked under his arm and his quilted coif stained with sweat. I sat with Lord Jasper and Lord Oxford at a long trestle covered in maps and diagrams in the guest parlour of Merevale Abbey, while our army was setting up camp around a lake and stream in the surrounding fields. We had stripped to our chemises on this warm cloudless afternoon, the shutters were open on the unglazed windows and the sound of bees working in the herb garden below the sill was carried in to us on a balmy summer breeze. Having marched unopposed from Pembrokeshire, we were now less than a hundred miles from England's capital city and the usurper had decided at last that it was time we were brought to a halt.

'I do not know you, sir, what is your name and why were you admitted?'

I asked the question with some irritation. Guards were positioned on every gate and door of the grey-walled abbey, with orders to admit no one. I had not brought thousands of men from France and Wales and overcome my own fears and doubts, only to be ignominiously murdered by some random stranger. Yet I was conscious that the closer we got to converging with Richard's army, the more likely it was that he might contrive to have me killed.

The interloper flushed and lowered his gaze. 'My name is John, your grace – John Hardwicke. The Abbot vouched for me with the guards.'

'You live locally then?'

He nodded. 'Yes, sire. I hold Lindley Manor a few miles from here and my true allegiance has always been to Lancaster. When I learned that you had brought your army to Merevale I thought Ambion Hill might be the place of choice for King Richard to set up his headquarters and I rode out to the edge of my domain to have a look. My guess was right. It is the highest hill in the area and a camp has appeared under the White Boar standard. You can see it from miles around and from there they can see any approach long before it reaches them. You have no chance of staging an ambush.'

Echoing my tone of irritation, Lord Jasper interjected, 'We have no intention of staging an ambush, my man. We intend to engage with the usurper's forces and defeat them.'

John Hardwicke nodded vigorously. 'That is why I have come, my lords. I was born and raised here and know the countryside intimately. If you trust me, I will show you the place where your army will gain the most advantage.'

'But why should we trust you?' It was Oxford who spoke.

He and Lord Jasper had been poring over local maps from the monastery's library. The maps, made by the monks, were not very accurate and difficult to decipher and I realised that possibly this John Hardwicke could be the answer to overcoming our ignorance of the terrain. On the other hand he could also place us in the perfect position for the usurper's army to decimate us with his guns. Backing up Lord Oxford's query about trust, I said so.

Still on his knees, the local man blushed but did not seem offended. 'I believe he does indeed have some mighty artillery, sire, and he may believe that by claiming the high ground he commands the best possible position to dominate Redemoor Plain, which is inviting as a battleground. But he has omitted to allow for, or is ignorant of, several crucial factors. Perhaps you will allow me to demonstrate on the maps you have in front of you?'

It was a reasonable request and I motioned him to rise and step to the other end of the table. Lord Oxford swung a map around and pushed it in front of him. John turned it so that it faced the way he preferred, which was giving us a south-to-north orientation, and pointed first to the usurper's chosen command post.

'This is Ambion Hill, where the White Boar standard flies, at the highest point in the immediate area, and undoubtedly the best place from which to dominate the flat open moorland to the southwest. We are here, at Merevale Abbey, about six miles away as the crow flies. To approach the enemy lines you will have to cross Watling Street.'

On the map he indicated the Roman road to London, running clear and straight on a southeast–northwest axis.

'And then there is the River Anker which runs along the other side of the road. The Yorkists will expect you to cross it at the Witherley Bridge, just here, a time-consuming and dangerous process that exposes you to enemy fire and surprise attack, which would weaken your numbers. Instead, I would guide you further down the Roman road to a ford, here at Caldecote. Because of a dip in the terrain, it is out of sight of the enemy, the ford is wide and the water is low; your carts and guns will cross more easily and quickly than over a bridge and the infantry will not get wet above the knee.

'Then you can turn north to traverse my lands here, to another Roman road running off Watling Street, here; a smaller road called Fenn Lane, which once led directly to Leicester I believe but is now no longer passable. Across the lane, between you and the enemy will be open moorland and, with respect, I would recommend a stand somewhere just about here,' he indicated where several tracks appeared to cross the lane at odd angles.

'These tracks take that pattern because they avoid a marsh in the middle of the moor, where various springs bubble up. It is not immediately obvious from above, being covered with moss and thorn bushes, but it is nevertheless treacherous ground, to be avoided by both men and animals. However, it might represent a useful tool for you to exploit. Operating from this particular location would put that mossy marsh between you and the king's army and, if you make the first move, you can choose on which side of it to advance. There is a small rise in the land here,' his finger moved again. 'It would make a good observation point from which to conduct your troop movements, and there is some firm ground to its left where you could deploy your guns. The enemy guns are already moving onto this flat ground here, but there is a copse of trees that will block their view of much of the battlefield if you choose the left-hand sweep around the marsh.'

The two earls were kept busy poring over the map, occasionally exchanging glances but making no remarks, allowing John Hardwicke to proceed uninterrupted, which he did.

'Perhaps the most important part of this approach now becomes apparent, my lords. You may have noticed that this location will place you directly south of Ambion Hill, with the sun behind you and in your enemies' eyes. Also the prevailing wind is southwesterly and will favour your archers, whilst theirs will be firing against both wind and sun.'

He stood back with what I could only describe as a triumphant look on his face.

'I hope you have followed my drift, my lords. Please ask if there is anything I can explain further.'

Lord Oxford and Lord Jasper both turned to me for a first reaction but I shook my head, indicating that they should comment. Personally I was very impressed with John Hardwicke's proposal and with his frank and open manner in making it; particularly in offering up his own lands to the carnage of marching feet and the wheels of heavy artillery, but I thought it politic to hand any military criticism to my commanders. To my surprise they were both cautiously in favour.

Lord Oxford considered the position of the marsh particularly interesting. 'Although I wonder whether it will present the obstacle you anticipate as the rivers are running very low. Will not the marsh also have dried up?'

John's weathered round cheeks crinkled in a smile. 'You are right to assume so, my lord, but that quagmire is probably half a mile deep and has never been known to dry out. Many a sheep has been swallowed before it could be rescued from its peaty grasp. I would advise your captains to warn the men of its dangers – and of course I will be there to show you its boundaries.'

'How long would it take us to march our men into that position, would you say? Given that we will have to skirt around the town of Atherstone and take into account the bottleneck at the ford?' Lord Jasper asked.

'I do not have any experience of marching with an army, my lord, but if I tell you it is a distance of about five miles over easy terrain, you can make your own calculation.'

Lord Jasper looked at me. 'The Bishop will want to say Mass for the men and they must break their fast. If we set off after that we should be in position around ten – eleven o'clock at the latest.'

John of Hardwicke nodded enthusiastically. 'A good time to engage with the enemy, my lords! The sun will be high and bright in their eyes. That might just win you the battle!'

'Then let us pray for the sun to shine,' I said.

47

Henry

Merevale and Redemoor Plain, 22nd August 1485

EMERGING FROM THE GATEHOUSE chapel soon after
dawn the next day I looked up at the sky and felt the
black dog of doubt descend on me once more. On this
significant day, I had invited a group of my most trusted
friends to join me at a Mass led by the Bishop of Exeter.
Some of the knights I had dubbed in Mill Bay were there,
including my boon companion of the Brittany days, Sir
Davy Owen. It was to him I expressed my misgivings as
I surveyed the mist that drifted around the gatehouse roof
and clung to the branches of the laden fruit trees in the
abbey orchard.

'God has not answered my prayers, Davy,' I murmured.
'The sun does not shine.'

Davy's blunt response took me straight back to our time
at Château Largoët. 'Well personally I have just prayed that
the mist hangs around until we reach the place of combat.
It is August, Harri, and when the sun does come out – as

it definitely will – there will be plenty of time to roast inside our armour.'

I glared at him, on the verge of accusing him of insolence, when I realised he was right. The place of combat. This was the day I had been anticipating for two years, ever since Richard of York had somehow disposed of his young nephews and usurped the throne. And although his army still outnumbered ours, there had been a change in the dynamic, which had given me hope of our advantage.

A message from Lord Stanley had been brought to me the previous evening, while I was riding through the camps calling encouragement to the troops and talking over problems with the captains. Stanley wanted to meet; he and his brother, Sir William, were only a mile away in Atherstone. I had immediately summoned Lord Jasper and my bodyguard and we rode through the dusk to the designated inn.

All the way there I pondered over what the stepfather I had never met would be like. In her letters my mother had given me little evidence to go on. I was not even sure what her own opinion was of the man of power and influence she had agreed to marry, telling me she did so primarily to boost my chances of returning to England and assuming what she considered my rightful place as a premier earl of the realm. In my own young mind I had speculated whether there had been coercion from King Edward and baulked at the idea of my mother being subject to a union that might have been repellent to her. Subsequent failure to achieve a successful agreement with the king, despite Lord Stanley's high position in the royal household, had led me to suspect a certain reluctance on the part of my stepfather to promote my cause.

I told myself firmly to banish these negative thoughts to

the back of my mind as we approached the inn, in the interests of obtaining the support of the Stanleys against the usurper. There was too much riding on this meeting to allow the distaste of a young son for his mother's new husband to muddy the waters.

At first sight he proved to be a nobleman of no great height but of considerable presence; a lofty brow, grey of beard and eye and broad of shoulder, with a high colour. And he, too, was conscious of the crucial matter in hand. After formal greetings he wasted neither time nor words.

'You showed courage in coming, Henry. It could have been a trap. But we need to compare strategies.'

Since he still had not yet actually committed his military support to my cause, I reacted accordingly. 'I am prepared to compare strategies with my allies, my lord,' I replied with a tight smile. 'But I need to be sure they will not immediately be relayed to the enemy.'

He stroked his thick beard pensively, studying my face under his bushy grey eyebrows. 'Let me make the first move then,' he said. 'We have received information that King Richard will deploy his troops tomorrow morning. His friend and close ally John Howard, Duke of Norfolk, will lead the van, having his archers on the right wing, so you had best put your vanguard on the left.'

I nodded, still frustrated by his failure to commit. 'So far we think alike. Lord Oxford has already opted for the left wing. He, too has archers to protect his advance – most of them Welsh.'

Sir William chose to interject at this time. 'So you have decided where to make your stand?' He appeared distracted, shuffling his feet like a man impatient to be elsewhere.

Hoping for more information, I decided to divulge further details. 'A local landholder has volunteered to guide us through his demesne to a good location off a causeway they call Fenn Lane – it runs through flat terrain between two villages called Dadlington and Stoke Golding. Are you aware of these?'

The two brothers exchanged meaningful glances and Lord Stanley spoke again. 'Our men are camped tonight around those very villages and we intend to deploy on the height overlooking that lane and with King Richard's camp to our right. So we will have a good view of the whole battleground.' He cleared his throat, hesitating before continuing. 'As far as I can tell that should place us precisely between your army and Richard's. You may not be aware that my son, Lord Strange, attempted to escape his detention but was unfortunately apprehended and compelled to reveal my brother's part in what York views as a rebel conspiracy. As a result Sir William is now declared a traitor and my son is in imminent danger of being summarily executed should I fail to place my troops under royal command tomorrow morning. I have told Richard that I prefer to keep command of my own men and that he will be able to see my four-thousand-strong company from his hilltop vantage. I pray that will be enough to persuade him to desist from carrying out his deadly threat.'

'You put much faith in the honour of a proven tyrant, my lord,' I observed dryly.

My stepfather shrugged. 'I am Richard's Steward. He knows full well that I have other sons.'

I made no response, puzzled and disturbed by his last remark but Lord Jasper intervened, barely containing his anger. 'We may assume then you will not be joining us tomorrow, my lord.'

Eyes locked, the two older men confronted each other, beards jutting.

'You may assume what you like,' Lord Stanley said in riposte. 'Tomorrow is another day. What I can tell you is that four of my best captains have expressed a wish to join your army. One of them is my nephew, Sir John Savage, and I can assure you that with their entourages they will make a significant addition to Lord Oxford's vanguard, should you agree to them returning with you tonight. Otherwise I am pleased to hear that your plans are made for the morrow and that you seem confident of victory.' He turned specifically to address me. 'I am grateful to you for coming to meet me tonight, Henry. Your lady mother looks forward to your reunion in the near future. Were she here now, I think I can safely say that she would be very proud of you.'

There seemed no point in continuing the meeting and when we rode back to the abbey forty more men at arms had swelled our ranks. But while I knew where Lord Stanley would be deploying his troops on the morrow, I still could not rely on their support, should I need to call on it.

Now the day of battle had dawned it was time to arm and put our trust in John Hardwicke and, true to his word, he did guide us without incident and in little more than two hours to the site off Fenn Lane with its comprehensive view over Redemoor Plain and the rush and thorn-covered marsh that he considered to be of such tactical significance.

When he had walked us up to its edge and shown my

commanders the features that marked its limits he added, 'If they should know it is there, the enemy will think you at a disadvantage, located so close to the evil ground and hampered by the need to avoid it, but in fact, as you see, it will keep the wings of your respective armies apart and forms just as much of a hazard for them in their efforts to attack you. That is if they even know it is there.'

Efficiently moving and spreading ever outwards on either side of the flat ground below their hilltop headquarters, the enemy filed into position, until there seemed to be miles of polished metal helmets glinting in the sun, as it finally emerged from behind the clouds. In that respect God had answered my prayers.

Lord Jasper clapped the small man on the back, almost knocking him over in his enthusiasm. 'John Hardwicke, you should be a general! Unlike common soldiers, generals come in all shapes and sizes. I have not seen the usurper since he was a boy but I hear he, like you, is quite a small man, unlike his brother Edward.'

'But an accomplished knight and commander, uncle,' I reminded him, 'with much battlefield experience.'

He flashed me a warning look, which said, 'Beware of sounding intimidated' – and I acknowledged inwardly that I was indeed daunted by the very sight of the enemy's lines. I thanked God for the bright sun, and asked Him further to grant me the courage to face the ordeal ahead, and the self-confidence to look like the king I had determined to be, and not the cringing rebel pretender my enemy had pronounced me.

Across the wide plain the tents of the usurper's retinue appeared more like tournament pavilions than military shelters, each flying its identifying banner but all dominated by the huge White Boar standard flapping in the lively breeze that swept up the ridge on its southern side. Directly ahead of our command hillock the marsh stretched for perhaps a quarter mile, deceptively covered by a mat of thick green sedge and dotted with clumps of rushes, swaying osier stems and stunted thorn bushes. It did not look threatening but I watched one of our mounted scouts approach it at a trot, only to have his horse come to a sudden halt and refuse to go any further as soon as the vegetation changed from rough sun-dried grassland to the intense yellowish-green of the marsh's carpet. All our men had been warned of the need to avoid straying into it.

Having no battlefield experience, I stuck close to Lord Jasper while he prowled the lines of his wing as they marched into position, uttering encouraging adages and witticisms as he went and raising nervous laughs and cheeky ripostes from the ranks. Lord Oxford had suggested that Sir John Savage, whom he described as 'a commander of renown', be put in charge of the van of the right wing, leaving Lord Jasper free to unite the considerable Welsh contingent, which so far had been uncomfortably bundled together under Rhys ap Thomas.

When we moved across to the left wing we found Oxford himself reminding the frontline troops of the orders their captains would give to bring them into his famous wedge formation.

'No man is to stray more than ten feet from his captain's banner,' he repeated at the top of his voice, as he moved down the lines. 'Keep the shape tight. When one man falls another is to move immediately into his place.'

Already deployed off to one side, the troop of Welsh archers were busy stringing and flexing their bows ready to fire and plunging the metal tips of their arrows down into the sandy soil beside them, the quicker to pluck them up and loose them off in a deadly fusillade, up to eleven or twelve a minute. 'Keep them flying until our men move into range, then we will change our stance to fire on the enemy's gunners,' their captain yelled. 'And collect stray arrows as you go. You will run out of ammunition if you do not.'

'If an archer does not know that, he should be shot with his own bow,' muttered one grizzled veteran to his mate.

I noticed that some of the frontline soldiers were equipped with the new hand-gonnes, the latest weapons acquired in France and reputed to be the infantry armament of the future, a replacement for both the reliable and deadly longbow and the cumbersome and creaky crossbow. I had experimented with one in Paris and found it heavy, noisy and slow to re-load but had been informed that, with practice, inserting the lead-covered wooden ball, priming the firing hole with gunpowder, aiming the barrel and applying the smouldering lighter could be done in less than half a minute. I had pointed out to the Master at Arms that an archer could fire five or six arrows in that time and passed the hand-cannon back. Anyway, like most knights I would be relying on my lance, my sword and my mace.

Our artillery, hauled so arduously over the Welsh mountains, was lined up ahead and to the left of Lord Oxford's 'wedge' under the command of Sir Richard Guildford, whose passion for these instruments of destruction had developed with alarming speed during the months preceding the expedition. He seemed to know instinctively, just by looking down the barrel of a cannon, how far it could fire a missile and how much damage it could inflict on flesh and bone.

I made a point of going to inspect the ordnance, turning my back on the dispiriting sight of the enemy's battery, which was considerably larger than ours. Aside from their main line of guns, others were dug in along the slope of the hill so that they would initially be able to fire over the heads of their own men, straight into our lines. I found myself praying for their missiles to fall short. Like me, many of the younger men fighting on this day might never have heard the thunder of a bombardment and although they had been warned of its intimidating noise and the random nature of its death-dealing, I wondered in trepidation how many of them might be tempted to turn and run when the fusillade began – and how many of them would never run again.

I was soon to find out. Lord Jasper returned to his command post on the right wing, where the English exiles and the Welsh footsoldiers stood ready to reinforce the efforts of Lord Oxford's 'wedge'. Davy, Will and I made our way on horseback to the raised ground behind our lines, where the rest of my mounted knights and squires were assembled, a cavalry of fifty horsemen and effectively our only form of rear-guard. As Lord Oxford had wryly pointed out when drawing up his battle-plan, 'We cannot spare troops to stand at the back and wait to be needed. If we have to call on a rear-guard, we have lost the battle!' As I took my stand, gazing in awed silence over the bristling pikes and halberds of our own packed ranks and across the empty marsh and grassland of the plain at the enemy crowding its far edge, the bombardment began.

48

Henry

The Battle of Redemoor Plain, 22nd August 1485

FIRST REACTIONS CAME FROM the horses. A single puff
of smoke went up from one enemy gun; I wondered why
there had been no sound, then a moment or two later it hit
my ears and Gwyn Eyrir shied and half-reared before I could
stop him, barging into Will's horse, which stood close behind
mine. All around us other horses reacted similarly and it was
a minute or two before calm was restored. Meanwhile the
cannonball that had been fired in that first salvo bounced its
way across the rough grass of the plain and came to a halt
fifty yards short of our lines. It had served as a signal: a series
of rounds blasted from both sides of the battlefield, none of
which reached their targets, but the sound was deafening and
drew loud yells from our lines as the men vented their fear
and anger with curses and oaths aimed at the opposition and
often, crudely, at the mother of every member of it. It was
also the signal for Lord Oxford to throw up his warder, the
official signal that battle was joined.

The next hour was the most dreadful I had ever known. If anyone had told me that I would sit on a horse, motionless, maintaining a facade of cold-blooded calm, watching men who had placed their hands between mine in loyal pledge mangled by spears and blades and smashed into pulp by speeding cannonballs, I would never have believed them. Those clashing lines of screaming, swearing, charging men consisted of fathers and husbands, uncles and sons and I had led them into this hellish maelstrom of blood and guts and madness, from which so many of them would never return to their families, or if they did they might be maimed or traumatised in the thundering, screeching chaos of it all. I had done it to rid their country of a murdering, cheating tyrant of a king, but only if I proved a better ruler and a more God-fearing monarch would I make it in any way excusable.

I itched to be part of the action, to lose myself in the heat of the battle rather than force myself merely to watch as the sun beat down and turned my armour into an oven and my body into a shaking, over-heated carcass.

'Water, lord king?' It was Roland de Belleville, offering me a leather bottle with the stopper dangling open. At first I did not hear him through the noise of combat but he attracted my attention by banging the bottle against my leg armour. 'Will you take water, sire?' he insisted.

I took the bottle from him and drank like a man in the desert. I was about to tell him that he might have saved my life when I remembered that I had banned him from the battle. 'What are you doing here, Roland?' I roared over the noise of the barrage. 'I forbade you to come.'

'I loaded a cart with barrels of water from the abbey

spring and asked one of the monks to drive it here,' he shouted back, without any sign of remorse. 'I thought it might be needed.'

The liquid was beginning to refresh my senses. I took a final draught from the bottle and handed it back to him, nodding. 'It was a good idea but do not venture onto the plain, Roland. The men have their own water skins.'

I could see his eyes widen as he turned to scan the carnage occurring on the flat ground out to the left, beyond the marsh. Within the last few minutes the enemy bombardment had slackened because Lord Oxford's wedge had split the usurper's vanguard and our right wing had moved in to surround the enemy's left section, cutting them off from the rest of their company, who had become targets of their own guns, stopping them from firing, while ours continued, raking the enemy archers and slowing their firepower. Lord Oxford and his men had pushed the right half of the enemy's vanguard back against a windmill on a rise in the ground; I could see their commander's standard, the white lion of Norfolk, waving beneath the mill's skeleton sails, and the gold and red standard of John de Vere, Earl of Oxford in close proximity. Bodies began to pile up under the windmill; the fighting was intense. Lord Jasper had led his Welsh troops around the bog to reinforce Oxford's push.

Richmond Herald came galloping up to inform me that the Duke of Norfolk, commander of the usurper's vanguard, had been killed – our left wing was turning back as Norfolk's men scattered. It was inevitable now that Richard would summon his rear-guard to attack our right flank and until Lord Jasper's Welsh brigade returned to its original position, my bodyguard and I were exposed.

At this point I turned my gaze up the hill to my right, beyond the Roman road, where the Stanleys' troops held their aloof position, remaining stationary and uncommitted to either side, lined up as spectators on the sloping common land that divided the villages of Dadlington and Stoke Golding. The greater number of their men wore my step-father's scarlet livery with its badge of a golden stag's head combined with the three-legged triangle of the Isle of Man, and were stationed separately from Sir William's lesser contingent, again in red but identified by a lone stag's head badge. Together they constituted a sizeable force and it probably infuriated Richard as much as it frustrated me that they did not show any sign of bringing their men to either side.

I could see one of Richard's heralds making his way across to the red-jacketed cohort and assumed he would be conveying a command to attack. Eager to take advantage of Oxford's elimination of the usurper's vanguard, I decided to take the matter into my own hands. At any cost I had to prevent the usurper's command reaching Stanley, and simply sending my own herald would not pack enough punch.

'We ride to the Stanleys!' I yelled to my knights, raising my sword to attract their attention and indicate the direction. 'Forward!'

Uncertain of the terrain, we set off at a trot, skirting the marsh and heading for the old Roman thoroughfare, which was on a raised causeway. The dry weather had made the marsh retreat a little, leaving a swathe of hardened ground alongside the road, and as soon as we reached it I realised that I had made a mistake. I had decided to risk exposure to any advance by the enemy rear-guard, thinking I could easily outrun it. However there was no sign of this happening; instead Richard had noticed my personal vulnerability and mobilised his own bodyguard cavalry into a charge. As we reached firm ground I looked up to the left and saw him leading them at a hectic gallop down the hill towards us. They were a terrifying sight, a hundred warhorses racing four abreast at full tilt, Richard's boar banner in the hands of his standard-bearer streaming out behind, Richard at the front, his gaping mouth screaming a battle cry through his open visor. Clearly he was intent on finishing off what he had called 'a treacherous little rebellion by a milksop Welshman' by personally putting an end to him.

But he was to discover that I was not that 'milksop Welshman'. The blood began to surge in my veins and I turned to face the onslaught, yelling my own curses and urging Gwyn Eyrir into a full gallop from almost a standing start. Behind me I could sense Will Brandon powering up his horse and big John Cheyne bellowing his own brand of invective at my other wing as he put his mount into a headlong charge. The ground shook with hoof beats and the air vibrated with the fury of my knights' battle cries as they gave united voice.

This was the moment when all our frustration and anger boiled over at what had been done to us and to England under the rule of the man who had been entrusted with the safety and honour of a boy king and his realm and had betrayed him and it in every aspect. The code of chivalry, for so long thought to have died in the past thirty years of civil conflict, was suddenly regenerated as the two opposing charges thundered down on one another in clouds of dust, with lances couched.

At the head of his knights, the usurper was aiming his charge directly at me, still screaming through his open visor. Reckoning that he might be underestimating my skill with the lance, I was concentrating all my attention on aiming at his unprotected face and so I will never know how Will managed to barge across me at the last moment, knocking me off my target and taking the full impact of Richard's thrust. Momentum carried me on into the mêlée of the enemy charge as my lance dealt a wounding blow to one of the usurper's knights and was torn from my grasp in the process. I swiftly drew my sword from its sheath and parried several more potential strikes before the charge swept past and I eased Gwyn Eyrir to a halt, turning him, certain that Richard would make another direct attack. With my visor closed I was unable to see what had happened to Will Brandon, only noticing that my standard was still flying but in the hands of another knight. Then, peering over the causeway I saw a sight that gave my already-pounding heart a heavy jolt. Sir William Stanley's troops were on the move and at some speed, pouring down the slope below Dadlington, through the small stream at its foot and over the Roman road, with his mounted men at arms well in the lead. It was evident that they were reacting to the clash of cavalries but it was not at all clear which side they would favour when they reached us. Were they coming to my aid or Richard's?

I had no time to ponder this vital question, being suddenly beset on all sides by Richard's knights, my armour taking strikes from sword and mace while I parried and slashed, at the same time trying to catch a glimpse of the gold coronet encircling the usurper's helm. Then I spotted the huge bulk of Sir John Cheyne engaged in close combat with the very man I sought; a David and Goliath duel, which against the odds resulted in victory for the gold coronet as Sir John took a huge hammer blow to the helm and was toppled from his horse. I readied myself once more to confront the usurper but three of my knights converged on him and were taken on by three of his retinue, effectively separating the two of us. I could not fault the chivalry of my bodyguards, whose job it was to protect their king, but even so I was frustrated in my intense desire to despatch Richard of York myself. To vent my spleen I rained blows of my sword on the helm of another of his entourage, whose coat of arms I recognised as that of Sir Richard Radcliffe, a close crony of his namesake.

It was at this stage that the red jackets began to arrive in serious numbers, surging in behind the usurper's knights, clearly fighting their way towards the helm with the gold coronet. My heartbeat slowed and my spirits rose as I realised that Richard's knights were now fighting on two sides, desperately protecting their leader, while being gradually forced back towards the marsh and its deceptively lush vegetation. Those of my own bodyguard who remained mounted began to converge, forming an impenetrable barrier around me and easily parrying any glory-seeking Yorkist who sought the final solution of my elimination. I risked lifting my visor to widen the scope of my vision and immediately noticed that the Percy blue lion still flew in its original place, behind the enemy camp. The Earl of Northumberland's rear-guard had not moved. On the other side of the marsh Oxford's vanguard troops were chasing

Yorkist footsoldiers, fleeing for their lives back up the hill to their base camp.

All along I had known it would be a fight to the death and that God would decide the outcome. Before my eyes His will became manifest as the usurper's horse stumbled backwards into the soft ooze of the marsh and flung its rider from the saddle. With apparently superhuman strength Richard hauled himself clear, raising the visor he had wisely closed in the thick of the fighting, to give himself clearer vision. The sun glinted off his gold crown as he drew his sword from its magnificent jewelled sheath; there was no denying his courage as he snarled defiance at his attackers. One of his knights leaped from his own horse and parried an enemy swipe as he offered the reins to his master but Richard shook his head violently, taking a wide-legged stance and snarling words that I could not hear. In response all his surrounding knights who were still on horseback abandoned their steeds and formed a human shield around him.

He could have mounted and made a run for it, back to his base camp with my men in hot pursuit but I think he knew that his reign was over. Major nobles he had thought his allies had failed to come to his aid; Northumberland and his men remained static up on the hill; Lord Stanley stood aloof from the battle and his brother was fighting for me. Only the Duke of Norfolk had remained faithful and now he was dead. God was not on Richard's side.

Nevertheless he was defiant and the words he shouted as he thrust his protectors aside and strode to the attack were clearly audible. 'Treason!' he yelled. 'Treason and betrayal beset me!' Across a sea of helms and blades his eyes met mine as I sat my white horse among my loyal knights.

I looked for hatred in his expression but could see only incredulity and resignation. He was a dead man walking and suddenly I did not wish any longer to be the man who killed him. I heard yells of triumph to my left and turned my head to see Jasper's Welsh contingent bearing down on us around the marsh. With a terrible wrench I also spotted Will Brandon's body sprawled in the trodden ground, with the tip of Richard's lance embedded in his right side. Holding my standard aloft, his unprotected armpit had been exposed to the usurper's thrust when he barged in front of me at full charge. The red dragon banner was now in the hands of another but I would always feel that I owed my life to Sir William Brandon.

From within the circle of my bodyguard I watched and grudgingly admired as the usurper resolutely engaged in the fight of his life and also, inevitably, his death. For what seemed an eternity he kept his attackers at bay, even though most of them were mounted. Without a shield but with extraordinary agility he dodged strikes by mace and battle axe, parrying with his gleaming sword and continuing to yell his mantra of 'Treason! Treachery!' every time a fresh attack was made. His armour took many blows without effect; it was hugely resilient, despite being constructed to allow him extraordinary freedom of movement and must have cost him a king's ransom. Nevertheless, like any attire, it had its vulnerable points. As he was forced back into the marsh once more he stumbled on to soft ground and his head jerked back, exposing the leather straps securing his helm. An opportunist slice from the sword of a Stanley knight cut it loose, injuring his beardless chin and allowing the heavy headgear to slip from his head. Undaunted Richard ducked forward and sliced through the horse's hamstring, bringing it crashing to the ground with an ear-splitting scream. Using the thrashing body as a screen, the now uncrowned monarch stood at bay, blood dripping from the wound which had silenced his yells of treason.

Suddenly a foot soldier yelling in Welsh dodged past my mounted knights, skirted the edge of the marsh and swung his vicious-looking halberd with deadly accuracy. Richard never even saw him, having briefly bent over to try and free his feet from the marsh's grip. The strike took him on the back of the head, smashing through his linen coif and into his exposed skull. Death snatched the light from his bulging blue eyes as his knees buckled and he sank slowly forward, falling on his face into the soggy morass with a clatter of steel. From the gaping wound in his skull, pale brain-matter oozed out over the sweat-darkened coif to stain the bright metal of his gorget.

Led by the Welsh halberdier, the cry went up and spread across the battlefield, 'The tyrant has fallen! Long live King Henry!'

49

Henry

The Battlefield of Redemoor Plain, Leicestershire, 22nd August 1485

ALL AROUND US THE battle seemed to hold its breath. The broad-shouldered halberdier who had dealt the death-blow stepped away from the scene of carnage and wiped the bloody blade of his weapon on the sedge. Richard's household knights had dismounted to defend him and several lay dead around his body. Those who still lived dropped their weapons and stood or knelt in the ooze, dazed and distraught.

I urged Gwyn Eyrir forward to congratulate the king-slayer on his action, even though I could have desired a more chivalrous end for a knight of skill and courage, as I had witnessed Richard of York to be.

The halberdier wore a kettle helm that protected against blows from mounted men at arms, the distinctive brim leaving his face open and I recognised him as the leader of one of the troops from North Wales, Rhys the Mighty, the butcher, or Rhys Fwar ap Maredudd to award him his full name in Welsh.

'You have served the dragon well today Rhys,' I shouted over the continuing clamour. Noble he was not, a common soldier, nevertheless, this Rhys had caused the usurper's inevitable and necessary death; not only that, his company had been one of those that brought with them from Wales a herd of stock animals, which fed us on the Welsh border. To mark his significance in this victory I ripped off one of the silver badges fixed to my horse's harness furnishings. 'I will not forget,' I told Rhys Fwar, and tossed the badge to him. It was stamped with the image of a dragon breathing fire, similar to the one on my battle standard. To mark the moment he and the men of his company gathered at the scene all bent the knee and raised their pole-weapons in salute. 'Hail to the dragon of Cadwallader!' they yelled. 'And God bless our Welsh King Harri!'

Behind them Lord Jasper and Rhys ap Thomas approached, leading the host of men from Pembroke and Carmarthen. They both dismounted and dropped a knee in homage. 'With the death of the usurper, the Almighty has decreed that the day is ours, your grace,' my uncle said and I saw bright tears swamp his eyes. 'May God bless your reign and your realm.'

I dismounted and handed my helm to Davy, who had been like my shadow throughout the battle. Then I reached out to take Lord Jasper's hand and raise him to his feet. With a clash of steel I pulled him into a heartfelt armoured embrace and when I finally drew back, I held both his shoulders, gazed into his familiar blue eyes and felt tears of gratitude prick the back of my own. 'Thank you, uncle; it is your wisdom and advice that has brought me here and your love and encouragement that has sustained me. I owe you my life and my kingdom and your selfless care will be rewarded above all others.'

As we released each other, Rhys ap Thomas suddenly rose beside Jasper and pointed urgently over my shoulder. 'The usurper's cronies are fleeing, your grace. Shall I send my men after them?'

I shook my head. 'No, let them go. We shall arrest the criminals later and deal with treacherous nobles through courts and Parliament. Lord Jasper and I have suffered from it for long enough to know very well the retributive power of the attainder. Instead I ask you, Rhys ap Thomas, to kneel once more and give me your sword.' He frowned fiercely but dropped back to one knee and obeyed my request. I passed the sword to Jasper. 'As true sons of a Welshman, I ask my uncle and his brother, Sir David Owen, to be your sponsors for knighthood. For at this memorable moment, in recognition of the service you and your compatriots have rendered to my crown and reign, I exercise my right as king of England and victor of this battle of Redemoor Plain to dub you knight.'

The sound of my gauntleted fist hitting his pauldron rang out and his followers gave a cheer as I motioned him to rise, as loud a cheer as any that had greeted me as king. Jasper formally pushed his sword into the sheath slung at his hip and Davy stepped forward to embrace him in brotherly recognition. 'You are welcome to the ranks of King Henry's knights, Sir Rhys; you will get your spurs later, we have none at present.'

Behind me my bodyguard was still mounted and dutifully

scanning the teeming battlefield in case a suicidal glory-seeker might yet pursue my death. However, I saw upon turning that our defeated enemies were running and stumbling up Ambion Hill, seeking the dubious safety of their now leader-less camp, while most of our soldiers had begun straggling back to the baggage carts.

It really was over. My thanks went to God, and perhaps He told me what I must do. 'I wish first to tour the battlefield, to see for myself what has been the result of the day, see the wounded and the dead and ensure they are properly attended,' I told my knights. 'When this essential task is completed, and after we have found refreshment, I invite you all to accompany me to celebrate Mass and give thanks to God for our glorious victory. Those among you who remain squires should also use that occasion to prepare yourselves to receive the honour of knighthood, as recognition of your loyal service in this place of combat.'

It was usually a squire's duty but as I went to remount, Davy stepped forward to hold my stirrup. Without speaking, we exchanged glances that were eloquent with personal meaning; many times as youths and young men we had imagined going into battle together and now we had done so and won. I sensed that he shared my relief and euphoria, tinged with uncertainty at what the future held. Before swinging into the saddle I reached out and gripped his shoulder in acknowledgement of our silent celebration.

Once mounted, I beckoned Rhys Fawr ap Maredudd forward. 'Your men will always hail you as the man who rid their country of a tyrant and so to you and them I grant the honour of attending to the dead and wounded of this historic scene. Please see that poor Sir John Cheyne is taken safely to the monks at Merevale Abbey, where I am sure he will be well cared for, and carry brave Sir William Brandon there too. His body will need preserving until his wife returns from France and can bring him home to Suffolk, where I am sure she will wish him to be buried. Tell the abbot all this will be at the king's expense.'

To the others assembled around I announced, 'Tonight I will rest in Leicester, the town where the usurper last lodged. I urge you to respect his body as you would that of a skilled, courageous knight and fix it on a horse to follow my procession, so that onlookers may witness and spread the word that he is dead.'

I sent Sir James Blount and Sir John Fortescue to marshal our victuallers and scurriers and accompany them in advance to Leicester, to warn the mayor and to arrange campsites for the men and nourishment and accommodation for my nobles and officers.

I wondered what the citizens would make of it: waving a king off to war on one day and welcoming another the following day, but I did not believe that they would close the gates on us as they had at Shrewsbury. When they learned that the usurper was dead, surely common sense would urge them to welcome the one to whom God had granted the throne by right and conquest.

Remarkably, the summer sun was still high in the sky when we finally left the battlefield and headed for the Stanley camps on the eastern slopes of Redemoor Plain. Reaching Sir William's tent first, I received his oath of loyalty and told him of my intention to continue onwards to celebrate Mass at the village church in Dadlington. However, he advised me that it would be too small for our numbers and that the larger church in Stoke Golding, only a mile further on, was more suitable.

'However, the priest at Dadlington has agreed to allow some of the dead to be buried in his churchyard,' he continued, 'and I have set men to dig a communal grave for the Yorkist casualties.'

I nodded approval. 'I trust they will keep a careful list of names. Though they were our enemies, their families still deserve to know where they are buried.'

He made a bow of acknowledgement. 'My clerks are seeing to that, your grace.'

I was conscious that the words 'your grace' applied to me sat strangely on his tongue but I was pleased that he had used them. It was important that my reign should start as if I had entered the battlefield as the rightful king. 'I hope you will attend the Mass with us,' I said. 'As we give thanks to Almighty God for our glorious victory, I will readily recognise that it would not have happened without your timely intervention, Sir William. I wonder, had you planned with my stepfather that it should be you who came to my aid, rather than him?'

Sir William's brow creased into a fierce frown. 'Support of a cause is not confined to the battlefield, your grace. My brother financed a good many of your ships and mercenaries with the gold he sent to France and we must never forget that his son and heir was a hostage in the usurper's power. One of the captured knights has revealed to us that when my brother refused to join Richard's ranks this morning, the usurper gave an order for Lord Strange's immediate execution but God be praised it was not carried out.'

'Then we have more than just our glorious victory for

which to give thanks, Sir William,' I responded, making the sign of the cross.

'There is another matter, my lord,' he said, a smile erasing his frown. 'When I returned to the scene of the usurper's death his helm was brought to me by one of my knights, who had spotted an opportunist Welshman grabbing it from among the branches of a hawthorn bush and making off with it. Being mounted, my man gave chase and the fellow took fright, dropped the helm and ran, as well he might for the gold coronet was still attached. I showed it to Lord Stanley before he left to claim his son. He suggested that he take it to one of his blacksmiths to detach and adjust it. Then he, as your stepfather, requests the honour of crowning you with it, on the day of conquest, and in the place of battle that has made you our king.'

50

Henry

Stoke Golding Church, Leicestershire, 22nd August 1485

S IR WILLIAM HAD BEEN right to suggest Stoke Golding as a suitable church in which to declare our gratitude to the Almighty and pronounce the start of a new reign. It was on hilly ground at the edge of the village and a steeple had been added to its bell tower, so that its dominating presence proclaimed the glory of God to all the other villages surrounding the Redemoor Plain.

The village priest told me that earlier in the day many of his parishioners had climbed the bell tower to view and tremble at the noise and blood of the battle; now they were awe-struck by the assembly of knights and nobles gathered in the churchyard. Permission was readily granted for the Bishop of Exeter to hold a victory Mass at the altar.

After being led in solemn procession down the nave, I knelt in the chancel with my knights and battle commanders around me as the bishop loudly acclaimed God's benevolence in granting us success in battle. Lulled by the familiarity of the litany that followed, I found my mind wandering from all the prayer and adulation to marvel at the transformation that two decisive hours had made in all our lives. Against the odds, my irregular army of miscellaneous nationalities had taken on the might of England's levy and won, thrusting those of us at the forefront, and me in particular, into a position we had scarcely dared to imagine, one that would require all the help and guidance God's favour could grant me.

In the absence of choirboy trebles Christopher Urswicke had been recruited to sing the Gloria in his deep, mellifluous voice, which lifted my heart. Accompanied by trumpeters and a piper, the words echoed around the aisles, in praise of God's presence among us, reminding me of the psalm I had so fervently recited on landing at Mill Bay. *Judica me, Deus, et discerne causam meam.* 'Judge me, O God, and favour my cause.' Truly the Lord had done so.

Outside in the churchyard, overlooking Redemoor Plain and the remnants of the historic battle that had been fought there, a carved wooden armchair had been placed in the dappled shade of a mighty oak, which spread its branches benignly over the gravestones of Stoke Golding's departed. Lord Stanley led me to it, preceded by a trumpeter and Richmond Herald, his colourfully embroidered tabard stained by the blood and mire of the battlefield, calling out 'Make way! Make way for the king!' Behind us my relieved stepbrother George, Lord Strange carried the gold coronet, released from its setting around the helm of the usurper. Remarkably it showed little evidence of the battle. The nobles drew close around my substitute throne, while my armoured knights and captains crowded to either side, taking care not to block my sweeping view of the plain.

Gunners on both sides still struggled to remove the heavy cannons that had dealt so much carnage. Many of the bodies they had shattered still lay like bloodied puppets on the ground between the lines. Cowled monks moved among them, making the sign of the cross and murmuring prayers that we could not hear, while lay brothers with their habits hitched up were lifting the dead and badly injured onto hurdles and carrying them to waiting carts. Once darkness fell I knew that shadowy figures with torches would move in to scavenge anything of value from the ground and from any corpses that still remained. As we celebrated victory on the hill, the scene before us was a sobering reminder of the other side of war.

My view of the battlefield was suddenly obscured by the solid armoured figure of Lord Stanley. He was holding the crown aloft. 'Your grace, as your stepfather and representative of your royal mother, from whom you derive your claim to England's throne, the honour has fallen to me of bestowing on you the symbol of kingship. In due course you will be crowned at Westminster Abbey, founded by the king we now call The Conqueror, but it should be remembered at this battlefield that your victory today makes you the only other king of England to achieve the throne by conquest, as well as by right through your mother's direct bloodline from King Edward the Third. England is now yours, therefore this crown and all the royal regalia and the privileges and responsibilities of monarchy, are also yours. May your reign be long and peaceful and prosperous, to the benefit of all your loyal subjects.'

There was another blast of the trumpet as Lord Stanley carefully placed the crown on my head. 'God save the King,

God Bless King Henry the Seventh!' he declared and the fierce expression in his eyes defied anyone to fail in his duty to take up his cries of acclaim.

Soon the churchyard echoed with voices raised and the sonorous sound of the church bell, rung on cue by the village priest and giving tongue from the tower. As the noise swelled and rolled out over the plain, so that the other villages nearby might hear it, I recognised full well that there would be opposition to my sudden and violent assumption of the throne, but for a short while on this first day, with the usurper's crown firmly on my head, I could enjoy the extraordinary achievement for which I had worked and prayed, but had never completely believed would come to pass. I gave Lord Stanley a careful nod of thanks, appreciating the unfamiliar weight of the heavy coronet as it shifted slightly on my head. I knew the task before me would be hard, with many pitfalls to avoid and I prayed silently that with God's help I might succeed; but there was one essential element I needed to achieve success.

I stood up and raised my hand for silence. The cheers reduced gradually to a murmur, but it took a little longer for the message to reach the bell ringer. When the last peal had faded away I cleared my throat. 'I thank you all for your courage and fighting skill today. The battle may have been relatively short but my journey to the throne has been a long and hard-fought campaign. Some of you will remember a vow I made at the main cathedral in Brittany two Christmases ago, while others may not be aware of it, but it was a vow important to you all. It was to unite the two royal Houses and bring a final end to the hostility between them by marrying Elizabeth of York, heiress of her late father, King Edward the Fourth. One of my first Acts will be the repeal of the slanderous Act of Royal Title, which the usurper used to manufacture his right to rule. Once King Edward's heirs are confirmed legitimate, and with the lady's consent, I intend to make good that vow.' Another cheer went up at this announcement, especially from the more recent recruits to my cause.

Before we left for Leicester I made a point of inspecting preparations to take the usurper's body there, and I felt a fierce jolt of dismay when I saw how Rhys Fwar ap Maredudd's men had treated the remains of the man who only that morning had worn the crown that I now wore. I was prepared to see those bruises and injuries I had witnessed during the battle but his body had been stripped and many more were visible. The man who had risen from his bed as King of England would be travelling naked, covered in bloody wounds and tied over the saddle of a mule like a hunted stag.

My stomach heaved at the sight and I turned to my companions, Lord Jasper and Lord Oxford, in some distress. 'They have mauled him like hounds! I did not sanction this.'

The two experienced campaigners did not appear surprised. Jasper shrugged. 'Do not be too squeamish, nephew,' he chided. 'Men who have fought and won tend to want to punish the loser.'

'It is no more than would have been done to you, had the battle gone the other way,' added Lord Oxford, 'and to your uncle and me too, probably. War is bloody, your grace; Richard could have fled but he chose to stay and fight to the death. Celebrate your victory, sire, and let the people see what happens to a tyrant and usurper.'

I could have overridden their advice and at least ordered a cloth to cover Richard's nakedness but I did not. Sovereignty was new to me and I would come to regret my weakness in the matter, when I had learned how to wield the power I had so recently acquired. All I did was to order that the body on the mule should be placed well behind me in the procession so that I should not hear the way onlookers reacted to it, or see whether they threw flowers or rotten fruit.

The fields of Leicestershire were still bathed in sunshine as we passed and crowds had gathered in the villages to gawp at the bright banners, the guns and the polished armour. After a few miles of country tracks we rode down the main street of a town where timbered houses lined the thoroughfare and a carved stone cross graced the central square. A good crowd had gathered to witness our passing.

Our local guide, Richard Hardwicke, was riding at my stirrup, identifying places and landmarks. 'This is our local market town, your grace,' he told me.

'And what is its name, Master Lindley?' I asked.

'Bosworth my lord, Market Bosworth.'

'The people who live here should remember this day,' I said, 'and tell their children that they witnessed the start of a new reign.'

51

Margaret

♕

Lathom House and Coldharbour Inn, 23rd August – 1st September 1485

MY STOOGE BROUGHT ME the letter from Henry. Since receiving his last missive I had been on my knees almost constantly, praying for his safety and success. The arrival of another should have filled me with elation, because it meant he was still alive, but having known a lifetime of violent turns of the Wheel of Fortune, God had granted me the fortitude to bear these variations without visible lurches of emotion.

> *To my beloved mother, Margaret, Countess of Richmond, greetings.*
>
> *I write in some haste but I desire above all things for you to be the first to know from my pen of our glorious victory over the usurper. God has seen fit to reward us for all our efforts to rid England of his illegal reign and*

Lord Stanley today crowned me with the coronet taken from the tyrant's battle helm. Soon, when it occurs, you will I hope be the proud and pre-eminent witness to my formal coronation in Westminster Abbey.

All restrictions on your liberty are now instantly rescinded and you are free to move about my kingdom entirely as you choose but I beg you to make all haste to London where the bells will ring out for our reunion and you will be hailed and installed as the first lady of the land. Your brother Sir John Welles will come immediately to Lathom to escort you with a suitable royal guard for My Lady the King's Mother, which is the title that shall be reserved for you, if my honoured and beloved mother approves.

I have also sent two leading knights of my household to Sheriff Hutton to bring Elizabeth of York south and I would be grateful if she could be lodged with you so that she and I might enjoy some private meetings under your propriety before a betrothal is made formal and a wedding can be arranged. With this in mind I intend to take back occupancy of Coldharbour Inn from the heralds of the College of Arms, which the usurper unwisely granted, and return it to your convenience. Once you are settled there I hope you will invite the dowager Queen Elizabeth to visit with you so that she and her royal daughter can be reunited in safety and comfort.

I will presently set aside time to write you a full and detailed account of our extraordinary and glorious victory. I have so many people to thank and of course I give thanks to God as the principal author of my ascent to the throne. But so much is due to you, my wonderful,

*indefatigable mother! I salute your tenacity,
determination and unfailing support over the years of
my exile and as sovereign I will do all that is in my
power to ensure that you are rewarded and honoured in
life, as you undoubtedly will be in Heaven.*

The signature and date blurred before my eyes and the letter fell from my shaking fingers as all my control dissolved, releasing the dammed-up tension of weeks, months and years. My husband sometimes accused me of being cold and unemotional. I was not cold now. My tears flowed.

When I reached London just three days after Henry, Richard's appointed heralds had already been ousted from Coldharbour and Reginald Bray, with his wife Kitty, was there to welcome me. The process of restoring the house to the home I had once so much enjoyed had already begun.

My long-awaited reunion with my son took place at Westminster Palace, where I was fêted and feasted and placed in the consort's throne.

'Until I marry, you are the queen of my court, my lady mother,' Henry informed me with one of his glorious smiles. 'The kingdom is as much yours as mine. I need your knowledge of English laws and ways and I know you will always tell me the truth. Your place is beside me.'

I cannot remember when I smiled so much. Lord Stanley was disconcerted but I paid no heed. Henry was to make him Earl of Derby and so he had his reward. Our marriage had suffered slings and arrows and survived and this precious time was Henry's and mine. Even when Elizabeth arrived he continued to put me first but I could not believe it would last.

In one of my many letters to Henry during his exile I had described Elizabeth of York as the loveliest damsel at court and time had not altered my opinion. She greatly resembled her mother, King Edward's beautiful and controversial queen. The same languorous, heavy-lidded brown eyes gazed out from under finely arched brows and she spoke softly in greeting through delicate bow-shaped lips, her rounded jawline accentuated by a slender white neck.

We dined alone together on her first day at Coldharbour and as we ate and talked I kept thinking that she reminded me of someone other than her mother. It was only a short time before it came to me. My former ward, Meg Woodville, was Elizabeth's first cousin; her adored husband Robert Poyntz had won a battlefield knighthood from Henry. I was rapidly discovering that Elizabeth of York, albeit ten years younger than Meg, was much like her in looks and just as quietly determined.

'When we spoke before, you said you wanted Henry to defeat your uncle Richard,' I ventured. 'Now that he has, are you still of the same mind? Will you willingly marry him?'

'I will tell you my mind when I have met him,' she answered with a smile. 'There is no doubt that my uncle loved me, as a man loves a woman, but any marriage between us was impossible, not only because he was my uncle but ironically because he had made me illegitimate. He knew the people would never accept a bastard as queen.' The word bastard was spat through gritted teeth.

Then I dared to ask the crucial question. 'Do you believe your father was contracted to marry Eleanor Butler?'

Elizabeth did not appear unwilling to reply but nor did

she answer directly. 'I think my uncle knew there was no impediment to my parents' marriage. My father would have confessed it on his deathbed and Richard never contested it during his brother's reign. But he was not prepared to spend six years as Protector of the realm and then meekly hand power to my brother Edward when he gained his majority.'

'Then why did he not release your brothers from the Tower, after they were disqualified from the succession?'

She shrugged. 'Put yourself in his shoes. He had been crowned king. He did not want two boys who were once Plantagenet princes let loose in his kingdom to become the focus for disaffected affinities. It was bad enough that the Duke of Buckingham decided he would start a rebellion and your son began to attract malcontents to his cause. But after the Act of Royal Title was passed, when my brothers did not emerge from the Tower, my mother and I began to fear not only for their lives but also for our own. We knew that sanctuary was not always considered sacrosanct when a throne is at stake.'

My eyebrows must have climbed to meet my headdress. 'Did you have reason to think your lives were at risk?'

Her eyes drilled into mine. 'Perhaps you can answer that better than I, Lady Margaret. After all you were attainted for treason and conspiracy after Buckingham's rebellion. He was executed. Did you fear for your life at that time?'

I met her accusing gaze with a steady calm I did not feel. 'Clearly your mother did not fear for me, Elizabeth, as we continued to conspire to join you and my son in marriage. A marriage to which you consented.'

Her gaze did not waver. 'I was betrothed to the Dauphin

of France for six years,' she said proudly. 'I have been reared and educated to be the wife of a king and now your son is on the throne of England.'

'Am I to conclude that if Henry had come back merely as Earl of Richmond you would not have been prepared to marry him?'

Her responding smile was dazzling. 'I do not have to answer that, my lady, because your son vowed to take the throne and to marry me. He needs me because I am the Yorkist heir and he is the heir of Lancaster. Together we can unite the two royal houses and bring peace to England. God has willed it and that is our destiny.'

Henry

I waited a few days before visiting Elizabeth at Coldharbour. She may have wished to be presented at court and fêted and praised as my mother had been but I had to consider my Lancastrian affinity. Suppose the crowds cheered her louder than me? London is her town. I would arrange a court presentation in due course, when we had come to know each other.

I had already decided that my reign would officially date from the day before our victory, which meant the Yorkists who had fought against us could be accused of treason against the king's grace, making the process of attainting them simpler. But it still required the ratification of Parliament. The worst offenders had been killed in the battle or fled into exile and there would be no need for mass executions or public hangings. Sometimes I wondered what justice might have been meted out to Richard, had he tried to run and been taken prisoner and I found myself giving thanks for his refusal to accept the horse that was offered. Most Yorkist knights and nobles, both those who had fought and those who had stayed away, were offered pardons and accepted them but they were put on a watch list. When the council met for the first time my coronation was planned for the end of October and a Parliament was called for November. Elizabeth and I would not have a joint coronation. I wanted no one to think she was the true heir and that I ruled only in her name. The throne and the crown were mine – by right and by conquest.

My lady mother looked proud as she ushered me into the beautiful hall at Coldharbour where Elizabeth waited. I bowed and took her hand to raise her from her curtsy. She was dressed in grey; a gesture of mourning for her missing brothers and executed Woodville relatives? Or perhaps some part of her regretted the death of her uncle Richard. I would never be sure.

She had not favoured me by sinking to her knees and I supposed she was making it clear that in her view we were of equal rank. Her hand felt small and soft in mine, which was calloused from daily weapon practice. 'You have suffered much during these last years, Lady Elizabeth,' I said, leading her to one of the chairs arranged for us in the long window overlooking the garden that led down to the river Thames. 'It is my hope that not only will our marriage fulfil the desires and expectations of the people but that we can also find mutual happiness together. I will certainly do all in my power to ensure that is so.'

I saw an eyebrow twitch in surprise and then the veil of her self-control dropped once more. 'Your grace is very kind,' she said. 'I have not been led to consider my personal happiness to be as important as my duty of support for my royal husband and the provision of heirs.'

I tried to inject some humour into my voice as I took the seat opposite her and made my reply. 'Very laudable sentiments, my lady, but I do not think mixing a little joy with the duty would cause any harm. I personally like music and laughter as much as prayer and solemnity and I do not intend that a smile as dazzling as yours should go unseen or unappreciated at my court.'

My mother had settled herself at a distance but not out of earshot and I saw her raise an eyebrow at my attempted gallantry. Elizabeth however rewarded me with a small hint of just how wondrous her smile would be when permitted full display. 'What would please me, if that is what you wish to do my lord, is to know when our marriage will take place. I look forward to my mother visiting tomorrow and I am sure she, too, would be interested to know.'

My shoulders lifted and I sighed. 'It would be next week if I had my way but we are not as free to choose as ordinary men and women. I have been on the throne for less than three weeks and although my dearest wish has been accomplished, in that I have set eyes on my beautiful bride-to-be, I have also learned the burden of the task ahead. First, Parliament must be summoned to repeal and destroy every copy of the appalling Act of Royal Title, so that you and your mother and sisters recover your royal status and privileges as soon as possible. I am sure the Dowager Queen will also be anxious to learn when that will happen.'

'Indeed she will, my lord.' She nodded eagerly and added, 'And also when her dower will be restored so that she can support herself and my younger sisters.'

'Yes, there is much to be done,' I said noncommittally. 'There are Privy Councillors to select, my administration requires staffing and the exchequer needs checking. Then there is the matter of the papal dispensation for us to marry, and of course my coronation. I cannot make you my queen consort until I am the anointed king.'

I paused for thought, which was when I discovered that my future queen had a sense of humour that chimed with mine. 'May Saint Valentine intercede for us!' she exclaimed, her smile at full charm. 'Without his help we could be old and grey before we plight our troth and then what will you do for a Tudor dynasty, your grace?'

I closed my eyes. 'Armel, lend me patience,' I begged my patron saint inwardly. I did not know whether my reaction to her was carnal or just that she had made me laugh, but I already desired to throw my arms around Elizabeth and smother her Aphrodite smile with kisses. However, in this matter, as in claiming my throne, it seemed that God might be testing me with yet another wait for His favour.

GLOSSARY

aft: The rear section of a ship.

aftcastle: A built-up section at the back of a medieval ship used as a steering and fighting platform – cabin underneath.

attainder: Confiscation of titles and revenues, punishment for treason.

bailiff: Monarch's representative in a town.

barding: Cloth covering of horse armour with heraldic decoration.

bezant: Heraldic gold 'roundel' or solid circle symbol.

blanc mange: Lit. 'white eating', often pounded fish and ground almonds.

bleaching pans: Shallow salt basins where sea water is dried and bleached.

bollard: A short post for securing ropes.

bow: Pointed front of a ship.

bowsprit: Protrusion from the bow, often carved and decorated.

brigandine: A protective padded canvas coat, often reinforced with metal.

bulwark: Solid side of a ship projecting up from the deck.

by-blow: Slang for an illegitimate child.

Calais Pale: English defended area around the castle and port of Calais.

chamfron: Armour protecting the head of a warhorse.

chantry: Chapel endowed for masses to be sung for the dead.

cleat: Protrusion of wood or metal for fastening ropes.

cloth of gold: Costly cloth 'shot' with fine threads of real gold.

cloth of state: An embellished canopy fixed or held over a ruler's head.

cog: Small medieval ship 'of all trades'.

commissioner of array: Official appointed to recruit for a royal army.

companionway: Ladder-like stair leading between a ship's decks.

Compline: The final Catholic Office (or 'Hour') of the day.

courser: A horse of 'status', used mainly for hunting.

corsair: A sailor who 'hunts' other shipping for profit, i.e. a pirate.

denier: Silver coin, worth about 2 pence.

destrier: A high-status warhorse – always a stallion trained from a colt.

donjon: The keep of a castle – from Norman French for a dungeon.

écranche: Target worn on the left shoulder in a joust.

galette: Dark Breton 'pancake' made with 'black' sarrasin flour.

gunwale: Upper edge of a ship's side.

Gwynedd: Northern area of Wales, once an ancient kingdom.

halberd: An axe-weapon with a hook on the back and a long shaft.

harpy: A rapacious woman. A pejorative term.

helm/kettle-helm: Armour for the head/one shaped like an upside-down bowl.

jetsam: Goods washed up on shore.

joust: Tilting competition for knights.

kirtle: Female 'dress' worn over the chemise and under the gown.

lancet: Narrow pointed window opening.

levée: Jousting term for aiming the lance at the *écranche*.

levy: The royal army, mustered for battle.

Malouins: Citizens of St Malo.

manège: An arena marked out for schooling horses.

minerva: Fur used as a trimming, mostly from the red squirrel.

minion: A servile person of lower class.

mullion: A division between the lights of windows, often carved stone.

oriel: A polygonal window recess built out from a wall.

Planta Genista: Latin name for gorse or broom, origin of name Plantagenet.

polearm: A weapon fixed to a long pole – a pike, halberd, axe or spear.

poop/poop-rail: Raised deck on ship to aid vision/its safety rail.

reiver: Cross-border raider, especially England/Scotland.

retainer: Paid or sworn servant or follower.

rouncey: Equine all-rounder – sturdy horse or pony of many uses.

round dance: A dance that starts with participants in a circle; many varieties.

sarrasin: Plant raised in poor soil; flowers dried and ground as a flour.

sanctuary: Claimed in consecrated ground as protection against arrest.

scupper: Hole to drain a ship's deck.

sheets: Nautical term for ropes used to control sails.

solar: A withdrawing room for privacy. (Lit. place in the sun.)

squint: A spyhole for secret observation.

stay: Nautical term for strong rope or wire which held up the mast.

St Anthony's rash or fire: Bright red rash caused by various allergies.

St Armel: Breton saint born in Wales. Henry's chosen patron.

St Elmo: Believed to protect sailors by sending fire from heaven.

surcôte: Sleeveless over-garment often worn to display coat of arms.

tack: Nautical manoeuvre used to sail against the wind.

tracery: Gothic decorative ornamentation.

turncoat: Person who changes sides.

uchelwr: Welsh gentry.

unguent: Ointment.

whipstaff: Strong wooden steering shaft connected to a ship's rudder.

widow's dower: A third portion of a dead man's property left to his widow.

Ynys Môn: The Isle of Anglesey, off North Wales.

AUTHOR'S NOTE

It is hard to find contemporary accounts of Henry Tudor's time in exile, except the odd mention in English sources of events affecting him and his uncle Jasper, such as when embassies were sent to the Duke of Brittany's court and attempts were made to repatriate them, where they were lodged and when their circumstances changed. There is one drawing believed to be of Henry as a young man and a few mentions of him by visitors to the duke's court but otherwise the only detailed account of his fourteen years in exile was of him being escorted to St Malo in order to be repatriated and how he managed to escape. With the odd exception, the people he met and the places he went to existed but their characters and descriptions are from my imagination.

I visited Nantes, where the ducal palace within its mighty castle walls is still intact and fascinating, and Vannes, where little remains of the Château de l'Hérmine except a section of curtain wall and the odd tower. The most atmospheric of the Tudor lodgings is Suscinio Castle, which has been completely renovated and returned to its medieval splendour – well worth a visit if you go to the south coast of Brittany. And I believe the tower at Château Largoët where Henry was lodged for two years is still standing but I arrived at the gate on the day after it had closed for the winter and was unable to gain access to the castle demesne – bad planning on my part – so I have had to rely on the accounts of others and some photographs. Château Trédion is larger and grander now than it was when the Comte de Rieux owned it but you can have your wedding there if you fancy it!

Having tried hard to remain separate from France for many years, Brittany finally succumbed to French rule after Duke Francis died, when his daughter Anne became Duchess and married Louis VIII, the young French king who features towards the end of *The Tudor Crown*. The border between France and Brittany is now only an administrative line, which has altered considerably since the fifteenth century, so the River Loire no longer forms any part of it, Nantes now being the capital of the French Département de Loire Atlantique.

Henry's romance with Catherine de Belleville is fictional. There is no evidence of any relationships with women during his exile, although a youth called Roland de Velleville is mentioned as being in Henry's retinue when he came to Bosworth and was a minor member of his court throughout his reign. For years historians struggled to find evidence that he was Henry's illegitimate son but to no one's conviction. I have taken the view that it is unlikely that Henry would have had no love life during his late teens and early twenties and so, after much digging around the French aristocracy I found Catherine de Belleville (not unlikely to have been written Velleville in English) in the ancestry of the Dukes of Luxembourg and used her as a possible candidate for his romantic interest. Her family history is accurate as I describe it, except for her job as governess to the daughter of the Comte de Rieux and the existence in my story of her illegitimate son Roland and the circumstances of his conception. The fact that he kept him at his court indicates that Henry was fond of Roland and he eventually granted him a small pension, making him Constable of Beaumaris Castle in Anglesey but these seem rather grudging grants by a royal father even to an illegitimate son. His legitimate son, who became King Henry VIII, granted his illegitimate son, Henry Fitzroy, a dukedom!

On first acquaintance with Lady Margaret Beaufort I considered her a somewhat dull character – full of good works but little personality. How wrong I was! More persistent research revealed an intelligent and complex character with a sense of purpose and a heart of gold. Her 'nestlings', as I call them, are all factual and she was generous towards them with her time and money, giving them the opportunity of a fine education and ensuring their futures with excellent marriages. It is my assumption that they filled the void left in her life by her barrenness and her long separation from her only son. Her letters reveal her unswerving loyalty to Henry, her generous advice and financial support throughout his exile and her fierce ambition for his future, which took a radical leap after the usurpation of Richard III. I believe it was her subtle handling of her marriage to Lord Stanley that eventually brought him round to Henry's side, radically affecting his victory at Bosworth. The physical image we have of her is of a nun-like figure who is constantly at prayer, and I am sure she did pray a great deal during the run-up to Bosworth and was liberal with alms and endowments but she was also a lady who loved dressing up and organising banquets and entertainments at her grand homes. The people who worked for her loved her and remained in her service for long periods. They were her friends as well as her servants and several of them fought at Bosworth. It is no surprise that her son kept her close to his side during the early years of his reign. She was his chief adviser when it came to England and its people, of which he was almost completely ignorant. She will feature again in a future novel I am planning, as will one of her 'nestlings'.

As is so common when tackling the medieval period, there are always too many people of the same name and Margaret is a case in point. I have granted Lady Margaret the privilege of her full name because I feel she deserves it – the other two Margarets had to become (Queen) Marguerite and Meg Woodville. Henry's lover remained Catherine but the other two Katherines became Kate and Kitty and, outranked by kings and princes, Edward Woodville had to be Ned. Thank goodness for unusual French names like Philibert and Guillaume!

It is over 530 years since Bosworth and there are remarkably few contemporary accounts of exactly how the battle was fought but recent research and archaeology have indicated that the original location was wrong and I explored the 'new' battlefield and discovered the role of Merevale Abbey on a tour organised by the Battle of Bosworth Visitor Centre. Richard III's death on the battlefield has also recently been described in detail since the discovery of his body and the evidence of the wounds found on the skeleton. I have never doubted that Richard was responsible for the deaths of the 'Princes in the Tower' and that he concocted the claim that his brother's marriage to Elizabeth Woodville was illegitimate and engineered the Act of Titulus Regius through Parliament. Therefore I believe him to have been a usurper and I have had Henry and his followers consistently refer to him as such. Whether or not Elizabeth of York would have married him I am not sure but what an insecure childhood she suffered. She must have been desperate for security!

Oddly there is no contemporary evidence that Jasper Tudor took part in the Battle of Bosworth but I cannot imagine that he was not closely involved in the planning and execution of the expedition and am sure he must ultimately have played a part in the military victory. Even though he was in his mid-fifties by that time many knights of his age still put on their armour and fought when the need arose. Once a knight always a knight and there were others of his age and older on that battlefield. He lived on into the first ten years of Henry's reign and was hugely rewarded for his kindness and loyalty – but that, again, is for another story.

Stay with me, kind reader! If you have questions I am on Facebook and Twitter @joannahickson.

ACKNOWLEDGEMENTS

I could name scores of research sources I have used for *The Tudor Crown* but for the straightforward historical record I relied heavily on *The Making of the Tudor Dynasty* by Ralph Griffiths and Roger S. Thomas, which has been revised, reprinted and updated many times and is the bible for many people on this section of England's history. Those two historians have also acknowledged the influence of the late Professor S. B. Chrimes's earlier definitive work, *Henry VII*, which I, too, consulted. More recently Thomas Penn has published a history of Henry Tudor called *The Winter King* and I have also read and much enjoyed Ruth Goodman's 'Dawn to Dusk Guide' on *How to be a Tudor*, which is full of fascinating detail about life as it was lived at every level of society in Tudor times.

I must mention the skill of the crew of the good ship *Loire Princesse*, which carried me and about eighty other passengers over the shoals and shallows of France's Loire River, at a time when the lack of rain had dangerously lowered the water level. Unfortunately we couldn't get as far up-river as Château Langeais, where Henry first entered the French royal court but the castles of the Loire that we did visit gave me a very good idea of the level of luxury its courtiers enjoyed and the good use to which they put their waterways for travel. The Loire itself also gave me inspiration for Henry's escape route when he made his hasty and dangerous exit from Brittany to France.

When it comes to research in England, I owe huge thanks to Eddie Smallwood, who was my guide around the Bosworth battlefield and its environs and tirelessly supplied detailed information on the latest archaeology which has now pin-pointed the exact location where the battle was fought and how the antagonists faced up to each other. If I have made any errors of a military or historical nature while describing this seismic event, then they are all mine and none of his. Also it was he who suggested that I stay at the Abbey Farm B&B, run by the lovely Jenny, which gave me 'open sesame' to the ruins of Merevale Abbey, where it is now believed Henry and his army made their HQ on the day before the battle. I can highly recommend it if you're visiting the Bosworth Battlefield Centre, which I encourage you to do! My thanks go to the staff at the centre for putting up with my myriad questions and to Pat in particular for the information-rich guided walk around Ambion Hill. For more information, go to www.bosworthbattlefield.org.uk

Getting a book like *The Tudor Crown* out into the world is very much a team effort. I am so lucky to have more or less the same core team at HarperFiction now as launched my debut novel in 2013 and I'm thrilled to say that I will be with them for another two novels at least. I thank them all enormously for their efforts and skill; Publisher Kimberley Young, Senior Commissioning Editor Kate Bradley (who fields all my joys and pains without discernible irritation and often throws in a lunch as well!), copy editor Joy Chamberlain, Publicity Manager Jaime Frost and Marketing Manager Emma Pickard. And those who have read *First of the Tudors* will probably recognise the super-limner hand of Holly MacDonald on the jacket once again. I love her eye-catching design!

HarperCollins annually rewards its authors with a fabulous party at the Victoria and Albert Museum and this is a good opportunity to say thank you for the good cheer to the friendly and sociable CEO Charlie Redmayne, who not only makes a fine speech but also keeps the company in sufficiently good order to give us all something to celebrate!

As usual I leave my gorgeous friend and super-agent Jenny Brown till last – but far from least! I am not only lucky to have the benefit of her sage advice on all crucial professional matters but also her unfailingly cheerful company on many hugely enjoyable bookish occasions. Lang may her lum reek!

Discover more page-turning
historical fiction
from Joanna Hickson

Available to buy now